W9-APN-740

VICIOUS

V. E. SCHWAB

TOR®

A TOM DOHERTY ASSOCIATES BOOK

NEW YORK

VICIOUS

Copyright © 2013 by Victoria Schwab

Edited by Miriam Weinberg

A Tor Book
Published by Tom Doherty Associates, LLC
175 Fifth Avenue
New York, NY 10010

www.tor-forge.com

Tor® is a registered trademark of Tom Doherty Associates, LLC.

The Library of Congress Cataloging-in-Publication Data is available upon request.

ISBN 978-0-7653-3534-0 (hardcover)
ISBN 978-1-4668-2217-7 (e-book)

Tor books may be purchased for educational, business, or promotional use. For information on bulk purchases, please contact Macmillan Corporate and Premium Sales Department at 1-800-221-7945, extension 5442, or write specialmarkets@macmillan.com.

First Edition: September 2013

Printed in the United States of America

0 9 8 7 6 5 4 3 2 1

*To Miriam and Holly, for proving time and again
that they are ExtraOrdinary*

Life—the way it really is—is a battle not between Bad and Good, but between Bad and Worse.

—Joseph Brodsky

1

Water, Blood, and Thicker Things

I

LAST NIGHT

MERIT CEMETERY

VICTOR readjusted the shovels on his shoulder and stepped gingerly over an old, half-sunken grave. His trench billowed faintly, brushing the tops of tombstones as he made his way through Merit Cemetery, humming as he went. The sound carried like wind through the dark. It made Sydney shiver in her too big coat and her rainbow leggings and her winter boots as she trudged along behind him. The two looked like ghosts as they wove through the graveyard, both blond and fair enough to pass for siblings, or perhaps father and daughter. They were neither, but the resemblance certainly came in handy since Victor couldn't very well tell people he'd picked up the girl on the side of a rain-soaked road a few days before. He'd just broken out of jail. She'd just been shot. A crossing of fates, or so it seemed. In fact, Sydney was the only reason Victor was beginning to believe in fate at all.

He stopped humming, rested his shoe lightly on a tombstone, and scanned the dark. Not with his eyes so much as with his skin, or rather with the thing that crept beneath it, tangled in his pulse. He might have stopped humming, but the sensation never did, keeping on with a faint electrical buzz that only he could hear and feel and read. A buzz that told him when someone was near.

Sydney watched him frown slightly.

"Are we alone?" she asked.

Victor blinked, and the frown was gone, replaced by the even calm he always wore. His shoe slid from the gravestone. "Just us and the dead."

They made their way into the heart of the cemetery, the shovels tapping softly on Victor's shoulder as they went. Sydney kicked a loose rock that had broken off from one of the older graves. She could see that there were letters, parts of words, etched into one side. She wanted to know what they said, but the rock had already tumbled into the weeds, and Victor was still moving briskly between the graves. She ran to catch up, nearly tripping several times over the frozen ground before she reached him. He'd come to a stop, and was staring down at a grave. It was fresh, the earth turned over and a temporary marker driven into the soil until a stone one could be cut.

Sydney made a noise, a small groan of discomfort that had nothing to do with the biting cold. Victor glanced back and offered her the edge of a smile.

"Buck up, Syd," he said casually. "It'll be fun."

Truth be told, Victor didn't care for graveyards, either. He didn't like dead people, mostly because he had no effect on them. Sydney, conversely, didn't like dead people because she had such a marked effect on them. She kept her arms crossed tightly over her chest, one gloved thumb rubbing the spot on her upper arm where she'd been shot. It was becoming a tic.

Victor turned and sunk one of the spades into the earth. He then tossed the other one to Sydney, who unfolded her arms just in time to catch it. The shovel was almost as tall as she was. A few days shy of her thirteenth birthday, and even for twelve and eleven twelfths, Sydney Clarke was small. She had always been on the short side, but it certainly didn't help that she had barely grown an inch since the day she'd died.

Now she hefted the shovel, grimacing at the weight.

"You've got to be kidding me," she said.

"The faster we dig, the faster we get to go home."

Home wasn't home so much as a hotel room stocked only with Sydney's stolen clothes, Mitch's chocolate milk, and Victor's files, but that wasn't the point. At this moment, home would have been any place that *wasn't* Merit Cemetery. Sydney eyed the grave, tightening her fingers on the wooden grip. Victor had already begun to dig.

"What if . . . ," she said, swallowing, ". . . what if the other people accidentally wake up?"

"They won't," cooed Victor. "Just focus on *this* grave. Besides . . ." He looked up from his work. "Since when are *you* afraid of bodies?"

"I'm not," she snapped back, too fast and with all the force of someone used to being the younger sibling. Which she was. Just not *Victor's*.

"Look at it this way," he teased, dumping a pile of dirt onto the grass. "If you do wake them up, they can't go anywhere. Now dig."

Sydney leaned forward, her short blond hair falling into her eyes, and began to dig. The two worked in the dark, only Victor's occasional humming and the thud of the shovels filling the air.

Thud.

Thud.

Thud.

II

TEN YEARS AGO
LOCKLAND UNIVERSITY

VICTOR drew a steady, straight, black line through the word *marvel*.

The paper they'd printed the text on was thick enough to keep the ink from bleeding through, so long as he didn't press down too hard. He stopped to reread the altered page, and winced as one of the metal flourishes on Lockland University's wrought-iron fence dug into his back. The school prided itself on its country-club-meets-Gothic-manor ambience, but the ornate railing that encircled Lockland, though *striving* to evoke both the university's exclusive nature and its old-world aesthetic, succeeded only in being pretentious and suffocating. It reminded Victor of an elegant cage.

He shifted his weight and repositioned the book on his knee, wondering at the sheer size of it as he twirled the Sharpie over his knuckles. It was a self-help book, the latest in a series of five, by the world-renowned Drs. Vale. The very same Vales who were currently on an international tour. The very same Vales who had budgeted just enough time in their busy schedules—even back before they were best-selling "empowerment gurus"—to produce Victor.

He thumbed back through the pages until he found the beginning of his most recent undertaking and began to read. For the first time he wasn't effacing a Vale book simply for pleasure. No, this was for credit. Victor couldn't help but smile. He took an immense pride in paring down his parents' works, stripping the expansive chapters on empowerment down to simple, disturbingly effective messages. He'd been blacking them out for more than a decade now, since he was ten, a painstaking but satisfying affair, but until last week he'd never been able to count it for anything as useful as school credit. Last week, when he'd accidentally left his latest project in the art studios over lunch—Lockland University had a mandatory art credit, even for budding doctors and scientists—he'd come back to his teacher poring over it. He'd expected a reprimand, some lecture on the cultural cost of defacing literature, or maybe the material cost of paper. Instead, the teacher had taken the literary destruction as art. He'd practically supplied the explanation, filled in any blanks using terms such as *expression, identity, found art, reshaping.*

Victor had only nodded, and offered a perfect word to the end of the teacher's list—*rewriting*—and just like that, his senior art thesis had been determined.

The marker hissed as he drew another line, blotting out several sentences in the middle of the page. His knee was going numb from the weight of the tome. If *he* were in need of self-help, he would search for a thin, simple book, one whose shape mimicked its promise. But maybe some people needed more. Maybe some people scanned the shelves for the heftiest one, assuming that more pages meant more emotional or psychological aid. He skimmed the words and smiled as he found another section to ink out.

By the time the first bell rang, signaling the end of Victor's art elective, he'd turned his parents' lectures on how to start the day into:

Be lost. Give up. give In. in the end It would be better to surrender before you begin. be lost. Be lost And then you will not care if you are ever found.

He'd had to strike through entire paragraphs to make the sentence perfect after he accidentally marked out *ever* and had to go on until he found another instance of the word. But it was worth it. The pages of black that stretched between *if you are* and *ever* and *found* gave the words just the right sense of abandonment.

Victor heard someone coming, but didn't look up. He flipped through to the back of the book, where he'd been working on a separate exercise. The Sharpie cut through another paragraph, line by line, the sound as slow and even as breathing. He'd marveled, once, that his parents' books were in fact self-help, simply not in the way they'd intended. He found their destruction incredibly soothing, a kind of meditation.

"Vandalizing school property again?"

Victor looked up to find Eli standing over him. The library-plastic cover crinkled beneath his fingertips as he tipped the book up to show Eli the spine, where VALE was printed in bold capital letters. He wasn't about to pay $25.99 when Lockland's library had such a suspiciously extensive collection of Vale-doctrine self-help. Eli took the book from him and skimmed.

"Perhaps . . . it   is . . . in . . . our . . . best   interest   to . . . to surrender . . . to give up . . . rather than waste . . . words."

Victor shrugged. He wasn't done yet.

"You have an extra *to*, before *surrender*," said Eli, tossing the book back.

Victor caught it and frowned, tracing his finger through the makeshift sentence until he found his mistake, and efficiently blotted out the word.

"You've got too much time, Vic."

"You must make time for that which matters," he recited, "for that which defines you: your passion, your progress, your pen. Take it up, and write your own story."

Eli looked at him for a long moment, brow crinkling. "That's awful."

"It's from the introduction," said Victor. "Don't worry, I blacked it out." He flipped back through the pages, a web of thin letters and fat black lines, until he reached the front. "They totally murdered Emerson."

Eli shrugged. "All I know is that book is a sniffer's dream," he said. He was right, the four Sharpies Victor had gone through in converting the book to art had given it an incredibly strong odor, one which Victor found at once entrancing and revolting. He got enough of a high from the destruction itself, but he supposed the smell was an unexpected addition to the project's complexity, or so the art teacher would spin it. Eli leaned back against the rail. His rich brown hair caught the too bright sun, bringing out reds and even threads of gold. Victor's hair was a pale blond. When the sunlight hit him, it didn't bring out any colors, but only accentuated the *lack* of color, making him look more like an old-fashioned photo than a flesh-and-blood student.

Eli was still staring down at the book in Victor's hands.

"Doesn't the Sharpie ruin whatever's on the other side?"

"You'd think," said Victor. "But they use this freakishly heavy paper. Like they want the weight of what they're saying to sink in."

Eli's laugh was drowned by the second bell, ringing out across the emptying quad. The bells weren't buzzers, of course—Lockland was too civilized—but they *were* loud, and almost ominous, a single deep church bell from the spiritual center that sat in the middle of campus. Eli cursed and helped Victor to his feet, already turning toward the huddle of science buildings, faced in rich red brick to make them seem less sterile. Victor took his time. They still had a minute before the final bell sounded, and even if they were late, the teachers would never mark them down. All Eli had to do was smile. All Victor had to do was lie. Both proved fright-eningly effective.

∞

VICTOR sat in the back of his Comprehensive Science Seminar—a course designed to reintegrate students of various scientific disci-plines for their senior theses—learning about research methods. Or at least being *told* about research methods. Distressed by the fact that the class relied on laptops, and since striking through words on a screen hardly gave him the same satisfaction, Victor had taken to watching the other students sleep, doodle, stress out, lis-ten, and pass digital notes. Unsurprisingly, they failed to hold his interest for long, and soon his gaze drifted past them, and past the windows, and past the lawn. Past everything.

His attention was finally dragged back to the lecture when Eli's hand went up. Victor hadn't caught the question, but he watched his roommate smile his perfect all-American-political-candidate smile before he answered. Eliot—Eli—Cardale had started out as a predicament. Victor had been none too happy to find the lanky, brown-haired boy standing in the doorway of his dorm a month into sophomore year. His first roommate had experienced a change of heart in the first week (through no fault of Victor's, of course) and had promptly dropped out. Due either to a shortage of students or perhaps a filing error made possible by fellow sophomore Max Hall's penchant for any Lockland-specific hacking challenge, the student hadn't been replaced. Victor's painfully small double was converted into a much more adequate single room. Until the start of October when Eliot Cardale—who, Victor had immediately decided, smiled too much—appeared with a suitcase in the hall outside.

Victor had initially wondered what it would take to recover his bedroom for a second time in a semester, but before he put any plans into motion, an odd thing happened. Eli began to . . . grow on him. He was precocious, and frighteningly charming, the kind of guy who got away with everything, thanks to good genes and quick wits. He was born for the sports teams and the clubs, but he surprised everyone, especially Victor, by showing no inclination whatsoever to join either. This small defiance of social norm earned him several notches in Victor's estimation, and made him instantly more interesting.

But what fascinated Victor *most* was the fact that something about Eli was decidedly *wrong*. He was like one of those pictures full of small errors, the kind you could only pick out by searching the image from every angle, and even then, a few always slipped by. On the surface, Eli seemed perfectly normal, but now and then Victor would catch a crack, a sideways glance, a moment when his roommate's face and his words, his look and his meaning, would not line up. Those fleeting slices fascinated Victor. It was like watching two people, one hiding in the other's skin. And their skin was always too dry, on the verge of cracking and showing the color of the thing beneath.

"Very astute, Mr. Cardale."

Victor had missed the question *and* the answer. He looked up as Professor Lyne turned his attention to the rest of his seniors, and clapped his hands once, with finality.

"All right. It's time to declare your thesis."

The class, composed mostly of pre-med students, a handful of aspiring physicists, and even an engineer—not Angie, though, she'd been assigned a different section—gave a collective groan, on principle.

"Now, now," said the professor, cutting off the protest. "You knew what you were getting into when you signed up."

"We didn't," observed Max. "It's a mandatory course." The remark earned him a ripple of encouragement from the class.

"My sincerest apologies then. But now that you're here, and seeing as there's no time like the present—"

"Next week would be better," called out Toby Powell, a broad-shouldered surfer, pre-med, and the son of some governor. Max had only earned a murmur, but this time the other students laughed at a level proportionate to Toby's popularity.

"Enough," said Professor Lyne. The class quieted. "Now, Lockland encourages a certain level of . . . industriousness where theses are concerned, and offers a proportionate amount of freedom, but a word of warning from *me*. I've taught this thesis seminar for seven years. You will do yourselves no favors by making a safe selection and flying under the radar; *however,* an ambitious thesis will win no points on the grounds of ambitiousness alone. Your grade is contingent upon execution. Find a topic close enough to your area of interest to be productive without selecting one you already consider yourselves expert on." He offered Toby a withering smile. "Start us off, Mr. Powell."

Toby ran his fingers through his hair, stalling. The professor's disclaimer had clearly shaken his confidence in whatever topic he'd been about to declare. He made a few noncommittal sounds while scrolling through his notes.

"Um . . . T helper 17 cells and immunology." He was careful not to let his voice wander up at the end into a question. Professor Lyne let him hang for a moment, and everyone waited to see if he would give Toby "the look"—the slight lift of his chin and the tilt of his head that he had become famous for; a look that said, *perhaps you'd like to try again*—but finally he honored him with a small nod.

His gaze pivoted. "Mr. Hall?"

Max opened his mouth when Lyne cut in with, "No tech. Science yes, tech no. So choose wisely." Max's mouth snapped shut a moment as he considered.

"Electrical efficacy in sustainable energy," he said after a pause.

"Hardware over software. Admirable choice, Mr. Hall."

Professor Lyne continued around the room.

Inheritance patterns, equilibriums, and radiation were all approved, while effects of alcohol/cigarettes/illegal substances, the chemical properties of methamphetamines, and the body's response to sex all earned "the look." One by one the topics were accepted or retooled.

"Next," ordered Professor Lyne, his sense of humor ebbing.

"Chemical pyrotechnics."

A long pause. The topic had come from Janine Ellis, whose eyebrows hadn't fully recovered from her last round of research. Professor Lyne gave a sigh, accompanied by "the look," but Janine only smiled and there wasn't much Lyne could say. Ellis was one of the youngest students in the room and had, in her freshman year, discovered a new and vibrant shade of blue that firework companies across the world now used. If she was willing to risk her eyebrows, that was her own business.

"And you, Mr. Vale?"

Victor looked at his professor, narrowing down his options. He'd never been strong in physics, and while chemistry was fun, his real passion lay in biology—anatomy and neuroscience. He'd like a topic with the potential for experimentation, but he'd also like to keep his eyebrows. And while he wanted to hold his rank in the department, offers from med schools, graduate programs, and research labs had been coming in the mail for weeks (and under the table for months). He and Eli had been decorating their entry hall with the letters. Not the offers, no, but the letters that preceded

them, all praise and charm, batting lashes and handwritten post-
scripts. Neither one of them needed to move worlds with their
papers. Victor glanced over at Eli, wondering what he would choose.

Professor Lyne cleared his throat.

"Adrenal inducers," said Victor on a lark.

"Mr. Vale, I've already turned down a proposal involving
intercourse—"

"No," Victor said, shaking his head. "Adrenaline and its physical and emotional inducers and consequences. Biochemical thresh-
olds. Fight or flight. That kind of thing."

He watched Professor Lyne's face, waiting for a sign, and Lyne
eventually nodded.

"Don't make me regret it," he said.

And then he turned to Eli, the last person to answer. "Mr.
Cardale."

Eli smiled calmly. "EOs."

The whole class, which had devolved more and more into muffled conversation as students declared their topics, now stopped.
The background chatter and the sound of typing and the fidgeting
in chairs went still as Professor Lyne considered Eli with a new
look, one that hung between surprise and confusion, tempered
only by the understanding that Eliot Cardale was consistently top
of the class, top of the entire pre-medical department, even—well,
alternating with Victor for first and second spot, anyway.

Fifteen pairs of eyes flicked between Eli and Professor Lyne as
the moment of silence lasted and became uncomfortable. Eli wasn't
the kind of student to propose something as a joke, or a test. But he
couldn't possibly be serious.

"I'm afraid you'll have to expand," said Lyne slowly.

Eli's smile didn't falter. "An argument for the theoretical feasibility of the existence of ExtraOrdinary people, deriving from laws of biology, chemistry, and psychology."

Professor Lyne's head tilted and his chin tipped, but when he opened his mouth, all he said was, "Be careful, Mr. Cardale. As I warned, no points will be given for ambition alone. I'll trust you not to make a mockery of my class."

"Is that a yes, then?" asked Eli.

The first bell rang.

One person's chair scraped back an inch, but no one stood up.

"Fine," said Professor Lyne.

Eli's smile widened.

Fine? thought Victor. And, reading the looks of every other student in the room, he could see everything from curiosity to surprise to envy echoed in their faces. It was a joke. It had to be. But Professor Lyne only straightened, and resumed his usual composure.

"Go forth, students," he said. "Create change."

The room erupted into movement. Chairs were dragged, tables knocked askew, bags hoisted, and the class emptied in a wave into the hall, taking Victor with it. He looked around the corridor for Eli and saw that he was still in the room, talking quietly, animatedly, with Professor Lyne. For a moment the steady calm was gone and his eyes were bright with energy, glinting with hunger. But by the time he broke away and joined Victor in the hall, it was gone, hidden behind a casual smile.

"What the hell was that?" Victor demanded. "I know the thesis doesn't matter much at this point, but still—was that some kind of joke?"

Eli shrugged, and before the matter could be pressed, his phone broke out into electro-rock in his pocket. Victor sagged against the wall as Eli dug it out.

"Hey, Angie. Yeah, we're on our way." He hung up without even waiting for a response.

"We've been summoned." Eli slung his arm around Victor's shoulders. "My fair damsel is hungry. I dare not keep her waiting."

LAST NIGHT

MERIT CEMETERY

SYDNEY'S arms were beginning to ache from lifting the shovel, but for the first time in a year, she wasn't cold. Her cheeks burned, and she was sweating through her coat, and she felt alive.

As far as she was concerned, that was the *only* good thing about digging up a corpse.

"Couldn't we do something else?" she asked, leaning on the shovel.

She knew Victor's answer, could feel his patience thinning, but she still had to ask because asking was talking, and talking was the only thing distracting her from the fact that she was standing over a body, and digging her way toward it instead of away from it.

"The message has to be sent," said Victor. He didn't stop digging.

"Well then, maybe we could send a *different* message," she said under her breath.

"It has to be done, Syd," he said, finally looking up. "So try to think of something pleasant."

She sighed, and started digging again. A few scoops of dirt later, she stopped. She was almost afraid to ask.

"What are *you* thinking of, Victor?"

He flashed a small, dangerous smile. "I'm thinking about what a lovely night it is."

They both knew it was a lie, but Sydney decided she'd rather not know the truth.

∞

VICTOR wasn't thinking of the weather.

He hardly felt the cold through his coat. He was too busy trying to picture what Eli's face would look like when he received their message. Trying to picture the shock, the anger, and threaded through it all, the fear. Fear because it could only mean one thing.

Victor was out. Victor was free.

And Victor was coming for Eli—just as he'd promised he would.

He sunk the shovel into the cold earth with a satisfying thud.

IV

TEN YEARS AGO

LOCKLAND UNIVERSITY

"YOU'RE seriously not going to tell me what that was about?" asked Victor as he followed Eli through the massive double doors and into the Lockland International Dining Suite, more commonly known as LIDS.

Eli didn't answer as he scanned the eating hall for Angie.

The whole place resembled a theme park, in Victor's opinion, all the mundane trappings of a cafeteria hidden beneath plastic and plaster facades that were out of scale and out of place beside each other. Circling a quad-sized stretch of tables, eleven eatery options each boasted different menus in different fonts with different decor. By the doors was a bistro, complete with a low little gate erected for a waiting line. Next to it Italian music played, several pizza ovens gaping behind the counter. Across the way the Thai, Chinese, and sushi places sat in paper-lantern colors, bright and primary and inviting. Joining these were a burger joint, a carving station, a comfort food kitchen, a salad bar, a smoothie shop, and a basic café.

Angie Knight was sitting near the Italian eatery, twirling pasta on her fork, her coppery curls wandering into her eyes as she read a book pinned beneath her tray. A small prickle ran through Victor when he spotted her, the voyeuristic thrill of seeing someone before they see you, of being able to simply watch. But the moment ended when Eli saw her, too, and caught her gaze without a word. They were like magnets, thought Victor, each with their own pull. They showed it every day in class, and around campus, people always drifting *toward* them. Even Victor felt the draw. And then when they got close enough to each other . . . well. Angie's arms were around Eli's neck in an instant, her perfect lips against his.

Victor looked away, giving them a moment of privacy, which was absurd considering their public display of affection was very . . . public. A female professor looked up from a folded paper several tables over, one eyebrow quirking before she turned the page with a loud crack. Eventually, Eli and Angie managed to pry themselves apart and she acknowledged Victor with a hug, a gesture that was simple but genuine, all the warmth, but none of the heat.

And that was okay. He was not in love with Angie Knight. She didn't belong to him. Even though he met her first, even though *he'd* been a magnet for her once, and she'd wandered toward him in LIDS that first week of school freshman year, and they'd had smoothies because it was still ungodly hot out even in September, and her face was red from track and his was red from her. Even though she hadn't even *met* Eli until sophomore year when *Victor* brought his new roommate to sit with him at dinner because it seemed like good karma.

Fucking karma, he thought as Angie pulled away and floated back to her seat.

Eli grabbed soup and Victor bought Chinese, and the three sat in the growing noise of the eating hall and ate and made mindless conversation, even though Victor desperately wanted to find out what the hell Eli was thinking picking *EOs* as a thesis. But Victor knew better than to interrogate him in front of Angie. Angie Knight was a *force.* A force with long legs and the most severe case of curiosity that Victor had ever encountered. She was only twenty, had been coveted by the top schools since she could drive, had been given a dozen business cards followed by a dozen offers and just as many follow-ups, both subtle and not-so-subtle bribes, and here she was at Lockland. She'd recently accepted an offer from an engineering firm, and upon graduation would be the youngest—and, Victor wagered, the brightest—employee of their company. She wouldn't even be able to drink yet.

Besides, judging by the looks the other students had given Eli when he made his thesis selection, word would reach her soon enough.

Finally, after a lunch dotted with pauses and occasional warning glances from Eli, the bell rang and Angie left for her next class. She wasn't even supposed to *have* a next class, but she'd taken on an extra elective. Eli and Victor sat and watched her cloud of red hair bob away with all the glee of someone off to eat cake, not explore forensic chemistry or mechanical efficacy or whatever she'd picked up as a pet project this time.

Or rather, Eli watched her go, and Victor watched Eli watch her, something twisting in his stomach. It wasn't just that Eli stole Angie from Victor—that was bad enough—but somehow Angie had stolen Eli from him, too. The more interesting Eli, anyway. Not the one with perfect teeth and an easy laugh, but the one beneath that was glittering and sharp, like broken glass. It was in those jagged pieces that Victor saw something he recognized. Something dangerous, and hungry. But when Eli was with Angie, it never showed. He was a model boyfriend, caring, attentive, and *dull,* and Victor found himself studying his friend in Angie's wake, searching for signs of life.

Several quiet minutes passed as the eating halls thinned and emptied, and then Victor lost patience and kicked Eli under the wood table. His eyes drifted lazily up from his food.

"Yes?"

"Why EOs?"

Eli's face slowly, slowly, began to open, and Victor felt his chest loosen with relief as Eli's darker self peeked through.

"Do you believe in them?" asked Eli, drawing patterns in what was left of his soup.

Victor hesitated, chewing on a piece of lemon chicken. *EO. ExtraOrdinary.* He had heard of them, the way people hear about any phenomena, from believer sites and the occasional late-night exposé where "experts" analyze grainy footage of a man lifting a car or a woman engulfed in fire without burning. Hearing *about* EOs and believing *in* EOs were very different things, and he couldn't tell by Eli's tone which camp he fell into. He couldn't tell which camp Eli wanted *him* to fall into, either, which made answering infinitely harder.

"Well," prompted Eli. "Do you believe?"

"I don't know," Victor said truthfully, "if it's a matter of believing . . ."

"Everything starts with belief," countered Eli. "With faith."

Victor cringed. It was a kink in his understanding of Eli, the latter's reliance on religion. Victor did his best to overlook it, but it was a constant snag in their dialogues. Eli must have sensed he was losing him.

"With wonder, then," he amended. "Do you ever *wonder?*"

Victor wondered about lots of things. He wondered about himself (whether he was broken, or special, or better, or worse) and about other people (whether they were all really as stupid as they seemed). He wondered about Angie—what would happen if he told her how he felt, what it would be like if she chose him. He wondered about life, and people, and science, and magic, and God, and whether he believed in any of them.

"I do," he said slowly.

"Well, when you wonder something," said Eli, "doesn't that mean part of you *wants* to believe in it? I think we want to prove things, in life, more than we want to disprove them. We *want* to believe."

"And you want to believe in superheroes." Victor's voice was carefully devoid of judgment, but he couldn't smother the smile that crept across his mouth. He hoped Eli wouldn't take offense, would only see it as good humor—levity, not mockery—but he didn't. His face snapped shut.

"Fine, yeah, it's stupid, right? You caught me. I didn't give a shit about the thesis. I just wanted to see if Lyne would let me get away with it," he said, flashing a rather hollow smile and pushing up from the table. "That's all."

"Wait," said Victor. "It's not all."

"That's *all*."

Eli turned, dumped his tray, and walked out before Victor could say more.

VICTOR always kept a Sharpie in his back pocket.

As he wandered the aisles of the library searching for books to kick-start his own thesis, his fingers itched to take it out. His failed conversation with Eli had set him on edge, and he longed to find his quiet, his peace, his personal Zen, in the slow obliteration of someone else's words. He managed to make his way to the medical section without incident, adding a book on the human nervous system to one he'd already picked up on psychology. After finding a few smaller texts on adrenal glands and human impulse, he checked out, careful to keep his fingertips—permanently stained from his art projects—hidden in his pockets or under the lip of the counter while the librarian looked over the books. There had been a few complaints during his time at Lockland about books being "vandalized," if not outright "ruined." The librarian looked at him over the stack as if his crimes were written on his face instead of his fingers, before finally scanning in the books and handing them back.

Back in the university-issued apartment he shared with Eli, Victor unpacked his bag. He knelt in his bedroom and slid the marked-up self-help book onto a low shelf beside two others he'd checked out and altered, silently pleased that no return calls had been placed on any of them yet. The books on adrenaline he left on his desk. He heard the front door open and shut and wandered into the living room a few minutes later to find Eli flopping down onto the couch. He'd set a stack of books and stapled printouts on the university-issued wooden coffee table, but when he saw Victor come in, he reached instead for a magazine and began to flip through it, feigning boredom. The books on the table were on everything from brain function under stress to human will, anatomy, psychosomatic responses . . . but the printouts were different. Victor picked up one of them and sank into a chair to read it. Eli frowned faintly as he did it, but didn't stop him. The printouts were captures from Web sites, message boards, forums. They would never been seen as admissible sources.

"Tell me the truth," said Victor, tossing the pages back onto the table between them.

"About what?" asked Eli absently. Victor stared, blue eyes unblinking, until Eli finally set the magazine aside, sat up, and pivoted, setting his feet firmly on the ground so he could mirror Victor's position. "Because I think they might be real," he said. *"Might,"* he emphasized. "But I'm willing to consider the possibility."

Victor was surprised at the sincerity in his friend's voice.

"Go on," he said, offering his best *trust me* face.

Eli ran his fingers over the stack of books. "Try to look at it like this. In comic books there are two ways a hero is made. Nature and nurture. You have Superman, who was born the way he was, and Spider-Man, who was made that way. You with me?"

"I am."

"If you do even a basic Web search for EOs"—here he gestured at the printouts—"you find the same divide. Some people claiming that EOs are born ExtraOrdinary, and others suggesting every-thing from radioactive goo and poisonous insects to random chance. Let's say you manage to find an EO, so you've got the proof they *do* exist, the question becomes how. Are they born? Or are they *made*?"

Victor watched the way that Eli's eyes took on a sheen when he spoke of EOs, and the change in his tone—lower, more urgent—matched with the nervously shifting muscles in his face as he tried to hide his excitement. The zeal peeked through at the corners of his mouth, the fascination around his eyes, the energy in his jaw. Victor watched his friend, mesmerized by the transformation. He himself could mimic most emotions and pass them off as his, but mimicking only went so far, and he knew he could never match this . . . *fervor.* He didn't even try. Instead he kept calm, listened, his eyes attentive and reverent so that Eli wouldn't be discouraged, wouldn't retreat.

The last thing Victor wanted him to do was retreat. It had taken nearly two years of friendship to crack through the charming, candy shell and find the thing Victor had always known lurked within. And now, slouching around a coffee table stacked with low-res screen shots of sites run by grown men in their parents' basements, it was as if Eliot Cardale had found God. Even better, as if he had found God and wanted to keep it a secret but couldn't. It shone through his skin like light.

"So," said Victor slowly, "let's assume EOs do exist. You're going to figure out *how*."

Eli flashed him the kind of smile a cult leader would covet. "That's the idea."

V

LAST NIGHT

MERIT CEMETERY

THUD.

Thud.

Thud.

"How long were you in prison?" asked Sydney, trying to fill the quiet. The sound of digging, when combined with Victor's absent humming, wasn't helping her nerves.

"Too long," answered Victor.

Thud.

Thud.

Her fingers hurt dully from gripping the shovel. "And that's where you met Mitch?"

Mitch—Mitchell Turner—was the massive man waiting for them back in the hotel room. Not because he didn't like grave-yards, he told them emphatically. No, it was just that *someone* had to stay behind with Dol, and besides, there was work to do. Lots of work. It had nothing to do with the bodies.

Sydney smiled when she thought of him scrounging for excuses. It made her feel a fraction better to think of Mitch, who was roughly the size of the car—and could probably lift one with ease—being squeamish about death.

"We were cellmates," he said. "There are a lot of very bad people in jail, Syd, and only a few decent ones. Mitch was one of them."

Thud.

Thud.

"Are you one of the bad ones?" asked Sydney. Her watery blue eyes stared straight at him, unblinking. She wasn't sure if the answer mattered, really, but she felt like she should know.

"Some would say so," he said.

Thud.

She kept staring. "I don't think you're a bad person, Victor."

Victor kept digging. "It's all a matter of perspective."

Thud.

"About the prison. Did they . . . did they let you out?" she asked quietly.

Thud.

Victor left the shovel planted in the ground, and looked up at her. And then he smiled, which she noticed he seemed to do a lot before he lied, and said, "Of course."

VI

PRISON was less important than what it afforded Victor. Namely, time.

Five years in isolation gave him time to think.

Four years in integration (thanks to budget cuts and the lack of evidence that Vale was in any way abnormal) gave him time to practice. And 463 inmates to practice on.

And the last seven months had given him time to plan this moment.

"Did you know," said Victor, skimming a book from the prison library on anatomy (he thought it particularly foolish to endow inmates with a detailed sense of the positions of vital organs, but there you go), "that when you take away a person's fear of pain, you take away their fear of death? You make them, in their own eyes, immortal. Which of course they're not, but what's the saying? We are all immortal until proven otherwise?"

"Something like that," said Mitch, who was a bit preoccupied.

Mitch was Victor's cellmate at Wrighton Federal Penitentiary. Victor was fond of Mitch, in part because Mitch was thoroughly unconcerned with prison politics, and in part because he was *clever*. People didn't seem to catch on because of the man's size, but Victor saw the talent, and put it to good use. For instance, Mitch was presently trying to short out a security camera with a gum wrapper, a cigarette, and a small piece of wire Victor had secured for him three days before.

"Got it," said Mitch a few moments later, when Victor was thumbing through the chapter on the nervous system. He set the book aside, and flexed his fingers as the guard came down the aisle.

"Shall we?" he asked as the air began to hum.

Mitch took a long look around their cell, and nodded. "After you."

VII

TWO DAYS AGO

ON THE ROAD

THE rain hit the car in waves. There was so much of it that the wiper blades did nothing to clear it away, only managed to move it around on the windows, but neither Mitch nor Victor complained. After all, the car was stolen. And obviously stolen *well*; they'd been driving it without incident for almost a week, ever since they swiped it from a rest stop a few miles from the prison.

The car passed a sign that pronounced MERIT—23 MILES.

Mitch drove and Victor stared out past the downpour at the world as it flew by. It felt so fast. Everything felt fast after being in a cell for ten years. Everything felt free. For the first few days they had driven aimlessly, the need to move outweighing the need for a destination. Victor hadn't known where they were driving. He hadn't decided yet where to start the search. Ten years was long enough to plan the details of the prison break down to the minutiae. Within an hour he had new clothes, within a day he had money, but a week out and he still didn't have a place to start looking for Eli.

Until that morning.

He'd picked up *The National Mark,* a nationwide paper, from a gas station, flipping absently through, and fate had smiled at him. Or at least, *someone* had smiled. Smiled straight up from a photo printed to the right of a news article titled:

CIVILIAN HERO SAVES BANK

The bank was located in Merit, a sprawling metropolis halfway between Wrighton's barbed-wire walls and Lockland's wrought-iron fences. He and Mitch had been heading there for no other reason than the fact that it was somewhere to go. A city full of people Victor could question, persuade, coerce. And a city that was already showing promise, he thought, lifting the folded paper.

He had bought the copy of *The National Mark,* but taken only that page, slipping it into his folder almost reverently. It was a start.

Now Victor closed his eyes, and tipped his head back against the seat while Mitch drove.

Where are you, Eli? he wondered.

Where are you where are you where are you where are you?

The question echoed in his head. He'd wondered it every day for a decade. Some days absently, and others with such an intense need to know that it hurt. It actually *hurt,* and for Victor, that was something. His body settled back into the seat as the world sped by. They hadn't taken the freeway—most escaped convicts knew better than that—but the speed limit on the two-lane highway was more than satisfactory. Anything was better than standing still.

Sometime later, the car hit a small pothole, and the bump jarred Victor from his reverie. He blinked, and turned his head to watch the trees that bordered the road zip past. He rolled down the window halfway to feel that speed, ignoring Mitch's protests about the rain splashing into the car. He didn't care about the water or the seats. He needed to *feel* it. It was dusk, and in the last dregs of the day Victor caught sight of a shape moving down the side of the road. It was small, head bowed and clutching at itself as it trudged down the narrow shoulder of the highway. Victor's car passed it before he frowned and spoke up.

"Mitch, go back."

"For what?"

Victor turned his attention to the massive man behind the wheel. "Don't make me ask again."

Mitch didn't. He threw the car into reverse, the tires slipping on the wet pavement. They passed the figure again, but this time going backward. Mitch shifted the car again into drive, and crawled up alongside the shape. Victor rolled down his window the rest of the way, the rain pressing in.

"You all right?" he asked over the rain.

The figure didn't respond. Victor felt something prickle at the edge of his senses, humming. Pain. It wasn't his.

"Stop the car," he said, and this time Mitch put the vehicle promptly—a little *too* promptly—into park. Victor got out, zipped his coat up to his throat, and began to walk alongside the stranger. He was a good two heads taller.

"You're hurt," he said to the bundle of wet clothes. It wasn't the arms crossed tightly over the form's chest that gave it away, or the dark stain on one sleeve, darker even than the rain, or the way the figure pulled back sharply when he reached out a hand. Victor smelled pain the way a wolf smelled blood. Tuned to it.

"Stop," he said, and this time the person's steps dragged to a halt. The rain fell, steady and cold, around them. "Get in the car."

The figure looked up at him then, and the wet hood of the coat fell back onto a pair of narrow shoulders. Water blue eyes, fierce behind smudged black liner, stared up at him from a young face. Victor knew pain too well to be fooled by the defiant look, the set jaw around which wet blond hair curled and stuck. She couldn't be more than twelve, thirteen maybe.

"Come on," he pressed, gesturing to the car that had stopped beside them.

The girl just stared at him.

"What's going to happen to you?" he asked. "Couldn't be worse than what already has."

When she made no motion toward the car, he sighed and pointed at her arm.

"Let me look at that." He reached out, letting his fingers graze her jacket. The air around his hand crackled the way it always did, and the girl let out a barely audible breath of relief. She rubbed at her sleeve.

"Hey, stop that," he warned, knocking her hand away from the wound. "I didn't fix it."

Her eyes danced between his hand and her sleeve, and back again.

"I'm cold," she said.

"I'm Victor," he said, and she offered him a small, exhausted flicker of a smile. "Now what do you say we get out of the rain?"

VIII

LAST NIGHT

MERIT CEMETERY

"YOU'RE not a bad person," repeated Sydney, flinging dirt onto the moonlit grass. "But Eli is."

"Yes. Eli is."

"But he didn't go to prison."

"No."

"Do you think he'll get the message?" she asked, pointing at the grave.

"I'm pretty sure," said Victor. "And if he doesn't, your sister will."

Sydney's stomach twisted at the thought of Serena. In her mind, her big sister was two different people, two images overlapping in a way that blurred both, and made her feel dizzy, ill.

There was the Serena from before the lake. The Serena who'd knelt on the floor in front of her the day she left for college—they both knew she was abandoning Sydney to the toxic, empty house—and who used her thumb to wipe tears from Sydney's cheek, saying over and over, *I'm not gone, I'm not gone.*

And then there was the Serena from after the lake. The Serena whose eyes were cold and whose smile was hollow, and who made things happen with only words. The one who lured Sydney into a field with a body, cooing at her to show her trick, and then looking sad when she did. The one who turned her back when her boyfriend raised his gun.

"I don't want to see Serena," said Sydney.

"I know," said Victor. "But I want to see Eli."

"Why?" she asked. "You can't kill him."

"That may be." His fingers curled around the shovel. "But half the fun is trying."

IX

TEN YEARS AGO
LOCKLAND UNIVERSITY

WHEN Eli picked up Victor from the airport a few days before the start of spring semester, he was wearing the kind of smile that made Victor nervous. Eli had as many different smiles as ice cream shops had flavors, and this one said he had a secret. Victor didn't want to care, but he did. And since he couldn't seem to keep himself from caring, he was determined to at least keep himself from showing it.

Eli had spent the whole break on campus doing research for his thesis. Angie had complained because he was supposed to go away with her; Angie, as Victor predicted, was not a fan of Eli's thesis, neither the subject matter nor the percent of his time it was occupying. Eli claimed the holiday research stint was a token to placate Professor Lyne, to prove he was taking the thesis seriously, but Victor didn't like it because it meant that Eli had a head start. Victor didn't like it because he had, of course, petitioned to stay over break, too, applied for the same exemptions, and had been denied. It had taken all his control to hide the anger, the desire to pen over Eli's life, and rewrite it into his. Somehow he managed only a shrug and a smile, and Eli promised to keep him in the loop if he made any headway in their—Eli had said *their,* not *his,* and that had helped placate him—area of interest. Victor had heard nothing all during break; then a few days before he was scheduled to fly back to campus, Eli called to say he'd found something, but refused to tell his friend what it was until the two were back on campus.

Victor had wanted to book an earlier flight (he couldn't wait to escape the company of his parents, who had first insisted on a Christmas together, and then on reminding him daily of the sacrifice they were making, since holidays were their most popular tour slots) but he didn't want to seem too eager, so he waited out the days, working furiously on his own adrenal research, which felt remedial by comparison, a simple issue of cause and effect, with too much documented data to make for much of a challenge. It was regurgitation. Competently organized and elegantly worded, yes, but dotted by hypotheses that felt, to Victor, uninspired, dull. Lyne had called the outline solid, had said that Victor was off to a running start. But Victor didn't want to run while Eli was busy trying to fly.

And so, by the time he climbed into the passenger seat of Eli's car, his fingers were rapping on his knees from the excitement. He stretched in an effort to still them, but as soon as they hit his legs again, they resumed their restless motion. He'd spent most of the flight storing up indifference so that when he saw Eli, the first words out of his mouth wouldn't be *tell me,* but now that they were together, his composure was failing.

"Well?" he asked, trying unsuccessfully to sound bored. "What did you find?"

Eli tightened his grip on the steering wheel as he drove toward Lockland.

"Trauma."

"What about it?"

"It was the only commonality I could find in all the cases of EOs that are even close to well-documented. Anyway, bodies react in strange ways under stress. Adrenaline and all that, *as you know.*

I figured that trauma could cause the body to chemically alter." He began to speak faster. "But the problem is, *trauma* is such a vague word, right? It's a whole blanket, really, and I needed to isolate a thread. Millions of people are traumatized daily. Emotionally, physically, what-have-you. If even a fraction of them became ExtraOrdinary, they would compose a measurable percentage of the human population. And if that were the case EOs would be more than a thing in quotation marks, more than a hypothesis; they'd be an actuality. I knew there had to be something more specific."

"A genre of trauma? Like car accidents?" asked Victor.

"Yes, exactly, except there weren't indicators of any common trauma. No obvious formula. No parameters. Not at first."

Eli let his words hang in the car. Victor turned the radio from low to off. Eli was practically bouncing in his seat.

"But?" prompted Victor, cringing at his own obvious interest.

"But I started digging," said Eli, "and the few case studies I could dig up—unofficial ones, of course, and this shit was a pain to find—the people in them weren't just traumatized, Vic. They *died*. I didn't see it at first because nine times out of ten when a person doesn't stay dead, it isn't even recorded as an NDE. Hell, half the time people don't realize they've *had* an NDE."

"NDE?"

Eli glanced over at Victor. "Near death experience. What if an EO isn't a product of just any trauma? What if their bodies are reacting to the greatest physical and psychological trauma possible? Death. Think about it, the kind of transformation we're talking about wouldn't be possible with a physiological reaction alone, or a psychological reaction alone. It would require a huge influx of adrenaline, of fear, awareness. We talk about the power of will, we talk about mind over matter, but it's not one over the other, it's both at once. The mind and the body both respond to imminent death, and in those cases where both are strong enough—and both would *have* to be strong, I'm talking about genetic predisposition and will to survive—I think you might have a recipe for an EO."

Victor's mind whirred as he listened to Eli's theory.

He flexed his fingers against his pant legs.

It made sense.

It made sense and it was simple and elegant and Victor hated that, especially because *he* should have seen it first, should have been able to hypothesize. Adrenaline was *his* research topic. The only difference was that he'd been studying temporary flux, and Eli had gone so far as to suggest a permanent shift. Anger flared through him, but anger was unproductive so he twisted it into pragmatism while he searched for a flaw.

"Say something, Vic."

Victor frowned, and kept his voice carefully devoid of Eli's enthusiasm.

"You've got two knowns, Eli, but no idea how many unknowns. Even if you can definitively say that an NDE and a strong will to survive are necessary components, think of how many other factors there could be. Hell, the subject might need a dozen other items on their ExtraOrdinary checklist. And the two components you do have are too vague. The term *genetic predisposition* alone comprises hundreds of traits, any or all of which could be crucial. Does the subject need naturally elevated chemical levels, or volatile glands? Does their present physical condition matter, or only their body's innate reactions to change? As for the mental state, Eli, how could you possibly calculate the psychological factors? What constitutes a strong will? It's a philosophical can of worms. And then there's the entire element of chance."

"I'm not discounting any of those," said Eli, deflating a little as he guided the car into their parking lot. "This is an additive theory, not a deductive one. Can't we celebrate the fact that I've potentially made a key discovery? EOs require NDEs. I'd say that's pretty fucking cool."

"But it's not enough," said Victor.

"Isn't it?" snapped Eli. "It's a start. That's something. Every theory needs a place to start, Vic. The NDE hypothesis—this cocktail of mental and physical reactions to trauma—it holds water."

Something small and dangerous was taking shape in Victor as Eli spoke. An idea. A way to twist Eli's discovery into *his*, or at least, into *theirs*.

"And it's a *thesis*," Eli went on. "I'm trying to find a scientific explanation for the EO phenomena. It's not like I'm actually trying to *create* one."

Victor's mouth twitched, and then it twisted into a smile.

"Why not?"

∞

"**BECAUSE** it's suicide," said Eli in between mouthfuls of sandwich.

They were sitting in LIDS, which was still fairly empty before the start of the spring semester. Only the Italian eatery, the comfort food kitchen, and the café were open.

"Well, yes, necessarily," Victor said, sipping a coffee. "But if it worked . . ."

"I can't believe you're actually suggesting this," said Eli. But there was something in his voice, woven through the surprise. Curiosity. Energy. That fervor Victor had sensed before.

"Let's say you're right," pressed Victor, "and it's a simple equation: a near death experience, with an emphasis on the *near*, plus a certain level of physical stamina, and a strong will—"

"But you're the one who said it's *not* simple, that there have to be more factors."

"Oh, I'm sure there are," said Victor. But he had Eli's attention. He liked having his attention. "Who knows how many factors? But I'm willing to admit that the body is capable of incredible things in life-threatening situations. That's what *my* thesis has been about, remember? And maybe you're right. Maybe the body is even capable of a fundamental chemical shift. Adrenaline has given people seemingly superhuman abilities in times of dire need. Glimpses of power. Perhaps there's a way to make the change a lasting one."

"This is mad—"

"You don't believe that. Not entirely. It's your thesis after all," said Victor. His mouth quirked as he stared down into his coffee. "Incidentally, you'd get an A on that."

Eli's eyes narrowed. "My thesis was meant to be theoretical—"

"Oh really?" said Victor with a goading smile. "What happened to believing?"

Eli frowned. He opened his mouth to answer, but was cut off by a pair of slender arms around his neck.

"What has my boys looking so stern?" Victor looked up to see Angie's rust-colored curls, her freckles, her smile. "Sad the holidays are over?"

"Hardly," said Victor.

"Hey Angie," said Eli, and Victor watched the light fold in behind his eyes even as he pulled her in for one of those movie-star kisses. Victor swore inwardly. He had worked so hard to bring it out, and Angie was undoing all of Eli's focus with a kiss. He pushed up from the table, annoyed.

"Where you going?" asked Angie.

"Long day," he said. "I just got back, still have to unpack . . ."

His voice trailed off. Angie was no longer paying attention. She had her fingers tangled in Eli's hair, her lips against his. Just like that, he'd lost them both.

Victor turned, and left.

X

TWO DAYS AGO

THE ESQUIRE HOTEL

VICTOR held the hotel door open while Mitch carried Sydney—wounded and soaking wet—inside. Mitch was massive, head shaved, almost every inch of exposed skin inked, and about as broad as the girl was tall. She could have walked, but Mitch had decided that carrying her would be easier than trying to get her arm up around his shoulders. He had also carried two suitcases, which he dropped by the door.

"This'll do, I think," he said, looking cheerfully around the luxurious suite.

Victor set down another, much smaller case, peeled his wet coat off, and hung it up, rolling his sleeves as he directed Mitch to put the girl in the bathroom. Sydney craned her head as she was carried through the room. The Esquire Hotel, located in downtown Merit, was bare in a way that made her wonder if they'd thrown pieces of furniture out, and she found herself looking down to see if there were indents where chair legs or couch feet had once been. But the floor throughout was wood, or something manufactured to look like it, and the bathroom was stone and tile. Mitch set her in the shower—a large, doorless marble space—and disappeared.

She shivered, feeling nothing but a dull, pervasive cold, and Victor appeared several minutes later, carrying an armful of miscellaneous clothing.

"One of these should fit you," he said, dropping the pile on the counter beside the sink. He stood outside the bathroom door while she pulled her own wet clothes off and examined the pile, wondering where these new clothes had come from. It looked as though they'd raided the contents of a laundry room, but the things were dry and warm and so she didn't complain.

"Sydney," she called at last, her voice muffled by the shirt caught halfway over her head and the door between them. "That's my name."

"Pleasure," said Victor from the hall.

"How did you do that?" she called out as she searched through the shirts.

"Do what?" he asked.

"Make the pain stop."

"It's a . . . gift."

"A gift," mumbled Sydney bitterly.

"Have you ever met someone with a gift before?" he asked through the door.

Sydney let the question hang, the ensuing silence punctuated only by the sound of clothes being ruffled, tugged on, discarded. When she finally spoke again, all she said was, "You can come in now."

Victor did, and found her in sweatpants that were too big and a spaghetti strap top that was too long, but both would do for now. He told her to sit very still on the counter while he examined her arm. When he cleaned away the last traces of blood, he frowned.

"What's wrong?" she asked.

"You've been shot," he said.

"Obviously."

"Were you playing with a gun or something?"

"No."

"When did this happen?" he asked, fingers pressed to her wrist.

"Yesterday."

He kept his eyes on her arm. "Are you going to tell me what's going on?"

"What do you mean?" she asked hollowly.

"Well, Sydney, you have a bullet in your arm, your pulse is several beats too slow for someone your age, and your temperature feels about five degrees too cold."

Sydney tensed, but said nothing.

"Are you hurt anywhere else?" he asked.

Sydney shrugged. "I don't know."

"I'm going to give the pain back, a little," he said. "To see if you have any other injuries."

She gave a small, tight nod. His grip tightened a fraction on her arm, and the dull, pervasive cold warmed to an ache, pinching into sharp pain at different points on her body. She gasped for breath, but bore with it as she told him the places where the pain was worst. She watched him as he worked, his touch impossibly light, as if he was afraid of breaking her. Everything about him was light—his skin, his hair, his eyes, his hands as they danced through the air above her skin, touching her only when absolutely necessary.

"Well," said Victor, once he'd bandaged her up and taken back what was left of the pain. "Aside from the bullet wound, and a twisted ankle, you seem to be in decent shape."

"Aside from that," said Sydney drily.

"It's all relative," said Victor. "You're alive."

"I am."

"Are you going to tell me what happened to you?" he asked.

"Are you a doctor?" she countered.

"I was supposed to be one. A long time ago."

"What happened?"

Victor sighed and leaned back against the towel rack. "I'll trade you. An answer for an answer."

She hesitated, but finally nodded.

"How old are you?" he asked.

"Thirteen," she lied because she hated being twelve. "How old are you?"

"Thirty-two. What happened to you?"

"Someone tried to kill me."

"I can see that. But why would someone try to do that?"

She shook her head. "It's not your turn. Why couldn't you become a doctor?"

"I went to jail," he said. "Why would someone try to kill you?"

She scratched her shin with her heel, which meant she was about to lie, but Victor didn't know her well enough to know that yet. "No idea."

Sydney almost asked about jail, but changed her mind at the last moment. "Why did you pick me up?"

"I have a weakness for strays," he said. And then Victor surprised her by asking, "Do you have a gift, Sydney?"

After a long moment, she shook her head.

Victor looked down, and she saw something cross his face, like a shadow, and for the first time since the car pulled up beside her, she felt afraid. Not an all-consuming fear, but a low and steady panic spreading over her skin.

But then Victor looked up, and the shadow was gone. "You should get some rest, Sydney," he said. "Take the room down the hall."

He turned, and was gone before she could say thank you.

VICTOR made his way into the suite's kitchen, separated from the rest of the main room by only a marble counter, and poured a drink from the stash of liquor he and Mitch had been assembling since departing Wrighton, and which Mitch had brought up from the car. The girl was lying and he knew it, but he resisted the urge to resort to his usual methods. She was a kid, and clearly scared. And she'd been hurt enough already.

Victor let Mitch take the other bedroom. The man would never fit on the couch, and Victor didn't sleep much anyway. If he did happen to get tired, he certainly didn't mind the plush sofa. That had been his least favorite thing about prison. Not the people, or the food, or even the fact that it was *prison*.

It was the damned cot.

Victor took up his drink and wandered the wooden laminate floor of the hotel suite. It was remarkably realistic, but gave no squeak, and he could feel the concrete beneath. His legs had spent long enough standing on concrete to know.

An entire wall of the living room was made of floor-to-ceiling windows, a set of balcony doors embedded in the center. He opened them, and stepped out onto a shallow landing seven stories up. The air was crisp and he relished it as he rested his elbows on the frozen metal rail, clutching his drink, even though the ice made the glass cold enough to hurt his fingers. Not that he felt it.

Victor stared out at Merit. Even at this hour, the city was alive, a thrumming, humming place filled with people he could sense without even stretching. But at that moment, surrounded by the cold, metallic city air and the millions of living, breathing, *feeling* bodies, he wasn't thinking about any of them. His eyes hovered on the buildings, but his mind wandered past them all.

XI

TEN YEARS AGO

"WELL?" asked Victor later that night. He'd had a drink. A couple drinks. They kept a stocked beer shelf in the kitchen for gatherings, and a supply of hard liquor in the drawer under the bathroom sink for the very bad days or the very good ones.

"There's no way," said Eli. He saw the tumbler in Victor's hand, and headed to the bathroom to pour himself one, too.

"That's not strictly true," said Victor.

"There's no way to create enough control," clarified Eli as he took a long sip. "No way to ensure survival, let alone any form of abilities. Near death experiences are still near *death*. It's too great a risk."

"But if it worked . . ."

"But if it didn't . . ."

"We could create control, Eli."

"Not enough."

"You asked me if I ever wanted to believe in something. I do. I want to believe in this. I want to believe that there's *more*." Victor sloshed a touch of whiskey over the edge of his glass. "That we could *be* more. Hell, we could be heroes."

"We could be dead," said Eli.

"That's a risk everyone takes by living."

Eli ran his fingers through his hair. He was rattled, unsure. Victor liked seeing him that way. "It's just a *theory*."

"Nothing you ever do, Eli, is meant to be theoretical. I see it in you." Victor was very proud of verbalizing the observation in one try, considering his level of inebriation. Nevertheless, he needed to stop talking. He didn't like people to know how closely he watched, matched, mimicked them. "I see it," he finished quietly.

"I think you've had enough."

Victor looked down at the amber liquid.

The moments that define lives aren't always obvious. They don't always scream *LEDGE,* and nine times out of ten there's no rope to duck under, no line to cross, no blood pact, no official letter on fancy paper. They aren't always protracted, heavy with meaning. Between one sip and the next, Victor made the biggest mistake of his life, and it was made of nothing more than one line. Three small words.

"I'll go first."

He'd thought about it in the car on the way back from the airport, when he asked *why not?* He'd thought about it as they ate lunch, and then as he walked around campus, finishing his coffee, thought about it all the way back to the residence halls and the upperclassmen's apartments beyond them. Somewhere between the third and fourth tumbler, the question mark had become a period. There wasn't a choice. Not really. This was the only way to be more than a spectator to Eli's great feats. To be a participant. A contributor.

"What do you have on you?" he asked.

"What do you mean?"

Victor quirked a pale eyebrow, unamused. Eli didn't do drugs, but he always had them, the fast way on Lockland's campus—and Victor wagered any campus—to make cash, or a few new friends. Eli seemed to see, then, where Victor was going.

"No."

Victor had already vanished back into the bathroom, and emerged with the bottle of whiskey, which was still very full.

"What do you have?" he asked again.

"No."

Victor sighed, crossed to the coffee table and swiped a piece of scrap paper, scribbling out a note. *See the books on the bottom shelf.*

"There," he said, handing it to Eli, who frowned. Vic shrugged, took another swig.

"I worked hard on those books," he explained, steadying himself on the arm of the couch. "They're poetry. And they're a better suicide note than anything I'd be able to come up with right now."

"No," said Eli again. But the word was distant and dull, and the light in his eyes was growing. "This isn't going to work." Even as he said it, he was walking toward his room, toward the side table where Victor knew he kept the pills.

Victor pushed off the couch, and followed.

∞

HALF an hour later, lying on the bed with an empty bottle of Jack and an empty bottle of painkillers side by side on the nearest table, Victor began to wonder if he'd made a mistake.

His heart jackhammered, forcing blood too fast through the veins. His vision swam and he closed his eyes. A mistake. He sat up suddenly, certain he'd vomit, but hands pushed him back to the bed and held him there.

"No go," said Eli, easing up only when Victor swallowed and focused on the ceiling tiles.

"Remember what we talked about," Eli was saying. Saying something about fighting back. About will.

Victor wasn't listening, couldn't hear much over his pulse, and how could his heart pound any harder? He was no longer wondering whether or not he'd made a mistake. He was certain. Certain that in twenty-two years of life, this was the worst plan he had ever come up with. This was the wrong *method,* the fading, rational part of Victor said, the part that had been studying adrenaline and pain and fear. He shouldn't have washed the amphetamines down with whiskey, shouldn't have done *anything* to dull the nerves and senses, to ease the process, but he'd been nervous . . . afraid. Now he was going numb, and that scared him more than pain because it meant he might just . . . fade.

Fade right into death without noticing.

This was wrong wrong wrong . . . but that voice was drifting off, replaced by a spreading, sinking—

It could work.

He forced the thought through the dulling panic. It could work, and if it *did* work, he wanted the chance to hold the power, the evidence, the proof. He wanted to *be* the proof. Without it, this was Eli's monster, and he was merely the wall off which Eli bounced his ideas. With it, he *was* the monster, essential, inextricable from Eli's theories. He tried counting tiles, but he couldn't keep track. Even though his heart was straining, his thoughts seeped in like syrup, new ones pouring through before the old had left. Numbers began to overlap, to blur. Everything began to blur. His fingertips felt numb in a worrying way. Not cold exactly, but as if his body were beginning to draw its energy in, to shut down, starting with the smallest parts. The nausea faded, too, at least. Only the rushing pulse warned him that his body was failing.

"How are you feeling?" asked Eli, leaning forward in a chair he'd pulled up to the bed. He hadn't had a drink, but his eyes were shining, dancing with light. He didn't look worried. He didn't seem afraid. Then again, he wasn't the one about to die.

Victor's mouth felt wrong. He had to focus too hard to form the words.

"Not great," he managed.

They'd settled for a good old-fashioned overdose for several reasons. If it failed, it would be the easiest to explain. Also, Eli could wait to call it in until they'd entered a crisis zone. Reaching the hospital too early meant it wouldn't be a near death experience, just a very unpleasant one.

The numbness was eating its way through Victor's body. Up his limbs, through his head.

His heart skipped, then slammed forward in a disconcerting way.

Eli was talking again, low and urgent.

Each time Victor blinked it got harder to open his eyes again. And then, for a moment, fear crackled through him. Fear of dying. Fear of Eli. Fear of everything that could happen. Fear of nothing happening. It was so sudden and so strong.

But soon the numbness ate that, too.

His heart skipped again and there was a space where pain should have been, but he'd had too much to drink to feel it. He closed his eyes to focus on fighting back but all the darkness did was eat him up. He could hear Eli speaking, and it must have been important because he was raising his voice in a way he never did, but Victor was sinking, straight through his skin and the bed and the floor, right down into black.

XII

VICTOR heard something break, and looked down to find he'd clutched his drink too tightly, and shattered the glass. He was gripping shards, ribbons of red running down over his fingers. He opened his fist, and the broken glass tumbled over the banister into the hotel restaurant's shrubbery seven stories below. He looked down at the fragments still embedded in his palm.

He didn't feel them.

Victor went inside and stood at the sink, picking the largest shards of glass out of his skin, watching the fragments glitter in the stainless steel basin. He felt clumsy, numb, unable to get the smaller pieces out, so he closed his eyes, took a low breath, and began to let the pain back in. Soon his hand burned, his palm painted with a dull ache that helped him determine where the lingering glass was embedded. He finished extricating the pieces, and stood staring at his bloodied palm, shallow waves of pain rippling up his wrist.

ExtraOrdinary.

The word that started—ruined, changed—everything.

He frowned, turning up his nerves the way one would a dial. The pain sharpened, spread to a pins-and-needles prickle radiating out from his palm, down his fingers and up his wrist. He turned the dial up again and winced as the pins-and-needles became a blanket of pain across his body, not dull but sharp as knives. Victor's hands began to shake but he continued, twisting the dial in his mind until he was burning, breaking, shattering.

His knees buckled, and he caught himself on the counter with a bloody hand. The pain switched off like a blown fuse, leaving Victor dark. He steadied himself. He was still bleeding, and he knew he should get the medical kit they'd brought up from the car for Sydney; not for the first time, Victor wished he could trade abilities with Eli.

But first he wiped the blood from the counter, and poured himself another drink.

XIII

TEN YEARS AGO
LOCKLAND MEDICAL CENTER

OUT of nothing came pain.

Not the pain Victor would later learn to know and hold and use, but the simple, too-human pain of a poorly executed overdose.

Pain and dark, which became pain and color, and then pain and glaring hospital lights.

Eli was sitting in a chair by Victor's bed, just as he had been in the apartment. Only now there were no bottles, no pills. Just beeping machines and thin sheets and the worst headache Victor Vale had ever experienced, including the summer he decided to raid his parents' special collections while they were on a European tour. Eli's head was down, his fingers clasped loosely the way they were when he prayed. Victor wondered if that's what he was doing now, praying, and wished he would stop.

"You didn't wait long enough," he whispered when he was sure Eli wasn't busy with God.

Eli looked up. "You stopped breathing. You almost flatlined."

"But I didn't."

"I'm sorry," said Eli, rubbing his eyes. "I couldn't . . ."

Victor sagged back into the bed. He supposed he should be thankful. Erring too early was better than erring too late. Still. He dug his fingernail under one of the censors on his chest. If it *had* worked, would he feel different? Would the machines go crazy? Would the fluorescent lights shatter? Would the bed catch fire?

"How do you feel?" asked Eli.

"Like ass, Cardale," snapped Victor, and Eli winced, more from the use of that last name than the tone. Three drinks in, high on the wave of discovery, before the pills kicked in, they'd decided that when they were done, Eli would go by Ever instead of Cardale, because it sounded cooler, and in the comics heroes had important, often alliterative names. So what if neither one of them had been able to think of any examples? In that moment, it seemed to matter. For once Victor had the natural advantage, and even though it was the smallest, most inconsequential kind of thing, the way a name fell from the tongue, he liked having something Eli didn't. Something Eli wanted. And maybe Eli didn't *really* care, maybe he was just trying to keep Victor conscious, but he still looked stung when Victor called him *Cardale,* and right now that was enough.

"I've been thinking," started Eli, leaning forward. There was a barely contained energy to his limbs. He twisted his hands. His legs bounced a little in his chair. Victor tried to focus on what Eli was saying with his mouth, not his body. "Next time, I think—"

He stopped when a woman in the doorway cleared her throat. She wasn't a doctor—no coat—but a small nametag over her heart identified her as something worse.

"Victor? My name is Melanie Pierce. I'm the resident psychologist here at Lockland Medical."

Eli's back was to her, and his eyes narrowed on Victor, warning. He waved at Eli dismissively, both to tell him to get out and to confirm that he wouldn't say anything. They'd come this far. Eli rose and mumbled something about going to call Angie. He closed the door behind him.

"Victor." Ms. Pierce said his name in that slow, cooing way, running a hand over her mousy brown hair. It was big in that middle-aged, Southern way. Her accent was unplaceable but her tone was clearly patronizing. "The staff here told me that your emergency contacts couldn't be reached."

What he thought was *thank god*. What he said was, "My parents, right? They're on tour."

"Well, in these circumstances, it's important for you to know that—"

"I didn't try to kill myself." Partial lie.

An indulgent twitch of her lips.

"I just partied a little too hard." Total lie.

A lean of her head. Her hair never moved.

"Lockland's pretty high stress. I needed a break." Truth.

Ms. Pierce sighed. "I believe you," she said. Lie. "But when we release you—"

"When is when?"

She pursed her lips. "We are obligated to keep you here for seventy-two hours."

"I have class."

"You need time."

"I need to go to class."

"It's not up for discussion."

"I wasn't trying to kill myself."

Her voice had tightened into something less friendly, more honest, impatient, normal.

"Then why don't you tell me what you *were* doing."

"Making a mistake," said Victor.

"We all make mistakes," she said, and he felt ill. He didn't know if it was an aftereffect of the overdose, or just her prepackaged therapy. His head fell back against the pillow. He closed his

eyes but she kept talking. "*When* we release you, I'm going to rec-
ommend that you meet with Lockland's counselor."

Victor groaned. Counselor Peter Mark. A man with two first
names, no sense of humor, and a sweat gland issue.

"That's really not necessary," he mumbled. Between his parents,
he'd had enough involuntary therapy to last several lifetimes.

Ms. Pierce's patronizing look returned. "I feel it is."

"If I agree to it, will you release me now?"

"If you don't agree to it, Lockland will not welcome you back.
You'll be here for seventy-two hours, and during that time you'll
be meeting with me."

He spent the next several hours planning how to kill someone
else—Ms. Pierce, specifically—instead of himself. Maybe, if he
told her, she'd see that as progress, but he doubted it.

XIV

THE drink dangled precariously from Victor's freshly bandaged hand as he paced. No matter how many times he made it from one wall of the hotel room to the other and back, the restlessness refused to ebb. Instead, it seemed to charge him, a mental static crackling in his head as he moved. The urge to scream or thrash or pitch his new drink against the wall came on suddenly, and he closed his eyes, and forced his legs to do the one thing they didn't want to do: stop.

Victor stood perfectly still, trying to swallow the energy and chaos and electricity and find in its place *stillness.*

In prison, he'd had moments like this, this same shade of panic peaking like a wave before crashing over him. *End this,* the darkness had hissed, tempted. How many days had he resisted the urge to reach out, not with his hands but with this *thing* inside him, and ruin everything? Everyone?

But he couldn't afford to. Not then, not now. The only way he'd even made it out of isolation was by convincing the staff, beyond a shadow of a doubt, that he was normal, powerless, no threat, or at least no more of a threat than the other 463 inmates. But in those cell-locked moments of darkness, the urge to break everyone around him became crippling. Break them all, and just walk out.

Now, just as then, he folded in, doing his best to forget he even had a power to wield against others, a whim as sharp as glass. Now, just as then, he ordered his body and mind to still, to calm. And now, just as then, when he closed his eyes and searched for silence, a word rose up to meet him, a reminder of why he couldn't afford to break, a challenge, a name.

Eli.

XV

TEN YEARS AGO
LOCKLAND MEDICAL CENTER

ELI slumped into the hospital chair beside Victor's bed, dropping a backpack to the laminate floor beside him. Victor himself had just finished his last session with the resident psych, Ms. Pierce, in which they had explored his relationship with his parents, of whom Ms. Pierce was—unsurprisingly—a fan. Pierce left the session with the promise of a signed book and the sense that they'd made serious progress. Victor left the session with a headache and a note to meet with Lockland's counselor a minimum of three times. He'd negotiated his seventy-two-hour sentence down to forty in exchange for that signed book. Now he was waging battle with the hospital bracelet, unable to pry it off. Eli leaned forward, produced a pocket knife, and snapped the strange paper-plastic-hybrid material. Victor rubbed his wrist and stood, then winced. Nearly dying, it turned out, had not been pleasant. Everything hurt in a dull, constant way.

"Ready to get out of here?" asked Eli, shouldering his backpack.

"God yes," said Victor. "What's in the bag?"

Eli smiled. "I've been thinking," he said as they wound through the sterile halls, "about my turn."

Victor's chest tightened. "Hmm?"

"This was indeed a learning experience," said Eli. Victor muttered something unkind, but Eli continued. "Booze was a bad idea.

As were painkillers. Pain and fear are inextricable from panic, and panic aids in the production of adrenaline and other fight or flight chemicals. As you know."

Victor's brow creased. Yeah, as he knew. Not that his drunken self had cared.

"There are only a certain number of situations," continued Eli as they passed through a pair of automatic glass doors and into the cold day, "where we can introduce both enough panic and enough control. The two are in most cases mutually exclusive. Or at least, they don't have much overlap. The more control, the less need to panic, etc. etc."

"But what's in the bag?"

They reached the car, and Eli tossed the item in question into the backseat.

"Everything we need." Eli's smile spread. "Well. Everything but the ice."

∞

IN fact, "everything we need" amounted to a dozen epinephrine pens, more commonly known as EpiPens, and twice as many one-use warming pads, the kind hunters keep in their boots and football fans in their gloves during winter games. Eli grabbed three of the pens and lined them up on the kitchen table beside the stack of warmers, and then stepped back, casting one sweeping motion over it as if offering Victor a feast. Half a dozen bags of ice leaned against the sink, small rivers of cold condensation wetting the floor. They'd stopped for it on the way home.

"You swiped this?" asked Victor, lifting a pen.

"Borrowed in the name of science," countered Eli as he took up a hand warmer and turned it over to examine the removable

plastic coating on the back that served as an activation mechanism. "I've been shadowing at Lockland Med since freshman year.
They didn't even blink."

Victor's head was pounding again.

"Tonight?" he asked, not for the first time since Eli had explained his plan.

"Tonight," confirmed Eli, plucking the pen from Victor's grip.
"I considered dissolving the epinephrine directly into saline and
having you administer it intravenously, since that would give a
more reliable distribution, but it's slower than the EpiPens, and
dependent on better circulation. Besides, given the nature of the
setup, I thought we'd be better off with a more user-friendly
option."

Victor considered the supplies. The EpiPen would be the easy
part, the compressions more difficult and more damaging. Victor
had CPR training, and an intuitive understanding of the body,
but it was still a risk. Neither pre-med clusters nor innate skill
could truly prepare a student for what they were trying to do. Killing something was easy. Bringing it back to life took more than
measurement and medicine. It was like cooking, not baking. Baking took a sense of order. Cooking took a flare, a little art, a little
luck. This kind of cooking took a *lot* of luck.

Eli took up two more EpiPens, and arranged the three in his
palm. Victor's gaze wandered from the pens to the warmers to the
ice. Such simple tools. Could it be that easy?

Eli said something. Victor dragged his attention back.

"What?" he asked.

"It's getting late," Eli said again, gesturing beyond the bags of
ice to the window behind the sink, where light was bleeding rap-
idly out of the sky. "Better get set up."

VICTOR ran his fingers through the ice water, and recoiled. Beside him, Eli slit the last bag open, watching it rupture and spill ice into the tub. With the first few bags, the ice had crackled and broken and half dissolved, but soon the water in the bath was cold enough to keep the cubes from melting. Victor retreated to the sink and leaned against it, the three EpiPens brushing his hand.

They'd talked through the order of operations several times by now. Victor's fingers trembled faintly. He gripped the lip of the counter to still them as Eli tugged off his jeans, his sweater, and finally his shirt, exposing a series of faded scars that hatched his back. They were old, worn to little more than shadows, and Victor had seen them before, but never asked. Now, as he faced the very real possibility that this would be the last conversation he'd ever have with his friend, curiosity got the better of him. He tried to shape the question, but it wasn't necessary, because Eli answered without prompting.

"My father did it, when I was a kid," he said softly. Victor held his breath. In more than two years, Eli had never once mentioned his parents. "He was a minister." There was a far-off quality to his voice, and Victor couldn't help but notice the *was*. Past tense. "I don't think I've ever told you that."

Victor didn't know what to say, so he said the most useless word in the world. "Sorry."

Eli turned away, and shrugged his shoulders, the scars on his back warping with the gesture. "It all worked out."

He stepped up to the tub, his knees resting against the porcelain front as he looked down at the shimmering surface. Victor watched him watch the bath, and felt a strange mixture of interest and concern.

"Are you scared?" he asked.

"Terrified," said Eli. "Weren't you?"

Victor could vaguely remember a flicker of fear, a matchstick's worth, fluttering before being gutted by the effects of the pills and the whiskey. He shrugged.

"You want a drink?" he asked. Eli shook his head.

"Alcohol warms the blood, Vale," he said, eyes still fixed on the icy water. "That's not exactly what I'm going for here."

Victor wondered if Eli would actually be able to do it, or if the cold would crack his mask of ease and charm, shatter it to reveal the normal boy beneath. The bath had handles somewhere beneath the icy surface, and they'd done a walk-through before dinner— neither had been terribly hungry—Eli climbing into the then-dry tub, curling his fingers around the handles, tucking his toes under a lip at the foot of the bath. Victor had suggested cord, something to bind Eli to the tub, but Eli had refused. Victor wasn't sure if it had been bravado or a concern for the state of the body should this fail.

"Any day now," said Victor, trying to diffuse the tension. When Eli didn't move, didn't humor him with even a hollow smile, Victor reached over to the toilet, where his laptop rested on the closed lid. He opened a music program and clicked play, flooding the small tiled room with the heavy base of a rock song.

"You better turn that shit down when you're searching for a pulse," said Eli.

And then he closed his eyes. His lips were moving faintly, and even though his hands hung at his sides, Victor knew he was praying. It perplexed him, how someone about to play God could pray to Him, but it clearly didn't bother his friend.

When Eli's eyes floated open, Victor asked, "What did you say to Him?"

Eli lifted one bare foot to the rim of the bath, gazing down at the contents. "I put my life into His hands."

"Well," said Victor, earnestly, "let's hope He gives it back."

Eli nodded, and took a short breath—Victor imagined he could hear the faintest waver in it—before he climbed into the tub.

∞

VICTOR perched on the tub, clutching a drink as he stared down at Eliot Cardale's corpse.

Eli hadn't screamed. Pain had been written across every one of the forty-three muscles Victor's anatomy class taught him twined together in the human face, but the worst Eli had done was let a small groan escape between clenched teeth when his body first broke the surface of the icy water. Victor had only brushed his fingers through, and the cold had been enough to elicit a spark of pain up his entire arm. He wanted to hate Eli for his composure, had almost hoped—*almost hoped*—that it would be too much for him to bear. That he would break, give up, and Victor would help him out of the tub, and offer him a drink, and the two would sit and talk about their failed trials, and later, when it was a safe distance behind them, they would laugh about how they'd suffered for the sake of science.

Victor took another sip of his drink. Eli was a very unhealthy shade of whitish-blue.

It hadn't taken as long as he'd expected. Eli had gone quiet several minutes ago. Victor had shut the music off, the heavy beat echoing in his head until he realized it was his heart. When he'd ventured a hand down into the ice bath to search for Eli's own pulse—fighting back a gasp at the biting cold—there had been none. He'd chosen to wait a few more minutes, though, which is why he'd poured the drink. If Eli did manage to come back from this, he wouldn't be able to accuse Victor of rushing.

When it became evident that the body in the bath wouldn't somehow revive on its own, Victor set the drink aside, and got to work. Dragging Eli from the tub was the hardest part, since he was several inches taller than Victor, stiff, and submerged in a basin of ice water. After several attempts and a good deal of quiet cursing (Victor was naturally quiet, but even more so under pressure, which gave his peers the distinct impression he knew what he was doing, even when he didn't), he tumbled back to the tiles, Eli's body hitting the floor beside him with the sickening thud of dead weight. Victor shivered. He bypassed the EpiPens for the stack of blankets and warmers, remembering Eli's instructions, and quickly toweled the body off. He then activated the warmers and placed them at the vital points: head, back of the neck, wrists, groin. This was the part of the plan that required luck and art. Victor had to decide at what point the body was warm enough to begin compressions. Too soon meant too cold and too cold meant the epinephrine would put too much stress on the heart and organs. Too late meant too long and too long meant a much greater chance of Eli being too dead to fix.

Victor snapped the bathroom's heat lamp on, despite the fact that he was sweating, and grabbed the three pens from the counter—three was the limit, and he knew that if there was no cardiac response by the third pen, it was too late—and set them on the tiles beside him. He rearranged them, returned them to their straight lines, the small behavior giving him a sense of control while he waited. Every few moments, he checked Eli's temperature, not with a thermometer, but against his own skin. They had

realized during their walk-through that they didn't own a thermometer, and Eli, in a rare display of impatience, had insisted on
Victor using his judgment. It could have been a death knell, but
Eli's faith in Victor revolved around the fact that everyone at
Lockland believed him to have an affinity for medicine, an effortless, nearly preternatural understanding of the human body (in
truth, it was far from effortless, but Victor did have a knack for
guessing). The body was a machine, only necessary pieces, every
component at every level, from muscle and bone down to chemical and cell, operating on action and reaction. To Victor it just
made sense.

When Eli felt warm enough, he began compressions. The flesh
beneath his hands was coming up to temperature, making the
body feel less like a Popsicle and more like a cadaver. He cringed as
the ribs cracked beneath his tangled hands, but didn't stop. He
knew that if the ribs didn't separate from the sternum, he wasn't
pushing hard or far enough to hit the heart. After several sets, he
paused to grab the first pen, and jabbed it down into Eli's leg.

One count, two count, three count.

No response.

He started pumping again, trying not to the think about the
breaking ribs and the fact that Eli still looked thoroughly, undeniably dead. Victor's arms burned and he resisted the urge to cast
sideways glances at his cell phone, which had tumbled from his
pocket in the struggle to extricate Eli from the tub. He closed his
eyes, continued counting and pressing his intertwined fists up and
down and up and down and up and down over Eli's heart.

It wasn't working.

Victor took up the second pen, and plunged it into Eli's thigh.

One count, two count, three count.

Still nothing.

For the first time, panic filled Victor's mouth like bile. He swallowed, and resumed compressions. The only sounds in the room were his whispered counts and his pulse—*his* pulse, not Eli's—and the odd sound of his hands trying desperately to restart his best friend's heart.

Trying. And failing.

Victor began to lose hope. He was running out of chances, out of pens. There was only one left. His hand slid from Eli's chest, shaking as his fingers curled around it. He raised the pen, and stopped. Beneath him, sprawled on the tiles, was the lifeless body of Eli Cardale. Eli, who showed up in the hallway sophomore year with a suitcase and a smile. Eli, who believed in God and had a monster inside just like Victor, but knew how to hide it better. Eli, who got away with everything, who had slipped into his life and stolen the girl and the top rank and the stupid holiday research grant. Eli, who, despite it all, meant something to Victor.

He swallowed, and drove the pen into his dead friend's chest.

One count, two count, three count.

Nothing.

And then, somewhere between Victor giving up and reaching for his phone, Eli gasped.

XVI

TWO DAYS AGO

THE ESQUIRE HOTEL

VICTOR heard the tread of barefoot steps behind him as Mitch came into the room. He saw the hulking figure in the reflective sheen of the windowpane, felt him the way he felt everyone, as if they were all under water, himself included, and every movement made ripples.

"You're wandering," said Mitch, meeting Victor's gaze in the glass.

It was a small, familiar phrase, one Mitch had often used when he'd found Victor staring off between the bars, squinting faintly, as if trying to see through the walls to something in the distance. Something important.

Now Victor blinked, eyes sliding from the window and Mitch's ghostly reflection to the fake wood floor. He listened to Mitch's footsteps recede into the kitchen, the soft sound of the fridge opening, a carton being taken out. Chocolate milk. It was all Mitch wanted to drink now that he was out, since they didn't have any at Wrighton. Victor had quirked a brow, but let the man have his whims. Prison left a hunger in you, a craving. The exact nature of the want depended on the person.

Victor wanted something, too.

He wanted to watch Eli bleed.

Mitch leaned his elbows on the counter, and drank his milk in silence. Victor thought his cellmate after getting out might have a plan of his own, people he'd want to see, but he had only looked at Victor over the hood of the stolen car and asked, "Where next?" If Mitch did have a past, he was clearly still running from it, and in the meantime, Victor was more than willing to give him something to run *to*. He liked making people useful.

His gaze eventually wandered past Mitch's reflection to the Merit night, the ice in his nearly empty drink clinking as the glass shifted in his grip. The two had been in each other's company for a long time. They knew when the other wanted to talk, and when they wanted to think. The only problem was that more often than not, Victor wanted to think, and more often than not, Mitch wanted to talk. Victor could feel Mitch beginning to fidget under the weight of the quiet.

"Quite a view," he said, tipping his glass toward the windows.

"Yeah," said Mitch. "Been a long time since I've seen a view that grand. Next place we go, I hope it has windows like this."

Victor nodded again, absently, brought his forehead to rest against the cool glass. He couldn't afford to think of *next*, or *after*. He'd spent far too long thinking of *now*. Waiting for *now*. The only *nexts* in his world were the short, quick ones standing between him and Eli. And they were falling away so fast.

Mitch yawned. "You sure you're okay, Vic?" he asked, returning the carton to the fridge.

"Dandy. Night."

"Night," said Mitch, wandering back to his room.

Victor watched Mitch go in the glass, before two pale smudges— his own eyes, ghosted against the darkened buildings—brought him back. Victor turned away from the wall of windows, and finished his drink.

A folder sat on a side table beside the leather couch, a handful of papers escaping from within. A face gazed steadily out from a picture, the right eye and cheek obscured by the folder's front, and Victor set the empty glass on the table and flicked the cover back to reveal the rest of the face. It was the page from the copy of *The National Mark* he'd bought that morning.

CIVILIAN HERO SAVES BANK

Below ran the article on the young, precocious man who had been in the right place at the right time and had risked his life to stop an armed robber at a local branch.

Smith & Lauder Bank, a landmark in the northern financial sector of Merit, was the sight of a foiled robbery yesterday when a civilian hero put himself between a masked assailant and the money. The civilian, who wishes to remain nameless, told authorities that he noticed the man behaving suspiciously several blocks from the bank, and that a bad feeling was all that led him to follow. Before he reached the bank, the man pulled on a mask, and by the time the civilian caught up, the robber had already plunged inside. In a fearless display, the civilian went in after him. According to the customers and employees trapped inside, the robber at first appeared unarmed, but then proceeded to fire an undetermined weapon up at the stained-glass ceiling, shattering it and raining shards down on the captured populace. He then took aim at the bank vault, but was derailed by the arrival of the civilian. The bank manager reports that the robber took aim at the civilian when he tried to intercede, and then chaos erupted. Shots were fired, and in the mayhem the customers and employees managed to escape the building. By the time the police reached the scene, it was over. The robber, later identified as a troubled man named Barry Lynch, had been killed in the firefight, but the civilian was uninjured. It was a bad day with a happy ending, a remarkable display of courage by a citizen of Merit, and there is no doubt the city is thankful to have such a hero on her streets.

Victor had blacked out most of the article in his usual fashion, and what was left, was this:

a

sight

a civilian hero

nameless,

a bad feeling

fear-

less

unarmed

and in the mayhem

████████████████████████████ uninjured. It was █

████████████████████████ a remarkable display ████

██

██████████████████████████████

It had calmed something in Victor, the blotting out of the words, but the revised state of the article didn't change the fact that several things about it were clearly amiss. First, the robber himself. Barry Lynch. Victor had had Mitch go scrounging, and from what little they could dig up, Barry had several EO markers. Not only had he suffered an NDE, but he'd racked up a string of arrests in the months following, each for theft with an unidentified weapon. The cops never found it on his person, so he was let go; Victor had to wonder if Barry *was* the weapon.

Even more concerning—and more intriguing—than a potential EO was the photograph of the civilian hero. He had asked to remain nameless, but nameless and anonymous are not the same, especially where papers are concerned, and there, below the article, was a picture. A grainy photo of a young man turning away from the scene and the cameras, but not before casting a last, almost cocky, glance back at the press.

The smile on the man's face was unmistakable, young and proud, the same smile he used to flash Victor. The *exact* same smile.

Because Eliot Cardale hadn't aged a day.

XVII

TEN YEARS AGO
LOCKLAND UNIVERSITY

ELI took several gulping breaths, cradling his chest. His eyes struggled open, fought to focus. He took in the room around him, the view from the blanketed floor, before leveling his unsteady gaze on Victor.

"Hey," he said shakily.

"Hey," said Victor, fear and panic still scribbled over him. "How do you feel?"

Eli closed his eyes, rolled his head from side to side. "I . . . I don't know . . . I'm fine . . . I think."

Fine? Victor had cracked his ribs, broken at least half by the feel of it, and Eli felt *fine?* Victor had felt like death. Worse than. Like every fiber of his being had been plucked or torqued or twisted or cramped. Then again, Victor hadn't *died,* right? Not the way he was certain Eli had. He'd sat and watched, made sure Eliot Cardale was nothing but a corpsicle. Maybe it was shock. Or the three shots of epinephrine. That's what it had to be. But even with shock and a nowhere near healthy dose of adrenaline . . . *fine?*

"Fine?" he asked aloud.

Eli shrugged.

"Can you . . ." Victor wasn't sure how to finish the question. If their absurd theory had worked and Eli had somehow acquired an ability by simply dying and coming back, would he even know it? Eli seemed to know the question's end.

"I mean, I'm not starting fires with my mind, or making earthquakes or whatever. But I'm not dead." There was, Victor could hear, a faint waver of relief in his voice.

As the two sat in a pile of damp blankets on the water-streaked bathroom floor, the whole experiment seemed *idiotic*. How could they have risked so much? Eli took another long, low breath, and got to his feet. Victor rushed to catch his arm, but Eli shook him off.

"I said I'm fine." He left the bathroom, eyes carefully avoiding the tub, and vanished into his room in search of clothes. Victor plunged his hand down through the icy water one last time and pulled the plug. By the time he'd cleaned up, Eli had reappeared in the hall, fully dressed. Victor found him examining himself in a wall mirror, frowning faintly.

Eli's balance faltered, and he put a hand on the wall to steady himself.

"I think I need . . . ," he started.

Victor assumed the line would end with "a doctor" but instead Eli met his eyes in the mirror, and smiled—not his best—and said, "A drink."

Victor managed to pull his own mouth into something like a smile, then, too.

"That I can do."

∞

ELI insisted on going out.

Victor thought they could just as easily get wasted in the comfort of their apartment, but since Eli had experienced the more recent of their two traumas and seemed rather intent on be-ing in public, perhaps wanting to live it up, Victor indulged him. Now the two were on the far side of drunk—or at least, Victor was; Eli seemed remarkably lucid considering the sheer quantity of alcohol he'd consumed—swaying and sauntering down the road that ran so conveniently from the local bar back to their apartment building, eliminating the need for a vehicle.

Despite a festive air, both had done their best to avoid the sub-ject of what had happened, and how lucky Eli—and really both of them—had been. Neither seemed eager to talk about it, and in the absence of any ExtraOrdinary symptoms—other than feeling ex-traordinarily *lucky*—neither had reason to gloat as much as thank their stars. Which they did freely, tipping imaginary but brim-ming glasses skyward as they stumbled home. They poured invis-ible liquor on the concrete as a gift to earth or God or fate or whatever force had let them have their fun and live to know it had been nothing more than that.

Victor felt warm despite the flurries of snow, alive, and even welcomed the last dregs of pain from his own unpleasant proxim-ity to death. Eli beamed dazedly at the night sky, and then he stepped off the sidewalk. Or tried to. But his heel caught the edge, and he stumbled, landing on his hands and knees among a patch of dirty snow, and tire tracks, and broken glass. He hissed, recoiled, and Victor saw blood, a smear of red against the dingy, snow-dusted street. Eli proceeded to sit on the lip of the curb, tilting his palm toward the nearest streetlamp to get a better look at the gash there, glittering with the remains of someone's abandoned beer bottle.

"Ouch," said Victor, leaning over him to examine the cut and nearly losing his balance. He caught himself on the streetlamp as Eli cursed softly and pulled the largest shard out.

"Think I'll need stitches?"

He held his bloody hand up for Victor to inspect, as if the latter's vision and judgment were any better than his own right now. Victor squinted, and was about to reply with as much authority as he could muster, when something happened.

The cut on Eli's palm began to *close.*

The world, which had been swaying in Victor's vision, came to an abrupt stop. Stray flakes hung in the air, and their breath hovered in clouds over their lips. There was no movement except that of Eli's flesh healing.

And Eli must have felt it, because he lowered his hand into his lap, and the two gazed down as the gash that had run from pinkie to thumb knitted itself back together. In moments, the bleeding had stopped—the blood already lost now drying on his skin—and the wound was nothing more than a wrinkle, a faint scar, and then not even that.

The cut was just . . . gone.

Hours passed in blinks as the two let it sink in, what that meant, what they had done. It was extraordinary.

It was ExtraOrdinary.

Eli rubbed his thumb over the fresh skin of his palm, but Victor was the first to speak, and when he did, it was with an eloquence and composure perfectly befitting the situation.

"Holy shit."

VICTOR stared up at the place where the lip of their apartment building's roof met the cloudy night. Every time he closed his eyes he felt like he was falling over, getting closer and closer to the brick, so he tried to keep them open, focusing on that strange seam overhead.

"Are you coming?" asked Eli.

He was holding the door open, practically bouncing in his eagerness to get inside and find something else that could physically wound him. Zeal burned in his eyes. And while Victor didn't exactly *blame* him, he had no desire to sit around and watch Eli stab himself all night. He'd watched him try all the way home, leaving a dotted red trail in the snow from the blood that escaped before the wounds could heal. He'd seen the ability. Eli was an EO, in the (regenerating) flesh. Victor had felt something when Eli had come back to life seemingly EO-free: relief. With Eli's new abilities being thrust into his wavering line of vision all the way home, Victor's relief had dissolved into a ripple of panic. He would be relegated to sidekick, note-taker, the brick wall to bounce ideas off of.

No.

"Vic, you coming or not?"

Curiosity and jealousy ate at Victor in equal parts, and the only way he knew to stifle both, to quell the urge to wound Eli himself—or at least to try—was to walk away.

He shook his head, then stopped abruptly when the world continued swinging side to side.

"Go on," he said, mustering a smile that came nowhere near his eyes. "Go play with some sharp objects. I need to take a walk." He descended the stairs, and nearly fell twice in three steps.

"Are you fit to walk, Vale?"

Victor waved him on inside. "I'm not driving. Just going to get some air."

And with that, he took off into the dark, with two goals on his mind.

The first was simple: to put as much distance as he could between himself and Eli before he did something he'd regret.

The second was trickier, and his body hurt to even think of it, but he had no choice.

He had to plan his next attempt at death.

XVIII

I want to believe that there's more. That we could be more. Hell, we could be heroes.

Victor's chest tightened when he looked at Eli's unchanging face in the newspaper photograph. It was disconcerting; all he had of Eli was a mental picture, a decade old, and yet it lined up perfectly, like duplicate slides, with the one on the page. It was the same face in every technical way . . . and yet it wasn't. The years had worn on Victor in more obvious ways, hardening him, but they hadn't left Eli untouched. He didn't appear a day older, but the arrogant smile he'd often flashed in college had given way to something crueler. Like that mask he'd worn for so long had finally fallen off, and this was what lurked behind it.

And Victor, who was so good at picking things apart, at understanding how they worked, how *he* worked, looked at the photo, and felt . . . conflicted. Hate was too simple a word. He and Eli were *bonded*, by blood and death and science. They were alike, more so now than ever. And he had missed Eli. He wanted to see him. And he wanted to see him *suffer*. He wanted to see the look in Eli's eyes when he lit them up with pain. He wanted his attention.

Eli was like a thorn beneath Victor's skin, and it hurt. He could turn off every nerve in his body, but Victor couldn't do a damned thing about the twinge he felt when he thought of Cardale. The worst part of going numb was that it took away everything but this, the smothering need to hurt, to break, to kill, pouring over him like a thick blanket of syrup until he panicked and brought the physical sensations back.

Now that he was so close, the thorn seemed to burrow deeper. What was Eli doing here in Merit? Ten years was a long time. A decade could shape a man, change everything about him. It had changed Victor. What about Eli? Who had *he* become?

He fidgeted under the sudden urge to burn the photo, to shred it, as if damaging the paper could somehow cause damage to Eli, too, which of course it couldn't. Nothing could. So he sat down, and set the page aside, beyond arm's reach so he wouldn't be tempted to ruin it.

The paper called Eli a *hero*.

The word made Victor laugh. Not just because it was absurd, but because it posed a question. If Eli really was a hero, and Victor meant to stop him, did that make *him* a villain?

He took a long sip of his drink, tipped his head back against the couch, and decided he could live with that.

XIX

TEN YEARS AGO
LOCKLAND UNIVERSITY

WHEN Victor got home from his labs the next day, he found Eli sitting at the kitchen table, carving up his skin. He was dressed in the same sweatpants and shirt Victor had found him in the night before when he had finally come home from his walk, several degrees closer to sober, and with the beginnings of a plan. Now Victor grabbed a candy bar and hung his bag on the back of a wooden kitchen chair before sinking into it. He peeled away the wrapper and tried to ignore the way his appetite fizzled as he watched Eli work.

"Shouldn't you be shadowing at the hospital today?" asked Victor.

"It's not even a conscious process," murmured Eli reverently as he drew the blade up his arm, the wound healing in the knife's wake, a blossom of appearing and disappearing red, like a sick magic trick. "I can't stop the tissue from repairing."

"Poor you," teased Victor coolly. "Now if you don't mind . . ." He held up the candy bar.

Eli paused midcut. "Squeamish?"

Victor shrugged. "Just easily distracted," he said. "You look awful. Have you slept? Eaten?"

Eli blinked, and set the knife aside. "I've been thinking."

"The body doesn't survive on thoughts."

"I've been thinking about this ability. Regeneration." His eyes glittered as he spoke. "Why of all the potential powers I ended up with this one. Maybe it's not random. Maybe there's some correlation between a person's character and their resulting ability. Maybe it's a reflection of their psyche. I'm trying to understand how this"—he held up a blood-stained, but uninjured hand—"is a reflection of me. Why He would give me—"

"*He?*" asked Victor incredulously. He wasn't in the mood for God. Not this morning. "According to your thesis," he said, "an influx of adrenaline and a desire to survive gave you that talent. Not God. This isn't divinity, Eli. It's science and chance."

"Maybe to a point, but when I climbed into that water, I put myself in His hands—"

"No," snapped Victor. "You put yourself in *mine.*"

Eli fell silent, but began to rap his fingers on the table. After several moments he said, "What I need is a gun."

Victor had taken another bite of chocolate, and nearly choked. "And why's that?"

"To truly test the speed of regeneration. Obviously."

"Obviously." Victor finished his snack as Eli pushed up from the table to pour himself some water. "Look, I've been thinking, too."

"About what?" asked Eli, leaning back against the counter.

"About my turn."

Eli's brow crinkled. "You had it."

"About my *next* turn," Victor said. "I want to try again tonight."

Eli considered Victor, head cocked. "I don't think that's a good idea."

"Why not?"

Eli hesitated. "I can still see the line from your hospital bracelet," he said at last. "At least wait till you're feeling better."

"Actually, I'm feeling fine. Better than. I feel wonderful. I feel like roses and sunshine and glitter."

Victor Vale did not feel like glitter. His muscles ached, his veins still felt strangely starved of air, and he couldn't shake the headache that had trailed him since he'd opened his eyes beneath the fluorescent white of the hospital lights.

"Give yourself time to recover, okay?" said Eli. "And then we'll talk about trying again."

There was nothing overtly wrong with the words, but Victor didn't like the way he said them, the same calm, cautious tone people use when they want to let someone down slowly, smoothing a "no" into a "not right now." Something was wrong. And Eli's attention was already drifting back toward his knives. Away from Victor.

He clenched his teeth against the curse on his tongue. And then he shrugged carefully.

"Fine," he said, swinging his bag back onto his shoulder. "Maybe you're right," he added with a yawn and a lazy smile. Eli smiled back, and Victor turned toward the hall and his room.

He swiped an epinephrine pen on the way, and closed the door behind him.

VICTOR hated loud music almost as much as he hated crowds of drunk people. The party had both, and was made more insufferable by Victor's own sobriety. No booze. Not this time. He wanted—needed—everything to be sharp, especially if he was going to do this alone. Eli was still, presumably, at the apartment, carving up his skin while he assumed Victor was in his room, sulking or studying or both. What Victor had actually been doing was climbing out his window.

He'd felt fifteen again, a kid sneaking out to a party on a school night while his parents sat in the living room and laughed at something mindless on the TV. Or at least, Victor imagined this was what it would have been like had he needed to sneak out. Had anyone ever been home to catch him at it.

Victor moved through the party largely unnoticed, but not unwelcome. He earned a few second glances, but those were mostly because he rarely made an appearance at these kinds of events. He was an outsider by choice, a good enough mimic to charm his way into social circles when he wanted, but more often than not he preferred to stand apart and watch, and most of the school seemed content to let him.

But here he was, winding his way through bodies and music and sticky floors, the epinephrine pen tucked into the inside pocket of his coat, a small Post-it affixed to it that read *Use Me.* Now, as he found himself surrounded by lights and noise and bodies, Victor felt as if he'd wandered into another world. Is this what normal seniors did? Drank and danced with bodies interlocking like puzzle pieces to music loud enough to drown out thoughts? Angie had taken him to a few parties freshman year, but those had been different. He couldn't remember anything about the music or the beer, only her. Victor blinked the memory away. Sweat coated his palms as he took a plastic cup, and dumped the contents into a withering house plant. Holding something helped.

At one point he found himself on the balcony, looking down at the frozen lake that ran behind the frats. The sight made him shiver. He knew for optimum results he should mimic Eli, recreate the successful scenario, but Victor couldn't—wouldn't—do that. He had to find his own method.

He pushed off the banister, and retreated back into the house. As he continued on a circuit through the rooms, his eyes flicked around, appraising. He was amazed at how myriad the options for a suicide were, and yet how limited the options for one with any certitude of survival.

But Victor was certain of one thing: he wasn't leaving here without his turn. He wouldn't go back to the apartment and watch Eli joyfully saw at his skin, marvel at this strange new immortality he hadn't even tried *that* hard to find. Victor wouldn't stand there and coo and take notes for him.

Victor Vale was not a fucking sidekick.

By his third lap around the house, he'd scored what he considered to be enough cocaine to induce cardiac arrest (he wasn't sure, having never engaged in that kind of activity). He'd had to buy from three separate students, since each only had a few hits on them.

On his fourth lap around the house, while working up the nerve to *use* the cocaine, he heard it. The front door opened—he couldn't hear that over the music, but from his place on the stairs, he felt the sudden burst of cold—and then a girl squealed and said, "Eli! You made it!"

Victor swore softly, and retreated up the stairs. He heard his own name as he wound through the bodies. He broke through and reached the second-floor landing, then found an unoccupied bedroom with its own bathroom at the back. Halfway through the room, he stopped. A bookcase lined one wall, and there in the center, his own last name leapt out at him in capital letters.

He pulled the massive self-help book from the wall, and opened the window. The sixth book in a series of nine on emotional action and reaction hit the thin coat of snow below with a satisfying thud. Victor shut the window and continued into the bathroom.

On the sink he set his things in order.

First, his phone. He punched in a text to Eli but didn't hit Send, and set the device to one side. Second, the adrenaline shot. He'd be up to temperature, so hopefully a single direct injection would suffice. It would be hell on the body, but so would everything else he was about to do. He set the needle beside the phone. Third, the coke. He made a neat pile, and began to separate it into lines with a hotel card he found in his back pocket, a relic from the winter trip his parents had dragged him on. Despite an upbringing that would have driven most kids to drugs, Victor had never been much inclined to do them, but he had a good idea of the steps, thanks to a healthy diet of crime dramas. Once the cocaine was in its lines—seven of them—he pulled a dollar from his wallet and rolled it into a narrow straw. As seen on TV.

He looked in the mirror.

"You want to live," he told his reflection.

His reflection looked unconvinced.

"You need to live through this," he said. "You need to."

And then he took a breath and bent over the first line.

The arm came out of nowhere, wrapped around his throat, and slammed him back into the wall opposite the vanity. Victor caught his balance and straightened in time to see Eli run his hand through several hundred dollars' worth of coke, brushing it all into the sink.

"What the fuck?" Victor hissed, lunging for it. He wasn't fast enough. Eli's coke-dusted palm shoved him back again, pinned him to the wall, leaving a white print on the front of his black shirt.

"What the fuck?" parroted Eli with shocking calm. "What the *fuck*?"

"You weren't supposed to be here."

"*You* come to a party, people notice. Ellis texted me when you showed up. And then Max texts and tells me you're buying out the coke. I'm not an idiot. What were you thinking?" His free hand grabbed the cell on the sink. He read the text. He made a sound like a laugh, but his fingers tightened around Victor's collar as his other hand pitched the phone into the shower, where it broke into several pieces on impact.

"What if I hadn't heard my phone?" He let go of him. "What then?"

"Then I'd be dead," said Victor with feigned calm. His eyes drifted to the EpiPen. Eli's attention followed. Before Victor could move, Eli grabbed the pen and drove it down into his own leg. A small gasp escaped his gritted teeth as the contents flooded his system, jarring his lungs and heart, but in moments he recovered.

"I'm only trying to protect you," Eli said, casting the used cartridge aside.

"My hero," growled Victor under his breath. "Now fuck off."

Eli considered him. "I'm not leaving you here alone."

Victor stared past him to the sink, the edge still dusted with cocaine.

"I'll meet you downstairs," he said, gesturing to his shirt, the sink, the phone. "I have to clean up."

Eli didn't move.

Victor's cool eyes tracked up to meet his. "I've got nothing else on me." And then, a ghost of a smile. "Frisk me if you want."

Eli gave a cough of a laugh, but then his face sobered. "This isn't the way to do it, Vic."

"How do you know? Just because the ice worked doesn't mean something else won't—"

"I don't mean the method. I mean *alone*." He brought his coke-free hand to rest on Victor's shoulder. "You can't do this alone. So promise me you won't."

Victor held his gaze. "I won't."

Eli walked past him, into the bedroom.

"Five minutes," he called as he left.

Victor listened to the party flood in as Eli opened the door, then cut out again when he slammed it behind him. Victor stepped up to the sink, and ran his hand along the surface. It came away white. His fingers curled into a fist, and hit the mirror. It cracked— one, long, perfect line down the middle—but didn't shatter. Victor's knuckles throbbed, and he ran them under the sink, reaching blindly for a towel as he wiped at the lingering powder. His fingers came across something, and a sudden shock of pain went up his hand. He recoiled, and turned to see a socket on the wall, a clumsy Post-it taped beside it that said *Bad outlet do not touch seriously.*

Someone had gone in with a red pen and added punctuation.

Victor frowned, his fingers tingling from the small jolt.

And then the moment froze. The air in his lungs, the water in the sink, the flurries just beyond the window in the other room. All of it froze, the way it had in the street last night with Eli, only it wasn't Eli's hand this time but Victor's, burning faintly from the shock.

He had an idea. Retrieving the three pieces of his cell from the shower floor and fitting them back together, he typed in the message. Victor had promised he wouldn't do it alone. And he wouldn't. But he didn't need Eli's help either.

Save me, he texted, along with the address of the frat.

And then he hit Send.

XX

DOWN the hall and behind a door, Sydney Clarke lay curled in a nest of sheets. She'd listened to the sounds of Victor's steps in the other room, slow and soft and even as dripping water. She'd heard the glass break, heard the sound of the tap running, and then again, the steps, drip drip drip. She'd heard Mitch, his heavy tread, the muffled conversation, only tones reaching her through the walls. She'd heard Mitch's retreat down the hall. And then, quiet. The *drip drip drip* of Victor's pacing replaced by an odd stillness.

Sydney didn't trust stillness. She had come to believe that it was a bad thing. A wrong, unnatural, dead thing. She sat up in the strange bed in the strange hotel, her watery blue eyes unfocused on the door, stretching to hear through the wood and silence beyond. When still nothing greeted her, she slid from the bed in her too-large stolen sweats, and padded barefoot from her room and into the hotel suite's spacious living room.

Victor's bandaged hand was now draped over the arm of a couch facing the windows, a shallow glass dangling loosely from his fingers, only a sip's worth of liquid left inside, and most of it melted ice. Sydney tiptoed around the couch to face him.

He was asleep.

He didn't look peaceful, but his breathing was low, even.

Sydney perched on a chair and considered the man who had

saved her . . . no, she had saved herself . . . but found her, taken her in. She wondered who he was, and if she should be afraid of him. She didn't feel afraid, but Sydney knew not to trust fear, and certainly not to trust the absence of it. She hadn't been afraid of her sister, Serena, or even her sister's new boyfriend (at least not afraid *enough*) and look where that had gotten her.

Shot.

So she sat on the balls of her feet atop the leather chair and watched Victor sleep, as if the frown lines that lingered even now would rearrange and tell her all his secrets.

XXI

TEN YEARS AGO
LOCKLAND UNIVERSITY

DURING their freshman year, before Eli had ever set foot on campus, Angie had been drawn to Victor. In some ways they were opposites—Angie didn't seem to take anything seriously, and Victor didn't seem to take anything lightly—but in more ways they were alike; both young, dangerously smart, and lacking in patience when it came to the usual college crowd and their juvenile reaction to the sudden freedoms from parental restraint. Because of their shared sentiments, Victor and Angie both found themselves in constant need of an out, a reliable escape from situations they'd rather not be in, people they'd rather not be with.

And so, sitting in the comfort food kitchen in LIDS one day, they devised a fairly rudimentary code.

Save me.

The code was understood to be used sparingly, but always respected. Save first, ask questions later. When texted, along with an address, it meant that one desperately needed the other to bail them out, be it from a party or a study session or a bad date. Victor himself never had the luxury of a *date* with Angie, bad or otherwise, unless you counted the food they sometimes grabbed after bailing each other out—which Victor did. Nights spent in the same burger joint off campus, splitting shakes. He preferred chocolate but she always wanted some awful concoction, all swirled flavors and toppings, and in the end he didn't really care because he'd never remember what it tasted like anyway, only how the cold of it made Angie's lips redder, and the way their noses almost touched whenever they tried to drink at the same time, and how from that close up he could see the flecks of green in her eyes. He'd pick at his fries and tell her about the idiots in his study session. She would laugh, and spoon out the last of her shake, and recount how awkward her date had been. Victor would roll his eyes as she ran through the particular offenses, and think of how he would have done things differently, and of how thankful he was that someone—anyone—had pushed Angie Knight into wanting to be saved.

And by him.

Save me.

It had been a year and a half since Victor had thought to use that code. The last time had been before Eli—and certainly before Eli and Angie became a fused entity—but she still came to save him.

She pulled up in the frat's parking lot in her hatchback, right to the spot where Victor was waiting after half climbing and half falling from the same window through which he'd thrown his parents' book. And for a moment, one very small moment, after he climbed into the car and before he explained, it had been like freshman year again, just the two of them escaping a bad night, and he wanted so badly to let her drive to their old burger joint. They would slump into a booth, and he would tell her that parties hadn't gotten any better, and she would laugh, and somehow it would make everything okay.

But then she asked where Eli was, and the moment passed. Victor closed his eyes, and asked her to drive him to the engineering labs.

"They're closed," she said even as she guided the car in that direction.

"You have a swipe card."

"What's this about?"

Victor surprised himself by telling her the truth. She knew about Eli's thesis, but he told her about the most recent discovery, about the role of NDEs. He told her about his own desire to test the theory. He told her about his plan. The only thing he didn't tell her was that Eli had already successfully done it. That he held on to for a moment. And to her credit, Angie listened. She drove, knuckles whitening on the wheel, lips pressed into a line, and let Victor talk. He finished as she was pulling into the parking lot of the engineering labs, and she didn't say anything until she'd parked, and shut the engine off, and shifted in her seat to face him.

"Have you lost your mind?" she asked.

Victor managed a tight smile. "I don't think so."

"Let me get this straight," she said. The short red hair framed her face, frizzing in the winter weather. "You think that if you die, and manage to come back, you'll turn into what, one of the X-Men?"

Victor laughed. His throat was dry. "I was hoping for Magneto." The attempt at levity failed, the look between shock and horror and annoyance still firmly scrawled across Angie's face. "Look," he said, sobering, "I know it sounds crazy—"

"Of course it does. Because it *is* crazy. I'm not going to help you off yourself."

"I don't want to die."

"You just told me you did."

"Well, I don't want to stay dead."

She rubbed her eyes, rested her forehead for a moment on the steering wheel, and let out a groan.

"I need you, Angie. If you don't help me—"

"Don't you *dare* spin it that way—"

"—I'll just end up trying by myself again—"

"Again?"

"—and doing something stupid I *won't* recover from."

"We can get you help."

"I'm not suicidal."

"No, you're delusional."

Victor tipped his head back against the seat. His pocket buzzed. Eli. He ignored it, knowing it would be a matter of moments before Eli contacted Angie instead. He didn't have much time. Certainly not enough to convince her to help him.

"Why can't you just . . . ," mumbled Angie into the steering wheel, ". . . I don't know, OD? Something peaceful?"

"The pain's important," explained Victor, inwardly wincing. She wasn't so upset at what he was doing, then. Only that he was involving her. "Pain and fear," he added. "They're both factors. Hell, Eli killed himself in an ice bath."

"What?"

A grim, triumphant smile itched on his lips as he played the card. Victor had known that Eli wouldn't have told Angie yet. He was counting on it. The betrayal showed in her eyes. She got out, slammed the door, and sunk back against it. Victor followed, rounding the car. He drew tracks in the snow as he went. Through the partially tinted glass he could see her phone on the driver's seat. A red light flashed on its front. Victor turned his attention toward Angie.

"When did he do it?" she asked.

"Last night."

She looked at the film of snow on the concrete between them.

"But I came by this morning, Vic. He looked fine."

"Exactly. Because it worked. It *will* work."

She groaned. "This is crazy. You're crazy."

"You know that's not true."

"Why would he . . ."

"He didn't tell you anything?" prodded Victor, shivering in his thin jacket.

"He's been weird lately," she mumbled. Then her attention narrowed. "What you're asking me to do . . . it's crazy. It's *torture*."

"Angie . . ."

She looked up, eyes blazing. "I don't even believe you. What if it goes wrong?"

"It won't."

"What if it *does*?"

His phone buzzed angrily in his pocket.

"It can't," he said as calmly as he could. "I took a pill."

Her eyebrows knitted.

"Eli and I," he began to explain, "we isolated some of the adrenal compounds that kick in during life-or-death situations. We fabricated them. Essentially the pill acts like a trigger. A jump start."

It was all a lie, but he could see that its feigned existence impacted Angie. Science, even completely fictional science, held sway. Angie swore, and tucked her hands into her jacket pockets.

"Fuck, it's cold," she muttered, turning toward the building's front doors. The engineering lab itself was a problem, Victor knew. Security cameras. If something did go wrong, there would be footage.

"Where's Eli now?" she asked as she swiped her access card. "If you're in this together, why are you here with me?"

"He's busy relishing his new status as a god," said Victor bitterly, following her through the key-coded entry, scanning the ceiling for the red light of recording equipment. "Look, all you have to do is use the electricity to turn me off. Then turn me back on. The pill will do the rest."

"I study currents and the effects on devices, Victor, not people."

"A body is a machine," he said quietly. She led the way into one of the electrical engineering labs and flicked a switch. Half the lights turned on. Equipment was stacked along one wall, a variety of machines, some that looked medical, others technical. The room was full of tables, long and thin but large enough to rest a body on. He could feel Angie waver beside him.

"We'd have to plan it out," she said. "Give me a couple weeks, and maybe I could modify some of the equipment in here for—"

"No," said Victor, crossing to the machines. "It has to be to-night."

She looked aghast, but before she could protest, he took the lie he'd started, and ran with it.

"That pill I told you about . . . I already took it. It's like a switch, whether on or off depends on what state the body's in." He met her gaze, held it, and sent up a silent prayer that she didn't know half as much about hypothetical adrenal compounds as she did about circuits. "If I don't do this soon, Angie"—he winced for good measure—"the compound will kill me."

She paled.

He held his breath.

His phone vibrated again.

"How long?" she asked at last.

He took a step toward her, letting one of his legs nearly buckle under some imaginary strain. He caught himself on the edge of a table with a grimace, and found her gaze as the buzzing in his pocket stopped.

"Minutes."

∞

"**THIS** is mad," whispered Angie over and over as she helped bind
Victor's legs to the table. He worried that even now, with the machines around them humming to life and her busy winding the
rubber strap around his ankles, she might back out, so he doubled
up in fake pain, curled in on himself.

"Victor," she said urgently. "Victor, are you okay?" There was
pain and panic in her voice and he had to fight the urge to stop, to
soothe her, and promise it would be okay.

Instead he nodded, and said through gritted teeth, "Hurry."

She rushed to finish the knots, showed him the rubber-coated bars
on the table where he could put his hands. Her halo of red hair had
always looked electrified, but tonight it rose around her cheeks. Victor thought it made her look haunting. Beautiful. The first day they
met, she'd looked like this. It had been hot for September; her face
was flushed, and her hair had a life of its own. He'd looked up from
his textbook and saw her, standing at the entrance to LIDS, clutching a folder to her front as her eyes wandered over the room in an
appraising way—lost but unconcerned. And then they landed on
Victor at his table with his book, and her face lit up. Not full-wattage
light, but a steady glow as she crossed the room, and slid without
preamble into the seat across from him. They didn't even talk, that
first day. Just passed the same hour in the same space. Angie had later
referred to the two of them as concordant frequencies.

"Victor." Her voice saying his name drew him back to the cold
table in the lab.

"I want you to know," she said as she began to fix sensors to his
chest, "that I will never, ever forgive you for this."

He shivered under her touch. "I know."

His coat and shirt were cast off on a chair, the contents of his pockets set on top. Amid the keys and a wallet and a pre-med lab badge, sat his phone, the ringer turned off. It blinked angrily at him, flashing first blue and then red and then blue again, and so on, signaling it had both voice mail and texts waiting.

Victor smiled grimly. *Too late, Eli. It's my turn.*

Angie was standing by a machine chewing the nails off one of her hands. The other rested on a set of dials. The machine itself was whirring and whining and blinking. A language Victor didn't know, which scared him.

Her eyes caught on something, and she took hold of it, crossing back to him. It was a strip of rubber.

"You know what to do," said Victor, surprised by the calm in his voice. Everything beneath his skin was trembling. "Start at the low setting, and go up."

"Turn off, turn on," she whispered, before holding the rubber above his mouth. "Bite down on this."

Victor took a last deep breath, and forced his mouth to open. The strap was between his teeth, his fingers testing their grip on the small table bars. He could do this. Eli held himself under. Victor could, too.

Angie was back at the machine. Their eyes met, and for an instant everything else vanished—the lab and the humming machines and the existence of EO and Eli and the years since Victor and Angie had shared a milkshake—and he was just happy to have her looking at him. Seeing him.

And then she closed her eyes, and turned the dial a single click, and the only thing Victor could think of was the pain.

VICTOR fell back against the table in a cold sweat.

He couldn't breathe.

He gasped, expecting a pause, a moment to recover. Expecting Angie to change her mind, to stop, to give up.

But Angie turned the dial up.

The need to be sick was overcome by the need to scream and he bit into the rubber strap until he thought his teeth would crack but a moan still escaped, and he thought Angie must have heard, and she'd turn the machine off now, but the dial went up again.

And again.

And again.

Victor thought he would black out but before he could, the dial turned up and the spasm of pain brought him back to his body and the table and the room and he couldn't escape.

The pain kept him there.

The pain tied him down as it shot through every nerve in every limb.

He tried to spit out the strap but he couldn't open his mouth. His jaw was locked.

The dial went up.

Every time Victor thought the dial couldn't go any further, the pain couldn't get any worse, and then it did and it did and it did, and Victor could hear himself screaming even though the strap was still between his teeth and he could feel every nerve in his body breaking and he wanted it to stop. He wanted it to *stop*.

He begged Angie but the words were cut short by the strap and the dial turning up again and the sound in the air like cracking ice and shredding paper and static.

The darkness blinked around him and he wanted it because it meant the pain would stop but he didn't want to die and he was

afraid that the darkness was death and so he pulled violently back
from it.

He felt himself crying.

The dial went up.

His hands ached where they gripped the table bars, cramped in
place.

The dial went up.

He wished for the first time in his life that he believed in God.

The dial went up.

He felt his heart skip a beat, felt it grind and then double.

The dial went up.

He heard a machine warn, then alarm.

The dial went up.

And everything stopped.

XXII

TWO DAYS AGO

THE ESQUIRE HOTEL

SYDNEY watched the lines in Victor's face deepen. He must be dreaming.

It was late. The night beyond the floor-to-ceiling glass was dark—or as dark as it could be, in a city like this—and she stood and stretched, and was about to go back to bed when she saw the piece of paper, and everything in her went cold.

The newspaper article sat open beside Victor on the couch. The heavy bars of black on the page were the first thing that caught her attention, but the photo beneath was what held it. Sydney's chest tightened, sudden and sharp, and she couldn't breathe. It felt like she was drowning, *again*—Serena calling from the patio, a picnic basket hooked on the elbow of her winter coat, telling Syd to hurry up, or the ice would be all melted, which it was, underneath that brittle shell of frost and snow—but when she squeezed her eyes shut, it wasn't the half-frozen water of the lake that folded over her, but the memory of the field a year later, the stretch of frozen grass and the body and her sister's encouragement and then the sound of the gunshot, echoing in her ears.

Two different days, two different deaths, overlapping, swirling together. She blinked both memories away, but the photo was still there, staring up at her, and she couldn't tear her gaze away, and before she knew what she was doing, her hand was reaching out, stretching past Victor, toward the paper and the smiling man on its front.

It all happened fast.

Sydney's fingers curled around the newspaper page but as she lifted it, her forearm grazed Victor's knee and before she could shift her weight or pull back he shot forward, eyes open but empty, hand vising around Sydney's small wrist. Without warning, pain tore up her arm and through her small body, crashing over her in a wave. It was worse than drowning, worse than being shot, worse than anything she had ever felt. It was like every one of her nerves was shattering, and Sydney did the only thing she could.

She screamed.

XXIII

TEN YEARS AGO

LOCKLAND UNIVERSITY

THE pain had followed him up again, and Victor came to, screaming.

Angie was fumbling with his hands, trying to coax them free of the bars. He shot forward, clutching his head. Why was the electricity still running? The pain was a wave, a wall, wracking his muscles, his heart. His skin was tearing with it, and Angie was talking but Victor couldn't hear anything through the agony. He curled in on himself and stifled another scream.

Why wouldn't the pain stop? WHY WOULDN'T IT STOP?

And then, as sudden as a flipped switch, the pain was gone, and Victor was left feeling . . . nothing. The machines were off, the lights sprinkled across their fronts all dead. Angie was still talking, her hands running over skin, unbuckling the ankle straps, but Victor didn't hear her as he stared down at his hands and wondered at the sudden hollowness, as if the electricity had gutted his nerves and left only shells.

Empty.

Where did it go? he wondered. *Will it come back?*

In the sudden absence of pain, he found himself trying to remember how it felt, to drum up the sensation, a shadow of it, and as he did the switch clicked again, and the energy was there, crackling like static through the room. He heard the crinkle of the air, and then he heard a scream. He wondered for an instant if it was coming from him, but the pain was beyond Victor now, outside of him, humming over his skin without touching it.

He felt slow, dazed, as he tried to process the situation. Nothing hurt, so who was screaming? And then the body crumpled to the lab floor beside his table, and the space between his thoughts collapsed, and he snapped back to his senses.

Angie. *No.* He jumped down from the table to find her writhing on the floor, still screaming in pain, and he thought *stop!* but the electrical buzzing in the room continued to grow around him. *Stop.* She clutched her chest.

Victor tried to help her up but Angie cried out even louder when he touched her and he stumbled back, confusion and panic pouring through him. *The buzzing,* he thought. He had to turn it down. He closed his eyes and tried to imagine it as a dial, tried to imagine turning some invisible device. He tried to feel calm. Numb. He was surprised by how easily it came to him in the midst of chaos, the calm. And then he realized how horribly quiet the room had gone. Victor opened his eyes, and saw Angie sprawled on the floor, head back, eyes open, red hair a cloud around her face. The humming in the air had faded to a tingle, and then to nothing, but it was still too late.

Angie Knight was dead.

XXIV

TWO DAYS AGO
THE ESQUIRE HOTEL

THE hotel room was pain and noise and chaos.

Victor came to, dazed, trapped between the school lab and the hotel room, Angie's scream in his head and Sydney's in his ears. Sydney? But the girl was nowhere to be seen, and he was being pinned back against the couch by Mitch, whose whole body was shaking visibly from the effort, but unbudging as the room hummed around them.

"Turn it off," growled Mitch under his breath, and Victor woke fully. His eyes narrowed, the humming died, and everything in Mitch slackened, all signs of pain gone. He let go of Victor's shoulders, and slumped back onto a chair.

Victor took a low, steadying breath, and ran his hand slowly over his face and through his hair, before his attention settled on Mitch.

"Are you all right?" he asked.

Mitch looked tired, unamused, but safe. It wasn't the first time he'd had to intervene. Victor knew that when he had bad dreams, other people always suffered.

"I'm swell," Mitch said, "but not too sure about her." He pointed to a nearby shape in too large sweats, and Victor's gaze swiveled to Sydney, who sat on the floor, dazed. He'd shut down their nerves the moment he realized what was happening, or at least dulled them as much as he was safely able, so he knew she was physically all right. But she did look shaken. A pang of guilt, something foreign after a decade in jail, nudged his ribs.

"Sorry," he said quietly. He reached out to help her up, but thought better. Instead he stood, and made his way toward the hall bathroom.

"Mitch," he called back. "See she gets to bed."

And with that he closed the door behind him.

XXV

TEN YEARS AGO
LOCKLAND UNIVERSITY

VICTOR didn't revive Angie. He didn't try. He knew he should, or should want to, but the last thing he needed was more evidence of himself at the crime scene. He swallowed hard, cringing both at his ability to be so rational at a moment like this, and at the thought of the term. Crime. Scene. Besides, he could *feel* that she was dead. No charge. No energy.

So he did the only thing he could think to do. He called Eli.

"Where the *hell* are you, Vale?" A car door slammed in the background. "You think this shit is funny—"

"Angie's dead."

Victor hadn't been sure whether or not he would say that, but the words had formed and spilled out before he could catch them. He'd expected them to hurt his throat, to lodge in his chest, but they flowed out unrestricted. He knew he should be panicking, but he felt numb, and the numbness made him calm. Was it shock, he wondered, this steadiness that came to him now, that had been so easy to summon with Angie dying at his feet? Or was it something else? He listened to the silence on the other end of the phone until Eli broke it.

"How?" growled Eli.

"It was an accident," said Victor, maneuvering his cell so he could pull his shirt back on. He'd had to step around Angie's body to reach it. He didn't look at her.

"What did you do?"

"She was helping me with a test. I had an idea and it worked and—"

"What do you mean it worked?" Eli's tone went cold.

"I mean . . . I mean it worked this time." He let it sink in. Eli clearly understood, because he stayed quiet. He was listening. Victor had his attention, and he liked that. But he was surprised that Eli seemed more interested in his experiment than in Angie. Angie, who had always kept his monsters back. Angie, who was always getting in the way. No, she had been more than a distraction to both of them, hadn't she? Victor looked down at the body then, expecting to feel some shade of the guilt that had washed over him when he'd lied to her before, but there was nothing. He wondered if Eli had felt this strange detachment, too, when he woke up on the bathroom floor. Like everything was real, but nothing mattered.

"Tell me what happened," pressed Eli, losing patience.

Victor gazed around the room at the table, the straps, the machines that had once hummed but now appeared to have burned out, fuses blown. The whole place was dark.

"Where are you?" he snapped when Victor didn't answer.

"The labs," he said. "We were—" The pain came out of nowhere. His pulse quickened, the air thrummed, and a breath later Victor doubled over. It crackled over him, through him, lit up his skin and his bones and every inch of muscle in between.

"You were *what*?" demanded Eli.

Victor clutched at the table, biting back a scream. The pain was horrific, as if every muscle in his body had cramped. As if he were being electrocuted all over again. *Stop,* he thought. *Stop,* he begged. And then he finally pictured the pain as a switch, and snapped it off, and it was gone.

His pulse dropped, the air thinned, and he felt *nothing.* Victor was left gasping, dazed. He'd dropped the phone to the linoleum. He reached down a shaking hand and lifted the cell back to his ear.

Eli was practically shouting. "Look," he was saying, "just stay there. I don't know what you've done, but stay there. You hear me? Don't move."

And Victor might have actually stayed put, if he hadn't heard the double-click.

The landline in their apartment had been provided by the university. It made a faint double-click when it was lifted from its spot on the wall. Now, as Eli spoke to him on his cell and instructed him to stay put, and as Victor tried to get his coat on, he could just make out that small double-click in the background. He frowned. A double-click, followed by three tonal taps: 9-1-1.

"Don't move," Eli said again. "I'll be right there."

Victor nodded carefully, forgetting how easy it was to lie when he didn't have to look Eli in the face.

"Okay," he said, "I'll be here." He hung up.

Victor finished pulling on his coat, and cast a last glance at the room. This was a mess. Aside from the body, the scene didn't scream murder, but the contorted shape of Angie's corpse showed it wasn't exactly natural, either. He took a sanitary wipe from a box in the corner and cleaned the bars on the table, resisting the urge to wipe down every object in the room. Then it *would* look like a crime. He knew he was written on this lab, somewhere, despite how careful he'd been. He knew he was probably on the security footage, too. But he was out of time.

Victor Vale left the lab, and then he ran.

AS he made his way toward the apartment—he needed to speak to Eli in person, needed to make him understand—he marveled at how good he felt physically. High from the chase, and from the kill, but free from pain. Then, at the edge of a streetlight, he looked down and saw his hand was bleeding. He must have caught it on something. But he didn't feel it. And not just in the adrenaline-blots-out-minor-injuries way. He didn't feel it at *all*. He tried to summon that strange humming air, tried to lower his own pain threshold a fraction, just to see how he was *really* faring, and ended up doubled over, bracing himself against a light post.

Not so good, then.

He definitely felt like he'd died. Again. His hands ached from gripping the handles on the table, and he wondered if any bones were broken. Every muscle in the rest of his body groaned, and his head hurt so much he thought he might be sick. When the sidewalk began to tip, he threw the switch back. Pain blinked out. He gave himself a moment to breathe, to regain himself, and straightened in the pool of light. He felt *nothing*. And right now, nothing felt amazing. Nothing felt heavenly. He tipped his head back, and laughed. Not one of those maniacal laughs. Not even a loud laugh.

A cough of a laugh, an amazed exhale.

But even if it had been louder, no one would have heard it, not over the sirens.

The two squad cars screeched to a stop in front of him, and Victor hardly had time to process their arrival before he was thrown to the concrete, cuffed, and a black hood thrust over his head. He felt himself being shoved into the backseat of the cop car.

The hood was an interesting touch, but Victor supremely

disliked the sensation of being blindfolded. The car would turn, and his weight would shift, and without any visual cues or physical discomfort to orient himself, he'd nearly topple over. They seemed to be taking the turns purposefully fast.

Victor realized that he could react. Fight back without having to touch them. Without even having to *see* them. But he restrained himself.

It seemed unnecessarily dangerous to hurt the cops while they were driving. Just because he could turn his own pain off didn't mean he wouldn't die if they wrecked the vehicle, so he focused his attention on staying calm. Which was, again, too easy, given all that had happened. The calm troubled him; the fact that the physical absence of pain could elicit such a mental absence of panic was at once unnerving and rather fascinating. If he weren't currently in the back of a cop car, he would have wanted to make a thesis note.

The car turned hard, slamming him against the door, and Victor swore, not out of pain so much as habit. The cuffs dug into his wrists and when he felt something warm and wet run down his fingers, he decided to lower his threshold. Feeling nothing could lead to injury, and he wasn't Eli. He couldn't heal. He tried to feel. Just a little and—

Victor gasped and tipped his head against the seat. Hot pain tore through his wrists where the metal dug in, and magnified, his threshold plummeting. He clenched his jaw and tried to find balance. Tried to find normal. Sensation was nuanced. Not on and off, but an entire spectrum, a dial with hundreds of notches, not a switch. He closed his eyes despite the darkness of the hood, and found a place between numb and normal. His wrists ached dully, something closer to stiffness than sharp pain.

This was going to take some getting used to.

Finally the car stopped, the door opened, and a pair of hands guided him out.

"Can you take the hood off?" he asked the darkness. "Don't you have to read me rights? Did I miss that part?"

The person guiding him nudged him to the right and his shoulder clipped a wall. Campus police, maybe? He heard a door open, and felt a slight change in the sounds of the space. This new room had almost no furniture and smooth walls, he could tell by the echo. A chair screeched back, someone pushed Victor down into it, uncuffed one of his hands and recuffed them both to a place on a metal table. Footsteps faded, and were gone.

A door closed.

The room was silent.

A door opened. Footsteps drew closer. And then at last the hood came off. The room was very, very bright, and a man sat down across from him, broad-shouldered, black-haired, and unamused. Victor looked around at the interrogation room, which was smaller than he imagined, and a bit shabbier. It was also locked from the outside. Any stunt in here would be an utter waste.

"Mr. Vale, my name is Detective Stell."

"I thought those hoods were only used for spies and terrorists and bad action movies," said Victor, referring to the pile of black fabric now sitting between them. "Is it even legal?"

"Our officers are trained to use their judgment in order to protect themselves," said Detective Stell.

"Is my eyesight a threat?"

Stell sighed. "Do you know what an EO is, Mr. Vale?"

He felt his pulse tick up at the word, the air buzzing faintly around him, but swallowed, willed himself to find his calm. He nodded slightly. "I've heard of them."

"And do you know what happens when someone shouts EO?"

Victor shook his head. "Every time someone makes a 911 call and uses that word, I have to get up out of bed, and come all the way down to the station to check things out. Doesn't matter if the call-in's a prank by some kids, or the ravings of a homeless man. I have to take it seriously."

Victor furrowed his brow. "Sorry someone wasted your time, sir."

Stell rubbed his eyes. "Did they, Mr. Vale?"

Victor gave a tight laugh. "You can't be serious. Someone told you I was an EO"—he already knew who, of course—"and you actually believe them? What the hell kind of ExtraOrdinary am I supposed to be?" Victor stood but the cuffs were locked firmly to the table.

"Sit down, Mr. Vale." Stell pretended to examine his papers. "The student who called in the report, a Mr. Cardale, also said that you confessed to the murder of student Angela Knight." His eyes flicked up. "Now, even if I want to overlook this EO business, and I'm not saying I do, I take a body pretty damn seriously. And that's what we've got on our hands over at Lockland's engineering school. So, is any of this true?"

Victor sat and took a few long, deep breaths. Then he shook his head. "Eli's been drinking."

"Is that so?" Stell sounded unconvinced.

Victor watched a drop of blood fall from the cuffs to the table. He was careful to keep his eyes on the one, two, three drops as he spoke. "I was at the labs when Angie died." He knew the security cameras would show as much. "I needed to get away from a party, and she came and picked me up. I didn't want to go home, and she said she had work to do . . . it's thesis time and all . . . so I went with her to the engineering school. I left the room for a couple minutes, just to get a drink, and when I came back . . . I saw her on the floor and called Eli—"

"You didn't call 911."

"I was upset. Distraught."

"You don't seem distraught."

"No, now I'm pissed off. And in shock. And cuffed to a table." Victor raised his voice, because now seemed like an appropriate time to do so. "Look, Eli was drunk. Maybe he still is. He told me it was my fault. I kept trying to explain that it had been a heart attack, or a malfunction in the equipment—Angie was always messing around with voltage—but he wouldn't listen. He said he'd call the police. So I left. Made my way home to *talk* to him. And that's where I was heading when the cops showed up." He looked up at the detective, and gestured to their current situation. "As for this EO stuff, I'm as confused as you are. Eli's been working too hard. His thesis is on EOs, did he tell you that? He's obsessed with them. Paranoid. Doesn't sleep, doesn't eat, just works on his theories."

"No," said Stell across the table, making a note. "Mr. Cardale neglected to mention that." He finished writing, and tossed the pen aside.

"This is insane," said Victor. "I'm not a murderer, and I'm not an EO. I'm a pre-med student." At least the last one was true.

Stell looked at his watch. "We'll keep you overnight in a holding cell," he explained. "Meanwhile, I'll send someone over to see Mr. Cardale, test his blood alcohol level, and get his full statement. If, in the morning, we have proof that Mr. Cardale's testimony is compromised, and no evidence ties you to the death of Angela Knight, we'll let you go. You'll still be a suspect, understand? That's the best I can do right now. Sound good?"

No. It didn't sound good at all. But Victor would make do. The hood stayed off as an officer led him to the cell, and on the way he made careful note of the number of cops and the number of doors and the time it took to reach the holding area. Victor had always been a problem-solver. His problems had certainly been growing bigger, but the rules still held. The steps to solving a problem, from elementary math to breaking out of a police station, remained the same. A simple matter of understanding the problem, and selecting the best solution. Victor was now in a cell. The cell was small and square and came complete with bars and a man who was twice his age and smelled like piss and tobacco. A guard sat at the end of a hallway reading a paper.

The most obvious solution was to kill the cellmate, call the guard over, and kill the guard. The alternative was to wait until morning, and hope that Eli failed a breathalyzer, that the security cameras were limited to the entryways, and that he'd left no material evidence in the lab to link him to the death.

Picking the best solution really depended on your definition of *best*. Victor examined the man slumped against the cot, and got to work.

HE took the long way home.

The first touches of dawn warmed the sky as he walked, rubbing the dried blood from his wrists. At least, he consoled himself, he hadn't killed anyone. Victor was, in fact, quite proud of his restraint. He thought, for a moment, that the chain-smoking cellmate might be dead, but he was still breathing, the last time Victor had checked. Admittedly, he hadn't wanted to get too close. As he made his way home, he felt a trickle of wet on his face and touched the place below his nose. It came away red. Victor wiped his face on his sleeve, and made a mental note to be more careful. He'd pushed himself a lot in one night, especially considering he'd died first.

Sleep. Sleep would help. But it would have to wait.

Because first, he had to deal with Eli.

XXVI

VICTOR stood in the bathroom and waited for the hotel to quiet around him. Beyond the door he heard Mitch lead Sydney back to bed, muttering an apology on his behalf. They should never have picked her up, but he couldn't shake the feeling that she would come in handy. She had secrets, and he planned to learn them. Still, he really hadn't meant to hurt her. He prided himself on control, but for all his efforts, he hadn't found a way to fully manage his power during sleep. Which is why he didn't sleep, or at least, not much.

He ran cold water over his hands and face, waiting for the faint electrical buzz to stop. When it didn't, he turned it inward, wincing as the humming vanished from the air around him and reappeared in his bones, his muscles. He clutched the granite counter as his body grounded the current, and several long moments later, the shudder passed, leaving Victor tired, but stable again.

He met his gaze in the mirror and began to unbutton his shirt, exposing the scars from the bullets of Eli's gun one by one. He ran his fingers over them, touching the three spots where he'd been shot the way a man might cross himself. One tucked under his ribs, one above his heart, and one that had actually hit him in the back, but at close enough range that it passed right through. He'd memorized their position so that when he did see Eli, he could repay the gesture. Hell, if the bullets lodged, there was a chance Eli would heal around them. It gave Victor a modicum of pleasure to think of that.

Perhaps the wounds would have earned him some respect in prison, but by the time he'd integrated, they were long faded. Besides, Victor had found other ways of asserting himself at Wrighton, from the subtle discomfort inmates felt when they displeased him to the instant agony he used more sparingly, the kind of pain that left them gasping at his feet. But he didn't only *cause* pain; Victor also took it away. He'd learned to gift painlessness, to trade it. Amazed by the lengths men would go to avoid any form of suffering, Victor had become a dealer in a drug only he could provide. Jail had, in some ways, been pleasant.

But even there Eli had haunted him, tarnished his enjoyment by clinging to his thoughts, whispering in his head, ruining his peace. And after ten years of waiting, it was Victor's turn, to get into Eli's head and do some ruining.

He rebuttoned his shirt, and the scars vanished again, from view but not from memory.

XXVII

TEN YEARS AGO

LOCKLAND UNIVERSITY

VICTOR hoisted himself up onto his windowsill, thankful that he'd left it cracked, and that they lived on the first floor and thus he was only forced to contend with the five steps' worth of height leading from the street up to the building's entrance. He paused on the sill, straddling it as morning light seeped into everything around him, and listened for sounds within the apartment. The place was quiet, but Victor knew Eli was home. He could *feel* him.

His heart fluttered gently with the thrill of what would happen next, but that was all it was, a flutter. No pounding panic. This new calm was becoming unsettling. Victor struggled to assess it. The absence of pain led to an absence of fear, and the absence of fear led to a disregard for consequence. He knew it was a bad idea to break out of the cell, just as he knew what he was about to do was a bad idea. A worse idea. He could track his thoughts better now, marveled at the way they circled round to solutions that bypassed caution and favored the immediate, the violent, the rash, the way a crippled man favors his good leg. Victor's mind had always been drawn to those solutions, but he had been impeded by an understanding of right and wrong, or at least what he knew others saw as right and wrong. But now, this . . . this was simple. Elegant.

He paused long enough to smooth his hair in the mirror, distressed by how grungy death and half a night in a cell had made him look. Then he met his own eyes—the new calm had made them a fraction paler—and his reflection smiled. It was a cold smile, a slightly foreign one, bordering on arrogant, but Victor didn't mind. He rather liked that smile. It looked like something Eli would wear.

Victor stepped out of his room and made his way gingerly down the hall to the kitchen. On the table were a set of knives and a notebook, half a page filled with Eli's tight script and dotted with blood. As for Eli himself, Victor could see him on the living room couch, head bowed forward in thought, or maybe prayer. Victor paused a moment to watch him. It seemed odd that Eli couldn't sense Victor's presence the way Victor sensed his. That was the problem with an inward ability like healing. Self-absorbed to the last, he thought as he took up a large knife and dragged its tip along the table, eliciting a high scratch.

Eli spun up from the couch in a fluid motion. "Vic."

"I'm disappointed," said Victor.

"What are you doing here?"

"You turned me in."

"You killed Angie." The words snagged slightly in Eli's throat. Victor was surprised by the emotion in his friend's voice.

"Did you love her?" he asked. "Or are you just mad I took something back?"

"She was a *person*, Victor, not a thing, and you murdered her."

"It was an accident," he said. "And it's your fault, really. If you had just helped me . . ."

Eli ran his hands over his face. "How could you do this?"

"How could *you*?" asked Victor, lifting the knife fully from the table as he spoke. "You called the cops and you accused me of being an EO. I didn't rat *you* out, you know. I could have." He scratched his head with the tip of the knife. "Why would you tell them something so silly? Did you know they have special people who come in if there's an EO suspected? Some guy named Stell. Did you know that?"

"You've lost it." Eli sidestepped, keeping his back to the wall. "Put the knife down. It's not like you can hurt me."

Victor smiled at the challenge. A quick step forward, and Eli tried to step back on instinct but met the wall and Victor met him.

The knife slid in. It was easier than he imagined. Like a vanishing act, one moment the metal glinted and the next it was gone, buried in Eli's stomach to the hilt.

"You know what I figured out?" Victor leaned into him as he spoke. "Watching you in the street that night, picking the glass from your hand? You can't heal yourself until I take the knife out." He twisted it, and Eli groaned. His feet went out from under him and he began to slide down the wall, but Victor hoisted him up by the handle.

"I'm not even using my new trick yet," he said. "It's not as flashy as yours, but it's rather effective. Want to see it?"

Victor didn't wait for a response. The air buzzed around him. He didn't worry about a dial. Up. That's all he cared about. Up. Eli screamed, and the sound made Victor feel good. Not in a sun-is-out-and-life-is-wonderful way, of course, but in a punishing way. A controlling way. Eli had betrayed him. Eli deserved a little pain. He would heal. When this was over, he wouldn't even have a scar. The least Victor could do was try to make an impression. Victor let go of the knife handle and watched Eli's body collapse to the floor.

"A note for your thesis," he said as his friend lay there, gasping. "You thought our powers were somehow a reflection of our nature. God playing with mirrors, but you're wrong. It's not about God.

It's about us. The way we think. The thought that's strong enough to keep us alive. To bring us back. You want to know how I know?" He turned his attention to the table, looking for something new and sharp. "Because all I could think about when I was dying was the pain." He cranked the dial up in his mind, and let the room fill with Eli's screams. "And how badly I wanted to make it stop."

Victor turned the dial down again, and heard Eli's screams fade as he reached the table. He was looking over the various blades when the room exploded with noise. A very sudden, very loud noise. Drywall crumbled a foot away, and Victor turned back to find Eli clutching his stomach with one hand and a gun with the other. The knife was on the floor in a satisfying amount of blood, and Victor wondered with a scientific curiosity how long it would take Eli's body to regenerate itself. Then the second shot rang out, much closer to Victor's head, and he frowned.

"Do you even know how to use that?" he asked, thumbing a long, thin knife. Eli's hands were shaking visibly around the gun's grip.

"Angie is dead—," said Eli.

"Yes, I know—"

"...but so are you." It wasn't a threat. "I don't know who you are, but you're not Victor. You're something that's crawled into his skin. A devil wearing him."

"Ouch," said Victor, and for some reason, the word made him laugh. He couldn't stop laughing. Eli looked disgusted, and it made Victor want to stab him again. He felt behind him for the nearest knife, and watched Eli's fingers tighten on the gun.

"You're something else," he said. "Victor died."

"*We* died, Eli. And we both came back."

"No, no, I don't think so. Not entirely. Something's wrong, missing, gone. Can't you feel it? I can," said Eli, and he actually sounded *scared*. Victor was disappointed. He'd hoped that maybe Eli felt it, too, this calm, but apparently he felt something else entirely.

"Maybe you're right," said Victor. He was willing to admit that he felt different. "But if I'm missing something, then so are you. Life is about compromises. Or did you think because you put yourself in God's hands that He would make you all you were and more?"

"He did," growled Eli, pulling the trigger.

This time he didn't miss. Victor felt the impact, and looked down at the hole in his shirt, glad he'd bothered to turn his pain off. He touched the spot and his fingers came away red. Distantly, he knew this was a bad place to be shot.

Victor sighed, looking up. "That's a little self-righteous, don't you think?"

Eli took a step closer. The wound in his stomach had already healed, and the color was back in his face. Victor knew he needed to keep talking.

"Admit it," he said, "you feel different, too. Death takes something with it. What did it take from you?"

Eli lifted the gun again. "My fear."

Victor managed a dark smile. Eli's hands were shaking, and his jaw was clenched. "I still see fear."

"I'm not afraid," said Eli. "I'm just sorry."

He fired again. The force nudged Victor back a step. His fingers closed around the nearest knife and he swung, digging it into Eli's outstretched arm. The gun clattered to the floor, and Eli lunged back to avoid another blow.

Victor meant to follow it up, but his vision blurred. Just for a moment. He blinked, desperate to refocus.

"You may be able to turn the pain off," said Eli, "but you can't stop the blood loss."

Victor took a step forward but the room leaned. He braced himself against the table. There was a lot of blood on the floor. He wasn't sure how much of it was his. When he looked up again, Eli was there. And then Victor was on the ground. He pushed himself to his hands and knees but couldn't seem to force his body farther up. An arm buckled beneath his weight. His eyes unfocused again.

Eli was talking, but he couldn't quite make out the words. And then he heard the gun scraping across the floor as it was lifted, cocked. Something hit him in the back, like a soft punch, and his body stopped listening. Darkness crept in at the edges of his sight, the kind he'd wanted so badly when the pain on the table had been too much.

A thick darkness.

He began to sink into it as he heard Eli moving around the room, talking into his phone, something about medical attention. He was twisting his voice to sound panicked, but his face, even the blur that was his expression, was calm, composed. Victor saw Eli's shoes walk away before everything faded.

XXVIII

MITCH led Sydney back to her room, and closed the door behind her. She stood in the dark for several minutes, dazed by the echo of pain, and the photo in the newspaper, and Victor's pale eyes, dead before he came back to himself. She shivered. It had been a long two days. She'd spent the night before under an overpass, tucked into the place where two concrete corners met, trying to stay dry. Winter had dissolved into a cold, wet spring. It had started raining the day before she'd been shot, and hadn't stopped since.

She tucked her fingers into the cuff of the stolen sweatshirt. Her skin still felt strange. Her whole arm had been on fire, the gunshot wound a blazing center in a web of pain, and then the power had been cut. That was the only way Sydney could think of it, like the thing connecting her to the pain had been severed, leaving in its place a pins-and-needles numbness. Sydney rubbed at her skin, waiting for the feeling to come back. She didn't like numbness. It reminded her of cold, and Sydney hated being cold.

She pressed her ear to the door and listened for signs of Victor, but the bathroom door stayed firmly shut, and finally, as the prickle left her skin, she crawled back to the too-big bed in the strange hotel, curled in on herself, and tried to find sleep. At first it wouldn't come, and in a weak moment she wished Serena were there. Her sister would perch on the edge of the bed, and stroke her hair, claiming the gesture made thoughts quieter. Sydney would close her eyes and let everything hush, first her mind and then the world as her sister's touch dragged her down into sleep. But Sydney caught herself, twined her fingers in the hotel sheets, and remembered that Serena—the one who would have done those things—was gone. The thought was like cold water, sending Sydney's heart into rapid fire all over again, so she decided not to think of Serena at all, and instead tried a counting trick one of her sitters had taught her. Not counting up, or counting down, just counting one-two-one-two as she breathed in and breathed out. One-two. Soft and steady, like a heartbeat, until finally the hotel room sank away, and she slept.

And when she did, she dreamed of water.

XXIX

LAST YEAR

BRIGHTON COMMONS

SYDNEY Clarke died on a cool March day.

It was just before lunch, and it was all Serena's fault.

The Clarke sisters looked identical, despite the fact that Serena was seven years older, and seven inches taller. The resemblance stemmed partly from genes and partly from Sydney's adoration of her big sister. She dressed like Serena, acted like Serena, and was, in almost every way, a miniature version of her sister. A shadow, distorted by age instead of sun. They had the same blue eyes and the same blond hair, but Serena made Sydney cut hers short so people wouldn't stare. The resemblance was that uncanny.

As much as they looked like each other, they bore little resemblance to their parents—not that they were often around to provide comparison. Serena used to tell Sydney that those people weren't their parents at all, that the girls had washed ashore in a small blue boat from some faraway place, or been found in the first-class compartment on a train, or been smuggled in by spies. If Sydney questioned the story, Serena would simply insist that her sister had been too young to remember. Sydney was still fairly sure they were just fantasies, but never *entirely* sure; Serena was very good at telling tales. She had always been convincing (that was the word her sister liked to use for *lying*).

It had been Serena's idea to walk out on the frozen lake and have a picnic. They used to have them every year, right around New Year's when the lake in the center of Brighton Commons was nothing but a block of ice, but with Serena off at college they hadn't had the chance. So it was a long weekend in March, toward the end of Serena's spring break, and a few days shy of Sydney's twelfth birthday, when they finally got to pack their lunch and head out onto the ice. Serena wore the picnic blanket as a cape and regaled her little sister with the latest tale of how the two had come to be called Clarkes. It involved pirates, or superheroes, Sydney wasn't paying attention; she was too busy taking mental pictures of her sister, shots she'd cling to when Serena left again. They reached what Serena deemed to be a good bit of lake, and she tugged the blanket from her shoulders, spread it out on the ice, and began to unload the eclectic assortment of food she'd found in the pantry.

Now, the problem with March (as opposed to January or February) was that even though it was still quite cold, the depth of the ice was waning, uneven. Small patches of warmth during the days caused the frozen lake by their house to begin to melt. You wouldn't even notice the change, unless it broke beneath you.

Which it did.

The cracks were small and silent beneath a film of snow as the two arranged their picnic, and by the time the sound of splitting ice had grown loud enough for them to hear, it was too late. Serena had just started another story when the ice gave way, plunging both into the dark, half-frozen water.

The cold forced all the air from Sydney's lungs, and even though Serena had taught her how to swim, her legs got tangled in the blanket as it sank, dragging her down with it. The icy water bit at her skin, her eyes. She clawed toward the surface and Serena's kicking legs but it was no use. She kept sinking, and kept reaching, and all she could think as she sank farther and farther away from her sister was *come back come back come back*. And then the world began to freeze around her, and there was so much cold, and that began to vanish, too, leaving only darkness.

Sydney later learned that Serena *had* come back, that she had pulled her up through the freezing water and onto the unfreezing lake before collapsing beside her.

Someone had seen the bodies on the ice.

By the time the rescue crew got out to them, Serena was barely breathing, her heart stubbornly dragging itself through every beat—and then it stopped—and Sydney was the cool blue-white of marble, just as still. Both girls were dead at the scene, but because they were also technically frozen, they couldn't officially be declared, and the paramedics dragged the Clarke sisters to the hospital to warm them up.

What followed was a miracle. The sisters came back. Their pulses started, and they took a breath, and then another—that's all living is, really—and they woke up, and they sat up, and they spoke, and they were, in every discernable way, alive.

There was only one problem.

Sydney wouldn't warm up. She felt fine, more or less, but her pulse was too slow, and her temperature too low—she overheard two doctors say that with her stats, she should be in a coma—and they deemed her too fragile to leave the hospital.

Serena was another matter entirely. Sydney thought she was acting strange, even moodier than usual, but no one else—not the doctors and nurses, not the therapists, not even their parents, who had cut a trip short when they heard about the accident—seemed to notice the change. Serena complained of headaches, so they gave her painkillers. She complained of the hospital, so they let her go. Just like that. Sydney had heard them talking about her sister's condition, but when she walked up and said she wanted to leave, they stepped aside and let her pass. Serena had always gotten her way, but never like this. Never without a fight.

"You're going? Just like that?" Sydney was sitting in her bed. Serena was standing in the doorway in street clothes. She had a box in her hands.

"I'm missing school. And I hate hospitals, Syd," she said. "You know that."

Of course Sydney knew. She hated hospitals, too. "But I don't understand. They're just letting you go?"

"Seems so."

"Then tell them to let me go, too."

Serena stood beside the hospital bed, and ran her hand over Sydney's hair. "You need to stay a little longer."

The fight bled out of Sydney, and she found herself nodding, even as tears slid down her cheeks. Serena brushed them away with her thumb, and said, "I'm not gone." It reminded Sydney of sinking beneath the surface, of wanting her sister so badly to *come back*.

"Do you remember," she asked her big sister, "what you were thinking in the lake? When the ice broke?"

Serena's brow crinkled. "You mean, besides *fuck, it's cold*?" Sydney almost smiled. Serena didn't. Her hand slid from Sydney's face. "I just remember thinking *no*. No, not like this." She set the box she'd been holding on the side table. "Happy birthday, Syd."

And then Serena left. And Sydney didn't. She asked to leave, and they refused. She pleaded and begged and promised she was fine, and they refused. It was her birthday, and she didn't want to spend it alone in a place like this. She couldn't spend it here. But they still said no.

Her parents both worked. They had to go.

A week, they promised her. Stay a week.

Sydney didn't have much choice. She stayed.

∞

SYDNEY hated evenings at the hospital.

The whole floor was too quiet, too settled. It was the only time the heavy panic set in, panic that she would never leave, never get to go home. She would be forgotten here, wearing the same pale clothes as everyone else, blending in with the patients and the nurses and the walls, and her family would be outside in the world and she would bleed away like a memory, like a colorful shirt washed too many times. As if Serena knew exactly what she'd need, the box by Sydney's bed contained a purple scarf. It was brighter than anything in her small suitcase.

She clung to the strip of color, wrapped the scarf around her neck despite the fact that she wasn't very cold (well, she was, according to the doctors, but she didn't *feel* very cold), and began to walk. She paced the hospital wing, relishing the moments when the nurses' eyes flicked her way. They saw her, and they didn't stop her, and that made Sydney feel like Serena, around whom the seas kept parting. When Sydney had walked the entire floor three times, she took the stairs to the next one. It was a different shade of beige. The change was so subtle that visitors would never notice, but Sydney had been staring at the walls on her own floor enough to pick out their paint chip on one of those walls with ten thousand colors, two hundred kinds of white.

People were sicker on this floor. Sydney could smell it even before she heard the coughing or saw the stretcher being wheeled from a room, bare but for a large sheet. It smelled like stronger disinfectants here. Someone in a room down the hall shouted, and the nurse wheeling the stretcher paused, left it in the hall, and hurried into the patient's room. Sydney followed to see what the fuss was about.

A man in the room at the end of the hall was unhappy, but she couldn't understand why. Sydney stood in the hall and tried to catch a glimpse, but a curtain was drawn in the room, bisecting it and shielding the shouting man from view, and the stretcher was blocking her way. She leaned on the gurney, just a little, and shivered.

The sheet she was touching had been put there to cover something. The something was a body. And when she brushed against it, the body twitched. Sydney jumped back, and covered her mouth to keep from shouting. Pressed against the beige wall she looked from the nurses in the patient's room to the body under the sheet on the stretcher. It twitched a second time. Sydney wrapped the tails of her purple scarf around her hands. She felt frozen all over again but in a different way. It wasn't icy water. It was fear.

"What are you doing here?" asked a nurse in an unflattering shade of beige-green. Sydney had no idea what to say, so she simply pointed. The nurse took her wrist and began to lead her down the hall.

"No," said Syd, finally. *"Look."*

The nurse sighed and glanced back at the sheet, which twitched again.

The nurse screamed.

∞

SYDNEY was assigned therapy.

The doctors said it was to help her cope with the trauma of seeing a dead body (even though she didn't actually see it) and Sydney would have protested, but after her unsupervised trip to the next floor up she found herself confined to her room, and there wasn't any other way for her to spend her time, so she agreed. She refrained, however, from mentioning the fact that she had touched the body a moment before it came back to life.

They called the person's recovery a miracle.

Sydney laughed, mostly because that's what they had called *her* recovery.

She wondered if someone had accidentally touched her, too.

∞

AFTER a week, Sydney's body temperature still hadn't come back up, but she seemed otherwise stable, and the doctors finally agreed to release her the next day. That night, Sydney snuck out of her hospital room and went down to the morgue, to find out for sure if what had happened in that hall was truly a miracle, a happy accident, a fluke, or if she somehow had something to do with it.

Half an hour later she hurried out of the morgue, thoroughly disgusted and spotted with stale blood, but with her hypothesis confirmed.

Sydney Clarke could raise the dead.

XXX

SYDNEY woke up the next morning in the too-large bed in the strange hotel, for a moment unsure of where, when, or how she was. But as she blinked away sleep, the details trickled back, the rain and the car and the two peculiar men, both of whom she could hear talking beyond the door.

Mitch's brusque tone and Victor's lower, smoother one, seemed to seep through the walls of her room. She sat up, stiff and hungry, and adjusted the oversized sweatpants on her hips before wandering out in search of food.

The two men were standing in the kitchen. Mitch was pouring coffee and talking to Victor, who was absently crossing out lines in a magazine. Mitch looked up as she walked in.

"How's your arm?" asked Victor, still blacking out words.

There was no pain, only a stiff feeling. She supposed she had him to thank for that.

"It's fine," she said. Victor set his pen aside and rolled a bag of bagels across the counter toward her. In the corner of the kitchen sat several bags of groceries. He nodded at them.

"Don't know what you eat, so . . ."

"I'm not a puppy," she said, fighting back a smile. She took a bagel and rolled the bag back across the counter, where it butted up against Victor's magazine. She watched him black out the lines of text, and remembered the article from last night, and the photo that went with it, the one she'd been reaching for when Victor woke. Her eyes drifted back to the couch. It wasn't there anymore.

"What's wrong?"

The question brought her back. Victor had his elbows on the counter, fingers loosely intertwined.

"There was a paper over there last night, with a picture on it. Where is it?"

Victor frowned, but slid the newspaper page out from under the magazine, and held it up for her to see. "This?"

Sydney felt a shiver, somewhere down deep.

"Why do you have a picture of him?" she asked, pointing at the grainy shot of the civilian beside the block of mostly blacked-out text.

Victor rounded the counter in slow, measured steps, and held the article up between them, inches from her face.

"Do you know him?" he asked, eyes alight. Sydney nodded. "How?"

Sydney swallowed. "He's the one who shot me."

Victor leaned down until his face was very close to hers. "Tell me what happened."

XXXI

LAST YEAR
BRIGHTON COMMONS

SYDNEY told Serena about the incident in the morgue, and Serena laughed.

It wasn't a happy laugh, though, or a light laugh. Sydney didn't even think it was an oh-dear-my-sister-has-brain-damage-or-delusions-from-drowning laugh. There was something stuck in the laugh, and it made Sydney nervous.

Serena then told Sydney, in very calm, quiet words (which should have struck Sydney as odd right then and there because Serena had never been terribly calm or quiet) not to tell *anyone else* about the morgue, or the body in the hall, or anything even remotely related to resurrecting dead people, and to Sydney's own amazement, she didn't. From that moment, she felt no desire to share the strange news with anyone but Serena, and Serena seemed to want nothing to do with it.

So Sydney did the only thing she could. She went back to middle school, and tried not to touch anything dead. She made it to the end of the school year. She made it through the summer . . . even though Serena had somehow convinced the faculty to let her do a trip to Amsterdam for credit, and didn't come home, and when Sydney heard this she was so mad she almost wanted to tell or show someone what she could do, just to spite her sister. But she didn't. Serena always seemed to call, just before Sydney lost her temper. They would talk about nothing, just filling up space with how-are-yous and how-are-the-folks and how-are-classes and Sydney would cling to the sound of her sister's voice even though the words were empty. And then, as she felt the conversation ending, she'd ask Serena to come home, and Serena would say *no, not this time,* and Sydney would feel lost, alone, until her sister would say *I'm not gone, I'm not gone,* and Sydney would somehow believe her.

But even though she believed those words with a simple, unshakeable faith, it didn't mean they made her happy. Sydney's slow-beating heart began to sink over the fall, and then Christmas came and Serena didn't, and for some reason her parents—who'd always been adamant about one thing, and that was spending Christmas together, as if one well-represented holiday could make up for the other 364 days—didn't seem to mind. They hardly even noticed. But Sydney noticed, and it made her feel like cracking glass.

So it's no surprise that when Serena finally called and invited her to come visit, Sydney broke.

∞

"COME stay with me," said Serena. "It'll be fun!"

Serena had avoided her little sister for nearly a year. Sydney had kept her hair short, out of some vague sense of deference, or perhaps just nostalgia, but she was *not* happy. Not with her big sister, and not with the deviant flutter in her own chest at her sister's offer. She hated herself for still idolizing Serena.

"I'm in school," she said.

"Come for spring break," pressed Serena. "You can come up and stay through your birthday. Mom and Dad don't know how to celebrate anyway. I always planned everything. And you know I give you the best gifts."

Sydney shivered, remembering how the last birthday had gone. As if reading her mind, Serena said, "It's warmer here in Merit. We'll sit outside, relax. It will be good for you."

Serena's voice was too sweet. Sydney should have known. Forever and ever after Sydney would know, but not then. Not when it mattered.

"Okay," said Sydney at last, trying to hide her excitement. "I'd like that."

"Great!" Serena sounded so happy. Sydney could hear the smile in her voice. It made her smile, too. "I want you to meet someone while you're here," added Serena, in an afterthought kind of way.

"Who?" asked Sydney.

"Just a friend."

XXXII

SERENA threw her arms around her little sister.

"Look at you!" she said, dragging her sister inside. "You're growing up."

Sydney had barely grown at all, actually. Less than an inch in the year since the accident. It wasn't just her height, either. Sydney's nails, her hair, everything about her crept forward. Slowly. Like melting ice.

When Serena teasingly mentioned her still-short hair, Sydney pretended the look had simply grown on her, implied that it had nothing to do with Serena anymore. Still, she wrapped her arms around her sister, and when her sister hugged back, Sydney felt as if broken threads, hundreds and hundreds of them, were stitching the two back together. Something in her started to thaw. Until a male voice cleared its throat.

"Oh, Sydney," said her sister, pulling away, "I want you to meet Eli."

She smiled when she said his name. A boy, college-aged, was sitting in a chair in Serena's apartment—one of the ones usually reserved for upperclassmen—and he stood up at the mention of his name, and stepped forward. He was handsome, with broad shoulders and a firm handshake and eyes that were brown but alive in that glittering, almost drunk sort of way. Sydney had a hard time looking away from him.

"Hi, Eli," she said.

"I've heard a lot about you," he said.

Sydney didn't say anything, because Serena had never mentioned Eli until the phone call, and then she'd only called him *a friend*. Judging by the way they looked at each other, that wasn't the whole truth.

"Come on," said Serena. "Put your stuff away and then we can all get to know each other."

When Sydney hesitated, Serena pulled the duffel from her sister's shoulder and walked away, leaving her alone with Eli for a moment. Sydney wondered why she felt like a sheep in a wolf's den. There was something dangerous about Eli, about the calm way he smiled and the lazy way he moved. He leaned on the arm of the chair he'd been sitting in.

"So," he said. "You're in eighth grade?"

Sydney nodded. "And you're a sophomore?" she asked. "Like Serena?"

Eli laughed soundlessly. "I'm a senior, actually."

"How long have you been dating my sister?"

Eli's smile flickered. "You like to ask questions."

Sydney frowned. "That's not an answer."

Serena came back into the room holding a soda for Sydney. "You two getting along?" And just like that the smile was back on Eli's face, broad enough that Sydney wondered how long until his cheeks would start to hurt. Sydney took the drink and Serena went to Eli and leaned against him, as if declaring allegiance. Sydney sipped the soda and watched as he kissed her sister's hair, his hand curling around her shoulder.

"So," said Serena, examining her little sister, "Eli wants to see your trick."

Sydney nearly choked on the soda. "I . . . I don't—"

"Come on, Syd," pressed Serena. "You can trust him."

She felt like Alice in Wonderland. Like the soda must have had a little *drink me* tag and now the room was shrinking, or she was growing, or either way there wasn't enough space. Enough air. Or had it been the cake that made Alice grow? She didn't know . . .

She took a step back.

"What's the matter, sis? You were pretty eager to show *me*."

"You told me not to . . ."

Serena's brow furrowed. "Well, now I'm telling you to do it." She pushed off Eli and came up to Sydney, wrapping her in a hug. "Don't worry, Syd," she whispered in her ear. "He's just like us."

"Us?" Sydney whispered back.

"Didn't I tell you?" cooed Serena. "I have a trick, too."

Sydney pulled away. "What? When? What is it?" She wondered if that had been the thing stuck in Serena's laugh the night she told her about raising the dead. A secret. But why didn't her sister tell her? Why wait until now?

"Uh-uh," Serena said, wagging her finger. "Trade you. You show us yours, and we'll show you ours."

For a very long moment, Sydney didn't know whether to run, or feel elated that she wasn't alone. That she and Serena . . . and Eli . . . had something to share. Serena took Sydney's face between her hands.

"You show us yours," she said again, smooth and slow.

Sydney found herself taking a deep breath, and nodding.

"Okay," she said. "But we have to find a body."

ELI held open the front passenger door. "After you."

"Where are we going?" asked Sydney as she climbed in.

"On a road trip," said Serena. She got behind the wheel and Eli took the backseat, directly behind Sydney. She didn't like that, either; didn't like that he could see her but she couldn't see him. Serena asked absently about Brighton Commons as the university buildings beyond the car gave way to smaller, sparser structures.

"Why wouldn't you come home?" asked Sydney under her breath. "I missed you. I needed you and you promised you weren't gone but—"

"Don't dwell," said Serena. "What matters is that I'm here now, and you're here, too."

The structures gave way to fields.

"And we're going to have a ball," said Eli from the backseat. Sydney shivered. "Isn't that right, Serena?"

Sydney glanced at her sister, and was surprised to see a shadow cross Serena's face as she met Eli's gaze in the rearview mirror.

"That's right," she said at last.

The road got narrower, rougher.

When the car finally stopped, they were at the seam between a forest and a field. Eli got out first, and led the way out into the field, the grass coming up to his knees. Eventually he stopped and looked down.

"Here we are."

Sydney followed his gaze, and felt her stomach lurch.

There, tucked amid the grass, was a corpse.

"Dead bodies aren't that easy to come by," explained Eli lightly. "You have to go to a morgue, or a cemetery, or make one yourself."

"Please don't tell me you . . ."

Eli laughed. "Don't be silly, Syd."

"Eli shadows over at the hospital," explained Serena. "He stole a cadaver from the morgue."

Sydney swallowed. The corpse was dressed. Weren't cadavers supposed to be naked?

"But what is the body doing out here?" she asked. "Why didn't we just go to the morgue?"

"Sydney," said Eli. She really didn't like the way he kept using her name. Like they were close. "There are *people* in a morgue. And not all of them are dead."

"Yeah, well, we didn't have to drive half an hour away," she shot back. "Aren't there any fields, or abandoned lots, near the college? Why are we all the way—"

"Sydney," Serena's voice cut through the chill March air. "Stop whining."

And she did. The complaint died in her throat. She rubbed at her eyes, and her hand came away with black smudges from the makeup she'd put on in the cab as it wove its way toward the University of Merit. She'd wanted to impress Serena by looking grown up. But right now, she didn't feel grown up. Right now, she wanted nothing more than to curl into a ball, or to crawl out of her own skin. Instead she stood very still and looked down at the corpse of a middle-aged man and thought of the last time she'd been with a body (she didn't count the dead hamster in school because no one even knew it had died and it was small and furry and didn't have human eyes). The memory of the morgue, of the cold, dead skin against her fingertips. The chill like taking a large gulp of ice water, so large that the shiver ran down to her toes. It had been harder to make them dead again. She'd panicked. The woman in the morgue had tried to get up off the table. She hadn't thought about what to do next so she'd grabbed the closest weapon she could find—a knife, part of an autopsy kit—and driven it down into the woman's chest. She had lurched, then slumped back to the metal slab. Apparently raising the dead didn't mean they couldn't be killed again.

"Well?" said Eli, gesturing at the body like he was offering Sydney a gift, and she wasn't being very grateful.

She looked to her sister for answers, for help, but somewhere between the car and the body, Serena had changed. She seemed tense, her forehead crinkling in a way that she'd always tried to avoid because she said she didn't want wrinkles. And she wouldn't meet her sister's eyes. Sydney turned back to the body, and knelt gingerly beside it.

She didn't see what she did as raising the dead, not really. They weren't zombies, as far as she could tell—she didn't have prolonged exposure to her subjects, aside from the hamster, and she wasn't sure how a zombie hamster's behavior would differ from that of a normal one—and it didn't matter what they'd died of. The man under the sheet in the hospital hall had apparently suffered a heart attack. The woman in the morgue had already had her organs removed. But when Sydney touched them, they didn't just come back, they *revived*. They were okay. Alive. Human. And, as she found out in the morgue, as susceptible to mortality as they'd been before, just not the form that killed them. It perplexed Sydney, until she remembered the day on the frozen lake when the ice water had swallowed her up and she'd reached for Serena's leg and been a fraction too late, too slow, to catch it—*come back, come back*—and how badly she'd wanted a second chance.

That's what Sydney was giving these people. A second chance.

Her fingers hovered over the dead man's chest for a moment as she wondered if he *deserved* a second chance, then chided herself.

Who was she to judge or decide or grant or deny? Simply because she could, did that mean she should?

"Any day now," said Eli.

Sydney swallowed and forced herself to lower her fingers onto the dead man's skin. At first, nothing happened, and panic swept over her at the thought of finally having a chance to show Serena, and failing to do it. But the panic fell away when, moments later, the ice-water chill flooded through her veins, and the man beneath her shuddered. His eyes flew open and he sat up, all so fast that Sydney went stumbling backward to the grass. The once-dead man looked around, confused and angry, before his eyes locked on Eli, and his whole face contorted with rage.

"What the hell is—"

The gunshot rang in Sydney's ears. The man fell back into the grass, a small red tunnel between his eyes. Dead again. Eli lowered his gun.

"Impressive, Sydney," he said. "That's quite a unique gift." The humor, along with that horrible false cheer and fake smile, was gone, wiped away. In a way, Eli wasn't quite as frightening, because she'd always been able to see the monster in his eyes. Now it had finally stopped hiding. But the gun, and the way he held it, made him scary enough.

Sydney got to her feet. She really wished he would put the weapon down. Serena had retreated several feet, and was toeing a patch of frozen wild grass.

"Um, thank you?" said Sydney, her voice wavering. Her feet slid backward through the grass without her meaning to. "Are you going to show me your trick now?"

He almost laughed. "I'm afraid mine lacks the showmanship." And then he raised the gun, and leveled it at her.

In that moment, Sydney felt no surprise, no shock. It was the first thing Eli had done that seemed *right* to her. Genuine. Fitting. She wasn't afraid to die, she didn't think. After all, she'd done it once. But that didn't mean she was ready. Sadness and confusion coiled in her, not toward him, but toward her sister.

"Serena?" she asked quietly, as if maybe she didn't notice her new boyfriend was pointing a gun at her little sister. But Serena had turned away, arms crossed tightly over her chest.

"I want you to know," said Eli, fingers flexing on the gun, "that it is my grim task to do this. I have no choice."

"Yes, you do," whispered Sydney.

"Your power is wrong, and it makes you a danger to—"

"I'm not the one holding a gun."

"No," said Eli, "but your weapon is worse. Your power is *unnatural*. Do you understand, Sydney? It goes against nature. Against God. And this," he said, taking aim, "this is for the greater good."

"Wait!" said Serena, suddenly turning back. "Maybe we don't have to—"

Too late.

It happened fast.

Shock and pain hit Sydney in one loud blast.

Serena's voice had stolen her a moment, a fraction of a moment, and as soon as she saw Eli's fingers tighten on the trigger Sydney had cut to the side, lunging for a branch as the gun fired. She had the broad stick in her grip and swung into Eli before she even felt the blood running down her arm. The branch knocked the gun to the ground and Sydney spun, and ran for her life. She reached the edge of the forest before the shots started again. As she tumbled through the trees, she thought she heard her sister calling her name, but this time she knew better than to look back.

XXXIII

VICTOR stood very, very still, as he listened to Sydney's story.

"Is that everything?" he asked when she was done, even though he could tell it wasn't, that by the time the account left Sydney's lips, it had bites taken out. He had watched her pause to filter out the specific nature of her power every time she opened her mouth. In the end she'd only conceded that she *had* an ability, and that her sister's new boyfriend, Eli, had demanded a demonstration, and then tried to execute her for it—*execute,* that was the word she used—but that was all. *Executing EOs,* Victor's mind spun. What was Eli playing at? Had there been others? There had to have been. The stunt in the bank with Barry Lynch, how did that tie in? Had he contrived a scene to kill the man in broad daylight?

A hero? Victor now scoffed at the word. That's what the paper had been so eager to call Eli. And for a moment, Victor had believed the headline. He had been willing to play the villain when he thought Eli was *actually* a hero; now that the truth of his old friend was proving itself to be much darker, Victor would relish the role as opposition, adversary, foe.

"That's all," lied Sydney, and Victor didn't get mad. He didn't feel the need to hurt her, to pry the final truths loose—he couldn't blame her for hesitating; after all, the last time she revealed her powers to someone, she'd nearly died for it—because even if she wasn't telling him everything, she'd told him something vital. Eli wasn't just close. He was *here*. In Merit. Or at least, he had been a day and a half before. Victor propped his elbows on the counter and took in the small girl whose path had crossed his own.

He had never believed in fate, in destiny. Those things lurked too close to divinity for Victor's taste, higher powers and the dispensation of agency. No, he chose to see the world in terms of probability, acknowledging the role of chance while taking control wherever it was possible. But even he had to admit that if there was a Fate, it was smiling on him. The newspaper, the girl, the city. If he'd possessed even a fraction of Eli's religious zeal, he might think God was pointing him on a path, a mission. He wasn't willing to go that far, to buy in, but he still appreciated the show of support.

"Sydney . . ." He tried to suppress his excitement, forcing a calm he didn't feel into his voice. "Your sister's college, what is it called?"

"It's U of Merit. On the other side of the city. It's huge."

"And the school apartment, the one your sister was staying in. Do you remember how to get there?"

Sydney hesitated, picking at the bagel still in her lap.

Victor gripped the counter. "This is important."

When Sydney didn't move, Victor took her by the arm, curling his fingers over the place she'd been shot. He'd taken away the pain, but he wanted her to remember, both what Eli had done, and what *he* could do. She froze beneath his touch as with his free hand, he tugged the collar of his shirt down so she could see the first of the three scars made by Eli's gun.

"That's two of us he's tried to kill." He let go of her arm and his shirt collar. "We got lucky. How many other EOs haven't? And if we don't stop him, how many other EOs *won't*?"

Sydney's blue eyes were wide, unblinking.

"Do you remember where your sister lives?"

For the first time, Mitch spoke up. "We won't let Eli hurt you again," he said over his glass of chocolate milk. "Just so you know."

Victor had opened Mitch's laptop, and pulled up a campus map. He turned the screen toward her.

"Do you remember?"

After a long moment, Sydney nodded. "I know the way."

∞

SYDNEY couldn't stop shaking.

It had nothing to do with the cold March morning and everything to do with fear. She sat in the front seat and navigated. Mitch drove. Victor sat in the back and fiddled with something sharp. It looked to Sydney, who'd glanced back once or twice, like a fancy knife that could be flicked open or closed. She turned forward and hugged her knees as the streets went by. The same streets that slid past the taxicab window a few days before as it took her to Serena. The same streets that slid past the window of Serena's car as she drove them to the field.

"Turn right," said Sydney, making a concerted effort to stop her teeth from chattering. Her fingers wandered to the spot on her arm where the bullet had passed through. She closed her eyes but saw her sister, felt her arms around her, the soda can cold in her hand and Eli's eyes on her when Serena said *Show us*. The field and the body and the gunshot and the woods and—

She decided to keep her eyes open.

"Turn right again," she said. In the backseat, Victor opened and closed the knife. Sydney remembered hating it when Eli sat be-

hind her, the weight of his eyes on the back of her seat, on her. She
didn't mind it now with Victor there.

"Here," she said. The car slowed, and stopped along the curb.
Sydney looked out the window at the apartment buildings that
hugged the eastern edge of campus. Everything looked the same,
and that felt wrong, like the world should have registered the
events of the last few days, should have changed the way *she* had
changed. Cool air blew against her face and Sydney blinked
and realized Victor was holding the car door open for her. Mitch
was standing on the path to the apartment, kicking a loose piece
of concrete.

"Coming?" asked Victor.

She couldn't will her feet to move.

"Sydney, look at me." He rested his hands on the car roof and
leaned in. "No one is going to hurt you. Do you know why?" She
shook her head, and Victor smiled. "Because I'll hurt them first."

He held the door open wide for her. "Now get out."

And Sydney did.

∞

THEY made an odd picture, knocking on the door to 3A: Mitch,
towering and tattooed; Victor in head-to-toe black—less like a
thief and more like a Parisian, groomed and elegant—and Sydney,
sandwiched between them, in blue leggings and a large red coat.
These clothes had appeared this morning, and still felt dryer-
warm. They even fit a little better. She particularly liked the
coat.

After several rounds of polite knocking, Mitch removed a set of
picks from his coat pocket, and was busy saying something about

how easy these school locks were in a way that made Sydney wonder more about his preprison life, when the door swung open.

A girl in pink and green pajamas looked at them, and her expression confirmed the oddness of the trio's collective appearance.

The girl, however, was not Serena. Sydney's heart fell.

"You selling cookies?" she asked. Mitch laughed.

"Do you know Serena Clarke?" asked Victor.

"Yeah, sure thing," said the girl. "She gave me the apartment, like, yesterday. Said she didn't need it anymore, and my roommate was driving me *up the wall* so Serena told me to take this one until the end of the year. I'm about to graduate anyway, thank *God*, I'm so done with this fucking school."

Sydney cleared her throat. "Do you know where she went?"

"Probably with that boyfriend of hers. He's a hottie, but kind of a dick, to be honest. He's one of those time-suck guys that always wants to be with her—"

"Do you know where *he* lives?" asked Victor.

The girl in the pink and green pajamas shook her head and shrugged. "Nope. Ever since they started dating last fall she's been so weird. I've hardly seen her. And we used to be tight! Like movies-and-chocolate-on-menstrual-time tight. And then he showed up and *bam*, it's Eli this and Eli that—"

Sydney and Victor both tensed at the name.

"No idea then," he cut in, "where we might find them?"

She shrugged again. "Merit's a big city, but I saw Serena in class yesterday—that's when she gave me the keys—so she can't have gone far." Her eyes flicked between them, and seemed to land on Sydney. "You look so much like her. You her little sister? Shelly?"

Sydney opened her mouth but Victor was already turning her away.

"We're just friends," he said, guiding her down the path. Mitch followed.

"Well, if you see them," called the girl, "thank Serena for the apartment. Oh, and tell Eli he sucks."

"Will do," called Victor as the three made their way back to the car.

∞

"THIS is hopeless," whispered Sydney, sliding onto the couch.

"Hey now," said Mitch. "A week ago, Eli could have been anywhere in the world. Now, because of you, we have him narrowed down to a city."

"If he's still here," said Sydney.

Victor paced the line of the couch. "He's here." The thorn dug deep beneath his skin. So close. How badly he wanted to walk out into the streets and shout his old friend's name until he came out. It would be so easy. Fast, efficient . . . and foolish. He needed a way to lure him out without leaving the shadows himself. He was catching up to Eli, but he wanted to be a step ahead before he turned to face him. He had to find a way to make Eli come to *him*.

"What now?" asked Mitch.

Victor looked up. "Sydney wasn't the first target. I'm willing to bet she won't be the last. Can you make me a search matrix?"

Mitch cracked his massive knuckles. "What kind?"

"I want a way to find potential EOs. See if there are others he's gotten to. And if there are any he hasn't found yet."

"Worried for their safety?" asked Mitch. Victor had been thinking more about using them as bait, but he didn't say it, not in front of Sydney.

"Limit the search to the last year, keep it in-state, and look for flags," he said, trying to summon Eli's thesis work. He'd prattled on about markers once or twice, in the spaces between other topics. "Search police reports, work evaluations, school and medical records. Search for any sign of near death experience—it will probably be classified under trauma—psychological instability in the aftermath, odd behavior, leave of absence, discrepancies in records made by shrinks, uncertainty in records made by cops . . ." He began to pace again. "And while you're at it, get Serena Clarke's school records, her class schedule. If Eli's tied himself to her in some way, then it might be easier to find her than him."

"Aren't all those records classified?" asked Sydney.

Mitch beamed and flicked open his laptop, settling in at the counter.

"Mitchell," said Victor. "Tell Sydney what you were in prison for."

"Hacking," he said cheerfully.

Sydney laughed. "Seriously? I had you pegged as more of a beat-someone-to-death-with-their-own-arm type."

"I've always been big," said Mitch. "That's not my fault." He cracked his knuckles again. His hands were larger than the keyboard.

"And the tattoos?"

"It's best to look the part."

"Victor doesn't look the part."

"Depends on what part you're going for. He cleans up well."

Victor wasn't listening. He was still pacing.

Eli was close. Eli was in this city. Or had been. What on earth could Sydney's sister do, that he had found her so valuable? If Eli was executing EOs, why had he spared Serena? Victor was glad he had, though. She had given him a reason to stay in Merit, and he needed Eli tethered. Mitch's large fingers were a blur across the keyboard. Window after window unfolded on his sleek black screen. Victor couldn't stop pacing. He knew the search would take time, but the air was humming, and he couldn't will his feet to stop, couldn't force himself to find stillness, to find peace, not now when Eli was finally in reach. He needed freedom.

He needed air.

XXXIV

YESTERDAY

SYDNEY followed him into the street.

Victor hadn't heard her, not for a block, but when he finally glanced back and saw her there, her expression turned cautious, almost scared, as if she'd been caught breaking a rule. She shivered and he gestured to a nearby coffee shop. "Care for a drink?"

"Do you really think we'll find Eli?" she asked several minutes later as they made their way down the sidewalk, gripping coffee and cocoa respectively.

"Yes," said Victor.

But he did not elaborate. After several long moments of Sydney's fidgeting beside him, it was clear that she wanted to keep talking.

"What about your parents?" he asked. "Won't they notice you missing?"

"I was supposed to stay with Serena all week," she said, blowing on her drink. "And besides, they travel." She glanced over at him, then trained her gaze on the to-go cup. "When I was in the hospital last year, they just left me there. They had *work*. They always have work. They travel forty weeks a year. I had a watcher, but they let her go because she *broke a vase*. They made time to replace the vase, because apparently it was a focal piece in the house, but they were too busy to find a new watcher, so they said I didn't need one. Staying alone would be good practice for life." The words spilled out, and she sounded breathless by the end. Victor said nothing, only let her settle, and a few moments later, she added, calmer, "I don't think my parents are an issue right now."

Victor knew far too well about those kinds of parents, so he let the matter fall. Or at least, he tried to. But as they rounded the corner, a bookstore came into view, and there in the front window, a massive poster announced the newest Vale book, on sale this summer.

Victor cringed. He hadn't spoken to his own parents in nearly eight years. Apparently having a convicted offspring—at least one that didn't show any inclinations toward being rehabilitated, especially not with the "Vale system"—wasn't great for book sales. Victor had pointed out that it wasn't that *bad* for book sales, either, that they might be able to capitalize on that niche—morbid curiosity buyers—but his parents hadn't been impressed. Victor wasn't terribly distraught about the falling-out, but he'd also been spared their window displays for nearly a decade. To their credit, they sent a set of books to his cell in isolation, which he'd cherished, rationing the destruction to make it last as long as possible. When he finally integrated he found that the penitentiary library had, not surprisingly, stocked a complete set of Vale self-help books, and he'd corrected those in his trademark fashion until Wrighton caught on and denied him access.

Now Victor wandered into the store, Sydney close behind, and bought a copy of the newest book, entitled *Set Yourself Free*, and subtitled *From the Prison of Your Discontent*. It felt like a pretty obvious jab. Victor also bought a handful of black Sharpies from the turnstile by the checkout counter, and asked Sydney if she wanted anything, but she simply shook her head and clutched her to-go cup of cocoa. Back out front, Victor considered the storefront

window, but he feared the Sharpies weren't big enough and besides, he didn't intend to get picked up for vandalism of all things,
so he was forced to leave the window untouched. It was a shame, he
thought, as they walked on. There had been an excerpt, blown up
large and pasted on the window, and in a passage studded with
overwrought gems—his favorite being "out of the ruins of our
self-made jails . . ."—he had seen the perfect opportunity to spell
out a simple but effective "We . . . ruin . . . all . . . we touch."

He and Sydney continued on their stroll. He didn't explain the
book, and she didn't ask. The fresh air felt good, the coffee infinitely better than even bribery and pain could get him in prison.
Sydney blew absently on her hot chocolate, small fingers curled
around it for warmth.

"Why did he try to kill me?" she asked quietly.

"I don't know yet."

"After I showed him my power, and he was about to kill me, he
called it a grim task. He told me he didn't have a choice. Why
would he want to kill EOs? He said he was one, too."

"He is an ExtraOrdinary, yes."

"What's his power?"

"Self-righteousness," Victor said. But when Sydney looked confused, he added, "He heals. It's a reflexive ability. In his eyes, I
think that makes it somehow pure. Divine. He can't technically
use his power to hurt others."

"No," said Sydney, "he uses guns for that."

Victor chuckled. "As for why he seems to think it's his personal
duty to dispose of us"—he straightened—"I suspect it has something to do with me."

"Why?" she whispered.

"It's a long story," said Victor, sounding tired. "And not a pleasant one. It's been a decade since I had a chance to philosophize

with our mutual friend, but if I had to guess, I'd say Eli believes he's somehow protecting people from us. He once accused me of being a devil wearing Victor's skin."

"He called me unnatural," said Sydney softly. "Said my power went against nature. Against God."

"Charming, isn't he?"

It was after lunch and the people had almost all slunk back into their offices, leaving the streets strangely bare. Victor seemed to be leading them farther and farther away from the crowds, onto narrower streets. Quieter streets.

"Sydney," he said some time later, "you don't have to tell me your power if you don't want, but I need you to understand something. I'm going to do everything I can to beat Eli, but he's not an easy opponent. His power alone makes him nearly invincible, and he may be crazy, but he's cunning. Every advantage he has makes it harder for me to win. The fact that he knows your power, and the fact that I *don't*, puts me at a disadvantage. Do you understand?"

Sydney's steps had slowed, and she nodded, but said nothing. It took all of Victor's patience not to force her hand, but a moment later, that patience was rewarded. The two of them passed an alley, and heard a low whine. Sydney broke away and turned back, and when Victor followed, he saw what she had seen.

A large black shape stretched on the damp concrete, panting. It was a dog. Victor knelt just long enough to run a finger down its back, and the whining faded. Now the only sounds it made were shuddering breaths. At least it wouldn't be in pain. He stood again, frowning the way he did whenever he was thinking. The dog looked mangled, as if it had been hit by a car and staggered the few feet into the alley before crumpling.

Sydney crouched down by the dog, stroking its short black fur.

"After Eli shot me," she said in a soft, cooing voice, as if speaking to the dying dog instead of Victor, "I swore I'd never use my power again. Not in front of anyone." She swallowed hard, and looked up at Victor. "Kill it."

Victor arched an eyebrow. "With what, Syd?"

She gave him a long, hard look.

"Please kill the dog, Victor," she said again.

He looked around. The alley was empty. He sighed and pulled a handgun from its place against his back. Digging in his pocket he retrieved a silencer, and screwed it on, glancing over it at the wheezing dog.

"Scoot back," he said, and Sydney did. Victor took aim, and pulled the trigger once, a clean shot. The dog stopped moving, and Victor turned away, already dismantling his gun. When Sydney didn't follow, he glanced back to find her crouching over the dog again, running her hands back and forth along its bloody coat and its crushed ribs in small, soothing motions. And then, as he watched, she went still. Her breath hovered in a cloud in front of her lips, and her face tightened in pain.

"Sydney—," he started, but the rest of the sentence died in his throat as the dog's tail *moved*. One slight swoosh across the dirty pavement. And then again, right before the body tensed. The bones cracked back into place, the chest inflated, the rib cage reformed, and the legs stretched. And then, the beast sat up. Sydney backed away as the dog pushed itself to its four feet, and looked at them, tail wagging tentatively. The dog was . . . huge. And very much alive.

Victor watched, speechless. Up until now he'd had factors, thoughts, ideas about how to find Eli. But as he watched the dog blink and yawn and breathe, a plan began to take shape. Sydney looked cautiously his way, and he smiled.

"Now *that*," he said, "is a gift."

She petted the dog between the ears, both of which stood roughly eye level with her.

"Can we keep him?"

VICTOR tossed his coat onto the couch as Sydney and the dog wandered in behind him.

"It's time to send a message," he announced, dropping the Vale self-help book he'd bought onto the counter with a flourish and a thud. "To Eli Ever."

"Where the hell did that dog come from?" asked Mitch.

"I get to keep him," said Sydney.

"Is that blood?"

"I shot him," said Victor, searching through his papers.

"Why would you do that?" asked Mitch, closing the laptop.

"Because he was dying."

"Then why isn't he dead?"

"Because Sydney brought him back."

Mitch turned to consider the small blond girl in the middle of their hotel living room. "Excuse me?"

Her eyes went to the floor. "Victor named him Dol," she said.

"It's a measurement of pain," explained Victor.

"Well, that's morbidly appropriate," said Mitch. "Can we get back to the part where Sydney *resurrected him*? And what do you mean you're going to send Eli a message?"

Victor found what he was looking for, and turned his attention to the hotel's floor-to-ceiling windows and the sun beyond them, trying to gauge the amount of light that stood between him and full night.

"When you want to get someone's attention," he said, "you wave, or you call out, or you send up a flare. These things are dependent on proximity and intensity. Too far away, or too quiet, and there's no guarantee the person will see or hear you. I didn't have a bright enough flare before, a way to guarantee his attention short of making a scene myself, which would have worked, but I'd have lost the advantage. Now, thanks to Sydney, I know the perfect method and message." He held up the news article and with it, the notes Mitch had made for him on Barry Lynch, the supposed criminal from the foiled bank robbery. "And we're going to need shovels."

XXXV

LAST NIGHT

MERIT CEMETERY

THUD.
 Thud.
 Thud.
The shovel hit wood, and stuck.

Victor and Sydney cleared the last of the dirt away, and tossed the shovels up onto the grass rim around the grave. Victor knelt and pulled the coffin lid back. The body within was fresh, well preserved, a man in his thirties with dark, slicked-back hair, a narrow nose, and close-set eyes.

"Hello, Barry," said Victor to the corpse.

Sydney couldn't take her eyes from the body. He looked slightly . . . deader . . . than she would have liked, and she wondered what color his eyes would be when they opened.

There was a moment of silence, almost reverent, before Victor's hand came down on her shoulder.

"Well?" he said, pointing to the body. "Do your thing."

∞

THE corpse shuddered, opened its eyes, and sat up. Or at least, it tried to.

"Hello, Barry," said Victor.

"What . . . the . . . hell . . . ?" said Barry, finding the lower two thirds of his body pinned beneath the bottom half of the coffin lid, which was presently being held shut by Victor's boot.

"Are you acquainted with Eli Cardale? Or maybe he goes by Ever now."

Barry was clearly still grasping the exact details of his situation. His eyes snapped from the coffin to the wall of dirt to the night sky, to the man with blond hair interrogating him and the girl sitting at the grave opening, swinging her small legs in their bright blue leggings. Sydney looked down, and was surprised and a bit disappointed to find that Barry's eyes were an ordinary brown. She'd hoped they would be green.

"Fucking Ever," Barry growled, banging his fist against the coffin. He flickered in and out of sight a little each time, like a shorting projection. The air made faint whooshing noises, like far-off explosions every time he did. "He said it was a tryout! Like, for a Hero League or some shit—"

"He wanted you to rob a bank to prove you were a hero?" Skepticism dripped from Victor's voice. "And then what?"

"What the fuck does it look like, ass hat?" Barry gestured down at his body. "*He killed me!* The bastard walks right up in the middle of a demonstration *he* told me to do, and he shoots me."

So Victor was right. It had been a setup. Eli had staged a killing as a rescue. He had to admit, it was one way to get away with murder.

"I mean, I'm dead, right? This isn't some shit prank?"

"You *were* dead," said Victor. "Now, thanks to my friend, Sydney, you're a bit less dead."

Barry was spluttering curses and crackling like a sparkler. "What did you do?" He spat at Sydney. "You broke me." Sydney frowned as he continued to short out, lighting up the grave in a strange, camera-flash kind of way. She had never resurrected an

EO before. She wasn't sure if all the pieces would—*could*—come back. "You broke my power, you little—"

"We have a job for you," cut in Victor.

"Fuck off, does it look like I want a *job*? I want to get out of this fucking coffin."

"I think you want to take this job."

"Blow me. You're Victor Vale, right? Ever told me about you when he was trying to recruit me."

"It's nice that he remembers," said Victor, his patience wearing thin.

"Yeah, think you're high and mighty, causing pain and shit? Well I'm not afraid of you." He flickered in and out again. "Got that? Let me out and I'll show *you* pain."

Sydney watched Victor's hand tighten into a fist, and felt the air hum around her, but Barry didn't seem to feel anything. Something was wrong. She'd gone through the motions, given him a second chance, but he hadn't come back the way the ordinary humans had, not all the way. The air stopped humming, and the man in the coffin cackled.

"Hah, see? Your little bitch messed up, didn't she? I don't feel a thing! You can't hurt me!"

At that, Victor straightened.

"Oh, sure I can," he said pleasantly. "I can shut the lid. Put the dirt back. Walk away. Hey," he called up to Sydney, who was still swinging her legs over the side of the grave. "How long would it take for an undead to become dead again?"

Sydney wanted to explain to Victor that the people she resurrected weren't *undead,* they were *alive,* and, as far as she could tell, they were perfectly mortal—well, aside from this little nerve issue—but she knew where he was going with this and what he wanted to hear, so she looked down at Barry Lynch, and shrugged dramatically. "I've never seen an undead go dead again on their own. So I'm guessing forever."

"That's a long time," said Victor. Barry's cursing and his taunts had died away. "Why don't we let you think on it? Come back in a few days?" Sydney tossed Victor his shovel, and a spray of dirt tumbled down on the coffin lid like rain.

"Okay, wait, wait, wait, wait," begged Barry, trying to claw his way out of the coffin and finding his feet trapped. Victor had nailed his pants to the wooden floorboards before they got started. It had been Sydney's idea, actually, just to be safe. Now Barry panicked and flickered and began to whimper, and Victor rested the spade under the man's chin and smiled.

"So you'll take the job?"

XXXVI

LAST NIGHT

"**WHAT** happened back there, Sydney?"

Victor was still knocking dirt off his boots as they climbed the stairs to the hotel room—he didn't like elevators—with Sydney taking the steps two at a time beside him.

"Why didn't Barry come back the way he should?"

Sydney chewed her lip. "I don't know," she said, winded from the climb. "I've been trying to figure it out. Maybe . . . maybe it's because EOs have already had their second chance?"

"Did it feel different?" pressed Victor. "When you tried to resurrect him?"

She wrapped her arms around herself, and nodded. "It didn't feel right. Normally, it's like there's this thread, something to grab onto, but with him, it was hard to reach, and it kept slipping. I didn't get a good hold."

Victor was quiet until they reached the seventh floor.

"If you had to try again . . ." but his question faded as they reached their room. There were voices beyond the door, low and urgent. Victor slid the gun from his back as he turned the key and the door swung open on the hotel suite, only the back of Mitch's tattooed head peering over the couch in front of a TV. The voices continued on the screen in black-and-white. Victor sighed, shoulders loosening, and put the gun away. He should have known it was nothing, should have felt the absence of new bodies. He chalked up the slipup to distraction as Sydney bobbed past him into the apartment and the people on the screen argued on in dapper suits and hushed voices. Mitch had a thing for classics. Victor had arranged on numerous occasions to have the TV in the prison commons, which was usually programmed to sports or old sitcoms, set to show old black-and-whites instead. He appreciated Mitch's incongruities. They made him interesting.

Sydney tugged off her shoes by the door and went to scrub the grave dirt and the lingering feel of the dead from beneath her fingernails. The giant black dog looked up from the floor beside the couch as she passed, tail thumping. Somewhere after reviving the dog and before leaving to revive Barry, Victor had cleaned the lingering blood and grime off Dol's fur, and the beast almost looked normal as it got to its feet and followed Sydney lazily from the room.

"Hey, Vic," called Mitch, waving without looking away from the tuxedoed men on the screen. The laptop sat beside him, and hooked up to it was a small, very new printer that hadn't been there when they left.

"I don't keep you around to warm the couch, Mitch," said Victor as he crossed into the kitchen.

"You find Barry?"

"I did." Victor poured himself a glass of water and slumped against the counter, watching the bubbles flee to the top of the glass.

"He agree to deliver your message?"

"He did."

"So where is he? I know you didn't actually let him *go*?"

"Of course not." Victor smiled. "I put him back for the night."

"That's cold."

Victor shrugged, and took a sip. "I'll let him out in the morning to run his errand. And what have you been up to?" he said, tipping the glass toward him. "I hate to interrupt *Casablanca* for business but . . ."

Mitch stood and stretched. "You ready for the world's biggest case of good news—bad news?"

"Go on."

"The search matrix is still sifting." He held out a folder. "But here's what we've got so far. Each one's got enough markers to make them EO candidates." Victor took it, and began to spread the pages out on the counter. There were eight in total.

"That's the good news," said Mitch.

Victor stared down at the profiles. Each page had a block of text, lines of stolen information—names and ages and brief medical summaries following brief lines on their respective accidents or traumas, psych notes, police reports, antipsychotic and painkiller prescriptions. Information distilled, messy lives made neat. Beside the text on each profile was a picture. A man in his late fifties. A pretty girl with black hair. A teenage boy. All of the photos were candids, the subjects' eyes looking at or around the camera, but never directly at the photographer. And all of the photos had been x-ed out with a thick black Sharpie.

"What's with the x's?" asked Victor.

"That's the bad news. They're all dead."

Victor looked up sharply. "All of them?"

Mitch looked sadly, almost reverently, at the papers. "Looks like your hunch about Eli was right. These are just the Merit area, like you asked. When I started getting hits, I opened a new search, and expanded the parameters to cover the last ten years and most of the country. I didn't print those results—too many—but there's definitely a pattern."

Victor's gaze drifted back down to the files, and stuck. He couldn't tear his eyes from the thick black x's on the photos. Perhaps he should feel responsible for unleashing a monster on the world, for the bodies that monster left in his wake—after all, he made Eli what he was, he urged him to test his theory, he brought him back from the dead, he took away Angie—but as he stared down into the faces of the dead, all he felt was a kind of quiet joy, a vindication. He'd been right about Eli *all along*. Eli could preach all he liked about Victor being a devil in stolen skin, but the proof of Eli's own evil was spread across the counter, on display.

"This guy is doing damage," said Mitch as he lifted another, much, much smaller stack from beside the printer, and set them on the counter, faceup. "But here's a positive postscript for you." Three pictures gazed, glanced, or stared up at Victor, unaware. A fourth was in the process of printing itself out with a soft buzzing sound. When the machine spit it out, Mitch paused the movie and delivered the sheet to the counter. None of the photos were crossed out.

"They're still alive?"

Mitch nodded. "For now."

Sydney reappeared just then in sweats and a T-shirt, trailed by Dol. Victor wondered absently if things brought back by the girl felt a connection to her, or if Dol simply possessed the usual unconditional affection inherent in most canines, and appreciated the fact that he was tall enough to look Sydney in the eyes. She patted his head absently and grabbed a soda from the fridge, climbing onto one of the counter stools, clutching the can in both her hands.

Victor was stacking the dead and set them aside. There was no need for Sydney to look at them right now.

"You okay?" he asked.

She nodded. "I always feel strange after. Cold."

"Wouldn't you rather have a hot drink, then?" asked Mitch.

"No. I like holding this. I like knowing at least I'm warmer than the can."

Mitch shrugged. Sydney leaned forward to look at the four profiles while the program plodded on in the background.

"They're all EOs?" she whispered.

"Not necessarily," said Victor, "but if we're lucky, one or two."

Victor's eyes skimmed the collage of private information that ran beside the photos. Three of the potentials were young, but one was older. Sydney reached over and took up one of the profiles. It was a girl named Beth Kirk, and she had bright-blue hair.

"How do we know which one he'll go after first? Where do we start?"

"Matrix can only do so much," said Mitch. "We'll have to guess. Pick one and hope we get there before Eli."

Victor shrugged. "No need. They're irrelevant now." He didn't care about the blue-haired girl, or any of them for that matter. He was more interested in what the dead proved about Eli than what the living offered *him*. He'd meant them only as bait anyway, to be dug up and used as lures, but Sydney herself—her gift, and the message they'd made with it—had rendered these EOs extraneous to his plans.

Sydney looked appalled by his answer. "But we have to warn them."

Victor plucked Beth Kirk's profile from her grip, and set it face-down on the counter.

"Would you rather I warn them," he asked gently, "or save them?" He watched the anger slide from her face. "It's a waste, going after the victims instead of the killer. And when Eli gets our message, we won't even need to hunt him down."

"Why's that?" she asked.

Victor's mouth quirked up. "Because he'll be hunting *us*."

2

An ExtraOrdinary Day

I

THIS MORNING

TERNIS COLLEGE

ELI Ever sat in the back of the history seminar, tracing the wood grain of the desk and waiting for the lecture to end. The class was being taught in an auditorium at Ternis College, an exclusive private school half an hour or so outside Merit city limits. Three rows in front of him, and two spaces to the left, sat a girl with blue hair named Beth. It wasn't such a strange thing, the hair, but Eli happened to know that Beth only started dying it that color after it had all gone white. The white was the product of trauma, a trauma that had nearly killed her. Technically it *had*, in fact. For four and a half minutes.

Yet here Beth was, alive and attentively taking notes on the Revolutionary War or the Spanish American War or World War II—Eli wasn't even sure what the name of the course was, let alone which conflict the professor was currently teaching—while the blue strands fell around her face, and trailed across her paper.

Eli couldn't stand history. He figured it probably hadn't changed that much in the ten years since he'd taken it, just another one of Lockland University's many prerequisites, meant to round every student into a smooth little ball of knowledge. He stared at the ceiling, then at the spaces between the professor's half-cursive, half-print notes, then back at the blue hair, then at the clock. Class was nearly over. His pulse quickened as he pulled the slim dossier out of his satchel, the one Serena had put together for him. It explained, in painstaking detail, the blue-haired girl's history, her accident—tragic, really, the sole survivor of a nasty crash—and her subsequent recovery. He brushed his fingertips over the photo of Beth, wondering where it had come from. He rather liked that hair.

The clock ticked on, and Eli slid the dossier back into his bag, and pushed a pair of thick-framed glasses up his nose—they were plain glass, not prescription, but he'd noticed the trend around the Ternis College campus and followed suit. Looking the part agewise was never a problem, of course, but styles changed, almost too fast for him to keep track. Beth could choose to stand out if she wanted, but Eli did everything in his power to blend in.

The professor finished his lecture a few blessed minutes early, and wished them all a good weekend. Chairs scraped. Bags were hoisted. Eli rose and followed the blue hair out of the auditorium and down the hall, carried on a wave of students. When they reached the outer door, he held it open for her. She thanked him, tucked a cobalt strand behind her ear, and headed across the campus.

Eli followed.

As he walked, he felt for the place in his jacket where his gun would be, a product of habit, but the pocket was empty. The dossier had told him enough to make him wary of anything that might succumb to magnetism, so he'd left the weapon in his glove box. He'd have to do this the old-fashioned way, which was fine. He didn't often let himself indulge, but he couldn't deny that there was something simple and satisfying about using his hands.

Ternis was a small school, one of those cozy private affairs made up of mismatched buildings and an abundance of tree-lined paths. Beth and he were both on one of the larger paths that bisected the campus, and there were enough students around to keep Eli's pursuit from seeming at all conspicuous. He crossed the campus at a safe distance, enjoying the morning, taking in the crisp spring air, the beauty of the late afternoon sky and the first green leaves. One of them pulled loose from a tree and landed on the girl's blue hair, and Eli admired the way it made both colors seem brighter as he slipped his gloves on.

When they were almost to the parking lot, Eli began to pick up his pace, closing the gap between them until he was within arm's reach.

"Hey!" he called behind her, feigning breathlessness.

The girl slowed, and turned to look at him, but kept walking. Soon he was beside her.

"It's Beth, right?"

"Yeah," she said. "You're in Phillips's history section with me."

Only for the past two classes, but he'd been sure to catch her eye both times.

"Sure am," said Eli, flashing his best college-kid grin. "I'm Nicholas." Eli had always liked the name. Nicholas and Frederick and Peter, those were the ones he found himself using the most. They were important names, the kind held by rulers, conquerors, kings. He and Beth passed through the parking lot, row after row of cars, the school shrinking in the distance behind them.

"Sorry, can I ask you a favor?" asked Eli.

"What's up?" Beth tucked a stray lock of hair behind her ear.

"I don't know where my head was during class," he said, "but I missed the assignment. Did you write it down?"

"Sure," she said as they reached her car.

"Thanks," he said, biting his lip. "I guess there were better things to look at than the board."

She giggled shyly as she set the bag on the hood and unzipped it, digging around inside.

"Anything's better than the board," she said, pulling out her notebook.

Beth had just turned to face him with the notes when his hand closed around her throat, and he slammed her back into the side of the car. She gasped, and he tightened his grip. She dropped the notebook and clawed at his face, raking the black-rimmed glasses off, carving deep scratches across his skin. He felt blood trickle over his cheek but didn't bother wiping it away. The car behind her began to shake, the metal trying to bend, but she was too new to her power and the car was too heavy, and she was running out of air and fight.

There had been a time when he spoke to the EOs, tried to impart to them the logic, the necessity, of his actions, tried to make them understand before they died, that they were already dead, already ash, held together by something dark but feeble. But they didn't listen, and in the end, his actions conveyed what his words had failed to. He'd made an exception for Serena's little sister, and look where that had gotten him. No, words were wasted on them all.

So Eli pinned the girl against the car, and waited patiently until the struggle slowed, and weakened, and stopped. He stood very, very still, and relished the ensuing moment of quiet. It always came to him, right here, when the light—he'd say the *life*, but that wasn't right, it wasn't life, only something *posing* as life—went out of their eyes. A moment of peace, a measure of balance being restored to the world. The unnatural made natural.

Then the moment passed, and he peeled his gloved fingers away from the girl's throat and watched her body slide down the warped metal of the car door and onto the concrete, blue hair falling across her face. Eli crossed himself as the angry red scratches on his cheek knitted and healed, leaving only smooth, clear skin beneath the drying blood. He knelt to retrieve his prop glasses from the ground beside the body. His cell rang as he straightened them on his nose, and he fished the phone from his coat.

"The Hero Line," he answered smoothly. "How can I assist you?"

ELI had expected Serena's slow laugh— the Hero bit was an inside joke—but the voice on the other end was gravelly and most certainly male.

"Mr. Ever?" asked the man.

"Who is this?"

"This is Officer Dane with the Merit PD. We got a call of a robbery in progress at Tidings Well Bank, at Fifth and Harbor."

Eli frowned. "I have my own job, Officer. Don't tell me the cops want me to do theirs, too. And how did you get this number? It's not how we agreed to communicate."

"The girl. She gave it to me." Something exploded in the background, showering the line with static.

"It better be urgent."

"It is," said Officer Dane. "The robber is an EO."

Eli rubbed his forehead. "Don't you have special tactics? Surely they teach you those somewhere. I can't exactly walk in and—"

"The fact he's an EO isn't the problem, Mr. Ever."

"Then do tell me," said Eli through gritted teeth. "What is?"

"He's been identified as Barry Lynch. You . . . that is, he's . . . he's supposed to be dead."

A long pause.

"I'm on my way," said Eli. "Is that all?"

"Not quite. He's making a scene. Shouting for you specifically. Should we shoot him?"

Eli closed his eyes as he reached his car. "No. Don't kill him until I get there." Eli hung up.

He opened the door and climbed in, hitting speed dial. A girl's voice answered, but he cut her off.

"We have a problem. Barry's back."

"I'm watching it on the news. I thought you—"

"Yes, I killed him, Serena. He was very dead."

"Then how—"

"How is he robbing a bank at Fifth and Harbor?" Eli snapped, gunning the car. "How is he suddenly *not* dead? That's a good question. Who could possibly have resurrected Lynch?"

There was a long quiet on the other end of the phone, before Serena answered. "You told me you killed her."

Eli gripped the wheel. "I thought I did." He had hoped, anyway.

"The way you killed Barry?"

"I may have been more certain about Lynch than I was about Sydney. Barry was definitely, undeniably dead."

"You told me you followed her. You told me you finished—"

"We'll talk about this later," he said. "I have to go kill Barry Lynch. Again."

∞

SERENA let the phone slip through her fingers. It landed on the bed with a soft thud as she turned back to the hotel television, where the robbery coverage continued. Even though the action was happening within the bank, and the cameras were stuck on the street behind a thick border of yellow tape, the scene was causing quite a stir. After all, it had been in all the papers, the robbery last week at Smith & Lauder. The civilian hero had come out of the firefight unscathed. The robber had come out in a body bag.

No surprise that the public was disconcerted, then, to find the robber alive and well enough to rob another bank. His name ran in ticker-tape fashion along the bottom of the screen, the bold-lettered scrawl announcing *Barry Lynch Alive Barry Lynch Alive Barry Lynch Alive . . .*

And that meant Sydney was alive. Serena had no doubt that the strange and disquieting feat had somehow been her sister's work.

She took a sip of too-hot coffee, and winced faintly when it burned her throat, but didn't stop. She clung to the fact that inanimate objects weren't subject to her power. They didn't have minds or feelings. She couldn't will the coffee *not* to burn her, couldn't will knives *not* to cut her. The people holding the things were hers, but not the things themselves. She took another sip, eyes wandering back to the television where a photo of the previously deceased EO now filled the right half of the screen.

But why had Sydney done it?

Eli had promised Serena that her sister was dead. She'd warned him not to lie, and he'd looked her in the eyes and told her that he'd shot Sydney. And that hadn't been a lie exactly, had it? She'd been standing right there when he pulled the trigger. Her jaw clenched. Eli was getting better at fighting back, finding little loopholes in her power. Redirections, omissions, evasions, delays. Not that she didn't appreciate the small defiance—she did—but the thought of Sydney, alive and hurt and in the city, made it hard to breathe.

It was never supposed to go like this.

Serena closed her eyes, and the field and the body and her sister's frightened face filled her vision. Sydney had done her best to look brave that day, but she couldn't hide the fear, not from Serena, who knew every line on her sister's face, who'd perched on the edge of her sister's bed so many nights, smoothing those lines one by one with her thumb in the dark. Serena should never have turned back, never called her sister's name. It had been a reflex, an echo of life before. She'd reminded herself over and over that the girl in the field wasn't her sister, not really. Serena knew the girl who looked like Sydney *wasn't* Sydney, the same way she knew that *she* wasn't Serena. But it didn't seem to matter the moment right before Eli pulled the trigger; Sydney had looked small and frightened and so very *alive* and Serena had forgotten that she wasn't.

Her eyes drifted open, only to settle on the still-streaming headline—*Barry Lynch Alive Barry Lynch Alive Barry Lynch Alive*—before she snapped the TV off.

Eli said it best. He called EOs *shadows,* shaped like the people who made them but gray inside. Serena felt it. From the moment she woke up in the hospital, she felt as if something colorful and bright and *vital* was missing. Eli went on to say it was her soul; he claimed *he* was different and Serena let him think that because the only other option was to tell him otherwise, and then he'd believe it.

But what if he was right? The thought of having lost her soul made Serena sad in a distant way. And the thought of poor small Syd all hollowed out made her ache, and made it easier to believe Eli when he said it was mercy, returning EOs to the earth. It had been harder when Sydney was standing in her doorway, flushed from the cold and blue eyes bright, like the light was still in them. Serena had faltered, tripped over the *what-ifs* whispering in her head as they trudged into the field.

Sydney's sin, Eli claimed, was double. Not only was she an EO, unnatural and wrong, but she also possessed the power to corrupt others, to poison them by filling their bodies with something that looked like life, but wasn't. Maybe that was what Serena had seen in Sydney's eyes, a false light she'd mistaken for her sister's life. Her soul.

Maybe.

Whatever it was that made her pause, the fact was that Serena had faltered, and now her sister—the shadow in her shape—was alive, and apparently here in the city. Serena pulled on her coat, and went to look for Sydney.

II

THIS MORNING

VICTOR savored the scalding water of the hotel shower as he rinsed the last of the grave dirt from his skin. Barry Lynch had been surprisingly receptive when he revisited the cemetery this morning. Victor had gone back just before dawn, scooped out the foot of dirt he'd put back on top of Lynch, to make the grave look empty if anyone chanced to walk by, and pried the lid off to find Barry's terrified eyes staring up at him. Pain and fear are inextricable—a lesson that went back to Victor's studies at Lockland—but pain has multiple forms. Victor might not be able to physically hurt Barry Lynch, but that didn't mean he couldn't make him suffer. Barry, for his part, seemed to get the message. Victor had smiled, and helped the once-dead man out of his coffin— even though he hated the way the man's strangely nerveless skin felt against his own—and as he passed him the note and sent him on his way, Victor felt confident that Lynch would follow through. But just to be certain, he'd told him one last thing. He'd taken several steps back, and then turned toward Barry, and said it as an afterthought.

"The girl, Sydney, the one who brought you back. She can change her mind at any point. Snap her fingers, and drop you like a stone. Or rather, like a corpse. Do you want to see?" he asked, digging the phone from his pocket. He began to dial. "It's really quite a clever trick."

Barry had paled, and shaken his head, and Victor had sent him on his way.

"Hey, Vale!" Mitch's voice reached him through the bathroom walls. "Get out here."

He snapped the shower water off.

"Victor!"

Mitch was still shouting his name when he stepped into the hall a minute later, toweling off his hair. Sun was streaming in through the tall windows, and he winced at the brightness. Late morning, at least. His message should be well on its way.

"What is it?" asked Victor, at first worried, but then he saw Mitch's face, the broad, open smile. Whatever the man had done, he was proud of it. Sydney appeared, with Dol close behind, his tail wagging lazily.

"Come see this." Mitch gestured to the profiles spread out on the kitchen counter. Victor sighed. There were more than a dozen now—and most of them dead-ends, he was sure. They couldn't seem to get the search matrix exact enough. He'd spent the previous evening, and most of the night, looking over the pages, wondering how Eli did it, if he followed every lead, or if he knew something Victor didn't, saw something Victor hadn't. Now before his eyes, Mitch began turning papers facedown, eliminating profile after profile from the mix until only three were left. One was the blue-haired girl, and the second an older man he'd studied last night, but the third was new, it must have been freshly printed.

"This," said Mitch, "this is Eli's current list of targets."

Victor's cool eyes flicked up. He began to shift his weight from foot to foot. His fingers tapped out a beat. "How did you figure that out?"

"It's a great story. Stand still and I'll tell you."

Victor forced himself to stop moving. "Go on," he said, scanning the names and faces.

"So, I'm seeing this pattern," said Mitch. "I keep ending up in police files. *Merit* police files. So I think, what if the cops are already working on their own database, right? Maybe we could compare it with ours. You mentioned, way back when, that one cop knowing about EOs. Or someone with the cops. And then I think, hey, maybe I can just borrow *their* data, instead of going through all the hassle—I mean it's nothing beyond my reach, but it takes time—but what if they've done some of the work for me? So I start browsing in Merit PD's 'Persons of Interest' database. And something catches my eye. I used to love those puzzles growing up where they ask you to spot the difference. I rocked that shit. Anyway—"

"They're flagged," said Victor, eyes skimming the profiles.

Mitch's posture fell. "Man, you always ruin a punch line. But yeah . . . and I made it easy for you to see," he said as he pouted. "I turned the pages down. Easy to see a pattern when it's all that's in front of you . . ."

"What do you mean, flagged?" asked Sydney, standing on her tiptoes to see the pages.

"Look," Victor said, gesturing to the profiles. "What do all these people have in common?"

Syd squinted at the paper, but shook her head.

"The middle names," said Victor.

Sydney read them aloud. "Elise, Elington, Elissa . . . They all have 'Eli' in them."

"Exactly," said Mitch. "They've been flagged. Specifically for our friend, Eli. Which means—"

"He's working with the cops," said Victor. "Here in Merit."

Sydney stared down at the photo of the girl with the blue hair. "How can you be sure?" she asked. "What if it's a coincidence?"

Mitch looked smug. "Because I did my homework. I cross-checked the theory by pulling up some of their old profiles, 'Persons of Interest' now deceased, all of which had conveniently found their way into the digital trash bin. Which is its own red flag, by the way, but I found matches to Eli's killings over the last four months." He dropped the dead EO folder on the table. "Including your man Barry Lynch. The one you just spent the night digging up."

Victor had started to pace.

"It gets better," said Mitch. "The flagged profiles were created by one of two cops." He tapped the top right corner of a page. "Officer Frederick Dane. Or Detective Mark Stell."

Victor's chest tightened. Stell. What were the odds? The man who'd had Victor arrested ten years ago, the one who'd been on EO duty at the Lockland precinct, and the one who, when Victor recovered from his multiple gunshot wounds, personally escorted him to the isolation wing of Wrighton Penitentiary. Stell's involvement, along with Eli's testimony, was the reason Victor spent five years in solitary confinement (he wasn't declared an EO on the records, of course, only an extreme danger to himself and others, and it had taken him half a decade of deliberately not hurting anyone—at least not in a conscious or appreciable way—to get himself integrated).

"You listening?" asked Mitch.

Victor nodded absently. "The men flagging the profiles, they are, or have been, in direct contact with Eli."

"Exactly."

Victor toasted the air with his water, his thoughts miles away. "Bravo, Mitch." He turned to Sydney. "You hungry?"

But Sydney didn't seem to be listening. She had taken up the folder with the dead EOs, and was flipping through, almost absently, when she stopped. Victor looked over her shoulder and saw what she saw. Short blond hair and water blue eyes stared up at her beside a cleanly printed name: Sydney Elinor Clarke.

"My middle name is Marion," she said quietly. "And he thinks I'm dead."

Victor stooped over and swiped the page. He folded the paper and tucked it inside his shirt pocket with a wink.

"Not for long," he said, tapping his watch. "Not for long."

III

THIS MORNING

ELI parked a block and a half from the yellow tape of the crime scene barrier, and repositioned the prop glasses on his nose before getting out. He could see, as he wound his way behind the eyes of the crowd of morbid spectators and the gathering photographers, to the back of the bank, and the crime was no longer in progress. People lingered, lights flashed, but the relative quiet—sirenless, gunless, shoutless—told him enough.

He stiffened when he saw Detective Stell, even though Serena promised it was safe. Still, the detective had come to Merit a few months before to investigate a string of killings in the area—Eli's handiwork, of course—and even Serena's assurances couldn't entirely wipe away Eli's doubt regarding the detective's loyalty. Stell, who now had salt-and-pepper hair and a permanent crease between his eyes, met him behind the building, and lifted the tape so he could pass. Eli pushed the prop glasses up his nose a second time. They were a fraction too big.

"How Clark Kent of you," said Stell drily. Eli was not in the mood.

"Where is he?"

"Dead." The detective led the way into the bank.

"I told you I wanted him alive."

"Didn't have a choice. He started firing, or whatever you want to call it. Couldn't aim worth a damn. Like that power of his was on the fritz. Didn't stop him from making a mess, though."

"Civilians?"

"No, he ordered those all out." They reached a black sheet cast over a vaguely human shape. Stell nudged it with his boot. "Media wants to know why a madman who's supposed to be dead enters a bank with a weapon, but doesn't try to rob it, and doesn't take any prisoners. All he does is kick everyone out, and fire at the air and scream and scream for someone named Eli Ever."

"You should have never let that story run last week."

"Can't stop the press from using their eyes, Eli. You're the one who wanted to make a scene."

Eli didn't like the man's tone, had never liked it, never trusted the thread of combativeness that ran through it.

"I needed a demonstration," Eli growled. He didn't want to admit that there was more to it than that, that he'd *wanted* an audience. It had been Serena's idea, he was sure, before it became his.

"A demonstration is one thing," said Stell. "But did you need a spectacle?"

"It covered up the murder," said Eli as he threw back the black sheet. "How was I supposed to know he wouldn't stay dead?" Barry Lynch's brown eyes gazed up at him, shallow and dead. He could hear the whispers from the other cops milling around, hushed voices wondering who he was, what he was doing there. He tried to look official as he stared down at the dead man.

"You dragged me out here for nothing," he said under his breath. "Now that he's dead."

"Forgive me, but he was dead before, remember? And besides," added Stell, "this time he left a note."

Stell handed Eli a plastic bag. Inside was a crumpled piece of paper. He withdrew the paper and unfolded it gingerly.

It was a stick-figure drawing. Two people holding hands. A thin man in black and a girl, half his height with short hair, and wide eyes. The stick-girl's head was cocked slightly, and a small red spot marked her arm. Three similar spots, no bigger than periods, dotted the stick-man's chest. The stick-man's mouth was nothing more than a faint grim line.

Beneath the drawing ran a single sentence: *I made a friend.*

Victor.

"You okay?"

Eli blinked, felt the cop's hand on his arm. He slid free, folded the paper, and put it in his pocket before anyone could see or say otherwise.

"Get rid of the body," he said to Stell. "Burn it this time."

Eli went back the way he'd come. He didn't stop, not until he was safely in his car. In the relative privacy of the side street in Merit, he pressed his hand against the drawing in his pocket, and a phantom pain started in his stomach.

Victor lifted the knife from the table. "You called the cops and you accused me of being an EO. I didn't rat you out, you know. I could have. Why would you tell them something so silly? Did you know they have special people that come in if there's an EO suspected? Some guy named Stell. Did you know that?"

"You've lost it." Eli sidestepped. "Put the knife down. It's not like you can hurt me."

Victor smiled then. He looked like someone else. Eli tried to step back, but the wall came up behind him. The knife buried itself in his stomach. He felt the tip scratch at the skin of his back. The pain had been sharp, persistent, dragging itself out instead of flashing forward and dissolving.

"You know what I figured out?" Victor growled. "Watching you in the street that night, picking the glass from your hand? You can't

heal yourself until I take the knife out." He twisted it, and pain exploded behind Eli's eyes, a dozen colors. He groaned and began to slide down the wall, but Victor hoisted him up by the handle.

"I'm not even using my gift yet," Victor said. *"It's not as flashy as yours, but it's rather effective. Want to see it?"*

Eli swallowed hard, and dialed Serena as he put the car in gear and headed for the hotel. He didn't wait for her to speak.

"We have a problem."

IV

TEN YEARS AGO

LOCKLAND UNIVERSITY

ELI Ever sat on the steps of his apartment in the cold morning and ran his fingers through his hair before realizing they were covered in blood. Caution tape surrounded him in streamers of yellow, too bright against the dull winter dawn. Red and blue lights dotted the icy ground and every time he looked at them, he ended up spending minutes trying to blink the colors away.

"If you could tell us one more time . . . ," said a young cop.

Eli touched his stomach, the echo of pain still there even though the skin had healed. He rubbed his hands together and watched blood flake off into the sidewalk snow. He wove a distress he wasn't sure he felt back into his voice as he recounted everything from Victor's panicked call the night before, confessing to Angie's murder, to his sudden appearance in their living room, gun in hand. Eli left out the knives, having scrubbed and returned them to their drawers before the police arrived. It was odd, the way his brain had made space around the weedy panic, helping his hands and legs do what needed to be done even as a fading voice in the back of his mind screamed and his best friend lay shot full of holes on their living room floor. Something in Eli had gone missing—fear, that's what he'd told Victor—right down the drain with the icy bath water.

"So you wrested the gun from Mr. Vale." Wrested had been Eli's word, not the officer's.

"I taught a self-defense seminar last summer," he lied. "It's not that hard."

And then he pushed himself shakily to his feet. He was covered in blood, arms curled carefully around his ribs to hide the knife hole in his shirt. Two other officers had already questioned him about it. He'd told them he got lucky. He didn't know how the weapon could have missed him. But it did. Obviously. Look, hole in shirt, no hole in Eli. Fortunately the cops had been too interested in Victor's bleeding out on the hardwood floor to care much about Eli's magic trick. *One lucky man,* they muttered, and he wasn't sure if they'd been talking about him, or Victor, who had managed to avoid dying, for now.

"And then you shot him three times."

"I was distraught. He'd just killed my girlfriend." Eli wondered if he was in shock, if that was the thing keeping Angie's death from sinking in the way the knife had. He wanted to care, he wanted to care *so badly,* but there was this gap between what he felt and what he wanted to feel, a space where something important had been carved out. And it was growing. He'd told Victor the thing he lost was his fear but that wasn't quite true because he was still scared. He was scared of that rift.

"And then?" prompted the cop.

Eli rubbed his eyes. "And then he came after me. I panicked. I didn't know what to do. I tried not to kill him." He swallowed, wishing he had a glass of water. "Look, do you think I could go clean up?" he asked, gesturing to his ruined clothes. "I need to go see Angie . . . her body." The officer called past the yellow tape, and was given the all-clear. The ambulance was long gone. All that was left was a mess. The officer held up the tape to let him pass.

A trail of red wound through the living room. Eli stopped and stared at it. The fight replayed behind his eyes as relentlessly as the police lights, and he forced himself to veer toward the bathroom. When he caught sight of himself in the bank of mirrors, he stifled a laugh. One of those ill, halfway-to-tears laughs. Blood stained his shirt. His pants. His face. His hair. Eli did his best to wash it off, scrubbing his arms OR-style in the sink. His favorite shirt, a bold red one that Victor always said made him look like a ripe tomato, was ruined.

Victor. Victor was wrong. About everything.

"If I'm missing something, then so are you. Life is about compromises. Or did you think because you put yourself in God's hands that He would make you all you were and more?"

"He did," said Eli aloud to the sink. He did. He would. He had to. Whatever this gap was, it was there for a reason, there to make him stronger. He had to believe that.

Eli washed his face, cupped water over his hair until the red ran out of it. He pulled on fresh clothes, and was just about to duck back under the yellow tape across his front door when he caught the end of the young officer's remark to another cop.

"Yeah, Detective Stell's on his way."

Eli paused, and stepped backward into the apartment.

"Did you know they have special people that come in if there's an EO suspected? Some guy named Stell. I bet you didn't know that."

Eli turned, made a line for the back door, only to find his path blocked by a very large cop.

"Everything all right, sir?" asked the cop. Eli gave a slow nod.

"Door's taped," he said. "Just trying to get out of everyone's way."

The large cop nodded, and stepped aside. Eli was through the back door and into the small communal courtyard by the time the large officer reached the younger one. He didn't look guilty, he told himself. Not yet.

Victor was the guilty one. The Victor that he knew was dead, replaced by something cold and vicious. A twisted, violent version of himself. Victor had never been good, or sweet—he'd always had a sharp edge; Eli had been drawn to the metallic glint of it— but he'd never been this. A murderer. A monster. After all, he'd *killed Angie.* How? How had it happened? With pain? Was that possible? The medical part of his mind tried to break it down. A heart attack? Would the pain cause a short-circuit, like electricity? Would the body shut down? Would the functions freeze? He dug his nails into his palms. This was *Angie.* Not a science experiment. A person. The one who'd made him feel better, saner, kept him afloat when his mind began to sink. Was that it, then? Was Angie the missing thing? Wouldn't it be lovely to make the gap another person instead of a part of himself? But no, that wasn't it. Angie had helped, she'd always helped, but he'd felt the hole before she died, felt it even before *he* died. The feeling—the *lack* of it—had only ever come in glimpses, like a cloud passing overhead. But from the moment he woke up on the bathroom floor, the shadow had settled over him, a sign that something was wrong.

Not wrong, he forced himself to think. *Different.*

Eli got to his car, thankful he'd parked two blocks away (less chance of getting a ticket there), and threw it into gear. He drove past the engineering labs, slowing only enough to see the yellow tape there, too—marking out Victor's path of destruction—and the huddle of emergency vehicles. He kept going. He needed to get to the pre-med buildings as fast as possible. He needed to find Professor Lyne.

ELI strode through the automatic doors and into the lobby of the three clustered buildings reserved for the medical sciences, an empty backpack slung on one shoulder. The lobby of the center lab had been painted an awful pale yellow. He wasn't sure why they insisted on painting labs such sickly shades—maybe to prepare the pre-med students for the equally sad palettes of most of the hospitals they aspired to work in, or perhaps on some misguided notion that pale meant clean—but the color made the place seem lifeless, now more than ever. Eli kept his head down as he made his way up two flights of stairs, until he reached the office where he'd spent most of his free time since the start of winter break. Professor Lyne's nameplate hung on the door, letters gleaming. Eli tried the handle. It was locked. He searched his pockets for something to use on the lock, and came up with a paper clip. If it worked on television, it could work here. He knelt before the handle.

Before Victor had come back to campus, Eli had taken his discovery to Professor Lyne, who had gone from skeptical to intrigued as his theories gained weight. Eli had enjoyed getting the professor's attention back in the fall, but it was nothing compared to the relish he felt earning Lyne's respect. His research, now *their* research, had taken on a new focus under the professor's guidance, reinterpreting the hypothetical qualities of existing EOs—the NDEs and their physical and psychological aftermath—into a potential system for *locating* them. A kind of search matrix. At least, that had been the charted course of study until Victor showed up and suggested that they could potentially *make* an EO instead. Eli had never shared this idea with Professor Lyne. He hadn't had the chance. After Victor's failed attempt, Eli had become too preoccupied with his own trial, and then after his success—and it *was* a success, missing pieces aside—he hadn't wanted to share. He'd been watching Lyne's interest sharpen from curiosity into fascination in a way that Eli knew well. Certainly well enough to distrust it.

Now he was glad he'd kept the new direction to himself. In less than a week, Eli's research had ended Angie's life, ruined Victor's (if he lived), and changed his own. Even though the dark turn in the thesis and the ensuing destruction had both been Victor's fault, his actions had also revealed the grim truth of their discoveries, and where they would inevitably lead. And now Eli knew exactly what he had to do.

"Can I help you?"

Eli looked up from his lock-picking, which wasn't going well, to find a janitor leaning on a broom, eyes flicking from Eli to his straightened paper clip. He forced a casual laugh and stood up.

"I hope so. God, I'm such an idiot. I left a folder in Lyne's office. He's my adviser. I need it for my thesis." He was talking too fast, the way actors did on TV when they wanted the audience to pick up on the fact they were lying. His hands were slick. He paused, forcing himself to breathe. "Have you seen him, by the way?" Inhale, exhale. "I can wait around a little while." Inhale, exhale. "Be the first rest I've had in weeks." He stopped and waited to see if the janitor would buy the story.

After a long moment, the man pulled a set of keys from his pocket and unlocked the door.

"I haven't seen him yet, but he should be in soon. And in the future," he offered as he turned away, "it takes two paper clips."

Eli smiled with genuine relief, waved his thanks, and went inside, urging the door closed with a click. He let out a low sigh, and got to work.

There are times when the marvels of scientific advancement expedite our processes, making our lives easier. Modern technology provides machines that can think three or five or seven steps ahead of the human mind, machines that offer elegant solutions, a selection of contingency plans, Bs and Cs and Ds in case A isn't to your liking.

And then there are times when a screwdriver and a bit of elbow grease are all that's necessary to get the job done. Eli admitted that it wasn't terribly creative, or aesthetically pleasing, but it was efficient. Their research was stored in two places. The first was a blue folder in the third drawer of the wall cabinet, which Eli removed and slid into his backpack. The second was on the computer.

He dismantled Professor Lyne's computer the simplest, most fail-safe way he knew how: by physically removing the hard drive and crushing it underfoot, then putting the remnants into his backpack alongside the folder with the intent of tossing the whole bag into some crematorium or wood-chipper for good measure. He'd have to hope Professor Lyne didn't think to store a copy of the research anywhere else.

Eli zipped the bag closed, and did his best to position the computer so that at first glance it didn't appear to be missing a hard drive at all. He had just shouldered the backpack and returned to the hall, and was in the process of trying to relock Lyne's office door when he heard a cough and turned to find the professor himself barring his path, coffee in one hand, briefcase in the other. They considered each other, Eli's hand still resting on the doorknob.

"Good morning, Mr. Cardale."

"I'm withdrawing my thesis," said Eli without preamble.

Lyne's brow crinkled. "But you'll fail."

Eli shifted the bag and pushed past him. "I don't care."

"Eli," said Professor Lyne, following. "What's this about? What's going on?"

They were alone in the hall. Eli spoke, but didn't slow his pace. "It has to stop," he said under his breath. "Right now. It was a mistake."

"But we're just getting started," said Professor Lyne. Eli shoved the door to the stairwell open and stepped onto the landing, Lyne trailing behind him. "The discoveries you've made," said Lyne, "the ones *we'll* make . . . they'll change the world."

Eli turned on him. "Not for the better," he said. "We can't pursue this. Where does it lead? We make it possible to find EOs, and then what? They get taken, examined, dissected, explained, and someone decides to stop studying and start creating." His stomach twisted. It would happen, just like that, wouldn't it? He was proof. Wooed by the prospect, the potential, the chance to prove something instead of disprove.

Do you ever wonder?

"Would that be so bad?" asked Lyne. "To create something ExtraOrdinary?"

"They aren't ExtraOrdinary," snapped Eli. "They're *wrong*."

Eli blamed himself. Victor was right, he'd played God, even as he asked for His help. And God in His mercy and might had saved Eli's life, but destroyed everything that touched it. "I won't give anyone the tools to make more of them. All these roads lean to ruin."

"Don't be dramatic."

"It's over. I'm done." Eli's grip tightened on the bag. Lyne's eyes narrowed.

"I'm not," said Lyne, his hand coming to rest on Eli's shoulder, fingers curling around the backpack strap. "We have an obligation to science, Mr. Cardale. The research must continue. And discoveries of this magnitude must be shared. Stop being so selfish."

Lyne gave a sharp tug on the bag, but Eli stood his ground, and before he knew what was happening, the two men were fighting over the backpack. Eli shoved Lyne off him and up against the railing, and somewhere in the struggle, Lyne's elbow met Eli's lip hard, splitting it. Eli wiped the blood away and ripped the bag from Lyne's grip, tossing it to the side only to realize that Lyne had stopped fighting for it. The professor stood, eyes wide, and Eli felt before he saw in Lyne's eyes what was happening. The skin of his lip knit cleanly back together.

"You . . ." Eli saw Lyne's expression shift from shock to glee. "You did it. You're one of them." He could already see the experiments, the papers, the press, the obsession. "You're an—"

Lyne didn't get a chance to finish, because at that moment, Eli gave him a sharp shove backward, down the stairs. The word was drawn out into a short cry, then cut off sharply by the first of several thuds as Lyne's body tumbled down the steps. He hit the bottom with a crack.

Eli stared down at the body, willing himself to feel horrified. He didn't. There it was again, that gap between what he knew he should feel and what he did, mocking him as he looked down at Lyne. Eli wasn't sure if he'd meant to push the professor down the stairs, or if he'd only meant to push him away, but the damage was done now.

"It was Victor's idea, putting the theory to the test," he found himself saying as he descended the steps. "The method took some tweaking, but it worked. That's why I know this has to stop." Lyne twitched. His mouth opened, made a sound between a groan and a gasp. "Because it works. And because it's wrong." Eli stopped at the base of the stairs beside his teacher. "I died begging for the strength to survive, and it was granted. But it's a trade, Professor, with God or the devil, and I've paid for my gift with the lives of my friends. Every EO has sold a part of themselves they can never have back. Don't you see?" He knelt beside Lyne, whose fingers twitched. "I can't let anyone else sin so heinously against nature."

Eli knew what he had to do, felt it with a strange and comforting certainty. He brought one hand almost gently under Lyne's jaw, the other cradling his chin. "This research dies with us."

With that, he twisted sharply.

"Well," said Eli softly. "With *you*."

Lyne's eyes emptied and Eli set his head gently back against the ground, sliding his fingers free as he stood. There was a moment of such perfect quiet, the kind he used to feel in church, a sliver of peace that felt so . . . right. It was the first time he'd felt like himself, like *more* than himself, since he'd come back to life.

Eli crossed himself.

Then he made his way back up the stairs, pausing a moment to consider the body, bent, neck broken in a way that looked believable considering the fall. The coffee had tumbled with the professor, and left a trail down the steps, the shattered cup beside his shattered body. Eli had been careful not to step in the liquid. He wiped his hands on his jeans, and retrieved the backpack from the landing, but couldn't bring himself to leave. Instead he stood there, waiting, waiting for the sense of horror, the nausea, the guilt, to come up to meet him. But it never came. There was only quiet.

And then a bell rang through the building, taking the quiet with it, and Eli was left with only a body and the sudden urge to *run*.

ELI crossed the parking lot as his mind spun over what to do next. The peace he'd felt in the stairwell had been replaced by a prickling energy and the voice in his head that whispered *go*. It wasn't guilt, or even panic, more like self-preservation. He reached his car, and slid the key into the door, and that's when he heard the steps behind him.

"Mr. Cardale."

Go growled the thing in his head, so clear and so tempting, but something else held him in place. He turned the key in the car door, locking it with a small click.

"Can I help you?" he asked, turning toward the man. He was broad-shouldered and tall, with black hair.

"My name is Detective Stell. Were you coming or going?"

Eli pulled the key from the door. "Coming. I thought I should tell Professor Lyne. About Victor, that is. They were close."

"I'll walk with you."

Eli nodded, and took a step from the car before frowning. "I'll leave my bag here," he said, unlocking the door and tossing the backpack—folders and hard drive and all—into the backseat. "I don't feel up to class today."

"I'm sorry for your loss," said Detective Stell automatically.

Eli counted the steps back to the pre-med labs. He got to thirty-four before he heard the sirens, and looked up sharply. Beside him, Stell swore and picked up his pace.

They'd found Lyne's body, then.

Run run run, hissed the thing in Eli's head. It sang in the same tone and speed as the sirens.

And he did run, but not away. His feet carried him toward the building's entrance, and through, following the emergency response team as it made its way to the base of the stairs. When Eli saw the body, he made a strangled sound. Stell pulled him away, and Eli let his legs go out beneath him, knees hitting the cold floor with a crack. He winced even as the bruises bloomed and faded under his pant legs.

"Come on, son," Stell was saying, pulling him back. But Eli's gaze was leveled on the scene. Everything was playing out as it should, as it *needed* to, the loose threads being snipped. Until he saw the janitor, leaning against the wall, watching, frowning in the way people frown when they're puzzling out a riddle.

Shit, thought Eli, but he must have said it aloud, because Stell tugged him to his feet and said, "Shit indeed. Let's go."

There were too many deaths too fast. He knew he'd be a suspect. Had to be. *Run,* said the thing in his head, urgent, and then pleading, plucking his muscles and nerves. But he couldn't. If he ran now, they'd follow.

So he didn't run. In fact, he played the part of victim pretty well. Devastated, angry, traumatized, and above all, cooperative.

When Detective Stell pointed out that everyone around him was either dead or close to it, Eli did his best to look heartbroken. He explained Victor's jealousy, both over his girlfriend, and over his rank in the class. Victor had always been a step behind. He must have snapped. People do.

When Detective Stell asked Eli about his thesis, he explained that it had been his, until Victor usurped it, went behind his back and started working with Lyne. And then he leaned in, and told Stell that Victor hadn't been himself the past few days, that something was different, wrong, and that if he survived—he was still in ICU—they should all be very careful.

Eli's thesis was waived, in light of the trauma. *Trauma.* The word haunted him through his police questioning and his academic meetings all the way to the school-sanctioned single apartment they'd moved him into. *Trauma.* The word that had helped him crack the code, helped him pinpoint the origins of EOs. *Trauma* became a kind of hall pass. If only they knew how much *trauma* he had sustained. They didn't.

He stood in the new apartment with the lights off, and let his backpack—they'd never searched the car for it—fall to the floor beside him. It was the first time he'd been alone—truly alone—

since he'd left the party in search of Victor. And for a moment, the gap between what he should feel and what he felt snapped shut. Tears began to stream down Eli's face as he sank to his knees on the hardwood floor.

"Why is this happening?" he whispered to the empty room. He wasn't sure if he meant the sudden and ferocious sadness or Lyne's murder or Angie's death or Victor's change or the fact that he was still here in the middle of all of it, unscathed.

Unscathed. That was exactly what it was. He had wanted strength, begged for it as the ice water leached the heat and life from his body, but he'd been given *this*. Resilience. Invincibility. But why?

EOs are wrong, and I am an EO, so I must be wrong. It was the simplest of equations, but it wasn't right. Somehow, *it wasn't right.* He knew in his heart with a strange and simple certainty that EOs *were* wrong. That they shouldn't exist. But he felt with equal certainty that *he* wasn't wrong, not in the same way. Different, yes, undeniably different, but not wrong. He thought back to what he'd said in the stairwell. The words had spilled out on their own.

But it's a trade, Professor, with God or the devil . . .

Could that be the difference? He'd seen a demon wearing his best friend's skin, but Eli didn't feel like there was any evil in *himself.* If anything, he felt hands, strong and steady, guiding him when he pulled the trigger, when he snapped Lyne's neck, when he didn't run from Stell. Those moments of peace, of certainty, they felt like faith.

But he needed a sign. God had seemed, in the past few days, like a match-light next to the sun of Eli's discoveries, but now he felt like a boy again, needing sanction, approval. He pulled a pocketknife from his jeans, and clicked it open.

"Would You take it back?" he asked the dark apartment. "If I were no longer of Your making, You would take this power back, wouldn't You?" Tears glistened in his eyes. "Wouldn't You?"

He cut deep, carving a line from elbow to wrist, wincing as blood welled and spilled instantly, dripping to the floor. "You'd let me die." He switched hands and carved a matching line down his other arm, but before he'd reached his wrist, the wounds were closing, leaving only smooth skin, and a small pool of blood.

"Wouldn't You?" He cut deeper, through to bone, over and over, until the floor was red. Until he'd given his life to God a hundred times, and a hundred times had it given back. Until the fear and the doubt had all been bled out of him. And then he set the knife aside with shaking hands. Eli dipped his fingertips in the slick of red, crossed himself, and got back to his feet.

V

AROUND NOON
THE ESQUIRE HOTEL

ELI parked on the street.

He hadn't trusted hotel garages since an incident with an earth-shaking EO three years earlier. It had taken him two full hours to heal, and that was only after he managed to dig himself out of the rubble. Besides, the check-ins and checkouts, tickets and tolls and barricades . . . garages made quick exits impossible. So Eli parked, crossed the road, and passed through the hotel's elegant entry, a stone and light marquee announcing Merit's pride, THE ESQUIRE. It had been Serena's choice, and he hadn't been in the mood to defy her. They'd only been there a couple days, since the *mishap* with Sydney. He'd really hoped the girl would bleed to death in the woods, that maybe one or two of the bullets he'd fired after her would find skin instead of wood and air. But the drawing in his pocket—and the dead-undead-dead-again Barry Lynch suggested otherwise.

"Afternoon, Mr. Hill."

It took Eli a moment to remember that *he* was Mr. Hill, and then he smiled, and nodded at the woman behind the front desk. Serena was better than a fake ID. He hadn't had to present *any* ID, in fact, when they checked in. Or a credit card. She did come in handy. He didn't like being so dependent on someone else, but he managed to twist it in his mind, to assure himself that while

Serena made things easier, smoother, she was sparing him effort that he was more than capable of exerting, if necessary. In this way, she wasn't essential, only terribly convenient.

Halfway to the elevator, Eli passed a man. He made a quick mental profile of the stranger, half out of habit and half out of a gut feeling of wrongness, a kind of sixth sense acquired over a decade of studying people as if they were all spot-the-difference pictures. The hotel was expensive, sleek, the majority of its clientele in suits. This man was wearing something that might pass for a suit, but he was massive, tattoos peeking out from his pushed-up sleeves and collar. He was reading something as he walked, and never looked up, and the woman behind the desk didn't seem concerned, so Eli shelved the man's face somewhere in mental reach, and went upstairs.

He took the elevator to the ninth floor and let himself in. The suite was pleasant yet sparse, with an open kitchen, floor-to-ceiling windows, and a balcony-aided view over Merit. But no Serena. Eli tossed his satchel onto the couch and sat down at the desk in the corner where a laptop sat on top of a daily paper. He woke the device and, as the Merit Police database loaded, pulled the folded drawing from his pocket and set it on the desk, smoothing its corners. The database gave a small chirp, and he entered through the digital back door Officer Dane and Detective Stell had set up for him.

He then scrolled through the folders until he found the file he was looking for. Beth Kirk stared at him, blue hair framing her face. He stared back at her for a moment, and then dragged the profile into the trash.

VI

TEN YEARS AGO
LOCKLAND UNIVERSITY

ELI was sitting in the school-sanctioned single apartment, eating Chinese takeout from LIDS, when the report came on the news. Dale Sykes, a custodian at Lockland University, had been involved in a fatal hit-and-run accident while walking home from work the night before. Eli speared another piece of broccoli. He hadn't meant to do it. That is to say, he hadn't set out in his car with the *intent* to kill the janitor. But he *had* unearthed Sykes's rotation schedule, and he *had* gotten in his car at the same time that Sykes clocked out of his once-a-week night shift, and he *had* seen him crossing the road, and he *had* sped up. But it was a series of circumstances lined up in such a way that any one of them could so easily have shifted in a matter of seconds and spared the man's life. It was the only way Eli could think of to give the janitor a chance, or rather, to give God a chance to intervene. Sykes wasn't an EO, no, but he was a loose end, and as Eli's car drove over him with a *thud-thud,* and that moment of quiet filled Eli's chest, he knew he'd done the right thing.

Now he sat slumped in a chair at the kitchen table while the story played out on-screen, and looked over his Chinese food at two stacks of paper. The first was made up of his own thesis notes, specifically early case studies—Web site stills, testimonies, and the like. The second stack held the contents of Lyne's blue folder. Eli's theory on the causation of EOness was there, but Lyne had added his own notes on the circumstances and factors used to identify a potential EO. To near death experiences the professor had added a term Eli had heard him use before, Post-Traumatic Death Disorder, or the psychological instabilities resulting from the NDE, and another one that must be new, Rebirth Principle, or the patients' desire either to escape the life they had before, or to redefine themselves based on their ability.

Eli had crinkled his nose at the second one. He didn't like recognizing himself in these notes. He had a good reason for reading them, though. Because what he'd felt when he drove over Dale Sykes was the same thing he felt when he tried to end Victor's life. Purpose. And he was beginning to figure out what that purpose was.

EOs were an affront to nature, to God; that he knew. They were unnatural and they were strong, but Eli would always be stronger. His power was a shield against theirs, impenetrable. He could do what ordinary people couldn't. He could stop them.

But he had to find them first. Which is why he was combing through the research, pairing Lyne's methods with the case studies, hoping one of them would give him a place to start.

Victor had always been better at these kinds of puzzles. He could take one look and see the connective threads, no matter how thin. But Eli persisted, scouring his files as the news in the background came and went and came again, and finally he found it. A lead. From a newspaper article Eli had saved on a whim. A man's family had been killed in a freak accident, crushed to death. It had happened only a few months after he himself had nearly died in a building collapse. Only his first name—Wallace—was given, and the paper, which came from a city about an hour away, called him a local. Eli stared at the name for several minutes before digging up a screenshot of an online forum, one of those sites where 99.5 percent of the people are hacks looking for a little attention. But Eli had been thorough, and printed it off anyway. He'd even found a list of members who belonged to the site. One of them, a Wallace47, had only posted once on a buried thread. It was dated last year, between his own accident and that of his family's. All it said was *No one is safe near me.*

It wasn't much, but it was a start. And as he tossed his takeout container in the trash and snapped the television off, Eli wanted to go, to run, not away, but *toward* something. He had a goal. A mission.

But he knew he had to wait. He counted down the days until graduation, all the while feeling the attention of the professors, the counselors, and the cops on him like the sun in summer. At first it was glaring, but eventually, as the months wore on, it lessened until, by the time he took his exams, most even forgot to look concerned when he entered the room. When the year finally ended, he packed casually, did a last, lazy pass through his place, and locked the door. He slid the key into a school-sanctioned white envelope and dropped it off in the mailbox outside residential services.

And then, and only then, when the campus of Lockland had vanished in the distance, Eli shrugged off the name Cardale in favor of Ever, and went out to seek his purpose.

ELI didn't enjoy killing.

He did quite like the moment after. The glorious quiet that

filled the air as his broken bones healed and his torn skin closed, and he knew that God approved.

But the killing itself was messier than he anticipated.

And he didn't like the term. *Killing.* What about *removal?* *Removal* was a better word. It made the targets sound less like humans, which they weren't really . . . semantics. Regardless, it was messy. The profusion of violence on television had led Eli to believe that killing was clean. The small cough of a gun. The quick jab of a knife. A moment of shock.

The camera cuts away and life goes on.

Easy.

And to be fair, Lyne's death *had* been easy. So had Sykes's, really, since the car had done the work. But as Eli peeled a blood-soaked pair of latex gloves from his hands, he found himself wishing the camera would cut to a more pleasant moment.

Wallace had put up a fight. Late fifties, but ox-strong. He'd even bent one of Eli's favorite knives before snapping it right in two.

Eli leaned against the brick wall and waited for his ribs to notch back into place before hauling the body toward the nearest pile of trash. The night was warm and he checked himself for blood before leaving the alley, the quiet already fading, leaving a strange sadness in its wake.

He felt lost again. Purposeless. Even with his lead, it had taken him three weeks to find the EO. It was a slow, clumsy pursuit. He'd wanted to be sure. He'd needed proof. After all, what if he guessed wrong? Eli had no desire to rack up a body count of humans. Lyne and Sykes had been exceptions, victims of circumstance, their deaths unfortunate, but necessary. And, if Eli was being honest with himself, sloppy. He knew he could do

better. Wallace had been an improvement. As with any pursuit, there was a learning curve, but he firmly believed in the old
saying.

Practice makes perfect.

VII

VICTOR and Sydney sat in the hotel room, eating cold pizza and looking over the profiles Mitch had set out for them. Mitch himself had gone to run an errand, and even though Victor's eyes tracked over the profile of a middle-aged man named Zachary Flinch, his mind was far more on the cell phone—ready and within reach on the counter beside him—and on the name Stell, than his papers. His fingers tapped out a quiet beat on his leg. On the opposite side of his phone sat the profile of a younger man named Dominic Rusher.

Sydney sat perched on a nearby stool, finishing her second slice of pizza. Victor saw her steal a glance at Eli's newspaper photo, tucked beneath the corner of the third profile, which belonged to the blue-haired Beth Kirk. He watched as she reached out and drew the article free, staring down at it with her wide, blue eyes.

"Don't worry, Syd," said Victor. "I'll make him hurt."

For a moment she was quiet, her face a mask. And then it cracked. "When he came after me," she said, "he told me it was for *the greater good.*" She spat the last three words. "He said I was unnatural. That I went against God. That was the reason he gave for trying to kill me. I didn't think it was a very good reason." She swallowed. "But it was enough for my sister to hand me over."

Victor frowned. The issue of Sydney's sister, Serena, still bothered him. Why hadn't Eli killed her yet? He seemed hell-bent on killing everyone else.

"I'm sure it's complicated," he said, looking up from the profile in his hands. "What can your sister do?"

Sydney hesitated. "I don't know. She never showed me. She was supposed to, but then her boyfriend kind of shot me. Why?"

"Because," he said, "Eli's keeping her around. There must be a reason. She must be valuable to him."

Sydney looked down, and shrugged.

"But," added Victor, "if it were based on value alone, he would have kept you around. His loss is my gain."

A ghost of a smile crossed Sydney's mouth. She tossed her pizza crust to the black mass on the floor. Dol perked and caught it before it hit the ground. He then hoisted himself to his feet, and made his way around the counter to Victor, eyeing his crust expectantly. Victor fed it to him, and gave the dog's ears—which came to his stomach, even sitting on the stool—a short scratch. He looked from the beast to Sydney. He really was collecting strays.

Victor's cell rang.

He dropped the paper and lifted the phone, all in one motion. "Yes?"

"Got him," said Mitch.

"Dane or Stell?"

"Dane. And I even found us a room."

"Where?" asked Victor, pulling on his coat.

"Look out your window."

Victor strode up to the floor-to-ceiling panes, and took in the view. Across the road, and two buildings down, was the skeleton of a high-rise. Wooden construction walls encircled the scaffolding, a banner that read FALCON PRICE was plastered on the front, but there were no workers. The project had either been paused, or abandoned.

"Perfect," said Victor. "I'm on my way."

He hung up, and saw Sydney already off her stool and clutching her own red coat, waiting. He couldn't help but think she had the same expression as Dol, expectant, hopeful.

"No, Sydney," he said. "I need you to stay here."

"Why?" she asked.

"Because you don't think I'm a bad person," he said. "And I don't want to prove you wrong."

VICTOR wound his way through the plastic sheeting that cordoned off the unfinished spaces of the high-rise's ground floor, his steps echoing off concrete and steel. The fine coat of dust on the more exposed outer rooms of the building suggested a recently abandoned project, but the quality of the materials and the prime location made him think it wouldn't stay abandoned for very long. Buildings in transition were perfect places for meetings like this.

A few veils of tarp later, he found Mitch and a man in a foldout chair. Mitch looked bored. The man in the chair looked indignant and, under that, terrified. Victor could practically feel the fear, a fainter version of the radarlike ripple caused by pain. The man was lean, with short dark hair, and a sharp jaw. His hands were bound behind his back with duct tape, and he was still in his uniform, the collar darkened in places by blood. The blood came from his cheek, or his nose, or perhaps both, Victor couldn't quite tell. A few drops had dripped onto the badge over his heart.

"I have to admit," said Victor, "I was hoping for Stell."

"You said either one would do. Stell was out. I caught this one on a smoke break," said Mitch.

Victor smiled beatifically as he turned his attention to the man in the chair. "Smoking's bad for you, Officer Dane."

Officer Dane said something, but the duct tape over his mouth made it unintelligible.

"You don't know me," continued Victor. He put his boot on the side of the foldout chair, and tipped it. Officer Dane tumbled out, hitting the floor with a crack and a muffled yelp, and Victor caught the chair before it fell, turned it in one lithe motion, and sat down. "I'm a friend of a friend. And I'd greatly appreciate your help." He sat forward, resting his elbows on his knees. "I want you to tell me your access codes to the police database."

Officer Dane frowned. So did Mitch.

"Vic," he said, hunching over so Dane wouldn't hear. "What do you need that for? I hacked you in."

Victor didn't seem to care if the officer overheard. "You gave me eyes, and I'm grateful. But I want to make a post, and in order to do that, I need a recognized ID." It was time to send another message, and Victor wanted every detail perfect. The flagged profiles had author tags, and as Mitch himself had pointed out, all of them belonged to one of two people: Stell or Dane.

"Besides," said Victor, sliding to his feet, "this way's more fun."

The air in the room began to hum, the exposed skeleton of the building reflecting back the energy until the whole space buzzed.

"You should wait outside," he said to Mitch.

Victor had perfected his art, could pick a person out of a crowd and drop them like a stone, but he still didn't like bystanders. Just in case. Now and then he got a touch too zealous, and the pain spilled over, leaked into others. Mitch knew him well enough, and didn't ask questions, just tugged a veil of plastic tarp aside, and left.

Victor watched him go, flexing his fingers as if he needed them supple. He felt a faint pang of guilt at involving Mitch in this at all. It's not as though hacking was the only reason the man had ended up in such a high security prison, but still. Abducting an officer was a serious offense. Not as serious as the crimes Victor himself was about to commit, of course, but given Mitch's record, it wouldn't look good. He'd considered dismissing his friend as soon as they were on the free side of the Wrighton Penitentiary fence, but the simple fact was that Victor didn't possess superhuman strength, and someone would have to help him dispose of bodies. That, and he'd grown rather accustomed to Mitch's presence. He sighed, and turned his attention to the officer, who was trying to speak. Victor crouched, his knee digging down into the man's chest as he peeled the duct tape back.

"You don't know what you're doing," growled Officer Dane. "You'll fry for this."

Victor smiled quietly. "Not with your help."

"Why should I help you?"

Victor returned the tape to his mouth, and stood.

"Oh, you shouldn't." The hum in the air sharpened, and Officer Dane's body spasmed, his scream muffled by the tape. "But you will."

VIII

ELI was still staring down at the gridded screen of the police database when he heard the door open behind him. He tapped the screen, closing the profile of a suspected EO named Dominic Rusher just as a pair of slim arms wrapped around his shoulders, and a pair of lips grazed his ear.

"Where have you been?" he asked.

"Looking for Sydney."

He tensed. "And?"

"No luck yet, but I've put the word out. At least we'll have a few more pairs of eyes. How was the bank?"

"I don't trust Stell," said Eli for the hundredth time.

Serena sighed. "How was Barry Lynch?"

"Dead again by the time I got there." He lifted the childlike drawing from the desk, handed it blindly back to her. "But he left this."

He felt the drawing plucked from his fingers, and a moment later, Serena said, "I didn't know Victor was so thin."

"This isn't a time for joking," snapped Eli.

Serena spun his chair to face her. Her eyes were cold as ice. "You're right," she said. "You told me you killed Sydney."

"I thought I did."

Serena leaned down, and slid the prop glasses from Eli's face.

He'd forgotten he was still wearing them. She tucked them into her hair like a makeshift headband, and kissed him, not on the lips, but between the eyes, the place that wrinkled whenever he resisted her.

"Did you really?" she breathed against him.

He forced his skin to smooth beneath her kiss. It was easier to think when she wasn't looking in his eyes.

"I did."

He sighed inwardly with relief as he said it. Two small words— half truth at most—and nothing more. It was hard, and it left him drained, but there was no doubt, he was getting better at holding back.

She pulled away enough to hold him with her cold blue eyes. He could see the devil in them, silver-tongued and cunning, and Eli thought, not for the first time, that he should have killed her when he had the chance.

IX

LAST FALL

THE music was loud enough to shake the pictures on the walls. An angel and a wizard made out on the stairs. Two naughty cats tugged a vampire between them, a guy with yellow contacts howled, and someone spilled a Solo cup of cheap beer near Eli's feet.

He snagged the horns from a devil by the front door, and set them on top of his head. He'd seen the girl walk in, flanked by a Barbie and a Catholic schoolgirl flaunting numerous uniform infractions, but *she* was in jeans and a polo, blond hair loose, falling over her shoulders. He'd lost sight of her for only a moment, and now her friends were there, weaving through the crowd with interlocking fingers held over their heads, but she was gone. She should have stood out, the lack of costume conspicuous at a Halloween party, but she was nowhere to be found.

He swept through the house, avoiding the attempts of several pretty undergrads to delay him. It was flattering, and after all, he looked the part—he'd looked the part for ten years—but he was here on business. And then, after several unsuccessful tours of the first floor, *she* found *him*. A hand pulled him onto the stairs, into the shadows.

"Hi there," whispered the girl. All the music, and the shouting, and somehow he could still hear her.

"Hi," he breathed against her.

Her fingers intertwined with his as she led him up the stairs, away from the deafening party, and into a bedroom that wasn't hers, judging by the way she glanced around before stepping through. *College girls,* thought Eli cheerfully. You had to love them. He pulled the door shut behind him and the world in the room became blissfully quiet, the music dulled into a kind of thrum. The lights were off and they left them off, the only illumination pouring in through the window in the form of moonlight and street lamps.

"A Halloween party and no costume?" teased Eli.

The girl pulled a magnifying glass from her back pocket.

"Sherlock," she explained. Her movements were slow, almost sleepy. Her eyes were the color of water in winter and he didn't know what her power was. He hadn't studied her long enough, hadn't waited for a demonstration, or rather, had been studying and waiting for weeks, but hadn't been able to catch sight of the ability, whatever it was, so he'd decided to get a bit closer. It broke his rules and he knew it, and yet here he was.

"And you are?" she asked. Eli realized he was too tall for her to see. He bowed his head and pointed to the horns balanced on top. They were red and sequined, and glittered in the darkened room.

"Mephistopheles," he said. She laughed. She was an English major. He knew that much. And it was fitting, he thought. One devil to lure another.

"Original," she said with a bored smile. Serena Clarke. That was the name in his notes. She was beautiful in the most careless way. The little makeup she wore looked like an afterthought, and Eli had a hard time breaking her gaze. He was used to pretty girls, but Serena was different, *more.* When she pulled him in for a kiss, he nearly forgot the chloroform in his back pocket. Her hands slid down his spine to his jeans and he peeled them away just before her fingers skimmed the bottle and the folded cloth. He guided her hands up the wall and over her head, pinning them there as they kissed. She tasted like cold water.

He'd meant to push her out the window.

Instead he let her push him back onto a stranger's bed. The chloroform dug into his hip, but when he looked away from her she guided his eyes and his attention back with only a finger and a smile and a whispered command. A thrill ran through him. One he hadn't felt in years. Longing.

"Kiss me," she said, and he did. Eli couldn't, for the life of him, *not* kiss her, and as his lips found hers, she pinned his hands above him playfully, her blond hair tickling his face.

"Who are you?" she asked. Eli had decided that tonight his name would be Gill, but when he opened his mouth what came out was, "Eli Ever."

What the hell?

"How alliterative," said Serena. "What brings you to the party?"

"I came to find you." The words came out before Eli even noticed he was talking. He stiffened under her, and somewhere in his mind, he knew that this was bad, knew he needed to get up. But when he went to free himself, the girl cooed, "Don't go, lie still," and his body betrayed him, relaxing beneath her fingers even as his heart hammered in his chest.

"You stand out," she said. "I've seen you before. Last week."

Actually, Eli had been following her for *two* weeks, hoping to catch a glimpse of her ability. No such luck. Until now. He willed his body to move, but it wanted to lie beneath her. *He* wanted to lie beneath her.

"Are you following me?" She said it almost playfully, but Eli answered, "Yes."

"Why?" she asked, letting go of his hands, but still straddling him.

Eli managed to push himself onto his elbows. He fought the answer down like bile. *Don't say to kill you. Don't say to kill you. Don't say to kill you.* He felt the words claw their way up his throat.

"To kill you."

The girl frowned decidedly, but didn't move. "Why?"

The answer poured out. "You're an EO," he said. "You have an ability that goes against nature, and it's dangerous. *You're* dangerous."

Her mouth quirked. "Says the boy trying to kill me."

"I don't expect you to understand—"

"I do, but you're not going to kill me tonight, Eli." She said it so casually. He must have frowned, because she added, "Don't look so disappointed. You can always try again tomorrow."

The room was dark and the party thudded on beyond the walls. The girl leaned forward and plucked the red sequined horns from his dark hair, nestling them in her own blond waves. She was lovely, and he struggled to think straight, to remember why she had to die.

And then she said, "You're right, you know."

"About what?" asked Eli. His thoughts felt slow.

"I'm dangerous. I shouldn't exist. But what gives you the right to kill me?"

"Because I can."

"Bad answer," she said, running her fingers along his jaw. And then she let her body slip down on top of his, jean to jean and hip to hip and skin to skin.

"Kiss me again," she ordered. And he did.

SERENA Clarke spent half her time wishing she were dead, and the other half telling everyone around her what to do, and wishing *someone* wouldn't do it.

She'd asked to leave the hospital, and the sea of staff had practically parted to let her pass before her IV was even out. It had been pleasant, at first, getting her way so easily, if not a little foreign. Serena had always been strong, always ready to fight for something she wanted. But suddenly there was no need, because the fight had gone out of everyone else. The world went limp around her, a complacent glaze filling the eyes of anyone she met and spoke to. The lack of opposition, of tension, became maddening. Her parents simply nodded when she said she wanted to go back to school. Her teachers ceased to be a challenge. Her friends bent and bent and bent to every whim. Boys lost their fire, gave her anything she wanted, and anything she didn't want, but was bored enough to ask for.

Where before Serena's world had bowed beneath the strength of her will, now it simply bowed. She didn't have to argue, she didn't have to try.

She felt like a ghost.

And worst of all, Serena hated to admit how easy and addictive it was, getting her way, even when it made her miserable. Every time she got tired of trying to make people fight her, she would slink back into the comfort of control. She couldn't turn it off. Even when she didn't order, even when she only suggested, only asked, they did it.

She felt like a god.

She dreamed of people who could fight back. Of wills strong enough to resist her.

And then one night, she got mad—truly mad—at the boy she was seeing, at the stupid, glazed look in his eyes that she knew too well, and when he refused to fight her, refused to deny her, because for some infuriating reason she couldn't order him to do *that,* his desire to bend superseding any attempt at violence, she told him to go jump off a bridge.

And he did.

Serena remembered sitting cross-legged on her bed and listening to the news, her friends huddled on the comforter around her—but not touching; there seemed to be a thin wall separating them from her, fear, or maybe awe—and it was then she realized that she wasn't a ghost, or a god.

She was a monster.

ELI examined the small blue card the girl had slipped in his pocket the night before. On one side she'd written the name of a café off the main library—the Light Post, it was called—along with a time, *2 p.m.* On the other side, she'd written *Scheherazade*—she'd even spelled it correctly. Eli knew the reference, of course. *Arabian Nights.* The woman who told the sultan stories and never finished at night, lest he kill her. Instead she drew the stories over until the next day.

As he made his way through U of Merit's campus, he felt hungover for the first time in a decade, his head heavy and his thoughts slow. It had taken him most of the morning to drag fully free of the girl's compulsion, to think of her as a target. Only a target.

He slipped the card back into his pocket. He knew Serena wouldn't show up. She'd be a fool to come anywhere near him after last night. After he'd admitted his intentions. And yet there she was, sitting on the patio of the Light Post wearing sunglasses and a dark blue sweater, her blond hair wisping around her face.

"Do you have a death wish?" Eli asked, standing beside the table.

She shrugged. "I've done it once. The novelty must be wearing off." She gestured to the empty chair across from her. Eli weighed his options, but he couldn't exactly kill her in the middle of campus, so he sat down.

"Serena," she said, sliding the sunglasses on top of her head. In the daylight, her eyes were even lighter. "But you already know my name." She sipped her coffee. Eli said nothing. "Why do you want to kill me?" she asked. "And don't say because you can."

The moment Eli's thoughts formed they were sliding across his tongue. He frowned as the words spilled out. "EOs are unnatural."

"You said that already."

"My best friend became one, and I saw the change. Like a devil had climbed into his skin. He killed my girlfriend, and then he tried to kill me." He bit into his tongue and managed to stem the flow of words. Was it her eyes, or her voice that was compelling him?

"So you go around blaming every other EO you can find," said Serena. "Punishing them in his place?"

"You don't understand," he said. "I'm trying to *protect* people."

She smiled behind her coffee. It wasn't a happy smile. "Which people?"

"The normal ones."

Serena scoffed.

"The natural ones," pressed Eli. "ExtraOrdinaries shouldn't exist. They haven't just been given a second chance, they've been given a weapon and no manual. No rules. Their very existence is criminal. They aren't whole."

The thin smile fell from Serena's red lips. "What do you mean?"

"I mean that when a person revives as an EO, not all of them comes back. Things are missing." Even Eli, blessed as he was, knew that he was missing pieces. "Important things like empathy and balance and fear and consequence. Those things that might temper their abilities, they're missing. Tell me I'm wrong. Tell me you feel all those things the way you did before."

Serena leaned forward, setting her coffee on a stack of books. She didn't contradict him. Instead, she said, "And what is your ability, Eli Ever?"

"What makes you think I have one?" He spat the words out as quickly as he could, filling the need to speak. It was such a small victory, countering like that, but he knew she registered it. And then her smile sharpened.

"Tell me your power," she said.

This time he answered. "I heal."

She laughed, loud enough that one or two students glanced over from tables across the patio. "No wonder you have a wicked sense of entitlement."

"What do you mean?"

"Well, your gift doesn't impact anyone else. It's reflexive. So in your mind *you're* not a threat. But the rest of us are." Serena tapped the stack of books, and Eli could make out psychology titles mingled in with the English books. "Am I close?"

Eli wasn't sure he liked Serena very much. He wanted to tell her about his covenant, but instead he asked, "How did you know I'm an EO?"

"Everything about you," she said, sliding her sunglasses back on, "is chock full of self-loathing. I'm not judging. I know the feeling." Her watch gave a small beep, and she dragged herself to her feet. Even that simple motion was lovely and fluid, like water. "You know, maybe I should let you kill me. Because you're right. Even though we come back, something stays dead. Lost. We forget something of who we were. It's scary and wonderful and monstrous."

She looked so sad in that moment, ringed with afternoon light, and Eli had to resist the urge to go to her. Something fluttered in him. She reminded him of Angie, or rather, how *he* had felt around Angie before everything had changed. Before *he* had changed. Ten years of staring across the chasm at the things he'd lost, and now, looking at this girl, it was like the chasm was shrinking, the gap pulling closed until his fingers could almost—*almost*—skim the other side. He wanted to be close to her, wanted to make her happy, wanted to reach across the rift and remember—he bit down again until he tasted blood to clear his mind. He knew the feelings weren't his, not entirely, not naturally. There was no going back. He was the way he was for a reason. A purpose. And this girl, this monster, had a dangerous, complicated gift. It wasn't a simple compulsion. It was an attraction. A want to please. A need to please. They were her feelings filtering through him, not his own.

"We're all monsters," she said, taking up her books. "But so are you."

Eli was only half listening, but still the words began to trickle through him, and he pushed them violently away before they could settle in his mind. He got to his feet, but she was already turning away.

"You can't kill me today," she called back. "I'm late for class."

ELI sat on a bench outside the psychology building, his head tipped back. It was a beautiful day, cloudy but not gray, cold but not bitter, and the breeze that tugged at his collar and wove through his hair kept him alert. His mind was clear again, now that Serena was gone, and he knew he had a problem. He needed to kill the girl without seeing her, without hearing her. If she were unconscious, he mused, then he might be able to—

"Aren't you picturesque." The voice was cool and warm at once. Serena clutched her books to her chest and looked down at him. "What were you thinking about?" she asked.

"Killing you," he said. It was almost freeing, not being able to lie.

Serena shook her head slowly and sighed. "Walk me to my next class."

He stood.

"Tell me," she said, weaving her arm through his. "At the party last night, how were you going to kill me?"

Eli watched the clouds. "Drug you and push you out the window."

"That's cold," she said.

Eli shrugged. "But believable. Kids get drunk at parties. After discretion, their balance is the next thing to go. They fall. Sometimes out of windows."

"So," she said, leaning against him. Her hair tickled his cheek. "Do you have a cape?"

"Are you mocking me?"

"More of a mask type, then."

"What are you getting at?" he asked as they reached her next building.

"You're the hero . . . ," she said, finding his eyes, ". . . of your own story, anyway." She started up the steps. "Will I see you again? Do you have me penciled in for a redo sometime this week? I just want to know, so I can bring my mace. Put up a fight at least, for realism's sake."

Serena was the strangest girl Eli had ever met. He told her so. She smiled, and went inside.

∞

SERENA'S eyes brightened when she saw him again the next day.

Eli was waiting on the building steps in the late afternoon with a cup of coffee in each hand. The dusk smelled like dead leaves and far-off fires; his breath escaped in small clouds as he held one of the coffees out to her, and she took it and slipped her arm through his again.

"My hero," she said, and Eli smiled at the inside joke. In nearly ten years he hadn't let anyone close. Certainly not an EO. Yet here he was, walking through the twilight with one. And he liked it. He tried to remind himself that the sensation was false, projected, tried to convince himself that this was research, that he was only trying to understand her gift, and how best to eliminate her, even as her let her guide him down the steps and away from the campus.

"So you protect the innocent world from the big bad EOs," she said as they made their way, arm in arm. "How do you find them?"

"I have a system." As they walked, he explained to her his method. The careful narrowing down of targets based on Lyne's three steps. The periods of observation.

"Sounds tedious," she said.

"It is."

"And then when you find them, you just kill them?" Her steps slowed. "No questions? No trial? No assessment of whether they're a danger or a threat?"

"I used to talk to them. Not anymore."

"What gives you the right to play judge and jury and executioner?"

"God." He hadn't wanted to say the word, hadn't wanted to

give this strange girl the power of knowing his beliefs, of twisting and bending them to her own.

She pursed her lips, the word hanging in the air between them, but she didn't mock him.

"How do you kill them?" she asked eventually.

"It depends on their ability," he said. "Default is a gun, but if there's a concern regarding metal, or explosives, or the setup, I have to find another method. Like with you. You're young and you'd probably be missed, which would be messy, and that therefore ruled out a crime. I needed to make it look like an accident."

They turned onto a side street lined with small apartment buildings and houses.

"What's the strangest way you've ever killed someone?"

Eli thought about it. "Bear trap."

Serena cringed. "No details necessary."

A few minutes passed in silence as they walked.

"How long have you been doing this?" asked Serena.

"Ten years."

"No way," she said, squinting at him. "How old are you?"

Eli smiled. "How old do I look?"

They reached her apartment and stopped.

"Twenty. Maybe twenty-one."

"Well, I guess I'm technically thirty-two. But I've looked this way for ten years."

"Part of that whole healing thing?"

Eli nodded. "Regeneration."

"Show me," said Serena.

"How?" asked Eli.

Her eyes glittered. "Do you have a weapon on you?"

Eli hesitated a moment, then withdrew a Glock from his coat.

"Give it to me," said Serena. Eli handed it over, but he had the self-possession to frown as he did it. Serena stepped away from him and took aim.

"Wait," said Eli. He looked around. "Maybe not out here, in the street? Let's go inside."

Serena considered him for a long moment, then smiled, and led him in.

X

"**VICTOR** sent you a message," said Serena, brushing her fingers over Sydney's stick figure in the drawing. There was a fleck of brownish red on the corner of the paper, and she wondered whose blood it was. "Are you going to send one back?"

She watched as the answer climbed up Eli's throat. "I don't know how," he said under his breath.

"He's here in the city," she said.

"So are millions of other people, Serena," growled Eli.

"And they're all on your side," she said. "Or they can be." She took Eli's hand, drew him up from the chair. Her hands slid around his back, pulled him close until his forehead rested against hers. "Let me help you."

She watched his jaw clench. Eli couldn't resist her, not really, but he was *trying*. She could see the strain in his eyes, in the space between his brows, as he fought the compulsion. Every time she asked a question. Every time she gave a small order. There was a pause, as if Eli were trying to reprocess the command, twist it until it was his. As if he could take back his will. He couldn't, but she loved to see him try. It gave her something to hold on to. She took it in, savored his resistance. And then, for his sake, she forced him to bend.

"Eli," she said, her voice, even and unmovable. "Let me help you."

"How?" he asked.

Her fingers slipped into his front pocket, and drew out his phone. "Call Detective Stell. Tell him we need a meeting with the Merit PD. *All* of them." Victor wasn't the only one in the city. Sydney was here, too. Find one, and they would find the other—the drawing told them as much. Eli stared down at his phone.

"It's too public," he said, fingers punching in the numbers even as he struggled to think. "It makes *us* too public. I haven't made it this long by standing in spotlights."

"It's the only way to flush them out. Besides, you shouldn't worry. You're the hero now, remember?"

He laughed drily, but didn't say *no* again.

"Do you want a mask?" she teased, pulling the glasses from her hair and sliding them back onto his face. "Or will these do?"

Eli ran his thumb over his phone, hesitating for one last moment. And then he connected the call.

XI

LAST FALL

SERENA Clarke lived alone. Eli could tell from the moment they walked in, when she slipped her shoes off by the door. The place was clean, calm, and unified. It had one cohesive taste, and Serena didn't look around for anyone before turning on him and raising the gun.

"Hold up," said Eli, shrugging his coat off. "This is my favorite. I'd rather not have holes in it." He took a small cylinder from the pocket, and tossed it to her.

"Do you actually know how to use a gun?" he asked.

Serena nodded as she screwed the silencer on. "Years of crime dramas. And I found my father's Colt once, and taught myself. Cans in the woods, and all that."

"Are you a decent shot?" Eli unbuttoned his shirt and took that off, too, draping it over the entry table with his coat. Serena gave him an appreciative head-to-toe-and-back look, and then she pulled the trigger. He gasped and staggered backward, red blossoming against his shoulder. The pain was brief and bright, the bullet passing straight through and lodging in the wall behind him. He watched Serena's eyes widen as the wound instantly began to close, his skin knitting back together. She gave a slow clap, the gun still in her grip. Eli rubbed his shoulder, and met her eyes.

"Happy now?" he grumbled.

"Don't be so sour," she said, setting the gun on the table.

"Just because I heal," he said, reaching past her for his shirt, "doesn't mean that didn't hurt."

Serena caught his arm in one hand and his face in the other, and held his gaze. Eli felt himself falling in. "Want me to kiss it?" she asked, brushing her lips against his. "Will that make it better?"

There it was again, in his chest, that strange flutter, like *want*, dusty and a decade old but there. Maybe it was a trick. Maybe this feeling—this simple, mortal ache—wasn't coming from him. But maybe it was. Maybe it could be. He nodded once, just enough to bring their lips together, and then she turned and led him toward to the bedroom.

"Don't kill me tonight," she added as she led him into the dark. And he never even thought of it.

SERENA and Eli were lying together in a tangle of sheets. They faced each other, and she ran her fingers down his cheek, his throat, his chest. Her hand seemed fascinated with the place where she'd shot him, now only smooth skin shining in the near dark of the room. Her hand wandered, then, over his ribs and around his back, and came to rest on the web of old scars there. She drew in a small breath.

"They're from before," he said softly. "Nothing leaves marks anymore." Her lips parted, but before she could ask what happened, he added, "Please. Don't ask."

And she didn't. Instead, she drew her hand back to his unscarred chest and let it rest over his heart.

"Where will you go, after you kill me?"

"I don't know," he said honestly. "I'll have to start again."

"Will you sleep with that one, too?" she asked, and Eli laughed.

"Seduction is hardly part of my method."

"Well, then, I feel special."

"You are." It came out in a whisper. And it was true. Special. Different. Fascinating. Dangerous. Her hand slid back to the bed, and he thought perhaps she'd fallen asleep. He enjoyed watching her this way, knowing he could kill her, but not wanting to. It made him feel like he was in control again. Or closer to it. Being with Serena felt like a dream, an interlude. It made Eli feel human again. It made him forget.

"There must be an easier way," she wondered sleepily. "To find them . . . if you could access the right networks . . ."

"If only," he whispered. And then they slept.

∞

THE sun streamed in but the room was cool. Eli shivered, and sat up. The bed was empty beside him. He found his pants, and spent several minutes searching for his shirt before he remembered he'd left it by the front door, and padded out into the apartment. Serena was gone. His gun was still on the table, and he tucked it into the back of his pants and went into the kitchen to make coffee.

Eli was fascinated by kitchens. By the way people ordered their lives, the cabinets they used, the places they kept food, and the food they choose to keep. He'd spent the last decade studying people, and it was amazing how much could be gleaned from their homes. Their bedrooms, and bathrooms, and closets, of course, but also their kitchens. Serena's coffee was in the lowest cabinet over the counter, just beside the sink, which meant she drank a lot of it. A small black, two-to-four-cup coffeemaker sat tucked along the tile backsplash, another clue she lived alone. The apartment was far too nice for an underclassman, one of those lottery-only wins, and Eli wondered absently as he pulled out a filter if she'd used her talents to get this, too.

He found the coffee cups to the left of the sink, and tapped the coffeemaker, eager for it to brew. As soon as it did, he filled his cup and took a long sip. Now that he was alone, his mind was making its way faithfully back to the topic of how he was going to eliminate Serena, when the front door opened and she walked in, flanked by two men. One was a police officer, and the other was Detective Stell. Eli's heart lurched in his chest, but he managed a careful smile over his mug as he leaned against the counter to hide the gun in the back of his pants.

"Good morning," he said.

"Morning . . . ," said Stell, and Eli watched confusion spread through his features beneath a glazed calm, which Eli quickly recognized as Serena's doing. It had been nearly ten years, during which the Lockland case had gone stone cold, and during which Eli had constantly thought of Stell, casting backward glances to see if he would follow. Stell hadn't, but he clearly recognized him now. (How could he not? Eli was a photograph, unchanging.) Yet neither he nor the officer reached for their weapons, so that was promising. Eli looked to Serena, who was beaming.

"I have a present for you," she said, gesturing to the men.

"You really shouldn't have," said Eli slowly.

"This is Officer Frederick Dane, and his boss, Detective Stell."

"Mr. Cardale," said Stell.

"I go by Ever now."

"You two know each other?" asked Serena.

"Detective Stell was on Victor's case," offered Eli. "Back at Lockland."

Serena's eyes widened in recognition. Eli had told her about

that day. He'd left out most of the details, and now, staring at the
only man who'd ever even had reason to suspect him of foul play,
potentially of *ExtraOrdinary* play, he wished he'd given her the
entire truth.

"It's been some time," said Stell. "And yet you haven't changed,
Mr. Card . . . Ever. Not at all—"

"What brings you to Merit?" cut in Eli.

"I transferred a few months ago."

"Change of scenery?"

"Followed a rash of killings."

Eli knew he should have broken up the path, the pattern, but
he'd been on a roll. Merit had attracted an impressive number of
EOs, by virtue of its population and its many dark corners. People
came to the city thinking they could hide. But not from him.

"Eli," said Serena. "You're ruining my surprise. Stell and Dane
and I, we've had a good long chat, and it's all been arranged. They're
going to help us."

"Us?" asked Eli.

Serena turned back to the men and smiled. "Have a seat." The
two men obediently sat down at the kitchen table.

"Eli, can you pour them some coffee?"

Eli wasn't sure how to do that without turning his back and his
gun on the cops, so he reached for Serena instead, and pulled her
close. Another small act of defiance. The motion had the easy movement of a lover's embrace, but his grip was tight. "What are you
doing?" he growled into her ear.

"I was thinking," she said, tipping her head back against his
chest, "about how tedious it must be, trying to find each EO." She
wasn't even bothering to lower her voice. "And then I thought, there
must be an easier way. It turns out the Merit Police Department
has a database for persons of interest. Of course, it's not meant for

EOs, but the search matrix, that's what it's called, right?" Officer
Dane nodded. "Yes, well, it's broad enough that we could use it for
that." Serena seemed thoroughly proud of herself. "So I went to
the station, and I asked to talk to someone involved with EO
investigation—you told me, remember, that some of them were
trained for it—and the man at the desk led me to these fine gentle-
men. Dane is Stell's protégé, and they've both agreed to share their
search engine with us."

"There's that *us* again," said Eli, aloud. Serena ignored him

"We've got it all figured out, I think. Right, Officer Dane?"

The lanky man with dark, close-cropped hair nodded and set a
thin folder on the table. "The first batch," he said.

"Thank you, Officer," said Serena, taking up the file. "This will
keep us busy for a little while."

Us. Us. Us. What on earth was happening? But even as Eli's
thoughts spun, he managed to keep his hand away from the gun
against his back and focus on the instructions Serena was now giving the cops.

"Mr. Ever here is going to keep this city safe," she told them,
her blue eyes shining. "He's a hero, isn't he, Officers?"

Officer Dane nodded. At first Stell only looked at Eli, but eventually, he nodded, too.

"A hero," they echoed.

XII

THIS AFTERNOON

THE FALCON PRICE PROJECT

DANE whimpered faintly from the floor.

Victor leaned back in the foldout chair, locking his fingers behind his head. A switchblade dangled loosely from one hand, the flat of the blade skimming his pale hair. It wasn't strictly necessary, but his talent was most effective when it amplified an existing source of pain. Officer Dane curled in on himself on the concrete floor, his uniform torn, blood streaking across the floor. Victor was glad Mitch had put some plastic sheeting down. He'd gotten a little carried away, but it had been so long since he'd stretched, so long since he'd let go. It cleared his head. It calmed him.

Dane's hands were still firmly bound behind his back, but the tape over his mouth had come off, and his shirt clung to his chest with sweat and blood. He'd given up the database's access codes, of course, and quickly at that—Victor had tested them on his phone to be sure. Then, with a bit more encouragement, he'd told Victor everything he knew about Detective Stell: his earlier days in Lockland, his transfer on the heels of a killing streak—Eli's work, no doubt—and Dane's own training. All cops these days, it turned out, learned an EO protocol, whether they were skeptics or believers, but at least one man in every precinct knew more than the basics, studied the indicators, and took charge of any investigation where an EO was even suspected.

Stell had been that man ten years ago at Lockland, and he was that man again here, and grooming Dane to follow. Not only that, but somehow, Eli had convinced the detective in charge of the investigation against him to *help* him.

Victor shook his head in wonder as he tortured the details out of Dane. Eli never ceased to amaze him. If he and Stell had been working together since Lockland, that would have been one thing, but this was a new arrangement—Stell and Dane had only been assisting Eli since last fall. How had Eli conned the Merit PD into helping him?

"Officer Dane," said Victor. The cop cringed at the sound of his voice. "Would you mind telling me about your interactions with Eli Ever?"

When Dane didn't answer, Victor stood and rolled the man onto his back with the tip of his shoe. "Well?" he asked calmly, leaning on the officer's broken ribs.

Dane screamed, but once the screams had given way to gasps, he said, "Eli Ever . . . is . . . a hero."

Victor let out a choked laugh, and put more weight on Dane's chest. "Who told you that?"

The officer's expression shifted. It was stern, but remarkably level when he answered. "Serena."

"And you bought it?"

Officer Dane looked at Victor as if he couldn't quite grasp the question.

And then Victor got it. "What else did Serena say?"

"To help Mr. Ever."

"And you did."

Officer Dane looked confused. "Of course."

Victor smiled grimly.

"Of course," he echoed, pulling the gun from his belt. He

rubbed his eyes, swore quietly beneath his breath, then fired two quick shots into Officer Dane's chest. This was the first person he'd killed since Angie Knight (if you didn't count that one man in prison, back when he'd been perfecting his technique, and Victor didn't), and certainly the first intentional *murder*. It wasn't that he shied away from killing; people simply weren't any good to him dead. After all, pain didn't have much effect on corpses. As for Dane's murder, it was unfortunate (albeit necessary), and the fact that a modicum of regret was all that Victor felt on the matter might have bothered him more, or at least been worth a moment of introspection, had he not been so preoccupied with bringing the dead man *back*.

Mitch ducked through the plastic sheeting and into the room at the muffled sound of the gunshots. He'd pulled on gloves, and already had a spare sheet of plastic tucked under one arm, just in case. He looked down at the officer's body, and sighed, but when he started taking up the plastic on the floor, and Dane with it, Victor held out a hand, and stopped him.

"Leave him," he said. "And go get Sydney."

Mitch hesitated. "I don't think . . ."

Victor spun on him. "I said, go get her."

Mitch looked profoundly unhappy, but did as he was told, leaving Victor alone with the officer's corpse.

XIII

LAST FALL
UNIVERSITY OF MERIT

SERENA ushered the detectives out, and returned to the kitchen to find Eli looking pale and bracing himself against the sink. Everything about him was coiled, the tension in his face something she hadn't seen, not in her presence, since the accident, and it sent a thrill through her. He looked *mad*. At *her*. She watched as he slid the gun from his back and set it on the kitchen counter, but left his hand on top.

"I should kill you," he growled. "I really, really should."

"But you won't."

"You're crazy. Those are my murders Stell's investigating and you just let him in."

"I didn't know about you and Stell," said Serena lightly. "Actually, it makes this even better."

"How so?"

"Because the whole point was to show you."

"That you've lost it?"

She pouted. "No. That I'm more use to you alive."

"I thought you had a death wish," said Eli. "And bringing back a man I've worked to avoid for a decade doesn't put you on my good side, Serena. Don't you think the cogs are turning in Stell's mind, somewhere past that spell you cast on him?"

"Calm down," she said simply. And sure enough, she could see the anger bleeding away, watched him try to cling to it as it thinned into nothing. She wondered what it felt like, to be under her influence.

Eli's shoulders loosened, and he let go of the counter while Serena flipped through the file Officer Dane had left for them. She plucked up a piece of paper, letting the rest fall to the table. Her eyes wandered absently over the page. A man in his twenties, handsome but for a scar that squinted one eye and carved a line down to his throat.

"What about your sister?" asked Eli, pouring more coffee now that his hands had stopped shaking.

Serena frowned, and looked up. "What about her?"

"You said she was an EO."

Had she? Had that been one of those confessions murmured in half sleep, the space where whispered thoughts and dreams and fears slipped out?

"Spin again," she said, trying to hide her tension as she nodded at the folder. She didn't like to think about Sydney. Not now. Her sister's power made Serena ill, not because of the talent itself but because it meant she was broken the way Serena was broken, the way Eli was broken. Missing pieces. She hadn't seen Sydney, not since leaving the hospital. She couldn't bear the thought of looking at her.

"What can she do?" pressed Eli.

"I don't know," lied Serena. "She's just a kid."

"What's her name?"

"Not her," she snapped. And then the smile was back, and she was passing the profile in her hands to Eli, "Let's try this one. He sounds like a challenge."

Eli looked at her for several long moments before he reached out and took the paper.

XIV

THIS AFTERNOON
THE ESQUIRE HOTEL

ELI sat waiting for the call to go through, and watching Serena as she crossed the hotel suite to the kitchen. Finally the ringing stopped, and a brusque voice answered.

"Stell here. What is it?"

"It's Ever," said Eli, taking the stupid glasses off. Serena was busying herself with the coffeepot, but he could tell from the way she tipped her head, the way she made so little noise, tiptoeing through the motions, that she was listening in.

"Sir," said the detective. Eli didn't like the way he said the word with a faint uptick at the end. "How can I assist you?"

Eli didn't know, when he dialed the number, if calling Stell was actually a good idea, or if it only seemed like one because it came from Serena. Now that he was talking to the detective, he realized that it wasn't a good idea at all. That it was, in fact, a very bad idea. For nine and a half of the last ten years, he'd been a ghost, managing to stay off radars despite his growing tally of removals and his unchanging face (the pairing of anonymity with immortality was no small feat). He'd managed to avoid Stell, until Serena involved him, and even then, everything Eli did, he did alone. He didn't trust other people, not with knowledge or with power, and certainly not with both. The risk here was high, probably too high.

And the reward? By indoctrinating an entire police force, he ensured both their support, with regard to Victor and his other targets, as well as sanction to continue his executions, his *removals*. But it meant tethering himself to the one person he knew he couldn't trust, and couldn't resist. The police wouldn't be listening to *him,* not really. They would be listening to Serena. She met his eyes across the room, and smiled, holding out a mug. He shook his head, *no,* a small action that made her smile. She brought the cup to him anyway, nested it right into his empty hand, and curled her fingers and his around it.

"Mr. Ever?" prompted Stell.

Eli swallowed. Whether it was a good idea or not, he knew one thing: he couldn't afford to let Victor get away.

"I need to set up a meeting," he told the detective, "with your entire police force. As soon as possible."

"I'll call them in. But it will take time for them to get here."

Eli looked at his watch. It was almost four. "I'll be there at six. And pass the word to Officer Dane."

"Will if I can find him."

Eli's brow furrowed. "What do you mean?"

"I just got back from the scene at the bank with your boy Lynch, and there's no sign of Dane. Must have stepped out for a smoke."

"Must have," echoed Eli. "Keep me posted." He hung up and hesitated a moment, turning the phone over and over in his hand.

"What's wrong?" asked Serena.

Eli didn't answer. He was able to resist answering, but only because he didn't *know.* Maybe nothing was wrong. Maybe the cop had gone on break, or cut out early. Or maybe . . . his senses tingled the way they did when Stell's words tipped up. The way they did when he knew he was following Serena's will instead of his own. The way they did when something was *off.* He didn't ques-

tion the feeling. He trusted it as much as the quiet that followed
his kills.

Which is why Eli dialed Officer Dane's number.

It rang.

And rang.

And rang.

∞

VICTOR paced the gutted room of the half-built high-rise and
pondered the problem of Serena Clarke who, it seemed, was quite
an influential person. No wonder Eli was keeping her around. Victor knew that he would have to kill her very, very quickly. He
looked around the space and considered its potential and his options, but his attention drifted invariably back down to Dane's
body, which lay sprawled in the middle of the floor on its plastic
sheeting. Victor decided to do what he could to minimize the signs
of torture, for Sydney's sake.

He knelt beside the corpse and began to straighten it up, align
the limbs, do what he could to give the body a more natural appearance. He noticed a silver wedding band on Dane's finger—he
slid it off, and into Dane's pocket—then placed the man's arms at
his sides. There was nothing he could do to make the body look
less dead; that would fall to Sydney.

Several minutes later when Mitch returned, holding aside a curtain of plastic and showing Sydney in, Victor was quite proud of
the job he'd done. Dane practically looked peaceful (aside from the
shredded uniform and the blood). But when Sydney's eyes snagged
on the body, she stopped and let out a small sound.

"That's bad, isn't it?" she asked, pointing to the badge on the
corpse's chest. "Killing a cop is bad."

"Only if it's a good cop," explained Victor. "And he wasn't one. This cop was helping Eli track down EOs. If Serena hadn't turned you over, this man would have." *So long as he was under Serena's spell,* he thought, but didn't say it.

"Is that why you killed him?" asked Sydney quietly.

Victor frowned. "It doesn't matter why I did it. What matters is that you bring him back."

Sydney blinked. "Why would I do that?"

"Because it's important," he said, shifting his weight from foot to foot, "and I promise to kill him again right after. I just need to see something."

Sydney frowned. "I don't want to bring him back."

"I don't *care,*" snapped Victor suddenly, the air humming to life around them. Mitch shot forward, putting his hulking form in front of Sydney, and Victor caught himself before he lost control. All three seemed surprised by the outburst, and guilt—or at least a pale version of it—tightened in Victor's chest as he considered the other two, the loyal guard and the impossible girl. He couldn't afford to lose them—their *help,* he corrected himself, their *cooperation*—certainly not today, so he drew the energy back into himself, wincing as he grounded it.

"I'm sorry," he said, letting out a low breath. Mitch took a small step to the side, but didn't abandon Sydney.

"Too far, Vic," he growled in a rare display of boldness.

"I know," said Victor, rolling his shoulders. Even with the energy grounded, the desire to hurt someone still coiled inside him, but he willed it to stay contained, just a little longer, just until he could find Eli. "I'm sorry," he said again, turning his attention to the small, blond girl still half-hidden behind Mitch. "I know you don't want to do this, Sydney. But I need your help if I'm going to stop Eli. I'm trying to protect you, and Mitch. And myself. I'm trying to protect all of us, but I can't do it alone. We have to work together. So will you do this for me?" He held his gun up for her to see. "I won't let the cop hurt you."

She hesitated, but finally crouched beside the body, careful to avoid the blood.

"Does he deserve a second chance?" she asked softly.

"Don't think of it that way," said Victor. "He only gets a moment. Just long enough to answer a question."

Sydney took a breath and pressed her fingertips to the clean spots on the officer's shirt. An instant later Dane gasped and sat up, and Sydney scrambled back to Mitch's side, gripping his arm.

Victor looked down at Officer Dane.

"Tell me again about Ever," he said.

The officer met his eyes. "Eli Ever is a hero."

"Well, that's discouraging," huffed Victor. He fired three more shots into the officer's chest. Sydney turned and buried her face in Mitch's shirt as Dane thudded back against the plastic-covered concrete, as dead as before.

"But now we know," said Victor, toeing the body with his shoe. Mitch looked at him over Sydney's pale hair, his face caught for the second time in as many minutes between horror and anger.

"What the fuck was that about, Vale?"

"Serena Clarke's power," said Victor. "She tells people what to do." He slid his gun back into his belt. "What to say, what to think." He gestured to the body. "And even death doesn't seem to sever the connection." Well, *the officer's* death, amended Victor silently. "We're done here."

Sydney stood very still. She'd let go of Mitch and now had her arms wrapped around her ribs, as if for warmth. Victor came over to her, but when he reached out to touch her shoulder, she cringed away. He sank to one knee in front of her so that he had to look up a fraction to meet her eyes.

"Your sister and Eli, they think they're a team. But they're nothing compared to us. Now come on," he said, straightening. "You look cold. I'll buy you a hot chocolate."

Her icy blue eyes found his, and she looked as though she had something to say, but she didn't get the chance, because that's when Victor heard the phone ring. It wasn't *his* phone, and he could tell by the look on Mitch's face, it wasn't his, either. And Sydney must have left hers back at the hotel because she didn't even reach for her pocket. Patting down the officer, Mitch found the device and drew it out.

"Leave it," said Victor.

"I think you want to take this one," said Mitch, tossing him the cell. In the place of the caller's name, there was only one word on the screen.

HERO.

Victor flashed a sharp, dark smile, cracked his neck, and answered the call.

"Dane, where are you?" snapped the person on the other end. Everything in Victor tensed at the sound, but he didn't answer. He hadn't heard that voice in ten years, but it didn't matter because the voice, like everything else about Eli Ever, hadn't changed at all.

"Officer Dane?" it said again.

"I'm afraid you just missed him," said Victor at last. He closed his eyes when he spoke, savoring the moment of quiet on the other end. If he concentrated, he could almost imagine Eli tensing at the sound of *his* voice.

"*Victor,*" said Eli. The word was a cough, as if the letters lodged in his chest.

"I admit, it's clever," said Victor, "using Merit's police database to find your targets. I'm a bit insulted that I haven't shown up on there yet, but give it time. I just got here."

"You're in the city."

"Of course."

"You won't get away," said Eli, the bravado dampening shock as it found its way back into his voice.

"I don't plan to," said Victor. "See you at midnight." He hung up, and broke the phone in two, dropping both parts onto Dane's body. The room filled with quiet as he considered the corpse, and then looked up.

"Sorry about that. You can clean up now," he said to Mitch, who was staring slack-jawed at him.

"Midnight?" growled Mitch. "Midnight? As in *tonight*?"

Victor checked his watch. It was already four. "Never put off till tomorrow what you can do today."

"I get the feeling that's not what Thomas Jefferson meant," muttered Mitch.

But Victor wasn't listening. His mind had spent the morning spinning, but now that it was set, now that there were only hours standing in his way, the violent energy quieted and the calm finally settled over him. He turned his attention back to Sydney. "How about that hot chocolate?"

∞

MITCH crossed his arms and watched them go, Sydney's short blond hair bobbing as she followed Victor out. When she'd taken hold of his arm, her fingers had been ice, and underneath the chill, she'd been shaking. That bone-deep kind of shiver that had less to do with cold, and more to do with fright. He wanted to say something, wanted to know what the hell Victor was thinking, wanted to tell him that he was playing with more lives than his own. But by the time he found the one word he should have said, one small, simple, powerful word—*STOP*—it was too late. They were gone and Mitch was alone in the plastic-shrouded room, so he did his best to swallow the word and the sinking feeling that went with it, then turned to the officer's body, and got to work.

XV

A LONG TIME AGO

VARIOUS CITIES

MITCHELL Turner was cursed.

Always had been.

Trouble followed him like a shadow, clinging to him no matter how much good light he tried to stand in. In his hands, good things broke and bad things grew. It didn't help that his mother died and his father bailed and his aunt took one look at him and waved him on, leaving Mitch to bounce between houses more like hotels, checking in and out, never putting down roots.

Most of his problems stemmed from the fact that people seemed to think size and intelligence were inversely proportional. They looked at him, at his hulking frame, and assumed that he was stupid. But Mitch wasn't stupid. In fact, he was smart. Very smart. And when you were that big, and that smart, it was easy to get into trouble. Especially when you were cursed.

By sixteen, Mitch had dabbled in everything from back-alley boxing to running books to roughing up thugs who owed money to people who liked money. And yet it wasn't any of those things that landed him his first stint in prison. In fact, he was innocent.

Mitch's curse, his *maldición,* as a Spanish foster mother had called it, was that bad things had a way of happening *around* him. The woman had never known its dark extent (she used the term to refer more to broken plates and baseballs through windows and tagged cars), but Mitch suffered from a cosmic case of wrong place, wrong time, and given his many, mostly illegal extracurricular activities, he didn't alibi out very easily.

So when a fight went wrong two streets over and left a man dead, and Mitch's knuckles were still raw from the back-alley match he'd won the night before, it didn't look good. He got off that time, but it was barely two weeks before it happened again. Another person died. It was uncanny and disturbing, and, though Mitch hated to admit it, a little thrilling. Or it would be, if Mitch didn't keep getting caught in the middle. It was becoming a problem, this trail of bodies, because even though he didn't make any of them, it certainly looked that way to the police, and by the third death, Metro PD seemed to think it would be easier to lock him up. Just in case. A hoodlum. A drain on society. Only a matter of time. The kinds of phrases tossed around by men playing catch with his life.

And just like that, with a curse and a rap sheet he didn't earn, Mitchell Turner went to jail.

FOUR years.

He didn't mind it so much, prison. At least he fit in. In the real world, people took one look at him and tightened their grip on their purses, quickened their pace. Cops took one look and thought *guilty or going to be.* But in prison people took one look and thought *I want him on my side,* or *I don't want to mess with him,* or *he could crack my skull in his elbow,* or any number of far more useful thoughts. His size became a status symbol, even if it denied Mitch the perks of worldly conversation, and even if the staff considered him with skepticism when he checked out a book and was surprised when he used a word with more than two syllables. He spent most of his time trying to hack the prison computers' various safety settings and firewalls, more out of boredom than a desire to cause any real trouble. But at least his curse left him alone.

By the time Mitch got out of jail, he looked more the part than ever. The imposing teen had graduated into a towering adult, flecked with the first of many tattoos. Once out, he lasted a month and a half before the curse caught back up with him. He'd gotten a job in food distribution, mostly because he could unload four times the weight of any other guy on the truck, and because he liked physical work. He might be mentally cut out for a desk job, but he doubted he'd *fit* behind most desks. And everything was going smoothly—shitty apartment and shitty pay but all legally valid—until a man was beaten to death a few blocks from where his crew was unloading peaches. The cops took one look at Mitch and booked him. No bloody knuckles, and two coworkers to swear he had his arms full of fruit the whole time, and none of it mattered. Mitch went straight back to prison.

Good behavior and a staggering lack of evidence got him out in a matter of weeks, but Mitch, in a rare display of cynicism, decided that if he was going to go to back to jail (and given his curse, it was a matter of *when,* not *if*), he might as well commit a crime, since serving time on behalf of others wasn't an entirely satisfying use of his life. And so, Mitch set out to plan the one crime he'd always wanted to commit, for no better reason than it was the subject of books and movies, an archetypal affair involving brains far more than bulk.

Mitchell Turner was going to rob a bank.

MITCH knew three things about robbing a bank.

The first was that, because of his easily identifiable appearance, he couldn't actually go *into* the bank. Even if he disabled the security cameras, the people inside would pick him out of a hundred-person lineup (with his luck, even if he wasn't *in* it). The second was that, given the advances in security-based technology—many of which he'd learned about through observation in prison, but knew to be far more evolved in the private sector—a large component of the heist's success would lie in hacking the bank's systems and codes to disable the vault, which could be done remotely. The third was that he would need help. And thanks to the two prison stints he'd served so far, Mitch had developed a fairly extensive list of acquaintances, many of whom would be stupid, desperate, or otherwise willing enough to take up some guns and set foot inside the bank.

What Mitch didn't count on was that while his hacking would succeed without a hitch, the partners with guns would fail spectacularly, be promptly arrested, and drop his name faster than a hat. And somehow, upon seeing Mitchell Turner in all his physical prowess, the police would pin the gun-laden part of the robbery on him, and the hacking on the three smaller men caught in the actual heist and clearly discernible, even masked, on the security footage. And so Mitch's third strike landed him not in a prison for tax-frauders and info-leakers, but in Wrighton, a maximum security facility where the majority of the inmates had actually committed crimes, and where his size, while impressive, was no guarantee of safety.

And where, three years later, he would come to meet a man named Victor Vale.

XVI

SIX HOURS UNTIL MIDNIGHT

MERIT CENTRAL PRECINCT

ELI stood against the pale gray wall of the police conference room, and readjusted the mask on his face. It was simple, partial, black, running from his temples to his cheekbones, and Serena had teased him for it, but as more than half of Merit's police force accumulated in the room and took him in (the other half would listen in) he was thankful for the disguise. His face was the one thing he couldn't change, and as bad an idea as this was, it would be infinitely worse if the entire force had a chance to memorize his features. Serena stood at the podium and smiled her slow smile and spoke to the gathering men and women.

"What happens at midnight?" she had asked as they drove to the station.

Eli had gripped the steering wheel, knuckles white. "I don't know." He hated saying those words, not just because they were true or because admitting them meant Victor was a step ahead, but because he couldn't *not* say them, because the confession crawled its way up his throat before he thought to swallow. Victor had hung up on him with only the promise of *midnight,* and Eli had been left fighting the urge to throw the phone against the wall.

"The man behind me is a hero," Serena was saying now. Eli watched the eyes of the people in the room glaze slightly at her words. "His name is Eli Ever. He has been protecting your city for months, hunting down the kinds of criminals you do not know about, the kind you cannot stop. He has been working to keep you and your citizens safe. But now he needs your help. I want you to listen to him, and do as he says."

She smiled and stepped away from the podium and its microphone, urging Eli forward with a nod and a lazy smile. Eli let out a low breath, and stepped forward.

"A little over a week ago, a man named Victor Vale broke out of Wrighton Penitentiary along with his cellmate, Mitchell Turner. If you're wondering why you didn't hear about the break on the news, it's because it was not *on* the news." Eli himself didn't know about it until he got Victor's note, until he heard his voice, until he contacted Wrighton. They'd refused to tell him more, but had been happy to inform Serena, when he handed her the phone, that they'd been ordered to keep the escape quiet, due to suspicions about one of the convict's nature, suspicions that had been put aside until the man in question, a Mr. Vale, incapacitated a good chunk of the Wrighton staff without laying a finger on them.

"The reason you did not hear about the prison break," continued Eli, "is because Victor Vale is a confirmed EO." Several heads cocked at the term, torn between Serena's order to listen to him and their own varying degrees of belief. Eli knew that all precincts were given a mandatory day of training on EO protocol, but most of them didn't take it seriously. They couldn't. Decades after the term was coined, EOs were still largely a thing of myths and online forums, kept that way by incidents like the one at Wrighton. Fires smothered instead of spread. It was better for Eli, that cases involving EOs were so readily tamped out instead of made public—it gave him an unobstructed path—but he was constantly amazed by how eager the officials were to have incidents forgotten, and how eager the people involved were to forget. Sure, there

would always be believers, but it helped that the vast majority of
EOs didn't want to be believed in, and those that did, well, they'd
saved Eli the trouble of hunting them down.

But who knows, maybe in another world EOs would have come
to light by now, and the huddle of uniforms before him would
have listened without a shred of disbelief, but Eli had done his job
too well. He'd had a decade to cull the crop, cut the numbers
down, and keep the monsters largely the stuff of stories. And so out
of the crowd, only Stell, who stood at the back of the room, gaze
trained on Eli, took in the words without surprise.

"But now," he continued, "Victor Vale and his accomplice,
Mitchell Turner, are in Merit. In *your* city. And it is imperative
that they are not allowed to escape. Imperative that they be found.
These men have abducted a young girl named Sydney Clarke, and
earlier today, they killed one of your own, Officer Frederick Dane."

The audience stirred at that, shock and anger spilling suddenly
across their faces. They hadn't heard the news—Stell had been
told, but he still looked gray with shock—and it got their attention. Serena could compel them, but this kind of report would do
something different. Agitate them. Motivate them.

"I've been led to believe that these men are planning something
tonight. By midnight. It is crucial that we find these criminals as
soon as possible. But," he added, "for the hostage's safety, we must
take them alive."

Ten years ago, Eli had faltered, and let a monster live. But tonight, he would correct his error, and end Victor's life himself.

"We have no photographic record for you," he added, "but you'll
find physical descriptions arriving on your phones. I want you to
blanket the city, block off the roads out, do whatever you have to
do to find these men before anyone else dies."

Eli took a single step back from the podium. Serena came

forward, and put a hand on his shoulder as she addressed the room.

"Eli Ever is a hero," she said again, and this time the collected Merit Police Department nodded and stood and repeated.

"Eli Ever is a hero. A hero. A hero."

The words echoed and followed them out. Eli followed Serena through the precinct, as the words sank in. A hero. Wasn't he? Heroes saved the world from villains, from evil. Heroes sacrificed themselves to do it. Was he not bloodying his hands and his soul to set the world right? Did he not sacrifice himself every time he stripped away an EO's stolen life?

"Where to now?" asked Serena.

Eli dragged his thoughts back. They were cutting through the precinct garage to a side street where they'd parked the car; he pulled a thin folder from his satchel, and handed it to her. Inside were the profiles for the two remaining EOs in the Merit area, or at least *suspected* EOs. The first was a man named Zachary Flinch, a middle-aged miner who'd suffocated in a tunnel collapse the year before. He'd recovered . . . physically. The second was a young soldier named Dominic Rusher, who stood too close to a buried mine and landed himself in a coma two years prior. He'd come to, and vanished from the hospital. Literally. No one saw him leave. He sprang up in three different cities—no path, no trail, just there and gone and there—before appearing in Merit two months earlier. And as far as Eli could tell, he hadn't vanished again, *yet*.

"Victor mentioned the database when he called," said Eli as they reached the car, "which means he has access to these files, too. Whatever he's planning, I don't need him adopting any more strays."

"I want to come this time," said Serena.

Eli frowned behind his mask. He always did this part alone.

His murders, his *removals,* weren't like golf or porn or poker, some stereotypically male hobby that he didn't want to share. They were rituals, sacrosanct. Part of his covenant. Not only that, but the deaths were a culmination of days, sometimes weeks, of research and reconnaissance and patience. They *belonged* to him. The planning and the execution and the quiet after were his. Serena knew that. She was pushing him. Anger crackled beneath his skin.

He tried to spin the demand in his mind, to regain control. He knew he didn't have time to savor these particular kills. Chances were, he wouldn't even have time to wait for a demonstration. Today the rituals would be broken anyway, defiled.

He could feel Serena watching him struggle, and she seemed delighted by it. But not subdued. She took the file from him, and held up Zachary Flinch's profile.

"Just once," she said, the words tipping the scale.

Eli checked his watch. It was well after six. And there was no question she would expedite the process.

"Just once," he said, climbing in the car.

Serena beamed, and slid into the passenger's seat.

XVII

SYDNEY was perched on the couch with Dol at her feet and the folder of executed EOs open in her lap when Mitch came in. The sun was setting beyond the floor-to-ceiling windows, and she looked up as he pulled the carton of chocolate milk from the fridge. He looked tired as he leaned his elbows—they were dusted with something chalkish and white—on the dark granite counter.

"Are you okay?" she asked.

"Where's Victor?"

"He went out."

Mitch swore under his breath. "He's crazy. The area is crawling with cops after that stunt."

"Which stunt?" asked Sydney, shuffling the papers in the folder. "Killing the cop or answering Eli's phone call?"

Mitch smiled grimly. "Both."

Sydney looked down at the face of a dead woman in her lap. "He can't mean it," she said quietly. "About meeting Eli at midnight. He doesn't mean it, right?"

"Victor means what he says," said Mitch. "But he wouldn't have said it if he didn't have a plan."

Mitch pushed off the counter, and vanished down the hall, and a moment later Sydney heard the bathroom door shut, and the shower snap on. She went back to reading the profiles, telling herself it was only because there was nothing good on television. The truth was, she didn't want to think about what would happen at midnight, or worse, what would happen *after*. She hated the *what-ifs* that crawled into her head the moment she lost focus. What if Eli won, what if Victor lost, what if Serena . . . she didn't even know what to think about her sister, what to hope for, what to fear. There were these traitorous parts of her that still wanted to feel Serena's arms around her, but she knew that now she had to run away from—not toward—her sister.

Sydney forced her eyes over the profiles in the folder, tried to focus on the EOs' lives and deaths—tried not to picture Victor's photo in among them, a black *x* across his calm, clear face—and guessed at what their powers were, even though she knew they could be anything. Victor had explained that it depended on the person, on their wants and wills and last thoughts.

The last profile was her own. She'd reprinted it after Victor took the first copy, and now her eyes wandered over the photo of her face. Unlike the other candid shots that filled the folder, hers was staged: head up, shoulders back, eyes leveled directly at the camera. It was a yearbook photo from last year, taken a week or so before the accident, and Sydney had loved it dearly because the camera had somehow, magically, caught her the moment before she smiled, and the proud upturn of her chin and faint crease in the corner of her mouth made her look *just* like Serena.

The only difference between this copy of the photo and the original was that this one had no *x* drawn through it. Eli knew by now that she was here, alive, and she hoped he felt sick when he'd heard about Barry's body walking back into the bank, when he'd put the pieces together and realized that it was her doing, that a few shots fired into the woods didn't equal a dead girl. Maybe it should have upset her, to see her own profile in the dead EO folder, and it had at first, but the shock had worn off, and the profile's existence in the digital trash bin, the fact that they'd underestimated her, assumed she was dead, and most of all the fact that she *wasn't*, made her smile.

"What's got you grinning?"

Sydney looked up to find Mitch freshly showered and dressed, a towel draped around his neck. She didn't realize how much time had passed. That happened to her more than she liked to admit. She'd blink, and the sun would be in a different position, or the show on TV would be over, or someone would be finishing a conversation she'd never heard them start.

"I hope Victor hurts him," she said cheerfully. "A lot."

"Jesus. Three days and you're already taking after him." Mitch sagged into a chair, ran his hand over his shaved head. "Look, Sydney, there's something you need to understand about Victor—"

"He's not a bad man," she said.

"There are no good men in this game," said Mitch.

But Sydney didn't care about *good*. She wasn't sure she believed in it. "I'm not afraid of Victor."

"I know." He sounded sad when he said it.

XVIII

THE third time Mitchell Turner went to jail, his curse followed him.

No matter where he went, or what he did (or didn't do), people kept dying. He lost two cellmates at the hands of others, one cellmate at the man's own hands, and a friend, who collapsed in the yard during the exercise period. So when the slim, polished form of Victor Vale appeared at the door of his cell one afternoon, pale in the dark gray prison uniforms, he figured the man was a goner. He was probably in for laundering, maybe a Ponzi scheme. Something heavy enough to make the right people angry and land him in max security, but light enough that he looked thoroughly out of place there. Mitch should have written him off but, still troubled by the death of his last cellmate, he became determined to keep Victor alive.

He assumed he would have his work cut out for him.

Victor didn't speak to Mitch for three days. Mitch, admittedly, didn't speak to Victor, either. There was something about the man, something Mitch couldn't place, but he didn't like it, in a primal, visceral way, and he found himself leaning vaguely away from Victor when the latter came near. The other inmates did it, too, on the rare occasions that first week when Victor ventured out among them. But even though it made Mitch uncomfortable, he followed the man, flanked him, constantly searching for an attacker, a threat. As far as Mitch could tell, his curse seemed firmly grounded in his proximity to people. When he was near them, they got hurt. But he couldn't seem to figure out how close was too close, how near he needed to be to doom a life, and he thought that maybe, if for once his proximity could save a person instead of somehow marking them . . . maybe then, he could break the curse.

Victor didn't ask him why he stayed so close, but he didn't tell him not to, either.

Mitch knew the attack would come. It always did. A way for the old to test the new. Sometimes it wasn't so bad, a few punches, a bit of roughing up. But other times, when men had a taste for blood or a bone to pick or even if they were just having a shitty day, it could get out of hand.

He followed Victor to the commons, to the yard, to the lunch-room. Mitch would sit on one side of the table, Victor on the other, picking at his lunch, while Mitch spent the entire time scanning the room. Victor never looked up from his plate. He didn't look at his plate, either, not exactly. His eyes had an unfocused intensity, as if he were somewhere else, unconcerned with the cage around him or the monsters inside.

Like a predator, Mitch realized one day. He'd seen enough nature specials on the common room set to know that prey had eyes on the sides of their head, were constantly on guard, but predators' eyes were forward-facing, close together, unafraid. Despite the fact that Victor was half the size of most inmates, and didn't look like he'd ever *been* in a fight, let alone won one, everything about him said predator.

And for the first time, Mitch wondered if Victor was really the one who needed protecting.

XIX

FOUR AND A HALF HOURS UNTIL MIDNIGHT
THE SUBURBS OF MERIT

ZACHARY Flinch lived alone.

That much Serena could tell before she ever set eyes on him. The front yard was a tangle of weeds, the car on the gravel strip of a driveway had two spares, the screen door was torn, and a coil of rope tied to a half-dead tree had been chewed through by whatever was once tied there. Whatever his power, if he even *was* an EO, it wasn't making him any money. Serena frowned, reconstructing his profile from memory. The entire page of data had been innocuous, except for the inversion—the Rebirth Principle, Eli had called it, a re-creation of self. It wasn't necessarily positive, or even voluntary, but always marked, and Flinch ticked off that box with a bold red check. In the wake of his trauma, everything about his life had changed. Not subtle changes, either, but full flips. He went from being married with three kids to being divorced, unemployed, and under a restraining order. His survival—or *revival*, rather—should have been cause for celebration, for joy. Instead, everything and everyone had fled. That, or he had pushed them away. He'd been to a slew of psychiatrists, and been prescribed antipsychotics, but judging by the state of his yard, he wasn't in a good place.

Serena knocked, wondering what would scare a man enough to throw his life away after he'd beaten death itself to keep it.

No one answered the door. The sun had dipped below the horizon, and when she exhaled it made small puffs of steam in the dusk. She knocked again, and could hear the sound of the television within. Eli sighed and pressed his back against the peeling paint of the siding by the door.

"Hello," she called. "Mr. Flinch? Could you come to the door?"

Sure enough, she could make out the shifting of feet, and a few moments later Zach Flinch appeared in the doorway wearing an old polo and a pair of jeans. Both were a size too big, making it look like he'd withered since putting them on. Over his shoulder she could see the coffee table littered with empty cans, the takeout boxes stacked on the floor beside it.

"Who are you?" he asked, dark rings beneath his eyes. There was a gruff tremor in his voice.

Serena clutched his dossier to her chest. "A friend. I just have a few questions."

Flinch grunted, but didn't shut the door in her face. She held his gaze so he wouldn't see Eli standing a couple feet to his right, still wearing his black hero's mask.

"Is your name Zachary Flinch?" she asked.

He nodded.

"Is it true you were involved in a mining accident last year? A tunnel collapse?"

He nodded.

She could feel Eli getting impatient, but she wasn't done. She wanted to know.

"In the wake of your accident, did anything change? Did you change?"

Flinch's eyes widened in surprise, but even as they did, he answered with a nod, his face caught between confusion and complacence. Serena smiled softly. "I see."

"How did you find me? Who are you?"

"Like I said, I'm a friend."

Flinch took a step forward, over the threshold. His shoes tangled in the stray greenish brown weeds that were trying to reclaim the porch. "I didn't want to die alone," he muttered. "That's all. Down there in the dark, I didn't want to die alone, but I didn't want this. Can you make them stop?"

"Make what stop, Mr. Flinch?"

"Please make them go away. Dru couldn't see them either till I showed her but they're everywhere. I just didn't want to die alone. But I can't take it. I don't want to see them. I don't want to hear them. Please make them stop."

Serena held out her hand. "Why don't you show me wha—"

The rest of the word was cut off by the gun as Eli swung it up to Zach Flinch's temple and pulled the trigger. Blood streaked across the siding of the house, flecking Serena's hair and dotting her face like freckles. Eli lowered the weapon and crossed himself.

"Why did you do that?" She spat, livid.

"He wanted to make them stop," said Eli.

"But I wasn't done—"

"I was merciful. He was sick. Besides, he confirmed he was an EO," said Eli, already turning toward the car. "A demonstration was no longer necessary."

"You have such a complex," she snapped. "You always have to be in control."

Eli gave a low, mocking laugh. "Says the siren."

"I just wanted to help."

"No," he said. "You wanted to *play*." He stormed away.

"Eli Ever, *stop*."

His shoe caught in the gravel, and stuck. The gun was still in his hand. For the briefest moment, Serena's temper got the best of her and she had to bite her tongue to stop herself from making him put the weapon to his own temple. The urge eased, and she stepped over Flinch's body and descended the stairs, coming up behind Eli. She wrapped her arms around Eli's waist and kissed the back of his neck.

"You know I don't want this kind of control," she whispered. "Now put the gun away." Eli's hand slid the weapon back into its holster. "You're not going to kill me today."

He turned to face her, wrapped his hands, now empty, around her back, and pulled her close, his lips brushing her ear.

"One of these days, Serena," he whispered, "you're going to forget to say that."

She tensed in his grip, and knew that he could feel it, but when she answered, her voice was even, light.

"Not today."

His hands fell away as he turned toward the car and held the door open for her.

"Are you coming with me?" he asked as they pulled out of the gravel drive. "To find Dominic?"

Serena chewed her lip, and shook her head. "No. Have your fun. I'm going back to the hotel to wash the blood out of my hair before it stains. Drop me off on your way."

Eli nodded, the relief written across his face as he gunned the engine, leaving Flinch on the porch, one lifeless hand trailing in the weeds.

FOUR HOURS UNTIL MIDNIGHT

DOWNTOWN MERIT

VICTOR made his way back toward the hotel, a bag of takeout beneath one arm. It had been a pretense, really, this errand, a chance to escape the confines of the hotel room, a chance to breathe and think and plan. He ambled down the sidewalk, careful to keep his pace casual, his expression calm. Since the meeting with Officer Dane, the call with Eli, and the midnight ultimatum, the number of cops on the streets of Merit had gone dramatically up. Not all in uniform, of course, but all alert. Mitch had carved out any photographic evidence from the system, from Lockland University profile pictures down to the mug shots that were logged at Wrighton. All the Merit cops would have to go on was a stick-figure drawing, Eli's own memory (ten years out of date, since unlike him, Victor *had* aged), and descriptions from the penitentiary staff. Still, the police weren't to be discounted. Mitch's size made him terribly conspicuous, and Sydney stood out for being a child. Only Victor, arguably the most wanted of the group, had a defense mechanism. He smiled to himself as he strode within reach of a cop. The officer never looked up.

Victor had discovered that pain was a spectacularly nuanced sensation. A large, sudden quantity could cripple, of course, but it had many more practical applications than torture. Victor found that, by inflicting a subtle amount of pain on those in a determined radius, he could induce a subconscious aversion to his presence. People didn't register the pain, yet they leaned ever so slightly away. Their attention, too, seemed to bend around him, lending Victor a kind of invisibility. It served him in prison, and it served him now.

Victor made his way past the abandoned Falcon Price site and checked his watch again, marveling at the structure of revenge, the fact that years of waiting and planning and wanting would come down to hours—minutes, even—of execution. His pulse quickened with the thrill of it as he made his way back to the Esquire.

∞

ELI dropped Serena off on the Esquire curb with the sole instruction to pay attention and let him know if she noticed *anything* unusual. Victor was going to send another message, it was only a matter of when, and as the clock ticked away the minutes until midnight, Eli knew that his level of control would depend almost entirely on how quickly he got the memo. The later it got, the less time he'd have to plan, prepare, and he was sure that was Victor's intent, to keep him in the dark as long as possible.

Now he idled on the painted pavement of the drop-off square in front of the hotel, sliding the mask free and dropping it onto the passenger seat before reaching for Dominic Rusher's profile. Rusher had only been in the city a few months, but he already had a history with the Merit Police, a list of misdemeanors consisting almost exclusively of drunk and disorderly conduct charges. The vast majority of the trouble had emanated not from Dominic's shitty hole of an apartment in the south part of the city, but from a bar. One particular bar. The Three Crows. Eli knew the address. He pulled away from the hotel, just missing Victor and his bag of takeout.

TWO cops stood in the Esquire's lobby, their full attention on a young blonde with her back to the hotel's revolving front doors. Victor wandered in unnoticed and headed for the stairs. When he reached the hotel room he found Sydney reading on the couch, Dol lying beneath her feet, and Mitch drinking straight from a carton at the counter while tapping out code one-handed on his laptop.

"Have any trouble?" asked Victor, setting the food down.

"With the body? No." Mitch set the carton aside. "But it was close with the cops. Jesus, Vale, they're everywhere. I don't exactly blend in as it is."

"That's what parking garage entrances are for. Besides, we just have to make it a few more hours," said Victor.

"About that . . . ," started Mitch, but Victor was busy scribbling something on a scrap of paper. He slid it toward him.

"What's this for?"

"It's Dane's ID and pass code. For the database. I need you to prepare a new flagged profile."

"And who are we flagging?"

Victor smiled, and gestured to himself. Mitch groaned. "I take it this has to do with midnight."

Victor nodded. "The Falcon Price high-rise. Ground floor."

"That place is a cage. You're going to get trapped."

"I have a plan," said Victor simply.

"Care to share?" Victor said nothing. Mitch grumbled. "I'm not using your photo. It took me ages to scrub it from the systems."

Victor looked around the room. His gaze settled on the latest Vale self-help tome he'd been inking out. He took it up, flashed the spine at Mitch, where VALE was written in glossy caps. "This'll do."

Mitch continued muttering even as he took the book and got to work.

Victor turned his attention toward Sydney. He carried a tub of noodles to the couch, and sagged onto the leather cushions as he offered it to her. Sydney set aside the dead EO folder and accepted the food, fingers curling around the still-warm container. She didn't eat. Neither did he. Victor stared past the windows and listened to the sounds of Mitch composing the post. His fingers itched to black out lines, but Mitch was using the book, so he closed his eyes and tried to find quiet, peace. He didn't picture sprawling fields or blue skies or water drops. He pictured squeezing the trigger three times, blood blossoming on Eli's chest in the same pattern it had on his, pictured carving lines into Eli's skin, watching them fade so he could do it over again, over and over and over. *Are you afraid yet?* he would ask when the floor was slick with Eli's blood. *Are you afraid?*

XXI

THREE AND A HALF HOURS UNTIL MIDNIGHT
THE ESQUIRE HOTEL

"DO you really have a plan?" asked Sydney sometime later.

Victor dragged his eyes back open, and said the same thing he'd said in the graveyard, when she asked if Wrighton Penitentiary had let him go. The same words and the same tone and the same look. "Of course," he said.

"Is it a good plan?" pressed Sydney. Her legs swung from the couch, boots grazing Dol's ears with every pass. The dog didn't seem to mind.

"No," said Victor. "Probably not."

Sydney made a sound, something between a cough and a sigh. Victor wasn't terribly fluent in her language yet, but guessed it was a kind of sad affirmative, the pre-teen version of *gotcha* or *okay*. The clock on the wall said it was almost nine p.m.. Victor closed his eyes again.

"I don't get it," said Sydney a few minutes later. She was scratching Dol's ear with her shoe. The dog's head rocked back and forth gently with the motion.

"What don't you get?" asked Victor, eyes still closed.

"If you want to find Eli, and Eli wants to find you, why do you have to go through all this? Why can't you just find each other?"

Victor blinked, and considered the small blond thing beside him on the couch. Her eyes were wide and waiting, but they were already losing their innocence. What little she'd clung to and brought with her down that road in the rain had faded in the face of Victor's pragmatic execution, his promises and his threats. She'd been betrayed, shot, saved, healed, hurt, healed again, forced to resurrect two men, only to witness the reassassination of one of them. She'd gotten tangled up in this, by Eli and then by Victor. She was like a child, but not a child, and Victor couldn't help but wonder if becoming an EO had hollowed her out the way it had him, had all of them—cut the ties of something vital and human. He wasn't protecting her, not by treating her like a normal kid. She wasn't normal.

"You asked me if I have a plan," he said, sitting forward. "I didn't, at first. I had options, yes, ideas, and factors, but not a plan."

"But you have one now."

"I do. But because of Eli, and because of your sister, I only have one shot to get it right. The first person to act sacrifices the element of surprise, and I can't afford to do that right now. Eli has a siren on his side, which means he could compel the entire city. Maybe he already has. I have a hacker, a half-dead dog, and a child. It's hardly an arsenal."

Sydney frowned and reached for the folder of living EOs. She held it out to him. "So make one. Or at least, make yours stronger. Try. Eli sees EOs—us—as monsters. But you don't, right?"

Victor wasn't sure how he felt about EOs. Up until he fetched Sydney from the side of the road, he'd only ever known one EO, himself excluded, and that was Eli. If he'd had to judge based on the two of them, then ExtraOrdinaries were damaged, to say the least. But these words people threw around—humans, monsters, heroes, villains—to Victor it was all just a matter of semantics. Someone could call themselves a hero and still walk around killing dozens. Someone else could be labeled a villain for trying to stop them. Plenty of humans were monstrous, and plenty of monsters knew how to play at being human. The difference between Victor and Eli, he suspected, wasn't their opinion on EOs. It was their reaction to them. Eli seemed intent to slaughter them, but Victor didn't see why a useful skill should be destroyed, just because of its origin. EOs were weapons, yes, but weapons with minds and wills and bodies, things that could be bent and twisted and broken and *used*.

But there were so many unknowns. Whether the EOs were still alive was an unknown. What their powers were was an unknown. Whether they would be receptive was an unknown, and while Victor possessed a compelling argument, since the other side wanted them dead and he had use for them alive, the fact remained that to recruit an EO would mean introducing unpredictable and unreliable elements into his equation. Add to that the fact that Eli was probably busy eliminating Victor's options, and it seemed more trouble than it was worth.

"Please, Victor," said Sydney, still holding out the folder. And so, to pacify her, and pass the time, he took it, and flipped the cover back. The page with the blue-haired girl had been removed, leaving only two profiles.

The first profile belonged to a man named Zachary Flinch. Victor had read through the man's page earlier that day, while waiting for Mitch's call, so he knew it was a dead end. Everything about the suspected EO was too ambiguous—an EO's ability seemed to have at least a tangential relationship to either the nature of death or the subject's mental state, but it was still a guessing game—and the fact that everyone had left in the wake of the accident suggested trouble. More trouble than Victor had time for.

He turned to the second profile, the one he hadn't gotten to yet, skimmed the page, and stopped.

Dominic Rusher was in his late twenties, an ex-soldier who'd had the misfortune of standing too close to a land mine overseas. The explosion had shattered many of Dominic's bones, and left him in a coma for two weeks, but it wasn't the coma or his new-found habit of disappearing that attracted Victor's attention. It was the brief medical note at the bottom of the page. According to the military hospital records, Rusher had been prescribed 35 milligrams of methahydricone.

It was a high dose of a fairly ambiguous synthetic opioid, but Victor had spent one rather slow summer in prison memorizing the extensive list of painkillers currently available via prescription, their purposes, dosages, and official names, as well as their medical ones, so he recognized the drug on sight. Not only that, but he felt sure that unless Eli had dedicated the same amount of time, he *wouldn't* recognize it.

Fate, it seemed, was smiling on Victor again.

With mere hours until his midnight meeting, he knew there was no time or place for building trust or loyalty, but perhaps these could be supplanted by *need*. And need, Victor had learned, could be as powerful as any emotional bond. The latter was neurotic, complicated, but need could be simple, as primal as fear or pain. Need could be the foundation of allegiance. And Victor had exactly what Dominic needed. He could supply, if Dominic's power was worth it. There was only one way to find out.

Victor folded the profile and put it in his pocket.

"Grab your coat, Mitch. We're going out."

"Car or foot?"

"Car."

"Absolutely not. Did you miss the memo about the cops? Last time I checked, that vehicle is stolen."

"Well, we'll just have to make sure we don't attract attention, then."

Mitch mumbled something unkind as he reached for his coat. Sydney ran to get hers from the bedroom where she'd abandoned it.

"No, Syd," said Victor when she reappeared, already tugging on her large red coat. "You need to stay here."

"But it was my idea!" she said.

"And it's a good one, but you still have to stay."

"Why?" she whined. "And don't tell me it's too dangerous. You said that about the cop, and then you dragged me in anyway."

Victor scoffed. "It *is* too dangerous, but that's not why you have to stay here. We stand out enough without a missing child, and I need you to do something for me."

Sydney crossed her arms and considered him skeptically.

"If I'm not back by ten thirty," he said, "I need you to hit the Post button on Mitch's computer, and upload my profile to the database. He has the window up and ready."

"Why ten thirty?" asked Mitch, buttoning his coat.

"Long enough for someone to see it, but hopefully not long enough for them to be prepared. It's a risk, I know."

"Not the biggest one you're taking," said Mitch.

"Is that all?" asked Sydney.

"No," said Victor. He patted down the pockets of his coat. His hand vanished, and then came out with a blue lighter. He didn't smoke, but it always seemed to come in handy. "At eleven, I need you to start burning the folders. All of them. Use the sink." He held out the lighter. "One page at a time, you understand?"

Syd took the small blue device, turning it over in her hands.

"This is really important," he said. "We can't be leaving evidence around, okay? You see why I need you here?" At last she nodded. Dol whined faintly.

"You're going to come back, right?" she asked when they reached the door.

Victor looked over his shoulder. "Of course I will," he said. "That's my favorite lighter."

Sydney almost smiled as the door shut.

"I get burning the papers, but why one page at a time?" asked Mitch as he and Victor were headed down the stairs.

"To keep her busy."

Mitch thrust his hands into his coat. "We're not coming back then, are we?"

"Not tonight."

XXII

THREE HOURS UNTIL MIDNIGHT

THE THREE CROWS BAR

ELI sat in a booth along the back wall of the Three Crows and waited for Dominic Rusher to show up. He'd checked with the bartender when he first arrived, and had been assured that Rusher came every night around nine o'clock. Eli had been early, but he had nothing else to do besides wait for midnight and whatever that would bring, so he'd ordered a beer and retreated to the corner booth, savoring the time away from Serena more than the booze.

The drink was mostly for appearances anyway, since regenerating negated its effect, and alcohol without inebriation was far less enticing (he'd been carded, too, and the novelty of *that* had long worn off). But the distance from Serena was important—vital, he'd found—to maintaining his slim hold on control. The longer he was with her, the more things seemed to blur, an intoxication Eli's body didn't overcome so easily. He should have killed her when he had the chance. Now, with the police involved, it was messy. Their loyalty was to her, not to him, and they both knew it.

A new city, that's what he needed.

After midnight and Victor and this whole mess was sorted out, he'd find a new city. Start over. Away from Detective Stell. Away from Serena, too, if he could help it. He didn't even mind the prospect of his old method, the time and dedication it took, the weeks of searching for the mere moments of payoff. Things had gotten too easy lately, and easy meant dangerous. Easy led to mistakes. Serena was a mistake. Eli took a sip of beer and checked his phone for messages. There were none.

Eli had hunted here once, a few years back, before Serena, when he was still a ghost, just passing through. The place was loud, and crowded, made for people who liked to surround themselves with chaos instead of quiet, ambient noise built of glass and shouting and music to which you could never discern the lyrics. It was an easy place to be invisible, to vanish, swallowed by the low light and the din of drunk and drinking and angry people. But even knowing that, Eli was neither bold enough nor foolish enough to perform a public execution. Serena might have secured him the police, but the people in the Three Crows weren't much for cops or conformity. A problem could escalate into a disaster in a place like this, especially without Serena to soothe the masses.

Eli reminded himself *again* that he was glad to be rid of her influence, both over others and over him. Now he could, out of want and necessity, do this his way.

He checked the time. Less than three hours until . . . until what? Victor had set the deadline to rattle him, put him on edge. He was disturbing Eli's calm, like a kid dropping rocks into a pond, making ripples, and Eli saw him doing it and still felt rippled, which perturbed him even more. Well, Eli was taking back control, of his mind and his life and his night. He drew his fingers through the ring left by his beer glass on the old wood table, before writing one word in the film of water.

EVER.

XXIII

"**WHY** Ever?"

Victor posed the question from across the table. Eli had just died. Victor had just brought him back. Now the two were sitting in the bar a few blocks down from their apartment, buzzed from several rounds (or at least Victor was) and the fact they'd been lucky enough to survive an acute attack of stupidity. But Eli felt odd. Not bad, just . . . different. Distant. He couldn't put his finger on it yet. Something was missing, though, he could feel the absence of it, even if he couldn't deduce the shape. Physically though—and he supposed that mattered most, all things considered—he felt fine, persistently so, suspiciously so, given that for some time that evening he had been an inanimate object instead of a living being.

"What do you mean?" he asked, sipping his beer.

"I mean," said Victor, "you could pick any name. Why pick Ever?"

"Why not?"

"No," said Victor, waving his drink. "No, Eli. You don't do anything like that."

"Like what?"

"Without thinking. You had to have a reason."

"How do you know?"

"Because I know you. I see you."

Eli drew his fingers through a ring of water on the table. "I don't want to be forgotten."

He said it so softly he worried Victor wouldn't hear, not over the chatter of the bar, but he clamped his hand down on Eli's shoulder. For a moment he looked so serious, but then he let go and slumped back in his seat.

"Tell you what," said Victor. "You remember me, and I'll remember you, and that way we won't be forgotten."

"That's shit logic, Vic."

"It's perfect."

"And what happens when we're dead?"

"We won't die, then."

"You make cheating death sound so simple."

"We do seem awfully good at it," said Victor cheerfully. He lifted his glass. "To never dying."

Eli lifted his. "To being remembered."

Their glasses clinked as Eli added, "Forever."

XXIV

DOMINIC Rusher was a broken man. Literally.

Most of the bones on his left side, the side nearest the IED, were pinned or screwed or synthetic, the skin pocked with scars beneath his clothes. His hair—for three years buzzed to military standards—had grown out, and now hung shaggy around his eyes, one of which was fake. His skin was tan and his shoulders strong, his posture still too straight to blend entirely with the bar's regulars, and despite it all he was clearly broken.

Eli didn't need the files to tell him any of that; he could see it as the man walked up to the counter, slid onto a stool, and ordered his first drink. Time was ticking past and Eli's grip tightened on his own glass, as he watched the ex-soldier kick off his night with a Jack and Coke. He had to resist the urge to abandon the booth and the beer and shoot Dominic in the back of the head, just to be done with it. Eli did his best to smother the flare of impatience; his rituals existed for a reason, and he would—and had—*compromised* them on occasion, but would not abandon them, even now. To slay without cause would be an abuse of power, and an insult to God. The blood of EOs washed from his skin. The blood of innocents would not. He had to get Dominic out of the bar, had to get a confession, if not a demonstration, before he executed him. Besides, Dominic would make fine bait. So long as he was instilled at the bar, and in Eli's sight, he was as useful alive as he was dead, because if Victor came looking for the broken man, and made his way here before midnight, Eli would be waiting, and he would be ready.

VICTOR drove, while Mitch lay sprawled across the backseat, as out of sight as possible given his mass. The city slid by, the greens and reds and office-window whites streaking past as Victor wove the car through the gridded streets, out of the downtown and into the old sector. They kept to the roads that curled through the side streets of Merit instead of the main grid that ran in and out of the city, avoiding any street that eventually led to a toll or a bridge or any other potential checkpoint. They watched their speed, pacing traffic when it went too fast because going slow would stand out just as much as speeding. Victor guided the stolen car through Merit, and soon the numbered avenues and lettered roads gave way to named streets. Real names, trees and people and places, clustered buildings, some dark, boarded, abandoned, and some bulging with life.

"Take a left," said Mitch, consulting the card-sized, shifting map on his phone. Victor checked his watch and ticked off the time it was taking to get to the bar, subtracted it from midnight to figure out how long they really had. He couldn't be late. Not tonight. He tried to find calm, find peace, but excitement rattled inside of him like loose change. He rapped his free hand on his leg and swallowed the whisper that this was a bad idea. It was better than sitting still. Besides, they had time. Plenty of time.

"Left again," said Mitch. Victor turned.

They'd spent the first half of the drive going over the plan, and now that it was laid out, and all that remained was to execute it, they drove in a silence punctuated only by Mitch's directions and Victor's restless tapping, and the roads rolling away beneath them.

∞

WHILE Victor drove, Mitch wondered.

Wondered if he would survive the night.

Wondered if Victor would, too.

Wondered what tomorrow would bring if they both did.

Wondered what Victor would do to occupy his thoughts once Eli was gone. If Eli was gone.

Mitch wondered what *he* would do next. He and Victor had never discussed their partnership, its terms and termination, but it had always been about this. About finding Eli. There was never any mention of what would come next. He wondered if there *was* a next, in Victor's mind.

The moving green dot on his phone reached the red still dot that marked the Three Crows Bar, and Mitch sat up.

"We're here."

∞

VICTOR parked in the lot across from the bar, even though it was crowded and narrow, and would prevent a quick exit, especially under pursuit. But with a stolen car and the cops on high alert, he didn't dare do anything that might stand out. He wasn't about to get picked up for a parking ticket on a stolen car. Not tonight. He shut off the engine, stepped out, and examined the huddle of bricks across the street that declared itself to be the Three Crows Bar, a trio of metal birds perching on the sign above the front doors. To the left of the bar was an alley, and as the two men crossed the street, Victor could make out the bar's side entrance set into the stained brick wall. When they reached the curb, he made his way toward the alley, and Mitch made his way toward the bar. Behind his eyes, Victor saw the pieces of his game lining up on the city-shaped board, chess and Battleship and Risk. His move.

"Hey," he called, as Mitch's hand gripped the front door. "Be careful."

Mitch smiled crookedly, and went inside.

XXV

"YOU want more milk?"

It was the first thing Victor Vale ever said to Mitchell Turner.

They were sitting in the cafeteria. Mitch had spent three days wondering absently what Victor's voice would sound like if he ever decided to talk. If he even *could* talk. Over the course of lunch, Mitch had actually taken to imagining that he couldn't, that beneath the collar of his prison-issued shirt some ghastly scar carved a smile across his throat, or that behind his curling lips there simply was no tongue. It sounded weird, but prison was boring, and Mitch found his imagination going to strange places more often than not. So when Victor finally opened his mouth and asked with perfect elocution if Mitch wanted another carton of milk, the latter was caught between surprise and disappointment.

He scraped his words together. "Uh. Yeah. Sure." He hated how stupid he sounded, how slow, but Victor only chuckled, and pushed up from the table.

"Keeps the body strong," he said before making his way across the cafeteria to the food counter. The moment he was gone, Mitch knew he should have followed. He'd spent three days shadowing his new cellmate, but the question had caught him off-guard, and now in its wake, he had a sinking feeling that he'd just sacrificed his chance to break the curse. He craned his neck in search of

Victor only to have someone slam him forward toward the table, and swing an arm around his shoulder. From across the room, the gesture might have looked friendly, but Mitch could see the sharpened metal in Ian Packer's hand, the edge angled toward his cheek. Mitch was twice the man's size but he knew the damage Ian could do before he'd be able to wrestle him off. Besides, Packer was one of those people who, despite his size, had power here, sway. Too much in a place this small.

"Hey, hey," said Packer, his breath foul. "Playing puppy dog?"

"What do you want?" growled Mitch, keeping his eyes on the tray in front of him.

"Been wanting you to play watchdog for my group for a year, been so kind and patient with your pacifistic shit"—Mitch was surprised (and a little impressed) that Packer knew the word *pacifistic*—"and suddenly this pointy prick shows up and you're all over the role." He tutted in Mitch's ear. "I should fuck him up just for wasting your time and talent, Turner."

A small carton of milk landed on his tray, and Mitch looked up to find Victor standing there, surveying the situation with mild interest. Packer's grip tightened on the sharpened metal as his attention flicked to the new man, and Mitch's heart sank. Another cellmate lost.

But Victor only tilted his head curiously at Packer.

"Is that a shiv?" he asked, bringing his shoe to rest on the bench, his hand to rest on his knee. "We didn't have those in isolation." *Isolation?* thought Mitch. "I've always wanted to see one."

"Oh, I'll show it to you close, you little fuck." Packer's arm vanished from Mitch's shoulders. He lunged for Victor, who did nothing more than set his foot back on the floor and curl his fingers into a fist, and Packer, halfway to him, buckled to the ground, screaming. Mitch blinked, confused by what had happened . . . and not happened. Victor had never even touched the guy.

The room broke into motion at the sound of the scream, the inmates on their feet and the guards on their way, as Mitch sat and watched and Victor stood and watched and Packer howled and writhed on the floor, hand bloody from clenching the sharpened sliver of metal as he twisted and screamed. There was a moment, before anyone else reached them, when Mitch saw Victor smile. A wolf's smile, thin and sharp.

"What's going on?" shouted a guard as he and another reached the table. Mitch looked to Victor, who only shrugged. The smile was gone, a faint crease of concern between his eyes.

"No idea," he said. "Guy comes over to talk. One minute he's fine and the next"—Victor snapped his fingers, and Mitch flinched—"just starts convulsing. Better get him checked out before he hurts himself."

The guards pinned the writhing Packer to the floor, and pried the blade from his shredded hand as his screams faded into groans and then into nothing. The convict had fainted. Somewhere between Packer attacking Victor, Victor dropping him with a look, and the guards reaching the scene, Mitch had extricated himself from the table bench, and now stood a few feet behind his cellmate, sipping his milk, and watching the events unfold, marveling in part at the scene, and in part at the fact that for once *he* hadn't been blamed.

But what the hell had happened?

Mitch must have whispered the question, because Victor honored him with a pale raised brow before turning back toward the cell blocks. Mitch followed.

"Well?" asked Victor as they made their way down the concrete halls. "Do *you* feel I'm wasting your time and talent?"

Mitch considered the impossible man beside him. Something

had changed. The discomfort, the aversion that he'd felt for three straight days had faded. Everyone else still seemed to bend away as they passed, but Mitch felt only wonder and, admittedly, a touch of fear. When they reached their cell, and he still hadn't answered, Victor stopped, rested his back against the bars, and looked at him. Not at his hulking shoulders or his meaty fists with their scarred knuckles, or the tattoos that ran up his neck, but at his face. He looked him in the eyes, even if he had to look up a bit to do so.

"I don't need a bodyguard," said Victor.

"I noticed that," said Mitch.

Victor let out a cough of a laugh. "Yes, well," he said, "I don't want everyone else to notice, too."

Mitch had been right. Victor Vale was a wolf among sheep. And it took a lot to make 463 hardened criminals look the part of prey.

"So what *do* you want then?" he asked.

Victor's lips curled into that same, dangerous smile. "A friend."

"That's all?" he asked, disbelieving.

"A good friend, Mr. Turner, is very hard to find."

Mitch watched Victor push off the bars and head into the cell, lifting a library book from his cot before settling onto it.

Mitch didn't know what had just happened back in the cafeteria, but a decade in and out of prison had taught him this: There were some people you had to stay away from, people who poisoned everything in reach. Then there were people you wanted to stick with, the ones with silver tongues and golden touches. And then, there were people you stood beside, because it meant you weren't in their way. And whoever Victor Vale was, whatever he was, and whatever he was up to, the only thing Mitch knew was that he did *not* want to be in his way.

XXVI

TWO HOURS UNTIL MIDNIGHT
THE THREE CROWS BAR

ELI tapped his phone awake, tensing when he saw the time. Still no Victor, and Dominic seemed to be an installation at the bar. Eli frowned, and dialed Serena, but she didn't pick up. When her voice mail kicked in, he hung up, eager to click End before her slow, melodic words could issue any instructions. He thought of Victor's threat: *It's clever, using the police database to find your targets. I'm a bit insulted I haven't shown up on there yet, but give it time. I just got here.*

Eli logged on to the database, hoping for clues, but it was after ten, and the only flagged profile belonged to the man currently stationed at the counter, nursing his third Jack and Coke. Eli frowned and put the phone away. His bait didn't seem to be drawing any fish. The seat beside Dominic emptied—it had been taken up and subsequently abandoned three times over the course of the hour—and Eli, tired of waiting, finished his beer and slid to the edge of the booth. He was about to make his way toward the target when a man appeared, approached the counter, and took the stool.

Eli stopped, and hovered at the edge of his booth.

He had seen the man before. In the lobby of the Esquire, and even though his presence here was less surprising—he fit in much better with the customers of the Three Crows than the suit-wearing clientele of the four-star hotel—his appearance still jarred Eli. There was something else about the man. He hadn't thought of it when he saw him before, but here, on the heels of the presentation to the Merit Metro Police Department, it seemed obvious. No photos existed of Mitchell Turner, Victor's partner in crime, but there had been generic thug descriptions: tall, burly, bald, tattooed. Dozens of men would fit the bill, but how many of them would cross Eli's path twice in as many days?

Eli had long since abandoned the notion of coincidence.

If this man was Turner, then Victor couldn't be far away.

He scanned the bar, searching for Victor's blond hair, his sharp smile, but he didn't see anyone who fit the bill, and by the time he turned his attention back to the counter, Mitchell was talking to Dominic Rusher. His hulking form leaned in over the ex-soldier like a shadow, and while the noise in the bar drowned out the conversation itself, Eli could see his lips moving quickly, could see Dominic stiffen in response. And then, mere moments after he sat down, Mitchell stood back up. Without ordering, without another word. Eli watched him scan the bar, watched the man's eyes pass blankly over him and settle on the sign that read RESTROOMS in neon yellow light. Mitchell Turner made his way, stepping between Dominic and the rest of the room, his massive form for a moment—a blink—hiding the man from view. By the time he'd finished the stride—crossed from one side of the ex-soldier to the other—Dominic was gone.

And Eli was on his feet.

The bar stool that had, for the better part of an hour, held his target was now suddenly empty, and there was no sign, to any side, of Dominic Rusher. *Not possible*, Eli's brain might have thought. Only Eli knew it was entirely possible, it was *too* possible. Where the man *went* took a backseat in Eli's thoughts to the question of *why* he went, and that was a question with only one answer. He'd been spooked. *Warned.* Eli's gaze swiveled across the room until he saw the door to the men's room swing shut behind Mitchell Turner.

He dropped a bill on the table beside his empty glass, and followed.

XXVII

NINETY MINUTES UNTIL MIDNIGHT
THE ESQUIRE HOTEL

SYDNEY perched on the desk chair, arms wrapped around her knees, attention flicking between the clock on the wall, the clock on the computer (the wall clock was a full ninety seconds faster), and the Post button glowing green in the open program on Mitch's screen. Just above the button was the profile they'd constructed. *Victor Vale* was typed in across the top, with *Eli* listed as his middle name. Where his date of birth should be, the current date was written. The space reserved for last known whereabouts was filled with the address of the Falcon Price high-rise project. Every other space—those reserved for background information, history, police notation—was filled with one word, repeated in every slot: *midnight*.

To the left of the profile was the photo, or the place where the photo would have been. Instead, the bold lettering of the book spine ran vertically, reading VALE.

The book they'd used for the picture, the one Victor had bought on their walk the day before, sat beneath the stack of papers Sydney was supposed to start burning soon, the blue lighter a spot of color resting on top. She slid the massive text out from under the folders, and ran a thumb over the book's cover. She'd seen it before, or one just like it. Her parents had a set in their study (spines uncracked, of course). Sydney opened the book, and turned to the first page, but it was a wall of black. Flipping through, she saw that every one of the first thirty-three pages had been systematically blacked out. The Sharpie nesting into the fold between pages thirty-three and thirty-four suggested that the only reason the remaining pages had been spared was because Victor hadn't gotten to them yet. It was only while flipping back through those thirty-three pages toward the front of the book that Sydney noticed two words exempt from the blackout.

For and *ever.*

The words were several pages apart, separated and surrounded by a sea of black. Not only that, but the word *ever* had been altered, part of a larger word, the *for-* preceding it blotted carefully out, which meant Victor was not trying to piece together the word *forever* from the text.

He clearly wanted it to be two separate words. Distinct.

For.

Ever.

She ran her fingers over the page, expected them to come away stained, but they didn't. Dol whined faintly beneath the desk chair, where he'd somehow crammed himself—or at least a good part of his front half—and Sydney shut the book and looked back at the clock. It was after ten thirty according to both the wall and the computer. Her index finger hovered over the screen.

She knew what it would mean to hit the button.

Even without knowing Victor's plan, she knew that if she clicked Post there would be no going back, and Eli would find Victor, and at least one of them would die, and tomorrow everything would be horrible again.

She would be alone.

One way or another, alone. An EO with a wounded arm and a sister who wanted her dead, with a sick, strange gift and absent parents, and maybe she would be running or maybe she would be killed, too—none of it sounded terribly appealing.

She considered *not* posting it. She could pretend the computer had crashed, could steal them another day. Why did Victor have to do this? Why did he and Eli have to find each other? But even as she asked it, she knew the answer. She knew because her own pulse still quickened defiantly at the thought of Serena, because even as reason told her to run as far from her sister as possible, the gravity of want drew Sydney back. She couldn't break the orbit.

But she could keep from falling. Couldn't Victor, just for a little while? Couldn't they all stay aloft? Alive? But then Mitch's warning echoed in her head—*there are no good men in this game*—and when she closed her eyes to block it out, she saw Victor Vale, not as he was in the rain that first day, or even as he was when she accidentally woke him, but as he was this afternoon, standing over that cop's body, pain crackling in the air around him as he ordered her to bring the dead man back.

Sydney opened her eyes, and hit the Post button.

XXVIII

SEVENTY-FIVE MINUTES UNTIL MIDNIGHT

THE THREE CROWS BAR

VICTOR was leaning back against the cold brick side of the bar's alley wall, consulting Dominic Rusher's profile, when a man matching the photo staggered out of nothing and into the narrow run between the buildings. Victor was impressed, especially considering the door to the bar had never opened, but did his best to hide it in the interest of maintaining the upper hand.

Dominic, for his part, took one look at Victor—he had a black eye and a blue one, and according to his file, the blue was fake—then staggered forward in pain, clutching his side, and crumpled, one knee cracking against the concrete. It wasn't Victor's doing. The man was in bad shape, and whatever disappearing stunt he'd pulled with the shadows hadn't helped his condition.

"You know, Mr. Rusher," said Victor, closing the folder, "you really shouldn't be mixing methahydricone with alcohol. And if you're this bad on 35 milligrams, a drink's not going to help."

"Who are you?" gasped Dominic.

"Where's my friend?" asked Victor. "The one who warned you?"

"Still in there. He just said there was a man—"

"I know what he said. I told him to say it. There's a man who wants to kill you."

"But why?"

Victor didn't enjoy persuasion nearly as much as coercion. It took so much longer.

"Because you're an EO," he said. "Because you're unnatural. Something to that extent. And I should clarify, the man doesn't just want to kill you. He *will* kill you."

Dominic struggled to his feet and met Victor's gaze. "Like I'm afraid to die." There was a stubborn intensity in his eyes.

"Well," said Victor, "how hard can it be, right? You've done it once. But being afraid and being unwilling are different things. I don't think you *want* to die."

"How do you know?" he growled.

Victor dropped the profile on top of a trashcan. "Because you would have done it. You're a mess. You're in constant pain. Every moment of every day, I'm guessing, but you don't end it, which speaks either to your resilience or your stupidity, but also to your wish to live. And because you came here." He gestured to the alley. "Mitch told you to come here if you wanted to live. You could have left and taken your chances, though how far you'd get given your condition, who knows. The point is, you didn't leave. You came here. So while I have no doubt you would face death again with all the honor of a soldier, I don't think you're eager to." Even as he spoke, he was picturing the game board, pieces shifting to accommodate a talent he'd only glimpsed, but already knew he wanted. "I'm giving you a choice," he added. "Go back inside and wait to die. Or go home and wait to die. Or stay with me and live."

"Why do you care?"

"I don't," said Victor, simply. "Not about you, that is. But the one who wants to kill you? I want him dead. And you can help me."

"Why would I?"

Victor sighed. "Aside from the obvious self-preservation?" He held out his empty hand, palm up, and smiled. "I'll make it worth your while."

When Dominic didn't take his hand, Victor brought it to rest on the man's shoulder. He could both feel and see as the pain left Dominic's body, watch it slide from his limbs and his jaw and his forehead and his eyes, which then widened in shock.

"What . . . what did you . . . ?"

"My name, Mr. Rusher, is Victor Vale. I am an EO, and I can take away your pain. All of it. Forever. Or . . ." His hand slid from the young man's shoulder, and a moment later Dominic's face crumpled as the pain swept back, redoubled. "I can give it back, and leave you here, to live in agony, or die at a stranger's hands. Not the best death for a soldier."

"No," hissed Dominic through gritted teeth. "Please. What do I have to do?"

Victor smiled. "One night's worth of work for a lifetime without pain. What are you *willing* to do?" When Dominic didn't answer, Victor clicked the dial up in his mind, watched the man wince, buckle.

"Anything," Dominic gasped at last. "Anything."

∞

MITCH stood at the bathroom sink, pushing the sleeves of his coat up to wash his hands. He turned the faucet on, and heard the door open over the sound of the water. His form filled the mirror, edge to edge, so he couldn't see the man behind him, but he didn't need to. He could hear Eli Ever cross the threshold, and slide the bolt on the bathroom door, locking the world out. Locking them in.

"What did you tell him?" came Eli's voice behind him.

Mitch turned the water off, but stayed at the sink. "Tell who?"

"The man at the bar. You were talking to him, and then he disappeared."

The paper towels were out of reach, and Mitch knew better than to make any sudden movements, so he wiped his hands on his coat, and turned to face the other man.

"It's a bar," he said with a shrug. "People come and go."

"No," snapped Eli. "He literally disappeared. Vanished."

Mitch forced a laugh. "Look, man," he said, walking past Eli toward the door as if he didn't notice the thrown bolt. "I think you've had a few too many—"

He heard Eli draw the gun from his coat, and his words cut off as his steps slowed, then stopped. Eli cocked the weapon. Mitch could tell it was an automatic by the metallic grating of the top half as it was shifted back and primed. He turned slowly toward the sound. The gun was in Eli's hand, the silencer already screwed on, but instead of being trained on Mitch, it hung at Eli's side. And that made Mitch more nervous, the casual way he held the weapon, fingers barely gripping it, not only comfortable with the gun, but in control. He looked like he felt in control.

"I've seen you before," said Eli. "At the Esquire downtown."

Mitch cocked his head and tugged one corner of his mouth up. "Do I look like I'd be caught in a place like that?"

"No. Which is exactly why I noticed you." Mitch's smile faded. Eli raised the gun, and took him in over the sight. "Someone swiped the visuals from the prison files and the police logs, but I'm willing to bet your name is Mitchell Turner. Now where is Victor?"

Mitch thought to feign ignorance, but in the end he decided not to chance it. He'd never been that great at telling lies, anyway, and he knew he'd have to make the few he needed count.

"You must be Eli," he said. "Victor told me about you. Said you had a thing for killing innocent people."

"They're not innocent," growled Eli. "Where is Victor?"

"Haven't seen him since we reached the city and split ways."

"I don't believe that."

"I don't care."

Eli swallowed, fingers drifting toward the trigger. "And Dominic Rusher?"

Mitch shrugged, but slid a step back. "Kid just vanished."

Eli took a step forward, settled his finger against the trigger. "What did you tell him?"

A smile twitched at the corner of Mitch's mouth. "I told him to run."

Eli's eyes narrowed. He twirled the gun in his hand, the barrel fetching up against his palm, and swung the handle hard against Mitch's head. His face cracked sideways, and blood poured from the gash above his eye, running into his vision as Eli brought his boot up, hard, and sent him sprawling backward to the bathroom floor. Eli spun the gun again, and trained it on Mitch's chest. "Where is Victor?" he demanded.

Mitch squinted through the blood. "You'll see him soon enough," he said. "It's almost midnight."

Eli bared his teeth, and bowed his head, and Mitch thought he could see him mouth the words *forgive me* before he looked up, and pulled the trigger.

VICTOR checked his watch. It was almost eleven p.m., and Mitch still hadn't come out.

Dominic stood nearby stretching, rolling his head and shoulders and swinging his arms forward and backward and side to side, as if he'd just set down a heavy burden. Victor supposed that in many ways he had. After all, Victor knew pain enough to know how much Dominic had been in, and was frankly impressed by the man's threshold. But while he might be able to function in pain, his powers clearly didn't flourish under it. So Victor had taken it away. Taken it all away. He had, however, left as much *sensation* as possible, which was tricky, given how tightly the two things were intertwined, but he didn't need his newest asset accidentally bleeding out just because he didn't notice he'd cut himself.

Victor's attention flicked between his watch and the ex-soldier, who was busy examining himself. People took their bodies and their health for granted. But Dominic Rusher seemed to savor every painless flexing of his hands, every stride. He clearly understood what a gift he'd been given. *Good,* thought Victor.

"Dominic," he said. "What I've done can be undone. And for the record, I do not need to touch you to do it. That was for effect. Do you understand? What I've taken can be given back in a blink, from a city away, or a world away. So do not cross me."

Dominic nodded solemnly.

In truth, Victor could only influence a person's pain threshold if they were within eyesight. The farthest he'd gotten in prison was dropping a man from across the football-field-sized yard with only a finger gun. Once he'd managed to crumple an inmate at the other end of the cell block, only his hand visible through the bars, but still. Out of sight, and his accuracy quickly vanished. Not that Dominic needed to know any of that.

"Your power," asked Victor. "How does it work?"

"I don't exactly know how to explain." Dominic looked down at his hands, and flexed and stretched them as if working out a lingering stiffness. "Yea, though I walk in the shadow of the valley of death—"

"Biblical allusions aside, please."

"After the mine blew, it was bad. I couldn't . . . it was inhuman, that pain. It was animal and everywhere. And I didn't want to die. God, I didn't, but I wanted quiet and dark and . . . it's hard to explain."

He didn't have to. Victor knew.

"I felt torn apart. I was. Anyway. They brought me back but they couldn't seem to pull me through, not all the way. I spent weeks in a coma. All that time, I could feel the world. I could hear it. Swore I could see it, too, but it was like everything was far away. Murky. And I couldn't reach out, couldn't touch any of it. And then I woke up, and everything was so sharp and bright and full of pain again, and all I wanted was to find that place, that dull, quiet place. And then I did. I call it walking in shadows, because I don't know any other term. I step into the darkness and can move from one place to another without being seen. Without time passing. Without anything. It looks like teleporting, I guess, but I have to physically move. I could cross a city in the time it takes you to blink, but it would take me hours. I'd have to walk the whole way. And it's hard. Like walking through water. The world resists, when you break its rules."

"Can you take others with you?"

Dominic shrugged. "I've never tried."

"Well then," said Victor, taking hold of Dominic's arm, ignoring the moment when the man winced intrinsically away. "Consider this your audition."

"Where are we going?"

"My friend is still inside," said Victor, nodding toward the bar. "He should have come out after you. But he didn't."

"That big guy? He said he'd cover me."

Victor frowned. "From who?"

"The one who wants to kill me," said Dominic, frowning. "I tried to tell you, that guy sat down next to me and said there was a man who wanted to kill me, and that he was *in the bar.*"

Victor's grip tightened on Dominic's sleeve. *Eli.* "Take me inside. *Now.*"

Dominic took a steadying breath, and put his hand over Victor's. "Don't know if this is even going to—"

The rest of the words dropped away, not fading out but plummeting into silence as the air around them shuddered, and split to allow the two men through. The moment Dominic and Victor stepped through the seam, everything hushed and darkened and stilled. Victor could see the man whose arm he was touching, just as he could see the alley around them, but all of it was cast in a kind of shadow, less like night and more like the world had been photographed in black and white and then the photo had aged, worn, grayed. When they walked, the world rippled thickly around them, the air viscous. It pressed in on them, weighed them down. When they reached the door to the bar, it resisted Dominic's pull before finally—slowly—giving way.

Inside, the photo world continued. People caught middrink, mid-pool-shot, midkiss, midfight, and mid-a-dozen-other-things, all stuck between one breath and the next. And all the sound caught, too, so that the space filled with a horrible, heavy quiet. Victor kept his hand on Dominic's arm like a blind man, but he couldn't take his eyes from the room. He scanned, searching the frozen faces of the crowd.

And then he saw him.

Victor ground to a halt, jarring Dominic backward. He glanced over his shoulder and asked what was wrong, the words mouthed, but never formed. And it didn't matter, anyway, because Victor didn't see his lips move. He didn't see anything but the dark-haired man caught midstride as he wove through the crowd, away from them and toward the front door, hand reaching out for the handle. Victor wondered how could he know that man without seeing his face. It was the posture, the broad shoulders and the arrogant way he held them, the edge of his sharp jaw visible as he turned away.

Eli.

Victor's hand began to slip from Dominic's arm. Eli Ever was *right there*. Half a room away. His back turned. His attention derailed and his body caught between seconds. Victor could do it. The bar was packed, but if he dropped every person at once, he'd have a shot—*No*. It took every ounce of focus for Victor to hold on to Dominic's sleeve. He had waited. Waited so long. He wasn't going to forfeit the planning, the lead, the control. It wouldn't work, not here, not the way it had to work. He dragged his eyes from Eli's back, and forced himself to search the rest of the room, but there was no sign of Mitch. His gaze swept through, and finally settled on the restrooms. A sign hung from the men's room. OUT OF ORDER in bold letters, a hand-drawn set of lines beneath to emphasize the point. He urged Dominic forward, through the heavy air until they reached the door, and went in.

Mitchell Turner was sprawled on the linoleum, his face stuck to the floor by a small puddle of blood emanating from a gash on his temple. Victor let go of Dominic's arm and winced as the room crashed into life around him all at once, a wave of color and noise and time. Dominic himself appeared a moment later, arms crossed, looking down at the body.

"Big guy," he said quietly.

Victor knelt carefully beside Mitch, and reconsidered his decision to leave Sydney at the hotel.

"Is he . . . ," started Dominic as Victor reached out and brought his fingertips to the gunshot hole in Mitch's jacket. His hand came away dry. He let out a breath and patted Mitch's jaw. The man groaned.

"Mother . . . fucker . . ."

"I see you met Eli," said Victor. "He's always been a bit trigger happy."

Mitch grunted as he sat up and touched his head, a bruise already blossoming beneath the drying blood. His gaze went to Dominic. "I see you're still alive then. Good choice."

He tried to stand, and got to one knee before pausing for breath.

"A little help?" he said, wincing. Victor's lips twitched, and the air hummed faintly for a moment before vanishing, taking Mitch's pain with it. The man got to his feet, swayed, and caught himself against the wall with a bloody hand before making his way to the strip of sinks to clean up.

"So he's like, bulletproof?" asked Dominic. Mitch laughed, and then pulled his jacket aside to reveal the vest beneath.

"Close enough," he said. "I'm not an EO, though, if that's what you're asking."

Victor wet a handful of paper towels and did his best to clean Mitch's blood off the floor and the wall while Mitch finished cleaning it off his face.

"What time is it?" asked Victor, tossing the ruined towels in the bin.

Dominic checked his watch. "Eleven. Why?"

Mitch snapped the faucet off. "Cutting it pretty close, Vic."

But Victor only smiled. "Dominic," he said. "Let's show Mitch what you can do."

XXIX

SIXTY MINUTES UNTIL MIDNIGHT

THE ESQUIRE HOTEL

SERENA toweled off her hair, holding strands up to the bathroom light to make sure Zachary Flinch hadn't stained them. She'd had to shower three times to get the feel of brain and blood off her skin, and even now, raw from scrubbing, with her hair probably damaged from the rinse repeat of it all, she didn't *feel* clean.

Clean was clearly not skin deep when it came to killing.

It was only the second execution she'd ever been to. The first had been Sydney's. Serena cringed at the thought of it. Maybe that's why she'd wanted to go, to wash the memory of her sister's almost-murder from her mind, replace it with some fresher horror, as if one scene could paint over the other.

Or maybe she'd asked to go along because she knew Eli would hate it—she knew how much his removals mattered to him, how much they *belonged* to him—and that he'd resist. Sometimes those moments when he fought back, when she could see the spark of defiance, were the only ones that made her feel alive. She hated living in such a limp world, every glazed eye and simple nod a reminder that nothing mattered. She would start to let go, and then Eli would fight back and force her to tighten her grip. She wondered with a thrill if maybe one day he would even break free.

Finally satisfied that the blood didn't stain, she dried her hair, pulled on a robe, and made her way into the living room, tapping the computer awake. She logged on to the police database, and filled out the "Middle Name" window of the search form with *ELI,* expecting it to return with no results, since Eli should have dispatched Dominic by now, but the search came back with two profiles. The first belonged to Dominic.

But the second belonged to *Victor.*

She read the profile three times, chewing her lip, then searched the room for her phone, which she'd lobbed onto the bed when she got in. She found it beneath a pile of clothes and towels, and was halfway through punching in Eli's number, when she stopped.

Less than an hour until midnight.

It was a trap. Eli would know it, too, of course, but he would go anyway. Why shouldn't he? Whatever Eli's enemy was planning, there was only one way this night would end, and that was with Victor Vale in a body bag. And Sydney? Serena's chest tightened. Her resolve had faltered the first time; she didn't know if she had the strength to watch Eli try again. Even if it wasn't really her sister, just a shadow of the little girl who'd clung to her side for twelve years, an imposter in her sister's shape. Even then.

Her fingers hovered over the screen. She could drag the file to the trash. Eli wouldn't find it in time. But it would only be a stay of execution. Victor wanted to find Eli, and Eli wanted to find Victor, and one way or another, they would succeed. She looked at Victor's profile one last time, and tried to picture the man who had once been Eli's friend, who had brought him back, made him what he was, saved her sister . . . and for a moment, as she finished dialing Eli's number, she almost wished he stood a fighting chance.

XXX

FIFTY MINUTES UNTIL MIDNIGHT
THE THREE CROWS BAR

ELI stormed through the front door of the Three Crows as he dialed Detective Stell and told him to send a cop over to the bar to clean up an incident.

"It was an EO, right?" asked Stell, and the question, as well as the shade of doubt that lined the officer's voice as he asked it, troubled Eli immensely. But he didn't have time to deal with the detective's resistance, not right now, not as the clock ticked down.

"Of course it was," he snapped, and hung up.

Eli paused beneath the metal sculpted crows on the bar's marquee, ran his fingers through his hair, and scoured the street for any sign of Dominic Rusher or Victor Vale, but all he saw were drunkards, and bums, and cars whizzing past too fast to see drivers or passengers. He swore and kicked the nearest trash can as hard as possible, relishing the blossom of pain even as it faded, whatever damage he'd done repairing, bone and tissue and skin knitting neatly back together.

He shouldn't have killed Mitch Turner.

He knew that. But it wasn't as though the man were innocent, not truly. Eli had seen the police records. Turner had sinned. And those who ally themselves with monsters are little better than monsters themselves. Still, he had felt no silence, no moment of peace, following the act, and Eli's chest tightened at being denied the calm, the assurance that he had not strayed.

Eli bowed his head, and crossed himself. His nerves were just beginning to smooth when his phone rang.

"What?" he snapped into the cell, heading for his car in the lot across the street.

"Victor posted to the database," said Serena. "That Falcon Price site. Ground floor." He heard the sound of the glass patio door sliding open. "It's right here, across from the hotel. Did you take care of Dominic Rusher?"

"No," he growled. "But Mitchell Turner's dead. Is the deadline still midnight?" His anger was cooling as he walked, focus knitting him closed the way his body knit together his skin. Things were on schedule. Not *his* schedule, but *a* schedule.

"Still midnight," said Serena. "What about the police? Should I call Stell? Have him send his men over to the high-rise?"

Eli rapped his fingers on his car and thought of Stell's question, his tone. "No. Not before midnight. Turner's dead, and Victor's mine. Tell them to be there at twelve, no sooner, and order them to stay outside the walls until we're done. Tell them it's not safe." He got inside, his breath fogging the windows. "I'm on my way. Should I pick you up?" She didn't answer. "Serena?"

After another long pause, she finally said, "No, no. I'm not dressed yet. I'll meet you there."

SERENA hung up.

She was leaning on the balcony, and she barely noticed the biting chill of the iron rail under her elbows because she was too busy looking at a trail of smoke.

Two floors down and several rooms over, the smoke curled through a pair of open doors, wafting up toward her. It smelled like burning paper. Serena knew because in high school she and her friends would always light a bonfire on the first night of summer vacation and pitch their essays and exams in, casting the old year into the flames.

But nice as the Esquire rooms were, none of them had fireplaces.

She was still wondering about the smoke when a large black dog wandered out onto the balcony. It stared out through the bars of the railing for a moment before a girl's voice called it back.

"Dol," called the girl. "Dol! Come back in."

A shiver ran through Serena. She knew that voice.

A moment later the small blond girl who so many people had mistaken for Serena's twin bobbed onto the porch, and tugged at the dog's neck.

"Come on," coaxed Sydney. "Let's go in."

The dog turned and obediently followed her back inside.

Which hotel room? Serena began to count. Two floors down. Three rooms over.

She spun on her heel, and went inside.

XXXI

FORTY MINUTES UNTIL MIDNIGHT

THE THREE CROWS BAR

DOMINIC took hold of Victor and Mitch, and led them in silence and shadow out of the restrooms, through the bar, and into the alley that ran beside it.

Victor gave a nod and Dominic let go, the world springing back into life around them. Even the deserted alley was a cacophony compared to the heavy quiet of the in-between; Victor rolled his shoulders, and checked his watch.

"That was . . . weird," said Mitch, whose mood seemed to have soured considerably since being shot.

"It was perfect," said Victor. "Let's go."

"So I passed?" asked Dominic, still flexing his hands. Victor could see the fear in his eyes, the desperate hope that the pain would stay away. He appreciated how transparent Dominic's desires were. It kept things simple.

"The night's not over yet," he said. "But you're doing well so far."

Mitch grumbled about the hole in his jacket as they made their way to the mouth of the alley. Victor knew that it was the first thing Mitch bought when they got out, a well-made coat, lined with dark-dyed goose down that now leaked in small puffs as he stepped off the curb.

"Look at the bright side," said Victor. "You're alive."

"Night's still young," said Mitch under his breath as they crossed the street.

He said something else, or started to, but it was cut off by the sudden shriek of sirens.

A squad car tore around a corner and down the street toward them in red and blue and white and blaring ripples of noise. Mitch spun, and Victor tensed, and time slowed. And then, time *stopped*. Victor felt the hand come down on his arm a breath before the sound and color went out of the night. The cop car froze, suspended between moments through the film of Dominic's shadows. Dominic's other hand rested on Mitch's wrist, and all three of them now stood in the darkness of his in-between world, frozen as if they, too, were caught in time. Victor might have admitted—if he *could* admit, if his words could take shape and sound—how useful Dominic Rusher was turning out to be, but since he couldn't, he simply nodded in the direction of the parking lot, and the three men waded through the thick air across the street.

Victor knew that they had a predicament.

Dominic, while much improved, was in no condition to drag them across the city. They needed the car. But they couldn't use the car until they stepped out of the shadows, and the moment they did that, reality would resume and the squad car would continue down the street to the Three Crows. Victor led the way to the stolen sedan, the other two in a trailing line behind, and when they got there he gestured for them to kneel in the gap between their vehicle and the next on the side of the cop cars' frozen approach, which had before been a convertible and was now a considerably larger truck. He took one last breath, and said a quiet curse, which was as close as Victor came to praying, and then he nodded at Dominic, whose hand vanished from his shoulder, stripping the stillness and plunging his world back into chaos.

The cop car careened up to the bar's entrance, where it slammed to a stop, sirens blaring. Victor held his breath and pressed his body against the metal side of their sedan and peered through the narrow space between his front bumper and the truck's as the sirens cut abruptly off, and left his ears ringing.

Two officers got out, and met at the front doors.

One cop vanished inside, but the other stayed on the curb and confirmed their arrival on a radio. Something about a body. They were here for Mitch's body. Which was problematic, since there *was* no body, a fact that would soon become readily apparent.

Go inside, he begged the second cop.

The cop didn't move. Victor freed his gun and trained it on the officer, tracking up until it was level with the man's head. He had a clear shot. He drew in a breath, and held it. Victor didn't feel guilt, or fear, or even a sense of consequence, not like normal people. All those things had been dead—or at least dulled to the point of uselessness—for years. But he'd trained his mind to reconstruct those feelings from memory as best he could, and assemble them into a kind of code. Nothing so elaborate as Eli's set of rules, just a simple wish to avoid killing bystanders, if possible. It didn't feel wrong, resting his finger on the trigger, but his mind provided the word *wrong.* He lowered the gun a fraction, knowing that sacrificing a kill shot would also sacrifice the certitude of their escape.

He let out his breath just as the radio crackled, and even if Victor couldn't make out the message, he could hear the officer's response—"What kind of problem?"—and, a moment later, "What do you mean? According to Ever and Stell . . . forget it. Hold on."

And just like that, the second cop turned toward the door. Victor lowered his weapon and his eyes drifted skyward, where thick gray clouds weakened the black of the night. He'd never been one for God, never had Eli's zeal, never needed signs, but if there were such things, if there was Fate, or some higher power, maybe it had an issue with Eli's methods, too. The second officer followed the first inside, and Victor, Mitch, and Dominic were on their feet, and in the car before the front doors of the bar had even swung shut.

A yellow ticket flapped against the windshield, pinned beneath a wiper blade, and Victor leaned out the window, plucked it free, and crumpled it, dropping the paper to the ground. The wind instantly caught it, and the ticket bounced away.

"Littering," said Mitch as Victor started the car.

"Let's hope that's not the worst crime I commit tonight," said Victor as they pulled out of the lot, away from the Three Crows and the squad car and back into the heart of the city as the minutes ticked away toward midnight. "Call Sydney. Make sure everything's okay on her end."

An ambulance soared past them toward the bar. It wouldn't be necessary.

"If I didn't know better," said Mitch, dialing. "I'd think you care."

XXXII

THIRTY MINUTES UNTIL MIDNIGHT
THE ESQUIRE HOTEL

BURNING the papers took longer than Sydney expected, and by the seventh or eighth page, the novelty of ruining something had faded, replaced by a tedious sense of obligation. She stood at the sink, boosted up by Victor's book, and fed one page at a time to the flame of the small blue lighter, waiting until each was a layer of ash in the sink before she began the next sheet, and strongly suspecting Victor had given her the task just to keep her busy. She didn't mind so much. It was better than sitting still, staring at the clock and wondering when they'd be back.

If they'd be back.

Dol stood beside her, nearly able to rest his nose on the counter by the remaining papers, and whimpering faintly every time she touched the lighter's flame to a page. She'd wait as long as she dared before dropping the burning paper into the sink—a little longer each time—and then watch as the crossed-out faces of Eli's victims blackened and curled, watch as the fire ate away their names, their dates, their lives.

Sydney shivered.

The room was freezing with the balcony doors open, and Dol had already wandered out once, unsettled by the fire, but she had to leave them that way, because of the smoke. It drifted out from the charred remains, and Sydney spent the whole task waiting for the alarms to go off. She had to resist the urge to burn the folder's remnants in one go and be done with it, but her concern about the alarms kept her slow, methodical. The amount of smoke created by a single page appeared too little to disrupt the systems, but lighting the whole folder at once would surely trigger something.

Dol soon lost interest, and wandered out once more onto the balcony. Sydney didn't like him out there, and called him back, nearly singeing her fingers when she forgot to let go of the latest page.

A phone rang in Sydney's pocket.

Victor had bought it for her. Or rather, Victor had bought it, and then given it to Sydney after he saw what she could do. The phone was, in Sydney's eyes, an invitation to stay. She and Mitch and Victor all had the same models, and somehow that made Sydney happy. It was like belonging to a club. She'd wanted to belong to a club in school, but she'd never been great at sports, didn't care about student government (it was a joke in middle school, anyway), and after resurrecting the science class's hamster, she was a bit shy about participating in the after-school nature club. High school clubs would be more fun anyway, she'd reasoned.

If she could stay alive that long.

The phone rang again, and Sydney set the lighter aside and dug the device from her pocket.

"Hello?" she answered.

"Hey, Syd." It was Mitch. "Everything okay there?"

"I'm almost done with the papers," she said, taking up the lighter and setting fire to another page. It was the blue-haired girl. The same blue, almost, as the lighter itself. Sydney watched as the girl's face curled into nothing. "Are you going to think up more ways to keep me busy?"

Mitch laughed, but he didn't sound very happy.

"You're a kid. Just watch some TV. We'll be home later."

"Hey, Mitch," said Sydney, softer. "You . . . you're coming back, right?"

"As soon as I can, Syd. Promise."

"You better." She lit another page. "Or I'll drink all your chocolate milk."

"You wouldn't dare," said Mitch, and she could almost hear the smile in his voice before he hung up.

Sydney put her phone away, and lit the last page. It was hers. She touched the lighter to the corner and held the paper up so the fire ate its way along one side before swallowing the photo, the paper-thin version of the girl with short blond hair and water blue eyes. It burned right through her and then there was nothing. She let the fire lick her fingers before she dropped the page into the sink, and smiled.

That girl was dead.

Someone knocked on the hotel door, and Sydney nearly dropped the lighter.

The knocking came a second time.

She held her breath. Dol stood, made something like a growl, and put himself squarely between her and the hotel door.

The knocking came a third time, and then someone spoke.

"Sydney?"

Even on her toes, Sydney wouldn't be able see out of the peephole, but she didn't need to. She knew the voice, knew it better than her own. She lifted her hand and brought it over her mouth to stifle the surprise, the reply, the sound of breathing, as if she couldn't trust her lips with anything.

"Sydney, please," came Serena's voice through the door, smooth and soft and low.

For a moment, Sydney almost forgot—the hotel and the

shooting and the broken lake—and it was like they were home and playing hide-and-seek, and Sydney was too good and Serena had given up, or gotten bored, and was imploring her little sister to give up, too, to come out. If they'd been at home, Serena would have said she had cookies, or lemonade, or why didn't they go watch that movie Sydney had been wanting to see? They could make popcorn. None of it was true, of course. Even then, Serena would say anything to coax her little sister out, and Sydney wouldn't mind, not really, because she'd won.

But they weren't at home.

They weren't anywhere near home.

And this game was rigged, because her sister didn't have to lie, or bribe, or cheat. All she had to do was say the words.

"Sydney, come open the door."

She put aside the lighter and stepped down from Victor's book, and crossed the room, pressing her hand against the wood for a moment before her traitorous fingers drifted over to the doorknob, and turned. Serena stood in the doorway wearing a green pea coat and a pair of leggings that vanished into heeled black boots. Her hands were braced against the frame to either side. One hand was empty, and the other held a gun. The hand with the gun slid down the door frame with a metallic hiss before coming to rest at her side. Sydney cringed away from the weapon.

"Hello, Sydney," she said, as she tapped the gun absently against her leggings.

"Hello, Serena," said her sister.

"Don't run," said Serena. It never occurred to Sydney to do so. She couldn't tell, though, if the thought had been there and bled away at her sister's words, or if she was brave enough to have never considered running, or if she was simply smart enough to know she couldn't outrun bullets twice, especially without a forest and a head start.

Whatever the reason, Sydney stayed very, very still.

Dol growled as Serena stepped into the hotel room, but when she told him to sit, he did, back legs folding reluctantly. Serena strode past her little sister, surveying the ashes in the sink, and the carton of chocolate milk on the counter (Sydney had silently resolved to drink it—at least some of it—if Mitch didn't come back soon), before turning back to Sydney.

"Do you have a phone?" she asked.

Sydney nodded, her hand drifting of its own accord to her pocket and retrieving the one Victor had given her. The one that matched his, and Mitch's. The one that made them a team. Serena held out her hand and Sydney's hand held out itself, depositing the device into her sister's palm. Serena then walked to the balcony, where the doors were still open to vent the smoke, and lobbed the phone over the railing and into the night.

Sydney's heart sank with the rectangle of falling metal. She'd really liked that phone.

Serena then shut the balcony doors and perched on the back of the couch, facing her sister, her gun resting on her knee. She sat the way Sydney did, or rather, Sydney sat the way *she* always had, with only half her weight, as if she might need to dash up at any second. But where Sydney's perching looked coiled, Serena somehow made the act look casual, even lazy, despite the weapon.

"Happy birthday," she said.

"It's not midnight yet," said Sydney quietly. *You can come up and stay through your birthday,* Serena had promised. Now she smiled sadly.

"You used to stay up until the clock turned, even though Mom told you not to because she knew you'd be tired the next day. You'd sit awake and read and wait and when the clock struck midnight you'd light a candle you'd stashed under the bed, and make a wish." There was a coat draped on the back of the couch, the red one Sydney had thrown off after Victor told her she had to stay behind, and now Serena fiddled with one of the buttons. "It was like this secret birthday party," she added softly. "Just for you, before everyone else could join in and celebrate."

"How did you know?" asked Sydney.

"I'm your big sister," said Serena. "It's my job to know things."

"Then tell me," said Sydney. "Why do you hate me?"

Serena held her gaze. "I don't."

"But you want me to die. You think I'm somehow wrong. Broken."

"I think we're all broken," said Serena, tossing her the red coat. "Put that on."

"I don't feel broken," Sydney said quietly as she tugged on the too-big sleeves. "And even if I am, I can fix other people."

Serena considered her sister. "You can't fix the dead, Syd. EOs are proof of that. And besides, it's not your place to try."

"It's not your place to control people's lives," snapped Sydney.

Serena raised a brow, amused. "Who taught you to sing so loud? The little Sydney I knew could barely chirp."

"I'm not that Sydney anymore."

Serena's face fell. Her grip tightened on the gun.

"We're going for a walk," she said.

Sydney cast glances around the room, even as her feet followed Serena toward the door with the same simple obedience that had possessed her hands to offer up the phone. Treacherous limbs. She wanted to leave a note, a clue, something, but Serena got impatient and grabbed her sleeve, shoving her toward the hall. Dol sat in the middle of the room, whining as they passed.

"Can I bring him?"

Serena paused, and ejected the magazine of the gun to check the number of rounds.

"Okay," she said, snapping it shut again. "Where's his leash?"

"He doesn't have one."

Serena held open the door and sighed.

"Follow Sydney," she said to Dol, and the dog sprang to his feet and loped over, pressing himself against the girl's side.

Serena led Sydney and Dol down the concrete stairs that ran beside the elevator, all the way to the parking garage, an open-walled structure pressed against the Esquire's spine. The place smelled like gas, the light was dim, and the air was biting cold, a sideways wind ripping through in short, sharp gusts.

"Are we driving somewhere?" asked Sydney, pulling the coat close around her.

"No," said Serena, turning on her sister. She brought the gun up to Sydney's forehead, rested it against her skin, between her watery blue eyes. Dol growled. Sydney brought a hand up and rested it against his back to quiet him, but didn't take her gaze off Serena, even though it was a struggle to focus her vision around the barrel of the gun.

"We used to have the same eyes," said Serena. "Yours are paler now."

"I like that we're finally different," said Sydney, fighting back a shiver. "I don't want to be you."

Silence fell between the sisters. A silence full of shifting pieces.

"I don't need you to be me," said Serena at last. "But I need you to be brave. I need you to be strong."

Sydney squeezed her eyes shut. "I'm not afraid."

∞

SERENA stood in the garage with her finger on the trigger, the barrel resting between Sydney's eyes, and froze. The girl on the other side of the gun was and was not her sister. Maybe Eli was wrong and all EOs weren't broken, at least not in the same way. Or maybe Eli was right and the Sydney she knew was gone, but still, this new Sydney wasn't hollowed out, wasn't dark, wasn't truly dead. This Sydney was alive in a way the other had never been. It shone through her skin.

Serena's fingers loosened on the gun, and she let it slide from her sister's face. Sydney kept her eyes squeezed shut. The gun had left a mark on her forehead, a small dent where she'd leaned into the weapon, and Serena reached out and smoothed it away with her thumb. Only then did Sydney's eyes drift open, the strength in them wavering.

"Why—," she started.

"I need you to listen now," cut in Serena in her even tone, the one that no one—not even Eli—knew how to refuse. An absolute power. "I need you to do as I say." She pressed the gun into Sydney's hands, and then took her by the shoulders and squeezed.

"Go," she said.

"Where?" asked Sydney.

"Somewhere safe."

Serena let go and gave her sister a small push backward, away, a gesture that once might have been playful, normal. But the look in her eyes and the gun in Sydney's hands and the cold night hardening around them served as a vivid reminder that nothing was normal now. Sydney tucked the gun into her coat, but didn't take her eyes from her sister, and didn't move.

"Go," snapped Serena.

This time, Sydney did as she was told. She turned, clutched the scruff of Dol's neck, and the two bolted between the cars. Serena watched until her sister was a speck of red, and then nothing. At least she'd have a chance.

A phone rang in the pocket of Serena's coat. She rubbed her eyes, and answered.

"I'm here," said Eli. "Where are you?"

Serena straightened. "I'm on my way."

XXXIII

TWENTY MINUTES UNTIL MIDNIGHT

SYDNEY ran.

She cut through the Esquire's parking garage and onto a side street that looped back around to the front of the hotel, and ended up a few yards to the left of the main doors. A cop stood several feet away, his back to her as he sipped a coffee and talked on his cell. Sydney felt the weight of the gun in her pocket—as if the hidden firearm would draw more attention than a missing girl in a bright red coat clutching the collar of a giant black dog—but the cop never turned around. It was late and the cars on the main road were sparse, the traffic clumping as the night wore on, and Sydney and Dol sprinted across the street, unnoticed.

She knew exactly where she was going.

Serena hadn't told Sydney to go *home*. She hadn't told her to run *away*. She'd told her to go somewhere *safe*. And over the course of the last week, *safe* had ceased to be a place for Sydney, and had become a person.

Specifically, *safe* had become Victor.

Which is why Sydney ran to the only place she knew Victor would be (at least, according to the profile he'd had her put up on the police database that night, the one she'd read through a dozen times while waiting and then working up the nerve to hit the Post button).

The Falcon Price high-rise project.

Down the block, the construction site was a spot of dark in the city, like a shadow between streetlights. There was a thin shell of wood surrounding the abandoned high-rise, two-story walls, the kind people loved to vandalize because they were both temporary and highly visible. The shell was plastered with posters and signs, tagged here and there by street art, and underneath it all, a few construction permits, and a building company logo.

Officially, there was only one way onto the construction site, through a front gate—also made of wooden sheeting—which had spent the last few months chained shut.

But earlier that day, when Mitch had brought her here to revive Officer Dane, he'd shown her another way in, not through the chained-off gate, but around the back of the building, through a place in the shell where two broad panels of wood overlapped slightly. He'd widened the gap between the sheets to let them through, the panels snapping shut again behind them. Sydney knew she could squeeze into the construction site without touching the walls, since even when the panels hung closed there was a small triangle of space near the bottom. She let go of Dol's neck, and worried the dog would bolt, but he didn't, only stood there watching Sydney crawl through the gap. Dol looked both distressed by Sydney's decision, and determined to follow her. When she made it to the other side and stood, brushing dirt from her pants, the dog crouched down, and squirmed through the gap in the boards.

"Good dog," she whispered as he stood and shook off.

Inside the wooden shell was a kind of yard, a large stretch of dirt strewn with bits of metal and plywood and bags of concrete. The yard was dark, shadows on shadows making the path from the wall to the building dangerous. The building itself towered, unfinished, a steel and concrete skeleton draped in layers of plastic sheeting like gauze.

But on the ground floor, several layers of plastic in, Sydney could make out a light.

It was diffused so much that if the yard hadn't been so dark, she might not have noticed it. But she did. Dol pressed himself against her side. Sydney stood in the yard, unsure what to do. Was Victor here already? It wasn't midnight yet, was it? She didn't have her phone, couldn't tell by the moon even if she knew *how* to read the moon because there was no moon above, only a thick layer of clouds, glowing faintly with reflected city light.

As for the light within the high-rise, it was steady, constant, more like a lamp than a flashlight, and somehow that gave Sydney comfort. Someone had set it there, had prepared, had planned. Victor planned things. But when she took a step toward the building, Dol barred her path. When she went around him, his jaws circled her forearm, and held fast. She twisted, but couldn't get free, and even though the dog was careful not to bite down, his grip was solid.

"Let go," she hissed. The dog didn't budge.

And then, on the other side of the building, beyond the thin wood shell, a car door slammed. Dol dropped Sydney's arm as his head snapped toward the sound. The noise, sharp and metallic, reminded Sydney of a gunshot, and sent her pulse spiking, the word *safe safe safe safe* pounding with the blood in her ears. She sprinted for the building, for the sheets and the steel and the shelter, tripping over a stray iron bar before reaching the hollow high-rise frame. Dol followed, and the two vanished into the Falcon Price as, somewhere, on the opposite side, someone dragged the front gate open.

∞

MITCH slammed the car door, and watched Victor and Dominic drive away. He'd planned to circle around to the back of the high-rise, pry open the loose wooden panel, and get in that way, but when he stepped up to the front gate, he saw it wasn't necessary. The chains had been cut, the snaking metal coiled on the ground at his feet. Someone was already inside.

"Great," whispered Mitch, withdrawing the gun Victor had given him.

Incidentally, Mitch had always hated guns, and the events of the evening hadn't made him any fonder. He pushed open the gate, wincing as the hinges screwed into the wood responded with a metallic whine. The yard was dark and, as far as he could tell, empty. He ejected the magazine on the gun, checked it, put it back, and rapped the barrel of the weapon nervously against his palm as he made his way to the center of the yard, halfway between the wooden shell of the fence and the steel skeleton of the high-rise, to a patch of dirt that was as open as possible.

A faint glow coming from the high-rise did little to illuminate him, but given his size and the sheer lack of other people, Mitch felt painfully confident he would be noticed, and soon. A stack of wooden beams, tarped against the weather, sat a few feet away, and Mitch sank onto them, checked his gun a second time, and waited.

SERENA'S phone rang again as she crossed the street, making her way down the now nearly deserted block toward the Falcon Price high-rise.

"Serena," said the caller. It wasn't Eli's voice.

"Detective Stell," she replied. She could hear the open and close of a car door.

"We're on our way now," he said. The line was muffled for a moment while the phone's speaker was covered and orders were given.

"Remember," she said, "you're to stay outside the fence—"

"I know the orders," he said. "That's not why I called."

Serena saw the signage of the abandoned high-rise, and slowed her pace. "Then what is it?"

"Mr. Ever had me send officers to a bar to clean up after an incident. There was supposed to be a body."

"Yeah, Mitchell Turner's," she said.

"Only I get a call from the officers just now. There was no body. No signs of a body, either." Serena's boots slowed, and stopped. "I don't know what's going on," said Stell, "but that's the second time things haven't lined up and—"

"And you didn't call Eli," she cut in softly.

"I'm sorry if that was wrong . . ."

"Why did you call me instead?"

"I trust you," he answered, without hesitation.

"And Eli?"

"I trust you," he said again, and Serena's heart fluttered a little, both at the officer's small display of evasion, the defiance of it, and at her own control over him. She started walking again.

"You did well," she said as she reached the wooden walls of the construction site. And there, through the gap in the broken gate, she saw Mitch's hulking form. "I'll take care of it," she whispered, "trust me."

"I do," said Detective Stell.

Serena hung up, and pushed the metal gate open.

XXXIV

TEN MINUTES UNTIL MIDNIGHT
THE FALCON PRICE PROJECT

MITCH thought he heard something from the building behind him, but when he strained to listen, the sounds that made it into the yard were so broken and faint that they could have been wind through the plastic sheeting, or a loose pipe. He might have gone to see, but Victor's orders had been explicit, and even if he felt like challenging them, it was at that moment that the front gate that surrounded the bones of the high-rise groaned inward again, and a girl stepped into the yard.

She looked like Sydney, thought Mitch. If Sydney had grown a foot taller and several years older. The same blond hair curled down into eyes that were somehow bright and blue, even in the dark. It had to be Serena.

When she saw Mitch waiting, she crossed her arms.

"Mr. Turner," she said, stepping forward, her black boots weaving effortlessly through the debris of the construction yard. "You have an impressive resilience to death. Is this Sydney's work?"

"Call me a cat," said Mitch, pushing up off the planks. "I'm still working through my own nine lives. And just so you know," he added, raising his gun, "I like to think there's a special place in hell for girls who feed their little sisters to wolves."

Serena's face fell. "You should be careful, playing with guns," she said. "Sooner or later you're going to get shot."

Mitch cocked the gun. "The novelty wore off when your boy-friend played target practice with my chest."

"Yet here you are," said Serena. Her voice had a slow, almost lazy sweetness to it. "Clearly his message wasn't *impactful* enough."

Mitch tightened his grip on the gun, and leveled it at her.

Serena only smiled. "Let's point that in a safer direction," she said. "Place the gun against your temple."

Mitch did everything he could to keep his hand still, but it was as if it no longer belonged to him. His elbow softened, his arm bent, and his fingers turned, shifting position until the barrel of the gun came to rest against the side of his head.

He swallowed.

"There are worse ways to die," said Serena. "And worse things to do than die. I promise I'll make it quick."

Mitch looked at her, this girl so much like Sydney, and yet so much less. He couldn't look at her eyes—at once brighter than her sister's, but empty in a bad way, a dead way—so he watched her lips as they formed the words.

"Pull the trigger."

And he did.

∞

SYDNEY and Dol were halfway toward the glowing center of the high-rise's ground floor when she heard the sound of footsteps—not hers, or the dog's, but heavier—and froze in her tracks. She'd only been with Victor and Mitch a few days, but it had been long enough to grow familiar with the sounds they both made. Not just their voices, but the way they sounded when they weren't speaking, the way they breathed and laughed and moved, the way they filled a space, and traveled through it.

Mitch was huge, but his steps were careful, as if he knew his size and didn't want to accidentally crush anything. Victor was almost silent, footfalls as smooth and hushed as everything else about him.

The steps Sydney heard now through several layers of plastic sheeting were louder, the proud clip of nice shoes. Eli had worn nice shoes. Despite the cold and the fact that he was dating a college girl, and the fact that he looked like a college boy, he'd had on leather shoes beneath his jeans when she met him. Shoes that made a sharp sound when he walked.

Sydney held her breath, and slid Serena's gun from her coat pocket, clicking the safety off. Serena had showed her once, how to use a gun, but this one was a little too big for her grip, too heavy and ill-weighted from the silencer screwed on to the end. She looked behind her, and wondered if she could find her way back through the maze of plastic curtains and into the lot before Eli would . . .

Her thoughts trailed off as she realized that the footsteps had stopped.

She checked the curtains to every side for moving shadows, but there were none, so she crept forward, through another plastic sheet, the light brighter here, only a few curtains between her and the source. Victor should be here by now. She couldn't hear him, but that was because he was so quiet, she told herself. He was always quiet. And safe.

Sydney, look at me, he'd said. *No one is going to hurt you. Do you know why? Because I'll hurt them first.*

Safe. Safe. Safe.

She pulled aside the last curtain. She just had to find Victor, and he would keep her safe.

Eli was sitting in a chair in the middle of the room, a table made of wooden planks on cinder blocks displaying what looked like a set of kitchen knives, all gleaming beneath the light of a lamp. The lamp had no shade, and the bulb lit the whole room, from curtain to curtain, and Eli in between. A gun dangled loosely from his hand, and his eyes were far-off, unfocused.

Until he saw Sydney.

"What's this?" he asked, standing. "A little monster."

Sydney didn't wait. She raised Serena's gun and fired once at Eli's face. The weapon was heavy and her aim was off, but even though the blowback knocked the gun from her grip, the bullet still found Eli's jaw and sent him reeling, clutching his face, blood and bone between his fingers. She spun, and tried to run away, but his hand shot out and caught her sleeve, and even though he couldn't keep hold, the sudden change of course sent her stumbling to her hands and knees on the concrete.

Dol lunged forward as Sydney rolled onto her back and Eli straightened, jaw cracking and snapping and healing, leaving only a smear of blood on his skin as he raised his gun and pulled the trigger.

CLICK.

One small sound after Mitch pulled the trigger, the sound made by the internal spring driving the firing pin to bypass the bullet and hit the mechanical stop. Because there were no bullets.

The gun was empty.

Mitch should know; he had checked it three times to make sure.

Now he watched the surprise spread across Serena's face, watched it turn to confusion, and begin to shift into something harder, but it never made it there, because that's when the darkness parted. The shadows behind Serena Clarke stirred and drew apart, and two men stepped into being out of nothing. Dominic stood, holding a red gas canister while Victor took a single stride up behind Serena, brought a knife to her throat, and drew it cleanly across.

There was a blossom of red, and her lips parted, but he'd cut deep, and no sound made it out.

"And Ulysses stopped up his ears against the siren's song," recited Victor, pulling the plugs from his own ears as Serena collapsed to the dirt lot, "for it was death."

"Jesus," said Dominic, looking away. "She was just a girl."

Victor looked down at her body. Blood was pooling beneath Serena's face, glistening and dark. "Don't be insulting," he said. "She was the most powerful woman in the city. Aside from Sydney, of course."

"About Sydney . . . ," said Mitch, looking down at the dead girl. From this angle she seemed smaller, and with her face turned like that, her hair caught in the collar of her coat, the resemblance was disturbing. "What are we going to do about this?"

Dominic set the plastic gas tank on the dirt beside the body.

"Burn the body," said Victor, closing his knife. "I don't want Sydney seeing it. And I certainly don't want her getting her hands on it. The last thing we need is Serena coming back to life."

Mitch had just taken up the gas canister when a gun fired within the building, lighting up the bones of the high-rise like a camera flash.

"What the hell?" growled Victor.

"Looks like Eli got here first," said Mitch.

"But if I'm out here," said Victor, "then what's Eli shooting at?" He grabbed hold of Dominic's shoulder. "Take me in there. Now."

∞

THE sound of Eli's gun rang off the concrete as Dol's body buckled, and even though he didn't seem to feel the pain of the shot, he
fell onto his side, panting for air. His chest went up and down and
up and down and then . . . stopped. Eli saw the girl reach for the
dog but he recocked the gun and leveled it on her.

"Good-bye, Sydney," he said.

And then the darkness moved around her, and a pair of hands
reached out of nothing and jerked her backward into nothing with
them. Eli pulled the trigger and the bullet hit the plastic sheeting
where the girl had been.

He let out a frustrated sound and fired two more shots into the
space that had been Sydney. But she was gone.

XXXV

MIDNIGHT

THE FALCON PRICE PROJECT

SYDNEY felt someone take hold and pull her into the dark.

One moment she was looking down the barrel of Eli's gun and the next she was standing hand in hand with the man from the profile she'd given Victor. She looked around, but didn't let go. They were still in the plastic-sheeted room, and yet they weren't. It was like standing outside of life, stuck in a too still world that scared her more than she would ever admit. She could see Eli, the bullet from his gun hovering in the air where she had been, and Dol, lifeless on the ground.

And Victor.

He hadn't been there a moment before, but now he was, standing several feet behind Eli, unseen, one hand reaching slightly forward and out, as if about to rest on Eli's shoulder.

Sydney tried to tell the man holding her hand that she had to get Dol, but her lips made no sound, and he didn't even look at her, only dragged her through the heavy world, winding back through the curtains of plastic until they reached the place where the building gave way to the dirt lot. There was a bright light across the lot, casting shadows up against the metal bones of the high-rise, but the man pulled her in the other direction, leading her to a darkened corner in the back of the construction site. They stepped back into the world, the bubble of quiet bursting into life and sound around them. Even just the sound of breathing, of time passing, was deafening compared to the quiet of the shadows.

"You have to go back," snapped Sydney, kneeling in the dirt.

"Can't. Victor's orders."

"But you have to get Dol."

"Sydney . . . it's Sydney, right?" The man knelt in front of her. "I saw the dog, okay? I'm sorry. It was too late."

She held his eyes, the way Serena had held hers. Calm and cold and unblinking. She knew she didn't have her sister's gift, her control, but even before, Serena got her way, and she was Serena's sister, and she needed him to see.

"Go back," she said sternly. "Go. Get. Dol."

And it must have worked because Dominic swallowed, nodded, and vanished into nothing.

ELI emptied the gun into the air, but all signs of them were gone. He growled and ejected the magazine. It clattered to the ground as he dug in his coat for a full one.

"I watch you, and it's like watching two people."

He spun at the sound of the voice and found Victor leaning back against a concrete pillar.

"Vic—"

Victor didn't hesitate. He fired three times into Eli's chest, mimicking the pattern of the scars on his own body, the way he had imagined he would for the last ten years.

And it felt *good*. He had been worried that after so much waiting and so much wanting the actuality of shooting Eli wouldn't live up to the dream, but it did. The air buzzed around them and Eli groaned and braced himself against the chair as the pain multiplied.

"It's why I let you stay," said Victor. "Why I liked you. All that charm outside, all that evil inside. There was a monster under there, long before you died."

"I'm not a monster," growled Eli as he dug one of the bullets out of his shoulder, and dropped the bloodied metal to the floor. "I am God's—" But Victor was already there, burying a switchblade in Eli's chest. He punctured a lung, he could tell by the gasp. Victor's mouth twitched, face patient but knuckles white around the blade's grip.

"Enough," said Victor. Behind his eyes, the dial turned up. Eli screamed. "You aren't some avenging angel, Eli," he said. "You're not blessed, or divine, or burdened. You're a science experiment."

Victor pulled the knife out. Eli went down on one knee.

"You don't understand," gasped Eli. "No one understands."

"When *no one* understands, that's usually a good sign that you're wrong."

Eli struggled up to his knees, reaching for the makeshift table as his skin knit together.

Victor's gaze shifted to it, taking in the row of knives. Just like that day. "How nostalgic of you." He put a foot on the table and knocked it over, sending the weapons scattering across the concrete. The dog's body, he noticed, was gone.

"You can't kill me, Victor," said Eli. "You know that."

Victor's smile widened as he buried his knife between Eli's ribs.

"I know," he said loudly. He had to speak up over the screams. "But you'll have to indulge me. I've waited so long to try."

A breath later, Dominic reappeared, half carrying half dragging a very large, very dead dog. He sank to the dirt lot beside its body, breathing heavily. Sydney hurried over, thanked him, and then asked him to get out of her way. Dominic sagged back, and watched as she ran a soothing hand over the dog's side, brushing the wound lightly. Her palm came away dark red, and she frowned.

"I told you," he said. "I'm sorry."

"Shhh," she said, and pressed her hands, fingers splayed, against the dog's chest. She drew in a shaky breath as the cold flooded up her arms.

"Come on," she whispered. "Come on, Dol."

But nothing happened. Her heart sank. Sydney Clarke gave second chances. But the dog had already had his. She'd fixed him once, but she didn't know if she could do it again. She pressed down harder, and felt the cold leeching something from her.

The dog still lay dead and stiff as the planks in the construction lot.

She shivered and knew it shouldn't be this hard as she reached not with her hands but something else, as if she could find a spark of heat within and take hold. She reached past the fur and skin and stiffness as her hands hurt and her lungs tightened and still she kept reaching.

And then she felt it, and took hold, and between one moment and the next, the dog's body softened, slackened. Its limbs twitched and its chest rose once, paused, fell, and a moment later rose again, before the beast stretched, and sat up.

Dominic scrambled to his feet. *"Dios mío,"* he whispered, crossing himself.

Sydney sat, gasping for breath, and rested her head against Dol's muzzle. "Good dog."

∞

VICTOR smiled. He was having a fabulous time killing Eli. Every time he thought his friend had given up, he pulled himself back together, and gave Victor the chance to try again. He wished it could go on awhile longer, but at least he was quite certain, as Eli's body buckled in pain, that he had his *full* attention. Eli gasped, and staggered to his feet, nearly slipping on the blood.

The floor was slick with it. Most of it was Eli's, Victor knew. But not all.

Blood ran down one of Victor's arms and over his stomach, both shallow cuts made by a wicked-looking kitchen knife Eli had managed to recover from the floor the last time Victor shot him. The guns were both empty now, and the two men stood bleeding, across from one another, each armed—Eli with a serrated knife, and Victor with a switchblade.

"This is a waste," said Eli, adjusting his grip. "You can't win."

Victor took a deep breath, wincing faintly. He'd had to turn his own threshold down because he couldn't afford to bleed out, not yet, and certainly not without noticing. He could hear the distant sirens of the cop cars. They were running out of time. He lunged for Eli, and managed to skim his shirt before Eli knocked the blow away and drove his own blade down into Victor's leg. He hissed as his knee buckled beneath him.

"What was your plan?" chided Eli, reaching out, not for Victor, but for the chair, for something coiled on it, something Victor hadn't noticed until Eli's hands took hold of it. "You hear the cops coming? They're all on my side here. No one's coming to save *you*."

"That's the idea," coughed Victor as his eyes focused on the thing in Eli's hand. Metal wire. Razor sharp.

"You and your ideas," hissed Eli. "Well, I've been planning, too."

Victor tried to find his feet, but he was too slow. Eli looped the

wire in the air, and brought it down around Victor's wrist, the one
with the knife, pulling hard. The wire dug in, slicing through skin
and drawing blood, forcing Victor to drop the blade, which clattered to the concrete. Eli caught his free hand in a crushing grip,
and wound the wire around that one, too. Victor pulled back,
but the cord only bit deeper into his skin.

The wire, he noticed then, was threaded through the chair itself, which Eli must have fastened to the ground because it never
moved, not during the fight, and not now when Eli yanked his
end of the cord and the slack drew in, forcing Victor's hands toward the bars of the chair back. Blood ran down his wrists, too
fast. His head was beginning to spin. He could hear the sirens now,
loud and clear, and thought that he could even see the red and
blue of the police lights through the plastic curtains. Color danced
before his eyes.

He smiled grimly, and shut off the last of the pain.

"You'll never kill me, Eli," he goaded.

"That's where you're wrong, Victor. And this time," he said,
cinching the wire, "I'm going to watch the life bleed out of your
eyes."

MITCH watched Serena's body burn, and tried not to listen to the
sounds of gunfire coming from inside the high-rise. He had to
trust Victor. Victor always had a plan. But where was he? And where
was Dominic?

He refocused on the body and the task at hand until red and
blue lights began to flash beyond the wood walls, colors cast up
against the darkened building. That wasn't good. The cops weren't
in the yard yet, but it was only a matter of minutes before they

swarmed the place. Mitch couldn't risk the broken gate of the front entrance so he rounded the building toward the gap in the walls, only to find Sydney leaning over a half-dead Dol, and Dominic standing over both, praying silently.

"Sydney Clarke," he snapped. "What the hell are you doing here?"

"She told me I had to go somewhere safe," whispered Sydney, petting Dol.

She, thought Mitch. The same *she*, he guessed, that was burning on the other side of the building. "And you came *here*?"

"The dog was dead," whispered Dominic. "I saw it . . . it was deader than dead . . . and now . . ."

Mitch took Dominic's sleeve. "Get us out of here. *Now*."

Dominic's eyes drifted up from the girl and the dog and seemed to register the flashing lights bouncing over the wooden walls and up against the high-rise for the first time. Car doors were slamming. Boots on pavement. *"Shit."*

"Yeah, exactly."

"What about Victor?" asked Sydney.

"We have to wait for him somewhere. Not here, Syd. We were never supposed to wait here."

"But what if he needs help?" she protested.

Mitch tried to smile. "It's Victor," he said. "There's nothing he can't handle."

But as Sydney took Dol, and Dominic took Sydney, and Mitch took Dominic, and they all vanished into the shadows, Mitch had a horrible feeling that he was wrong, and his curse had followed him all the way here.

ELI heard the footsteps, the men shouting orders as they tore toward them, through room after room of the plastic sheeting. Victor slumped on the floor, the area around the chair slick with his blood. His eyes were open, but losing focus. Eli wanted this kill to be his, not the Merit Police Department's, and certainly not Serena's.

His.

He saw Victor's knife on the floor a few feet away and took it up, crouching in front of him.

"Some hero," he heard Victor whisper with his two last, labored breaths. Eli rested the blade carefully beneath Victor's ribs.

"Good-bye, Victor," he said.

And then he drove the knife in.

DOMINIC buckled.

He went down on his hands and knees in an alley four blocks from the high-rise, a safe distance from the flood of cops and the burning girl and the guns. He cried out, and at the same time, Sydney clutched her arm, and Mitch rubbed at his bruised ribs. Pain swept over the three like a current, like a breath, something held back and now returned. And then, one by one, they realized what that meant.

"No!" shouted Sydney, turning back toward the high-rise.

Mitch caught her around the waist, wincing as she kicked and screamed and told him to put her down.

"It's over," he whispered as she fought. "It's over. It's over. I'm sorry. It's over."

ELI watched Victor's eyes widen, and then empty, his forehead slumping forward against the metal bars of the chair. Dead. It was so strange that Eli of all people had thought Victor was invincible. And he'd been wrong. Eli drew the knife out of Victor's chest and stood there in the blood-slicked room, waiting for the telltale quiet, the moment of peace. He closed his eyes, and tipped his head back, and waited, and he was still waiting when the cops tore into the room, led by Detective Stell.

"Step away from the body," ordered Stell, raising his gun.

"It's okay," said Eli. He opened his eyes and let his gaze drift down over them. "It's over."

"Get your hands on your head!" shouted another cop.

"Put the knife down!" ordered another.

"It's okay," said Eli again. "He's no danger now."

"Hands up!" demanded Stell.

"I took care of him. He's dead." Eli grew indignant as he gestured to the blood-soaked room, and the dead man bound by wire to the chair bars. "Can't you see that? I'm a *hero*."

The men leveled their guns and shouted and looked at Eli as if he were a monster. And then it hit him. There was no glaze in their eyes. No spell.

"Where's Serena?" he demanded, but the question was swallowed up by the sirens and the shouting cops. "Where is she? She'll tell you!"

"Put the weapon *down*," demanded Stell above the noise.

"She'll tell you. I'm a hero!" he shouted back, throwing the knife aside. "I saved you all!"

But as the blade hit the floor, the cops rushed forward, and slammed him to the ground. He could see Victor's dead face from there, and it seemed to be smiling at him.

"Eli Ever, you're under arrest for the murder of Victor Vale . . ."

"Wait!" he shouted as they cuffed him. "The body."

Stell read him his rights as two cops wrenched him to his feet. Another cop hurried to Stell's side, and said something about a fire out in the lot.

Eli fought their grip. "You have to burn the body!"

Stell gave a signal, and the cops dragged Eli back through the plastic curtains.

"Stell!" shouted Eli again. "You have to burn Vale's body!"

His words echoed on the concrete as the detective and the blood-soaked room and Victor's corpse vanished from his view.

XXXVI

TWO NIGHTS LATER

MERIT CEMETERY

SYDNEY readjusted the shovel on her shoulder.

The air was cold but the night was clear, the moon overhead illuminating the broken gravestones and the dips in the grass as she wove through the cemetery, Dol trotting along beside her. It had been harder to bring him back the second time, but he flanked her now, as if his life were truly tied to hers.

Mitch followed close behind, carrying two more shovels. He'd offered to carry hers, too, but Sydney felt it was important she hold her own. Dominic lagged several yards behind them, buzzed on painkillers and whiskey and tripping every few steps on a clump of weeds or a bit of dislodged rock. She didn't like him this way—useless from all the liquor and mean from all the pain—but she tried not to think of that. She tried not to think of her own pain, either, of the gunshot still burning a hole in her arm as the muscle and skin slowly healed. She hoped it left a scar, the kind she could see, the kind that would remind her of the moment when everything changed.

Not that Sydney thought she'd ever forget.

She readjusted the shovel on her shoulder, and wondered if Eli would live forever, and how much of forever someone could reasonably remember, especially when nothing left a mark.

Eli, incidentally, had been a press field day.

She and Mitch had seen it on the news. The madman who'd murdered two people at the Falcon Price building, all the while claiming to be some monster-slayer, some *hero*. The press said he'd killed a young woman in the construction lot, and burned her body before torturing and then murdering an ex-con on the ground floor. The woman's identity hadn't been made public—they'd have to go by dental records—but Sydney knew it was Serena. She knew even before she made Mitch hack the coroner's reports. She could feel the absence of her sister, the place in her where the threads had been. What she didn't know was why Eli would have done it. But she meant to find out.

The members of the press weren't nearly as interested in Serena as they were in Eli.

Apparently Eli had stood there over Victor's body, covered in blood, still holding the knife and shouting that he was a hero. That he'd saved them all. When no one bought the hero line, he tried to claim it had been a fight. But since his opponent was shredded and he didn't have a scratch on him, that line hadn't worked so well, either. Add that to the papers found in the satchel in Eli's hotel room—he clearly didn't have Victor's foresight to burn anything that could be construed as evidence—and the profiles on his computer, and Eli's body count quickly jumped into double digits. The news never touched on the Merit Police Department's own involvement in a good number of the recent killings, but Eli was now awaiting trial and a psych evaluation.

There was no mention of him being an EO, of course, but then again, why would there be? All it meant for Eli was that if someone shanked him in prison, he'd live to have it happen again. If he were lucky they'd put him in isolation, like Victor. Sydney hoped they didn't put him in isolation. She thought that maybe if they found out he could heal himself, hurting him would become the most popular game in the facility.

Sydney made a mental note to leak that detail wherever he ended up.

It was too quiet in the cemetery, what with only the sounds of grass muffled steps in the dark, so Sydney tried to hum the way Victor had when they'd gone to dig up Barry. But it sounded wrong in her mouth, eerie and sad, so she stopped and focused on finding her way by the map drawn in Sharpie on the back of her hand. She'd drawn it in daylight, but the Merit Cemetery, like most things, looked different at night.

Finally she caught sight of the fresh grave, and quickened her pace. The grave was unmarked except for Victor's book, which Sydney had set like a stone at the top of the patch of dirt that morning, waiting in the shadow of a stone angel for the diggers to finish and go away. That detective, Stell, had been there, too. He'd stayed long enough to watch the simple wood coffin get lowered down into the hole and covered with dirt.

Mitch caught up to her, and the two looked down at the grave for a moment before Sydney drove her shovel into the ground, and set to work. Dol wandered the plots nearby, but never let Sydney out of his sight, and Dominic eventually wandered over, and sat on a gravestone, keeping an eye out for trouble as the other two dug.

Thud.

Thud.

Thud.

They drove their shovels in the ground until the air seemed warmer and the night seemed thinner, and light grazed the far edges of the sky where it met the buildings of Merit. Sometime before dawn, Sydney's shovel hit wood, and they scraped the last dirt from the top of the coffin, and heaved the lid up.

Sydney looked down at Victor's body. Then she perched on the edge of the coffin, and pressed her hands against his chest, reaching as far as she could. A moment later, the cold ran up her arms, and caught her breath, and beneath her hands a heartbeat fluttered, as Victor Vale opened his eyes, and smiled.

ACKNOWLEDGMENTS

To my family, for not giving me strange looks when I told them what I wanted to write.

To my agent, Holly, for not giving me a strange look when I told her what I'd written.

To Patricia Riley, for loving every member of my motley crew (especially Mitch and his chocolate milk).

To Ruta Sepetys, who listened to me babble on and then told me very seriously to *finish this book*.

To Jen Barnhardt, for accompanying me to every comic book movie, even the not-so-great ones.

To Rachel Stark, for always asking hard questions, and for pushing me to do the same.

To Matthew Leach and Deanna Maurice, for the medical knowledge.

And to Sophie, for the term EO.

To my readers, for following me over moors and through dark halls and now into the heart of Merit.

And to my editor, Miriam, for making every step of this journey marvelous. From the first narwhal doodle to the last late-night discussions on morality, mortality, and villainy, I wouldn't have wanted to do this book with anyone else.